"YOU ARE SAFE HERE, HAVEN. NEVER DOUBT IT."

Peering up at Dare, Haven nodded, all kinds of words sitting on the tip of her tongue, challenging her to let them fly. "It's weird feeling safe—or at least safer—after a lifetime of not. It makes me want to try things I could never let myself try before. It makes me . . ." She shook her head and dipped her chin.

Dare stepped closer, his thighs coming up against her hip. He lifted her chin and made her look at him. The contact combined with the command in the gesture lanced white-hot desire through her veins. "Makes you what?"

"Want to feel alive," she whispered, her heart suddenly racing in her chest.

Dare's jaw ticked again as his gaze swept over her face.

She didn't think she was imagining the raw emotion pouring off of him and wrapping around her, but she wasn't sure if she was reading that emotion right or projecting her own desire onto him.

"Just once," she whispered, not sure what she was asking him for.

But he seemed to know. Because his hand was suddenly tangled in her hair and his mouth was suddenly on hers, claiming, probing, tasting.

By Laura Kaye

LAURA KAYE

Ride HARD

A RAVEN RIDERS NOVEL

AVONBOOKS

An Imprint of HarperCollinsPublishers

Excerpt from *Ride Rough* copyright © 2016 by Laura Kaye.

Chapter opener raven illustration © Fun Way Illustration/Shutterstock, Inc.

First Avon Books mass market printing: May 2016

ISBN 978-0-06-240333-9

Avon Trademark Reg. U.S. Pat. Off. and in Other Countries, Marca Registrada, Hecho en U.S.A.
Avon, Avon Books, and the Avon logo are trademarks of Harper-Collins Publishers.
HarperCollins® is a registered trademark of HarperCollins Publishers.

16 17 18 19 20   OPM   10 9 8 7 6 5 4 3 2 1

To my readers,
May you always find the beauty in life.
And when you can't find it,
create it from the beauty inside you.

CHAPTER 1

To say that Haven Randall's escape plans were not going as she'd hoped was quite possibly the understatement of the century. Especially since she wasn't at all sure her current situation was any better than the one she'd run from three weeks before.

But today could be the day she found that out for sure.

Staring out the window through the slats of the blinds, Haven watched as another group of motorcycles roared into the parking lot below. They'd been coming in groups of four or five for the past hour or so. And, *God,* there were a lot of them. Not surprising, since she was currently holed up at the compound of the Raven Riders Motorcycle Club. A shiver raced over her skin.

"Don't worry," Haven's friend Cora Campbell said. Sitting on the bed, her back against the wall, and her choppy, shoulder-length blond hair twisted up in a messy bun, Cora gave Haven a reassuring smile.

"I don't know what I'd do without you," Haven said. And it was the truth. Without Cora's bravery, encouragement, and fearless you-only-live-once attitude, Haven never would've put her longtime pipe dream of escaping from her father's house into action. Of course, those actions had landed her here, among a bunch of strange bikers of questionable character and intent, and Haven didn't know what to make of that. Yet.

But it had to be better than what would've happened if she'd stayed in Georgia. She had to believe that. *Had to.* If nothing else, for the first time in her life she could begin to consider what *she* wanted. Even if she didn't yet know what that was.

"Well, you won't ever have to find out," Cora said, flipping through an old gossip magazine that had been on the nightstand. "Because you're stuck with me."

"I wouldn't want to be stuck with anyone else," Haven said in a quiet voice.

Outside, the late-day sun gleamed off the steel and chrome of the motorcycles slowly but surely filling the lot. The bass beat of rock music suddenly drummed against the floor of their room. Now the Ravens' clubhouse, the building where they'd been staying for just over two weeks had apparently once been an old mountain inn. Their rooms were on the second floor, where guests used to stay, and though Cora had been more adventurous, Haven had stayed in her room as much as possible since they'd arrived. And that was while the majority of the guys had been away from their compound on some sort of club business.

Men's laughter boomed from downstairs.

Haven hugged herself as another group of bikers tore into the lot. "There are so many of them."

Cora tossed the magazine aside and climbed off the bed. She was wearing a plain gray tank top and a pair of cutoff shorts that Bunny, an older lady who was married to one of the Ravens, had lent her. Haven's baggy white T-shirt and loose khaki cargo pants were borrowed, too. They'd run away with a few articles of clothes and cash that Haven had stolen from her father, but they'd lost all of that—and their only vehicle—two weeks ago. Haven and Cora literally had nothing of their own in the whole world.

Haven's belly tossed. Being totally dependent on anyone else was the last thing she wanted. She was too familiar with all the ways that could be used against her to make her do things she didn't want to do.

Standing next to her at the window, Cora said, "We're not prisoners here, Haven. We're their guests. Remember what Ike said."

Haven nodded. "I know." She hadn't forgotten. Ike Young was the member of the Ravens who had brought them there, who'd told them they were welcome to stay as long as they needed to, who said that no one would give them any trouble. Who said the Ravens helped people like them all the time.

People like them.

So, people like someone who'd grown up as the daughter of the head of a criminal organization? Someone who'd been homeschooled starting in tenth grade so her father could control her every move—and make sure she never saw her first and only boyfriend again? Someone whose father used her for a maid and a cook and planned to barter her off in a forced marriage to another crime family to cement an alliance? Someone who, after managing a middle-of-the-night escape, ended up being captured by a drug-dealing gang seven hundred miles away—a gang that had apparently received notice of a reward for capture from her father? Someone who was then rescued by soldiers and bikers at war with that gang?

Because that was Haven's reality, and she really doubted the Ravens had helped someone like her before. Or, at least, she hoped not. Because she wouldn't wish the life she'd lived so far on her worst enemy.

Knowing that her father was looking for her—that he just wouldn't let her go—*and* that he had others hunting her, too . . . her stomach got a sour, wiggly sensation that left her feeling nauseous. She couldn't go back to him. Not ever.

"I'm okay," she said, giving Cora another smile. "Really." Maybe if she kept reassuring Cora of that, she'd begin to believe it herself.

"Listen, it's almost seven. Bunny said there'd be a big celebratory dinner tonight to welcome everyone back. Let's go down." Cora's bright green eyes were filled with so much enthusiasm and excitement.

Haven hated nothing more than disappointing her friend—her longest friend, her *only* friend, really. They bonded in the fifth grade when Haven noticed that Cora didn't have anything in her lunch box for the second day in a row. Haven gave Cora half her sandwich and all of her chips. Cora said her father forgot to go food shopping, which he apparently did a lot. So Haven got into the habit of taking extra for her new friend every day, and soon they were besties. Which was why Cora didn't give up on her when Haven was forced to drop out of school in tenth grade. And why Cora didn't shy away from visiting when she arrived to find Haven with a busted lip or a fresh bruise. Cora's father occasionally worked for Haven's, which paved the way for Cora to be allowed to visit and even sleep over. Haven lived for those visits, especially when her father's tight control didn't let up even after she turned eighteen. Or twenty-one.

"I don't know, Cora. Can you just bring me some food later?" Haven asked, dubious that her appetite was going to rebound but knowing Cora liked taking care of her, running interference for her, protecting her. Despite how tense things were at Haven's house, Cora slept over more and more in the time before they'd finally ran. Because she'd known it cheered Haven up so much. "I'm not hungry right now anyway."

"Oh," Cora said. "You know what? I'm not that hungry, either. I'll just wait." Her stomach growled. Loudly.

Haven stared at her, and they both chuckled. "Just go," Haven said. "Don't stay here because I'm too chicken to be around a bunch of strangers. Really. I'm so used to being alone. You know I don't mind."

Cora frowned. "That's exactly why I don't like leaving you."

"I'll feel bad if you stay. Go. Eat, visit, and meet every-body. Maybe . . . maybe I'll come down later," she said. Yeah. Maybe after the dinner was over, she could sneak down to the kitchen and help Bunny clean up. That might allow her to get a feel for some of the club members with-out being right in the middle of them, without feeling like she was under a microscope with everyone looking at her and wondering about her.

Grasping her hand, Cora's gaze narrowed. "Are you sure? You know I don't mind hanging out."

"Totally sure." Besides, Haven couldn't help but feel she held Cora back. Cora was adventurous and outgoing and pretty much down for anything at any time, which was one of the main reasons Haven was here and not in Georgia married to a horrible stranger. But now Cora was on the run, too, though every time Haven expressed guilt about that, Cora told her it was better than waitressing at the truck stop back home and watching her father drink too much. "I might actually take a nap anyway. I didn't sleep great last night . . ." Because Bunny had told them all the bikers would be returning to the club today.

Cora just nodded. She didn't have to ask Haven to explain. She knew her too well. "Okay, well, I'll bring food back later. But come down if you think you can. Even for a few minutes. Okay?"

"Yup." Haven sat on the edge of the bed and threw a wave when Cora looked back over her shoulder. The door clicked shut behind her friend. On a huff, Haven flopped backward against the hard mattress. Why couldn't she be more like Cora? Or, at least, more normal?

Because what did gaining her freedom mean if she was too scared to ever actually live?

DARE KENYON SHOULD'VE been happy—or at least content. The huge fight his club had joined with the team of Special Forces Army veterans operating out of Baltimore's Hard Ink Tattoo was over, the drug-dealing mercenaries who'd been responsible for killing two of his brothers were either dead or in custody, and all Dare's people were here at the compound, safe and sound and partying it up like tomorrow might never come.

Which made sense, since today was all anyone was ever guaranteed to get.

Standing at the far end of the carved wooden bar in the club's big rec room, Dare contemplated the tumbler of whiskey in his hand. Tilting it from side to side, he watched the amber liquid flow around the ice, the dim lighting reflecting off the facets in the cut glass. Around him, his brothers busted out in laughter as rock music filled the room with a pulsing beat. Couples danced and drank and groped. In shadowy corners here and there, people were pairing up, making out, getting hot enough to find a room upstairs. Hell, some of them didn't mind witnesses, either.

Finally, Dare tossed back a gulp of whiskey, savoring the biting heat as it seared down his throat.

"Hey, Dare." A woman with curly blond hair, a deep V-neck, and huge heels stepped up to the counter beside him. She ordered a drink from Blake, one of the prospects working the bar tonight, then turned her big smile and a generous eyeful of her cleavage toward Dare.

"Carly," he said, giving her a nod and already considering whether he was interested in what she no doubt was about to offer. He'd been with her a few times, though not much lately, since it had become more and more clear she was holding out hope to be his Old Lady.

"I'm sure glad you all are back," she said, sidling closer until she was leaning against him, her breasts against his arm, her hand rubbing his back. She was pretty, but she was also a sweet thing, the club's nickname for the attractive women who partied at the clubhouse and hung out at their track on race nights, seeking attention from and offering themselves to the brothers. Dare didn't mind having friends like Carly in the community, but he knew her interest was as much in being a part of the MC scene as it was in him. At thirty-seven, he wasn't sure he was ever going to settle down with one woman, but if he did, it certainly wasn't going to be with someone half his brothers had enjoyed, too.

And, anyway, he wasn't looking.

Dare just nodded to Carly as she pressed her way in closer until the whole front of her was tight against his side. Her hands wandered to his chest, his ass, his dick. Her lips ghosted over his cheek. "I missed you." Her hand squeezed his growing erection through his jeans. "Missed you a lot."

"Did you, now?" he said, taking another swig of Jack. The friction of her hand was luring him out of his head, out from under the strain of being responsible for so many people. It was an honor, one he'd built his life around, but he felt the weight of it some days more than others.

Losing Harvey and Creed almost two weeks before, he felt that weight like a motherfucker. Hell if every new loss in his life didn't whip up his guilt from the first two . . .

Sonofabitch.

Carly combed her fingers through the length of his brown hair, pushing it back off his face so she could whisper into his ear. "I did. Would you like me to show you how much?" Her fingers slowly worked at his zipper, tugging him from his thoughts.

Exactly what he needed. "What is it you have in mind?" He peered down at her, really appreciating the easy, lighthearted expression on her face. Nothing too deep, nothing too heavy, but full of life all the same.

Her fingers undid the button on his jeans and slipped in against his skin, finding and palming his now rigid cock. Fuck, that felt good. Warm and tight and full of promise.

Smiling, Carly slid herself in front of Dare, pinning her body between his and the hard wooden counter. Her eyes were full of heat and need. "I could drop to my knees right here. Suck you off. Let you fuck my face. Or we could go upstairs, baby. Whatever you want." She wrapped her other arm around his neck, her fingers playing with the long strands of his hair. "You seem . . . tense, upset. Let me make you feel better?"

And now, on top of everything else, he had a warm, willing woman wanting to make him forget all his troubles. So, yeah, he should've been content.

Dare emptied his glass and slammed it down on the counter. Fuck it. Grasping her face in his hand, he trailed his thumb over her bottom lip, stroking, dipping inside so she could suck on his flesh. "Always did love that mouth," he said.

She grinned around his thumb and nodded, then she slowly slid down his body.

Dare closed his eyes, wanting nothing more than to lose himself in the moment, the sensation, the physical. But his gut wouldn't stop telling him that some part of their recent troubles was going to come back and bite them in the ass. The past had a way of doing that. Which was why Dare always kept one eye trained over his shoulder. But this particular past was only weeks old and way bigger than their typical fights. The Ravens had just played a role in taking down longtime enemies and Baltimore's biggest heroin dealers—the Church Gang. In the process, they'd exposed an international drug smuggling conspiracy involving a team of former soldiers turned hired mercenaries and at least one three-star, active-duty general. The Ravens had initially come into the fight as hired help, but they'd taken up the cause as their own when Harvey and Creed had been killed.

Given all that, Dare had a really fucking hard time believing the dust would just settle and life would go back to normal without any blowback.

As Carly got into a crouched position at his feet, Dare opened his eyes and tried to shake away all the churn and burn in his head. But then his gaze snagged on a girl in the doorway across the room. Clarity stole over him, pushing away the fog of lust and the haze of troubled thoughts. The girl had the longest blond hair he'd ever seen, like some fairy-tale princess, or a fucking angel. Pale, small, almost too beautiful to look at. She stood out so starkly that it was almost as if she glowed in the dim room. Like a beacon. Bright and shiny and new.

One of these things is not like the other. And it was the timid beauty wearing too-big clothes and no makeup, hovering on the edge of the room.

And Dare wasn't the only man who noticed.

CHAPTER 2

Without thinking, Dare stepped back from Carly's reach and did up his jeans.

"What's wrong?" Carly said. "Dare?"

He gave her a hand up, but his eyes were all for the angel-faced beauty Joker was currently bearing down on, his walk full of swagger, his expression like he'd just won the lottery. Gut-deep protectiveness rose up inside Dare, the instinct as well-tuned as the engine on his bike. "Sorry, sweetie," Dare said. "Duty calls."

Carly's expression was pure exasperation and not a little pissed off. He gave her shoulder a squeeze, then worked his way through the crowd, trying like hell not to get pulled into any storytelling or jokes or conversations along the way.

Crossing the room felt like it took forever, and by the time he got clear, Joker had the girl pinned up against a wall in the hall. Not because he'd put her there, necessarily, but because she'd retreated as he'd advanced and backed herself into a corner.

Jesus, she looked terrified. Who the hell was this woman? Or was she just a girl? He honestly couldn't tell how old she was, but her skittishness was crystal clear.

Dare put a hand on his brother's shoulder. The guy was as big as a mountain but as harmless as a mouse. Well, mostly. "Joker, how's it going?"

"Goin' good, D. I was just introducing myself to . . ." His words trailed off, encouraging her to fill in the blank. Only she looked like she was two seconds from having a full-blown panic attack.

"Hey, whoa," Dare said, stepping closer to the blond. "You okay?"

She gave a quick nod, but the movement was jerky and forced, like she thought she was supposed to say she was fine. Dare frowned as a flush poured into her cheeks.

He eyeballed Joker and nodded for him to clear out. A concerned expression on his face, the big guy shrugged and made his way back into the thick of the party.

"I'm Dare, the club president. You're okay here," Dare assured her. "You know that, right?" Who the hell was she, anyway? He knew all the regulars, and she certainly wasn't one of them. Frankly, it was usually outgoing, confident women who gravitated to an MC, not shy girls. . . .

All of a sudden, he realized who he was talking to. "Wait. Are you Haven?" One of the two women who, in the midst of the club's fight against enemies in Baltimore, had been rescued from a gang and given refuge at the Raven Riders' compound. In all the chaos of the past few weeks, Dare hadn't met the women when they'd arrived at the compound, which was out of the norm for him. He'd only met the other woman, Cora, at dinner earlier in the night.

Her eyes went wide, the blue color so vivid it was almost electric. "Y-yes," she said, closing her eyes and shaking her head like she was frustrated. "Yes. I'm Haven," she said again, stronger, clearer.

"Haven," Dare repeated. "Well, okay." He held out a hand, gesturing down the hall. "Can I show you something? Something I think might help make you feel more comfortable here?"

Wariness crept into her gaze, but finally she nodded and followed him down the hall. She walked almost huddled against the wall, her body as far from his as she could make it given the width of the hallway. Anger curled into Dare's gut. Someone had taught her that fear, had given her a good reason to keep her distance. He saw it so damn often. And even though he wouldn't do it, her anxiety made him want to comfort her, to take her hand or put his arm around her shoulders. But he kept his distance, too.

He guided her toward the front door of the clubhouse, which had once been a mountain inn connected to the Green Valley Race Track his club owned and operated as one of their primary business ventures. Now the building housed the club's main social spaces, a kitchen and mess, meeting room, workout room, and a dozen rooms upstairs where people could crash or fuck or otherwise find some privacy.

In the big front lounge that had previously served as the inn's reception area, Dare paused and pointed to the wall across from the door. "See that?" he asked, pointing to one of the many pieces of work Bandit had done around the place.

Haven's gaze followed his hand to where the club's motto had been carved into the thick wooden molding above the old registration desk. Foot-high words inscribed permanently in the building's very fabric:

Ride. Fight. Defend.

"Yes," she said, the turning of her head pulling thick strands of long blond waves over her shoulder. Her hair hung to her hips over clothes so baggy Dare wondered how they stayed on. "What does it mean?"

Only everything—to him and all the Ravens. He'd built his life around those three words these past twenty years. "I don't know what you know about motorcycle clubs, but we're not your typical MC." And that had been by design. Dare had grown up inside an outlaw MC, inside a group of self-proclaimed One Percenters—the nickname coming from the American Motorcycle Association having once declared that ninety-nine percent of all MCs were law abiding. Which of course meant that one percent weren't. The son of Butch Kenyon, the Arizona Diablos' vice-president, who was also known as The Sandman for the number of men he was responsible for sending to their final sleep, Dare had been groomed to help lead that club one day. Which meant he knew exactly what things he hadn't wanted replicated here, thank you very much.

"I don't know a lot," Haven said in a quiet voice.

He walked to the side of the room, where a collection of framed photographs hung in a tight cluster on the wall. The club's patched members. Almost forty in total, not including a few older members who'd retired from active status, the two prospective members they currently had, and the extended family of all their wives and girlfriends and kids. "We live by our own rules and values, just like most clubs do. And we protect our own, whatever it takes. This MC is a brotherhood. It's a family," he said, crossing his arms. "But a long time ago we also made it our mission to be something more. To serve the community we live in. And we do that by fighting for those who can't fight for themselves, and by defending those who can't defend themselves." Dare looked Haven in the eye, wanting her to believe what he was saying. "Sometimes that means that we give people who need it a safe haven here, and sometimes that means that we provide protection for people in their lives. But either way, we intend to make it clear that in our backyard, there is no tolerance for bullying the weak, and absolutely no intention to fear those who think they're powerful."

"Okay," Haven said. She lowered her chin and nodded. "Thank you."

He appreciated the sentiment, but he didn't need it. None of this had started to stroke his own ego, anyway. Just the opposite, in fact. No matter how many people he and the Ravens helped, it never made up for the first two people he'd failed and let die—while he'd run for his life. Hell if twenty-plus years had done a damn thing to take the sharp edges off that reality. "Hey," he said, his voice suddenly full of gravel. He reached out a hand to nudge her chin up, but pink flooded her cheeks at the near touch, so he stepped back and folded his arms. "You don't owe me any thanks."

Eyes on the photographs, she hugged herself. "I . . . I do." Something about the way she said the words made Dare think she didn't often put herself out there by contradicting people, which made him even more curious about why she was doing it now. "Kindness isn't common, in my experience. Which means it's something to acknowledge." She brought her gaze back to his.

What the hell had happened to her to lead her to that conclusion? Not that he disagreed. Her words resonated inside Dare for a reason. He'd seen so damn much ugliness in his life. But why had she? And who the hell did he have to beat the shit out of for teaching her that particular lesson? "Well, you're welcome," he managed, and then he heaved a breath. "Listen, we can be a rowdy bunch, especially when we're blowing off steam like tonight. And we aren't angels by any stretch of the imagination. But there isn't a single man here who wouldn't help you. So if you need something, all you have to do is ask."

"ASK," HAVEN REPEATED. "Right." Only, while her ears heard the words, the racing of her heart and the prickling on her scalp told her she wouldn't be putting that advice into action any time soon. Assuming she even believed it.

She peered up at Dare. The man was intimidation personified. Tall. Shoulder-length dark brown hair. Muscular, but lean, like a back-alley brawler. Piercing eyes so dark they were almost black, so penetrating she felt like he could look inside her and read all her deepest fears. A scar cut a wide swath through his left eyebrow, and the crookedness of his nose said it had been broken at least once. There was a ruggedness about his face that bordered on harsh and an arrogance to the way his body moved that said he feared absolutely no one. Unlike her. Tattoos on his arms and peeking out of the neck of his black T-shirt added to the roughness of his appearance, as did the well-worn denim cutoff jacket he wore that was all decked out in black leather patches, symbols, and words.

Haven had grown up with men who looked every bit as intimidating, harsh, and rough as Dare. Men who got off on asserting their power, on toying with people's fears, on exploiting people's weaknesses.

Except . . .

Except Dare's words belied the image. Didn't they?

A lifetime of living around men, not all of whom had good intentions, had honed Haven's instincts. Being shy meant she was an observer, and that had helped her learn to read which men she had to be vigilant around and which she could trust not to jump her when they thought her father wasn't looking. It was in their eyes. In the way they treated those less powerful than them. In how they acted when her father wasn't in the room.

Still, Haven was just starting to get a read on Dare. The fact that he'd backed off from touching her before was a good sign, but only time would tell for sure. Butterflies whipped through her belly at the thought of believing him, trusting him, actually putting herself out there enough to put his words to the test. Oh, God, why had she come downstairs? Why had she thought she could actually handle a party full of strangers? Even standing on the outside looking in to the room where most of the people were hanging out had had her feeling like all the oxygen had suddenly disappeared, until she'd been gasping, suffocating, panicking.

"Haven?"

Dare's deep voice snapped her from her thoughts. "I'm sorry," she rushed out, sure she'd missed something important. Muscle memory had her bracing for a blow— verbal or physical. She had experience with both.

His face was suddenly in her line of vision, revealing that he'd leaned down to make her look at him. Tension roared through her, as did the desire to put more space between them. But she forced her feet to remain planted. Showing fear in the face of aggression usually just encouraged even more of it. Back in Georgia, she'd learned never to give her father or his men the satisfaction of her fear when they got in her face about something. Pretending to be unaffected usually made her less interesting to harass.

"You don't owe me that, either," he said, a gruffness to his tone she didn't know how to read.

"Sorry," she repeated, wincing when she realized she'd

done again what he told her not to do. She shook her head at herself, frustration rolling through her. *Pull it together, Haven.*

Dare winked. "Old habits die hard, huh?"

She met his gaze as surprise flowed through her. Surprise that he'd responded with a wry humor instead of irritation. Or worse. "Uh, yeah. Guess so."

He just nodded as his eyes searched hers. She could barely breathe with him so close, so observant, so . . . overwhelming. Finally, he relented, straightening to his full height and putting space between them again. "That's okay. But I need to ask something of you, Haven."

Her stomach dropped to the floor. Here it came. She knew there'd be a catch. "What?" she said, her tone breathy with rising dread. Her brain screamed at her to get the heck out of there. But how could she? She literally lived under Dare's roof right now and had not a cent to her name. Not to mention that she wouldn't begin to know where to go or who to trust with her father hunting her.

"I need you to try to judge me on my actions and my words, not on the actions and words of the people who came before me in your life."

The words were so different from what she'd expected that at first they wouldn't sink in.

"Think you can try to do that for me?" His dark eyes blazed down at her with an emotion she couldn't name or begin to understand.

But it had her nodding. Not because she felt she had to but because she suddenly wanted to . . . to what? To give him what he wanted, to ease whatever it was she saw shining from his eyes, to somehow thank him for surprising her. It wasn't often that someone failed to live down to her expectations. But Dare had. By a lot. "I'll try. I just . . ." Her throat went dry at the near admission of something she wouldn't normally say to a complete stranger—especially someone who looked the way Dare did and on whom she was dependent.

He tilted his head to the side, his eyes locked on hers. "Just what?"

Haven swallowed around the knot of fear in her throat. "I just usually expect the worst. That way . . . it doesn't . . ." She shrugged and rubbed her hands over her suddenly cold arms. ". . . it doesn't hurt as much when it happens." Her heart played like a bass drum against her breastbone.

Dare's expression didn't change. He didn't move, didn't speak, didn't blink. It gave Haven the impression that he'd just donned a mask, or closed the blinds over the windows of his true reaction. Finally, he gave a single tight nod. "I imagine you have a good reason for feeling that way. Just try to remember that those who've seen the most ugliness are also most able to recognize beauty. It comes down to trusting yourself as much as other people."

Tears pricked against the backs of Haven's eyes. She'd never heard someone say something so powerful, so challenging, so . . . scary in her life. Not scary because it threatened her, but because of its promise. That beauty existed. That she could see it. That she could *choose* to see it.

And it all started with her.

It was almost hopeful. But embracing hope was one of the scariest things of all.

She couldn't believe she was having a conversation like this, but now she was dying to know. "But how do you—"

"Oh, my God, Haven! You came down!" Cora bounded into the big lounge.

Haven spun, hand over her pounding heart. "Crap, you scared me," she said.

Cora laughed. "Sorry. I was just excited. Actually, I was headed to the kitchen to grab you some food," she said.

"That's why I came down," Haven said. She peered at Dare, and her manners suddenly kicked in. "Oh, have you met Dare? He's the club president."

Smiling, Cora nodded. "At dinner. I think I've met just about everybody now."

"I don't doubt it," Haven said, giving her friend a smile. Where Haven would rather do just about anything other than meet new people, Cora thrived on it. Even back when Haven still attended school, Cora had always been the one to pull her into new things and introduce her to new people.

"So, let's go get you something to eat," Cora said, taking her hand and tugging her toward a door next to the grouping of Ravens photographs. "See ya later, Dare."

"Yeah," he said.

Haven looked back over her shoulder toward him, wanting to say something, to offer something. But Cora pulled her into the dining room, where two big long tables sat in front of a large stone fireplace. Over the mantel, the Ravens' logo hung, carved into a giant slab of wood—a black raven sitting on the handle of a knife that was buried in the eye socket of a skull. Holy creepiness. Over the tables, American and black Prisoner of War/Missing in Action flags hung straight down from the rough-hewn exposed beams that ran across the ceiling. In the two weeks since they'd arrived there, Haven had most visited this part of the clubhouse, so all this was familiar to her.

Chattering as she led them into the kitchen, Cora finally dropped her arm and turned to her. "So everybody's really nice. You're going to like them. I promise."

"Okay," Haven said, tugging the fridge door open. She'd helped work in the kitchen more than once while they'd been there, so it was probably the one place outside her room where she actually felt comfortable making herself at home. She found lunch meat and cheese for a sandwich. "You can go back to the party, you know. I don't mind."

A chair scraped the tile floor. "I don't mind, either," Cora said, sitting at the small table along the kitchen's back wall. Like the rest of the clubhouse, the room itself was older, and its architectural details felt like they'd been inspired by a cabin—lots of wood paneling, exposed beams, and giant fireplaces, but the space had been ret-rofitted with a modern kitchen equipped to cook for a big group.

Haven set everything she needed on the table and put together a turkey and cheese sandwich with mustard and lettuce.

As she worked, Cora snatched a slice of American and nibbled at it. "So, what were you and Dare talking about? Seemed intense."

"He was just telling me about the club," Haven said. Although Cora was right, it *had* been way more intense than that. At least, it had felt that way to Haven. She took a bite of her dinner.

Cora nodded and waggled her eyebrows, a mischievous expression coming over her face. "He's hot in a tall, dark, and scary kinda way."

Haven almost choked on the food. She gulped at a glass of water until she forced the bite down. "You are so bad."

Laughing, Cora shrugged. "Not bad, just observant. But Dare's nowhere near as hot as Phoenix, whose butt I totally kicked in a game of pool, which he got all pouty over." She laughed. "He's hugely annoying, but pretty nice to look at."

Shaking her head, Haven chuckled. At least Cora had moved on from talking about Dare's hotness. Her stomach did a loop-the-loop because Cora . . . wasn't wrong. It was just that he was equally intimidating, which made the hotness harder for Haven to appreciate. "Who else did you meet?" she asked to keep Cora talking—about someone other than Dare.

As her friend ticked off a long list of names—well, nicknames, mostly—of Ravens she'd met, Haven finished her food and found it easier and easier to lose the anxiety she'd felt when she'd peeked in on the party and spoken with Dare.

Finally, Haven cleaned up her mess and put everything away.

"Come meet some people," Cora said, face expectant.

But Haven knew her limits. Tonight had been adventurous enough already. "No. The party's just too much for me. But you should totally go back."

Cora gave her a sad puppy face, complete with a fat bottom lip and all. "Please, I promise I'll stay by your side the whole time."

With a small smile, Haven shook her head. "You know I'm the worst partygoer ever. So go have fun and don't worry about me. I'm gonna sit out on the porch for a while and then head back up." One of her favorite things about being there was the peacefulness of the woods, the Blue Ridge Mountains, and the valley vista below. And despite the fact that the darkness would keep her from appreciating the view, she could still enjoy the peacefulness and put off holing herself up in her room for a little while longer. Apparently, she was also the oldest twenty-two-year-old ever.

"Okey dokey," Cora said. "But if you change your mind . . ."

Haven wouldn't, and they both knew it, but she just smiled. "If I change my mind, I'll come find you."

Nodding, Cora winked. "Okay. Stay out of trouble."

Haven smiled even though she wondered just how possible that actually was, for either of them. "Ha ha. Would you go already?"

Cora stuck her tongue out and left.

Haven made for the back door that led to the building-long covered back porch. Honestly, Cora was going to go party with an entire motorcycle club, and Haven was going to go sit by herself in the night air. Of the two of them, she was hardly the one who needed to worry about finding trouble. At least for tonight.

CHAPTER 3

A knock on the office door. "Hey, D?" Maverick leaned in as Dare looked up from the bag of
patches on the desk. "Was looking for you, man." The
club's vice-president and Dare's cousin, Maverick Rylan
was the light, good-looking, and upbeat yin to Dare's
dark, beat-to-hell, and brooding yang. The fucker. Good
thing he was one of Dare's best and most trusted friends
in the world.

"What's up, Mav?" Dare asked, letting his head fall
back heavily against the tall leather desk chair. Hands
linked over his gut, ankles crossed, shitkickers resting on
the desk's far corner, Dare was almost considering just
sleeping there for the night—the party providing com-
forting white noise in the background, the warm spring
air blowing through the open office window. The insanity
of the clubhouse was a helluva lot better than the solitude
of his own place sometimes.

Maverick dropped his big-ass frame into the beat-up wooden chair on the desk's far side. "You should be out there with everyone." The words were more question than criticism, more concern than censure.

Dare shrugged. "I was out there."

The droll stare was pure smart-ass Maverick. "It's a fucking celebration."

"I know what the hell it is," Dare said.

"Then you should be out there," Maverick said, shaking his shaggy sandy-blond hair out of his face. Intelligent dark blue eyes glared at Dare. "We need you out there, D."

"Get off my back, Maverick. I'm here. I'm always here. Everything I do, I do for this club." Dare's boots thudded loudly as he shifted position, all his peace from moments before gone now. Well, as close as he got to peace, anyway.

They glared at each other for a long moment, neither of them needing to explain why Maverick was hassling him. Harvey and Creed. The two brothers they'd lost and buried two weeks before. The two brothers whose loss they all still felt. The two brothers whose loss made tonight's celebration just a little bit hollow despite a fight won, justice served, vengeance claimed.

Heaving a sigh, Maverick's expression softened. "You're a moody motherfucker."

Now Dare was the one with the droll stare. "Oh, good. You've met me before." Only thirty-four years ago. Back before Dare's first family had been destroyed, back when Dare's father wasn't yet estranged from his grandfather and still returned to the East Coast for occasional visits. When they were kids, Dare and his brother, Kyle, and their cousin, Maverick, ran these mountains like the hellions they grew up to become. Well, Dare and Maverick got to grow up.

Maverick smirked and shook his head, his gaze falling on the bag of badges Dare had been studying earlier. The guy's eyes went wide upon realizing what he was seeing. He sat forward and tugged the clear plastic closer. "Gonna give these out tonight?" he asked, voice solemn, all the sarcasm gone.

Dare nodded. "Was just in here pulling my thoughts together." He wasn't one for grandstanding and speech giving, though certain occasions called for it—like honoring the death of a fallen brother. Or two.

His veep reached into the bag and pulled out two of the narrow, curved black patches. White stitching spelled out Harvey's name on one and Creed's on the other, along with the date they both died. It had been a while since the Ravens had last had to add a memorial patch to their colors, or cuts—the sleeveless riding vests that proclaimed their club affiliation and loyalty.

"All right, D." Maverick tapped the stiff patches against his palm and rose. "Sorry I hassled you."

"If you didn't hassle me, how would I know you loved me?" Dare smirked as his brother chuckled. "Now get the fuck out."

Flipping him the finger, Maverick left and closed the door behind him.

Dare pulled two patches out for himself and set them on the corner of the ancient, well-scribbled, coffee-stained blotter buried under papers and bike parts and about a dozen figurines of dogs riding motorcycles that people had given him as jokes over the years because he'd once given his German shepherd Indy, named after the vintage Indian motorcycles, a ride on his bike. Indy had been a good dog, the best. He'd died in his sleep of old age a few years before.

They should all be so lucky to go that way.

Shit. No sense putting this off. Dare grabbed the bag of patches and made his way to the rec room. He caught Blake's attention behind the bar and gestured to cut the music. The blond-haired prospect held up an empty glass in question. Dare nodded, and the loss of the tunes pretty quickly had everyone looking Dare's way—his brothers, their girlfriends, ladies and friends from town. From a grouping of couches in the back corner, Dare's grandfather gave him a nod, no doubt knowing what he was about to do.

Frank "Doc" Kenyon had whitish-gray hair and a beard. A hip and knee replacement a few years before made it difficult for him to ride much anymore, but there was absolutely no one else in the world that Dare respected or trusted more. After all, the man had once saved his life. And then he'd helped Dare build a whole new life—based around this club and this compound—when Dare hadn't thought it possible to go on after losing so much.

Glass of whiskey in hand, Dare scanned the room. Despite the festive atmosphere, the group's collective grief hummed just below the surface. He breathed it in and spoke. "It's a terrible tragedy when a brother takes his final ride. But Harvey and Creed haven't left us behind. Their spirits live on. In this family they loved. In each of you. In Phoenix," he said, raising his glass to Creed's cousin.

Despite the scary-looking jagged scar that ran from the guy's eye and through the side of his short brown hair, Phoenix almost always wore a smile that made him look younger than his thirty years, and he was nearly as often chasing skirts. But just then he wore an uncharacteristically solemn expression. The guys around him clapped him on the back and offered quiet words of support.

"I miss them both," Dare continued. "And I know each

of you do, too. But I won't shed a tear for them. Because they lived free. They lived the life they wanted. They died helping others. And they died with honor." Nods all around. Dare raised his glass high, and others joined him as he spoke. "So ride on, my brothers, and rest in peace. Wherever you are, may you always have the sun on your back, your fists in the wind, and the road stretching out before you." Dare raised his glass higher, then threw back the whiskey.

"Hear, hear," rang out in the room, and everyone drank in honor of Harvey and Creed. The bag of badges made the rounds.

"Now let's turn the music up, keep the liquor flowing, and celebrate a job damn well done. Because every one of you deserves it," Dare said to a round of raucous cheers. Music, conversation, and laughter filled the room once more. Stopping to talk to everyone as he went, Dare made his way across the room until he finally found Phoenix, Maverick, Caine McKannon, and Jagger Locke hanging out near the pool table. These four men made up most of the club's executive committee, with Phoenix serving as Road Captain in charge of all club runs and travel, Maverick running the club's chop shop, Caine serving as Sergeant-at-Arms in charge of rule enforcement and threat assessment, and Jagger serving as Race Captain in charge of organizing and running the club's racing activities.

"Hey, D," Maverick said, an approving look in his eye. "Good speech." He lifted his beer in salute.

Dare gave a nod, but he didn't want to put any more focus on their losses. Not tonight. And the look Phoenix wore said he felt the same way. Dare's gaze landed on Caine. "I want us to keep our ear to the ground for a while. Make sure nothing's coming back on us, given everything we've been involved with the past few weeks." Namely, taking down Baltimore's Church Gang, their longtime enemies, and helping expose a major military conspiracy. Officially, the authorities proclaimed that they'd rounded up all the conspirators, but you could never be too careful.

"Agreed," Caine said, answering in the fewest possible syllables, just like he always did. Scrubbing a hand over the dark scruff on his jaw, his gaze was calculating and filled with lethal intent toward anyone looking to harm them. From his six-four height, to his shaved black hair, which he always covered with a black knit cap, to the all-black ink covering a lot of his skin, to the small, round gauges in both ears, everything about Caine read intimidating—which often suited their purposes well. The only spot of lightness on him were the blue eyes so pale they didn't look real. "I'll make contacts on it in the morning."

"We have a run on Friday," Phoenix said, his voice flat and so unlike his normal smart-ass self. "I'll do some quiet asking while we're out."

Dare nodded. "Sounds good."

With his wavy mess of dark brown hair, his ability to play the hell out of any guitar, and his habit of humming under his breath, Jagger had come by his handle honestly. The guy took a swig of his beer. "I think I'm gonna need two weeks to get the races running again. We'd cleared the calendar when we didn't know how long the shit in Baltimore would take. That work for you?" Hosting stock-car and dirt-bike racing at the racetrack they owned was their main business, along with more occasional demolition derbies and less formally organized quarter-mile drag racing at a strip constructed on their property for that specific purpose. Three-hundred-plus acres gave them all kinds of room to move.

"Sounds good. Let's make sure Ike's in the loop so he can open betting again." As his day job, Ike Young was a tattoo artist at Hard Ink Tattoo in Baltimore, not to mention the guy who did most of the club's official ink when he was here, but he was also the Ravens' longtime betting officer and their point man in the city for racing bets and debt collection. Ike made the Ravens lots of coin. Dare did a quick sweep of the room but didn't see Ike around.

"Will do," Jagger said, his fingers moving with the chord changes in the rock song that was playing. The guy was brilliant. He could equally pick up an unfamiliar instrument or take apart an engine and perfect either within a day. Two at most.

Dare put in another hour of face time at the party and didn't feel bad for cutting out as people passed out, couples paired off, and the whole shindig started to wind down. Sometimes he felt like the years he'd spent alone and drifting had transformed him into an incurable loner. Because there were moments when he could stand in a roomful of people and feel totally alone, and other times when being social took more effort than he had to give and he absolutely craved his solitude. Like now.

On the way back to his office, Dare heard voices coming from the small room Ike used for his studio. Dare knocked.

A pause, and then, "Come in."

Dare opened the door to find Ike sitting on his stool, a tattoo machine in his hand and the tattoo on his bald head visible. Jessica Jakes sat in the chair next to Ike, the red skin on her neck revealing where Ike had been working moments before. Dare didn't know much about Jess besides that she worked at Hard Ink with Ike. "Sorry. Didn't mean to interrupt," Dare said, before looking to Jessica. "How are you, Jess?"

The woman had jet black hair with thick red strands and pretty much as many tats as Ike. "Good now that everything's over in Baltimore. Glad you all are back and we can all get back to normal."

Dare nodded. "Hope so." No doubt Ike and Jess were anxious in their own way about what would happen now. The tattoo shop's building had been heavily damaged in a firefight—the same attack that had claimed the lives of Harvey and Creed.

"We were just finishing," Ike said. "Need me?" A big mountain of a guy, Ike had found his way to the Ravens a decade before, and he and Dare had bonded over a fuckton of unfortunate shit they had in common. Evil fathers. Lost loved ones. Long years drifting on their own. The usual.

"Jagger's looking for you. Find him about the race schedule tonight if you can," Dare said.

"As soon as I finish up with Jess I'll get on it." Ike gave the petite woman a look, and her answering smile suddenly clued Dare in. They were together. Well, damn. In all the years Dare and Ike had known each other, neither of them had gotten serious about a woman. But good for Ike. Given everything the guy had been through, he deserved it.

"That works," Dare said. With a nod, he stepped out of Ike's studio and closed the door.

Back in his own office, Dare shut himself in, turned on the desk lamp, and dropped his ass into his chair. For a long time, he sat in the dim golden light, staring at the two remembrance patches on the desk. Slowly, he became aware of a soft sound—music? Or humming, maybe? He shifted toward the window that looked out over the clubhouse's big back porch. The darkness kept him from seeing much, but the sound—definitely a woman humming—was coming from someone out there for sure.

He stretched further, far enough to see the moonlight reflect off of long blond hair.

Haven. Sitting with her head lying on folded arms on the porch railing. Her face was totally in shadows, but her humming continued on. Soft. Sweet. Peaceful.

Dare clicked off the desk lamp and settled back into his chair, arms crossed, feet up. In the darkness, Haven's song seemed a little louder, more distinct. As tired as he was and as calming as her singing was, Dare was surprised he didn't nod off sooner. Instead, he hung there, right on the edge of sleep. The image of Haven standing in the doorway of the rec room played against the inside of his eyelids.

He hoped their talk had put her more at ease. She and Cora had nothing to their names as far as Dare knew, and, though he hadn't yet learned all their details, it seemed pretty clear they were runaways from something or someone. Until he got the backstory on them, he wouldn't know fully how to help them. So they were probably here to stay for at least a little while.

I just usually expect the worst. That way it doesn't hurt as much when it happens.

Her words from earlier came back to him in the quiet. In some ways—and certainly in that sentiment—she reminded him so much of himself. Or, at least, of the person he'd been back before he'd found his grandfather and a home at the clubhouse. The Raven Riders MC had already existed back then, headed up by Doc and a small group of his friends. But it wasn't until Dare arrived that the organization started to grow and take in new blood. First Dare. Then Maverick. Then Bandit. Then Caine. And many others, too.

Now these men were his family of choice if not by blood. Though they'd spilled plenty of that together over the years, too.

Finally, Haven's humming lured him into a state of semiconsciousness devoid of thoughts, free of concerns, and increasingly unaware of the world around him. And then he was out altogether.

IT STARTED THE way it always did. With Dare standing in the doorway of Kyle's bedroom.

"Mom's home from the bank," Dare said. "And Dad just pulled in after her."

"What?" Kyle asked, his eyes going wide. Their father was supposed to be on an overnight ride with the club. That's why they'd picked today for this.

"Shit, the bags," Kyle said, already in motion.

They scrambled down the steps to the living room, where three suitcases and two duffel bags sat packed for the new life their mother wanted for them. There'd been a time when she'd been fully supportive of the Diablos—after all, she'd married the man who became the club vice president. But that was before Kyle had been forced to kill two men—his first kills—as a way of proving his loyalty to an outlaw motorcycle club that viewed jail time as a badge of honor. When Mom found out what her seventeen-year-old son, the youngest Diablos prospect, had done, she'd been angry, then terrified, then resolved—she wanted her boys as far away from Arizona as they could get. Kyle might not have gone along with it if their father's alcohol-induced rages hadn't been getting worse and worse—landing both Dare and their mom in the ER in pretty quick succession.

Kyle shoved a duffel bag onto Dare's shoulder and a suitcase into his hand. "Gotta get these outta here," he said, grabbing the rest. Raised voices outside said their parents were close to the front porch of the old split-level. He and Kyle had just reached the top of the stairs when the front door crashed against the wall in the small foyer.

Yelling. Arguing. Crying.

Kyle all but shoved them into their parents' room and raced to the window which faced the backyard. He lifted the sash and squeezed the releases to lift the screen, too. "Climb out. I'll drop the bags down to you. Just make sure you catch them so they don't make noise," Kyle whispered.

Willing to follow his older brother to the ends of the earth, Dare was already half out the window. The house's split-level style meant that the drop wasn't as high as a regular second-story would be, but it was still enough that Dare's ankles, knees, and elbows took a beating when he hit the ground. One by one, Kyle dropped the bags out of the window, both of them trying like hell to be quiet and ignore the escalating noise coming from the living room.

Yelling. Arguing. Crying. Crashes.

Gunshot.

Dare got dizzy as all the blood rushed down to his feet. "Mom!" he cried, looking up at his brother.

Kyle's eyes were wild with anger and fear. "Get out of here, now," he rasped. "We'll meet you. You know where."

"No, Kyle," Dare said. "I'm not going without you." They could disappear together into the woods surrounding their house. That's what their mom would want them to do. She'd catch up when she could. *If* she could. God, the thought tore through him as hotly as any bullet would.

"Kyle! Dean! Get your asses down here!" Their dad's voice. "Dare" had been Kyle's nickname for him, one Dare had used without exception since that day. Dean Kenyon didn't exist. And hadn't for over twenty years.

Kyle's expression was livid. "Get the fuck out, Dare. Now!" Then he disappeared from the window.

Seconds later, a new round of chaos erupted. More yelling. More arguing. A scream.

Then nothing. The silence hung heavy and suffocating over Dare as if it had a physical form.

More screams.

Another gunshot.

Dare gasped awake.

For one heartbeat, his brain remained unaware enough to hope it'd all been a dream. And then reality came crashing back down. Kyle and Mom were dead. And Dare hadn't done a single thing to save them.

CHAPTER 4

When the horror of the dream faded away and his heart finally stopped hammering, Dare became aware of the silence. No music or voices came from the direction of the rec room, which probably meant the party had finally wrapped up. He woke up his phone to see that it was nearly 2:30 A.M.

At this rate, he might as well just spend the night right where he was.

He settled back into his chair, but the second he closed his eyes, *another* silence suddenly loomed large. Haven's humming. Gone.

Dare shifted his boots to the floor and leaned toward the window, but he couldn't tell if she remained out there. Probably not, given the late hour, but not knowing was going to bug his ass until he found out for sure. On a weary sigh, he hauled himself up and made his way through the mostly dark clubhouse. Brothers had passed out here and there, but Dare was the only one vertical.

Just as he stepped out onto the back porch, thunder rumbled in the distance and golden flashes of lightning lit up the night sky. And in the next light show, he spotted Haven. Curled up in a ball in one of the cushioned lounge chairs.

Should he wake her? Or should he just leave her alone?

Thunder rumbled again, closer this time. Rain fell, softly at first, then in a steadier downpour that drummed against the aluminum roof. A gust of wind whipped warm, humid air through the porch and the rain started blowing at an angle, wetting the railing and chairs along it.

Well, hell. Dare couldn't leave her out there in this.

He leaned over the chair, using a hand on her shoulder to shake her. "Hey, Haven."

Thunder boomed so loud it shook the porch floor under Dare's boots.

Haven's eyelids flew open and her eyes went wide with terror. She screamed and scrabbled backward, but the reclined back of the chaise lounge kept her from getting very far away from him. "No, no, no!" she yelled, her arms and legs striking out.

"Shit. Whoa, Haven. It's okay," he said, reeling back. "It's just me. Dare. I didn't mean to scare you."

Her breathing was nearly hoarse it was so labored. Her gaze darted around. "Dare," she finally managed, looking up at him.

"Yeah," he said, gesturing to the rain. "Just thought we should get you inside."

Thunder crashed and lightning lanced the sky.

Haven flinched, her hands white-knuckling it around the arms of the chair. "Yeah," she said with a quick, jerky nod. "I'm sorry."

Her propensity to apologize for things that either weren't her fault or didn't require apologies made him feel protective of her—even more protective than he normally felt of the women who sought the Ravens' help. Dare knew from the firsthand experience of having a controlling dickhead of a father that someone had ingrained that knee-jerk reaction into her. "Don't worry about it."

The downpour became torrential and the wind whipped water under the cover of the porch roof. Long tendrils of hair blew around her head, and Haven gathered them in her fist as she rose.

She seemed shaky on her feet, and Dare leaned down and put his mouth near her ear so she could hear him over the deluge. "Are you okay?"

A quick nod. "Yes," she said, though he just barely heard her. A fantastic explosion of thunder kept him from hearing her next words at all. She shrieked in fright and buried her face against his chest.

The contact shocked him, and it wasn't often that that happened. She'd given some pretty good cues earlier that she didn't want to be touched, and Dare had been around enough people with bad histories to know to respect their boundaries. Yet Haven touched him, taking shelter against his body.

Another clap of thunder had her pressing harder against him. One hand clutched at the edge of his cut.

Probably made him an asshole, but something about the way her hand fisted around the denim shot heat through him. Not that she'd meant to do it, of course. Not that she was probably even aware.

Shaking away the whole train of thought, Dare debated and then finally put an arm around her shoulders. When she showed no signs of minding the contact, he hugged her in tighter. God, she was a slender little thing in his arms. "Come on," he said, his lips against her ear. Keeping his arm around her, he guided her into the kitchen.

Inside, he secured the door and hit the kitchen lights.

Her shoulders sagged like she'd just been freed of a great weight. "Thanks," she said, hugging herself. "It's stupid, but I'm afraid of thunderstorms."

Dare looked at her, at the way her eyes skated away on the admission. Another story right there, no doubt. "We're all scared of something, Haven."

"Even you?" she asked, that electric-blue gaze filled with what looked like hope.

He gave a tight nod. "Even me."

HAVEN WAS COLD, wet, and embarrassed for freaking out in front of Dare. Again. Waking to a dark figure looming over her, she'd been sure her father had found her, would drag her back to a life she'd hated, would never let her go.

But her fear had given way to curiosity—about what a man like Dare could possibly fear. She was dying to know . . . but she chickened out of asking, and then he was heading toward the mess hall door.

"You heading up?" he asked, turning to peer at her over his shoulder.

The way he paused there perfectly highlighted the square edge of his jaw and had Haven thinking back to Cora's assessment earlier in the evening. Dare *was* hot. And his kindness made him even hotter, though he still intimidated the heck out of her. "Uh, yeah," she said. "In a minute. I need to get something to drink first."

With a nod, he disappeared through the door. Haven released a long breath and sagged into one of the chairs at the table. Something occurred to her in the quiet stillness. She'd burrowed against Dare's chest. She could still smell his scent, all leather and warm skin. And he hadn't flipped out on her. Or taken advantage of her vulnerability.

How sad was she that his decency made him note-worthy?

From there, her thoughts quickly spiraled. How long would she and Cora be welcome there? How would they get the resources they needed to start a new life, one where her father couldn't find her? What would that new life even look like? God, she was almost twenty-three years old with no skills, no money, and not even a high school diploma, since her father hadn't thought it important to officially withdraw her from public school or do anything to create an actual home school experience for her.

Between the storm and her troubling thoughts, Haven knew she had absolutely no chance of falling back to sleep. Her brain was wide awake and going a mile a minute. And there was only one thing that helped when middle-of-the-night anxiety settled in. Baking.

She loved cooking and was good at it, but baking was the thing that made her feel the best. That calmed her. That took her away from all the crap. Growing up without a mother, Haven had become responsible for cooking as soon as she'd been old enough to do it. In her father's quest to *look* respectable, they had a big, beautiful kitchen in their big, beautiful house, which he'd stuffed it full of his collections—of guns and knives, of World War II collectibles, of Atlanta Falcons memorabilia, of rare books he never read. She thought of him that way—as a collector. And she was just one more thing he owned. For her, the new plantation-style house, complete with pretentious white columns along the front, had been nothing more than a gilded cage.

Poking around in the pantry, Haven gathered ingredients until she decided what she'd make—cinnamon rolls. Bunny had told Haven to make herself at home in the clubhouse's kitchen, so she didn't feel like she'd upset anyone by baking away her troubles. Made from scratch, the rolls took a while because the dough had to rise, but that was one of Haven's favorite things about them. Besides how rich and decadent they were.

Slowly and methodically, she prepared a double batch of dough, then buttered and covered the dough balls and left them to rise in mixing bowls. Her father's intolerance for messes had taught her to clean up right behind herself, so once she'd tidied up, she set about making the filling with all its buttery, brown sugary, cinnamony goodness. Taking a peek at the dough, she found it risen, which meant it was time for the fun part. Haven dusted the counter with a healthy covering of flour and worked the dough out with her hands and a rolling pin until she had a big rectangle in front of her. She brushed melted butter over the dough and sprinkled lots of the cinnamon-sugar mix over it, then she rolled and stretched it until she had one superlong log of dough. She cut the log into slices and repeated the process with the second dough ball, giving her three dozen buns total.

The dough needed one more resting period before baking, which gave her plenty of time to clean up errant flour, wash dishes, and make her killer cream cheese frosting. An hour later, she slid the buns into the double ovens, already in love with this kitchen and planning what she'd make next. Assuming no one minded her using so many supplies.

One day . . . one day she was going to live in a place with an amazing kitchen where she could bake to her heart's content. She might not know what her future held yet, but she promised herself that much. She could dream, right?

The gray light of dawn was rising as she pulled the rolls

out to cool. They smelled incredible and filled the entire kitchen with the warm aroma of cinnamon. After being there for a few weeks, Haven knew there were usually at least some Ravens around for every meal, but most especially on the weekends. Last Sunday hadn't been too busy because a lot of the club had still been in Baltimore, but now with everyone back, maybe there'd be more.

As she slathered on the icing, Haven decided she really liked the idea of the club sitting down to a Sunday breakfast that included her rolls. It was a small way to give back to them for taking her and Cora in. When she was done with the icing, she left the rolls to cool on the big stove top, plating one to take for herself.

And then, before it got much later and she chanced running into anyone, she slipped out of the kitchen and upstairs to her room, more than a little delighted that the whole clubhouse smelled good. In the solitude of her room, she bit into the warm roll on a sigh, and the creamy icing and buttery cinnamon nearly melted in her mouth. Haven didn't know how to do many things, but these were perfection.

And in a life where so very little was ever good, let alone perfect, it gave her some solace to be able to make something good—to *do* good—with her own two hands.

HAVEN WASN'T ENTIRELY sure why Cora ever knocked, since her knock happened at the same instant that she opened the door and walked on in. But it was pure Cora, so it made Haven smile even though it chased away the last vestiges of the nap she'd been trying to take.

"Hey," Haven said.

"You're still in bed," Cora said, stretching out next to her. "Was that because you were up all night baking the world's best cinnamon buns?"

Haven wrenched into a sitting position. "You didn't tell anyone it was me, did you?"

Cora rolled her eyes. "Knowing you'd probably ask me that question in that very tone, I refrained from sharing that you are a goddess of all things sweet and ooey-gooey."

"Good," Haven said, reclining back onto her elbow. "They *were* good, weren't they?"

"Your best yet. Seriously. But why don't you want anyone to know? The guys were nearly fighting over them. Two guys arm-wrestled for the last one. I'm not even kidding."

Shrugging, Haven finally said, "I do it because it makes me feel good and I enjoy it. I don't need anything more from it than that."

"Well," Cora said, reaching up and swiping her fingers over Haven's eyebrow, "you might want to get rid of the flour-y evidence, then."

"Oh," Haven said, scrubbing her hands over her face. She'd been so tired after eating her bun that she'd lain down and fallen immediately asleep. At last.

"Besides, Bunny said she'd take us to the mall to get some clothes and so I can get this stupid hair fixed." Cora fingered at the choppy, blunt ends of her hair. When they ran away, Cora's hair had been halfway down her back, and one of the first things she did was take a pair of scissors to it. Haven had been shocked at how violently Cora hacked at it at a truck stop along I-95, but Cora laughed off her concern. It signified the new her, she said. So far, Haven had declined the offer to lose her long locks. It was one of the few parts of herself she thought was truly pretty. "Maybe you should get yours done, too?"

Haven fingered her hair, the thought of going out in public taking her belly on a loop-the-loop. There was no way her father could know where she was—heck, *she* barely knew where she was—but that didn't keep her from worrying. "Maybe. You really think that's wise? Going out, I mean?"

Cora twisted her lips, her expression going serious. "I think it's okay. We're a long way from Georgia here, and Ike said no one has any way of knowing that we're with the Ravens anyway."

"I guess that's right," Haven said, wishing she shared Cora's certainty. But Haven knew her father well enough to know he had to be livid that she'd defied him—and that she'd gotten away with some of his money to boot. *No one* crossed him. Or, at least, no one remained around to tell the tale if they did. "Okay. Well, I should grab a quick shower if we're going out."

An hour later, they were at Frederick's mall with Bunny McKeon, an older firecracker of a lady who'd gone out of her way the past few weeks to make them feel at home at the Ravens' compound. The mall was bigger and busier than Haven expected. The compound was so secluded that it made it feel like they were in the middle of nowhere, when in reality they were less than an hour away from the cities of Baltimore and Washington.

Haven hadn't been out in public like this in years. Her father's controlling possessiveness of her had started when her body began to visibly mature and worsened when he discovered she'd slept with her first and only boyfriend. Once her father had pulled her from school, he'd slowly but surely walled off her life until she could only leave the house with his permission and in the company of one of his drivers, usually Jack Carter. On the positive side, Jack was never mean to her, but the fact that he followed her everywhere revealed that his true purpose was to make sure she didn't run.

Not ready to cut her hair, Haven declined an appointment at the salon, but she enjoyed watching her friend's excitement as the stylist shaped Cora's blond hair into a cute and sassy shoulder-length cut full of soft waves and long layers.

"So, I have two questions for you," Bunny said as they waited in the chairs nearest the stylist's station. As Dare's great-aunt, Maverick's mother, and Doc's sister, Bunny had earned a ton of influence and respect from the club. She was also married to one of the Ravens—an older guy named Rodeo. And she was the person Haven had gotten to know best during their two-week stay with the Ravens.

But that didn't mean Haven had a clue what Bunny could want to ask her. "Okay," Haven said, equal parts curious and nervous.

"Were those your cinnamon rolls, and, if so, what do I have to do to get the recipe?" The older lady gave her a knowing smile.

Heat filled Haven's face as she nodded. "I don't really work off of written recipes, but I can probably write it down."

"That would be lovely, hon, because I haven't stopped thinking about them all day. The guys treated me like royalty thinking I made them and hoping I'd do it again soon, but now that I know it was you, I'll make sure to give credit where it's due." Bunny patted her arm.

"You really don't have to do that," Haven said. "I mean, I'm happy to make them again. And, in fact, helping in the kitchen makes me feel like I'm earning my way a little, especially with all this." Haven gestured at the salon and the three big shopping bags of clothes that sat at their feet.

Bunny's pale blue eyes narrowed. "Are you saying you don't mind if I don't tell anyone or that you don't want me to tell anyone?" As usual, she saw right through Haven.

Haven just hadn't decided yet if she really liked that about Bunny or wished the woman wasn't quite so perceptive.

"I guess I'd prefer no one knew. I just like to do it, not get, I don't know, praised for it."

Bunny laughed, and it made her look younger. Haven guessed the lady was probably in her sixties, but between her wavy pale blond hair and the jeans, black T-shirt, and black ankle boots she was wearing, she made sixties look good. "See, that's where we're different," Bunny said with a wink. "I love to get praised."

Haven couldn't help but laugh, too. "I'll remember that."

Cora joined them at the chairs, her face bright with happiness. "What do you think?"

"Fun and flirty, hon. She did a real nice job," Bunny said.

Rising, Haven gestured for Cora to spin around. Her new style hung in soft waves to just above her shoulders. "Oh, Cora. It looks so pretty. Do you like it?"

Cora beamed. "I do. Now it's your turn." She grabbed Haven's hand.

"Not today," Haven said, laughing and trying to resist Cora's pull toward the hairdresser's chair.

Finally, Cora stopped pulling her and planted her hands on her hips. "Okay, here's the deal. You either get your hair cut, or you have to go back and get those outfits you tried on."

Haven had picked out two cute but conservative summer dresses, two pairs of shorts, a few T-shirts, a pair of sandals, and some underthings. But she'd resisted the clothes that Bunny had picked out—skinny jeans with a sparkly pattern on the back pockets and the clingy black V-neck shirt that actually made her look like she had some boobs. That outfit seemed to scream *Look at me!*

when Haven was used to doing almost anything to blend into the background. More than that, not dressing in a way that attracted attention had become a survival skill in her father's house, where some number of his goons were always hanging around. So she'd taken to wearing boring clothes that were too big, keeping her face plain, and letting her hair shield her expressions.

"That's not fair," Haven said as she debated the options. She knew Cora well enough to know her friend wouldn't let this go until she picked. Weird thing was, back before her father had forced her to drop out of high school, Haven had liked wearing pretty, fashionable things. But that girl had been gone for a long, long time.

Pulling at the oversized T-shirt she wore, Haven huffed. "I'll get the clothes," she finally said. Getting them didn't mean she had to—

"Yay! And don't think that means I won't make you wear them," Cora said.

Haven's shoulders sagged. "Sometimes I think you know me too well."

Bunny laughed as she paid for Cora's haircut. "With friends, there's no such thing. Everyone needs someone who calls them on their shit. Now, let's go get you that outfit before you change your mind."

CHAPTER 5

"Church is now in special session," Dare said, banging a gavel against the old wooden table. The club's meetings, which had long been referred to as Church, officially took place on the first Monday evening of the month, but their recent activity in Baltimore had disrupted their normal routines, making them cancel May's regular meeting. Now they needed to regroup and strategize, so Dare had called the extra session of fully patched members.

Bear Lowry took attendance. The Old Timer had a full brown beard and was round through the middle, but he'd been doing the combined jobs of secretary and treasurer for the past few years because he was good with numbers, better with investments, and someone Dare and Doc trusted without question. "We've got twenty-four in attendance," he said. Decent number given the fact that everyone had been away from home more than usual lately.

They never had a full house anyway because some guys had part-time jobs or worked night shifts that didn't allow them to come.

Dare nodded as his gaze scanned over his brothers. Some were seated at the fifteen-foot-long table, and some were seated around the back of the long rectangular space that had probably been a sitting room when the clubhouse had been an inn. A mammoth stone fireplace spanned from floor to ceiling behind Dare, a carved Ravens logo like the one that hung in the mess hall centered over the mantel. At the other end of the room hung a mounted deer head wearing a brain bucket and sunglasses with its hooves placed on mounted handlebars.

"First thing I want to say is job well done in Baltimore. That situation was red hot, and all of you handled yourselves," Dare said. Words of agreement all around. "I want everyone to stay vigilant the next few weeks. Keep your eyes open for anything out of the ordinary in our backyard. Keep your ears open for any unusual activity. Given the caliber of the conflict we were engaged in, I just want us on the lookout for any possible repercussions."

"I put out some feelers," Caine said, his pale gaze ice-cold serious. In addition to their racing/betting activities at the track, the other major business the club ran was a trucking escort service. Mostly this involved providing escorts for container trucks or convoys carrying sensitive cargoes of one type or another. They had a few regulars they worked with and also took on one-offs on a case-by-case basis. When the money was right. This gave the club contacts and associates not just in central Maryland, but along the Interstate 95, 70, and 81 corridors into Pennsylvania, West Virginia, and Virginia. "Haven't heard anything, but I'll keep you posted."

"What is it you're anticipating?" Doc asked. If anybody

considered the men around this table family as much as Dare, it was his grandfather, one of the Ravens' founders. Frank Kenyon had gotten his nickname not because he had any medical expertise, but because he'd gained a reputation for fixing or figuring ways out of problems and had a knack for giving the kind of advice and tough love the guys needed.

"To be honest, I'm not sure, but my instincts tell me I'm missing something about what went down in Baltimore, missing some loose end. Maybe I'm being paranoid given the strength of the groups we were up against. Though the Church Gang was pretty well obliterated, someone else will rise in their place. If nothing else, that's something to keep an eye on," Dare said, wishing his gut could nail down what was bugging him.

Ike sat at the far end of the table, the ink on his head and neck making him look like the hard-ass he could sometimes be. "Since I'll be heading back to the city this week, I'll make sure any intel Nick's team acquires gets passed on here, too." Nick Rixey was a good friend of Ike's and the unofficial leader of the team of former Green Berets the club had fought alongside in Baltimore these past weeks.

"Good," Dare said. "That's real good."

"How worried do you think we gotta be?" came a deep, quiet voice from the back corner of the room. Sam "Slider" Evans, his nickname earned almost a dozen years before when his back tire hit a patch of gravel on an old country road and he went off into a ditch. He'd missed a huge tree by inches, skidded over the root system, and ultimately laid down his bike in a gully. Not a single serious scratch to rider or machine. For years they'd referred to him as one lucky SOB for coming out of that wreck without sustaining any damage, but no one had said that about him since his wife died of breast cancer three years before, leaving him with two young sons to care for on his own. Slider even attending a club meeting was noteworthy, as he'd nearly withdrawn from everything but his job and caring for his boys.

"Not worried, just cautious," Dare said. He fucking hoped he was right.

Wearing a black doo-rag knotted around unkempt, light brown hair that probably hadn't seen a haircut since before his wife died, Slider heaved a breath, a troubled frown on his face, but he said no more.

"One other thing we probably ought to hash out while everyone's here," Dare said, his shoulders heavy with the weight of this topic. "The guns we picked up during the ops in Baltimore." The Ravens had taken the hardware in partial payment for providing muscle in the Hard Ink team's fight—that was back before losing two of their own had brought the Ravens into the fight of their own free will. No payment required.

Doc sighed and scrubbed his hand over the whitish-gray hair of his beard. "Guns stolen from the Church Gang. This is dirtier shit than normal, Dare."

Dare nodded, knowing Doc hadn't agreed with the club taking possession of the weapons captured during an ambush of the Church Gang a few weeks before. It had been one of their most heated meetings and most divided votes. And Dare understood why. From the very beginning, going all the way back to when Dare first pushed to rebuild the Ravens' membership in the years after he'd arrived there, he'd made a commitment to Doc that he wasn't trying to recreate the Diablos' way of life in Maryland. That meant he didn't want to turn the Ravens into One Percenters who prized violence as proof of loyalty and a rite of passage, and who fought and killed to defend territory, usually because they wanted to control drug and gun sales in that territory. Dare's father's full embracing of the hardest parts of the hard-core MC culture was what had created the ice-cold rift between Doc and his son when Dare was just a snot-nosed kid.

So those had been easy commitments for Dare to make—because he didn't want to become his father. Ever.

None of that meant the Ravens were squeaky clean, though, because they weren't. But Dare was more than comfortable with the places where the legality of their actions became blurred or outright crossed the line, because it made the protective work they did possible. Ends justifying means and all that. Sometimes doing a little wrong allowed you to do an even greater good. His version of morality probably seemed like splitting hairs to some, but Dare had lived both lives—he *knew* there was a difference, a big one. And it mattered a helluva lot.

So, yeah, Dare wasn't in love with having these guns or needing to sell them. But the club had voted on it, and now they had to deal with that. "I don't disagree. But now that we have them, I don't want us holding on to them longer than we have to." That weight he'd been feeling on his shoulders pushed down on him ever harder as the tension in the room thickened.

Phoenix sat up straight in his seat and jabbed his finger into the table. "I say we should keep a small cache for ourselves. Just in case. And when we sell them, we do it way outside of our own backyard. We don't want all that heat on the market here. We don't want it associated with us. And we sure as fuck don't want it used against us."

"Amen," Ike said. "And keep it out of Baltimore while we're at it. Don't want it traced back to the original source with the Church Gang either."

Nods all around, though not all of those nodding looked happy about it.

"You gonna take this on, then, son?" Doc asked Phoenix. "If we gotta have our hands in this, then I agree with your thinking on it. As Road Captain, you're best positioned to make the contacts and orchestrate the sale. Maybe Caine, too."

Phoenix's brown-eyed gaze cut from Doc to Caine and back again. "Count on it. Whatever the club needs me to do. Always." To look at him, you might think Phoenix was just a laid-back player, joking and rarely serious. But the guy had a deep-seated sense of loyalty and protectiveness as intense as any man Dare knew. When it mattered, he was solid through and through and knew how to get shit done while staying shiny side up. Dare didn't doubt his word for a minute.

"I'm in," Caine said.

"Then Phoenix, Caine, and I will stay in touch on this and keep everyone informed," Dare said. After that, they moved on to less divisive business—this Friday's escort run, next Friday's return to racing, and the restoration of open betting. "Anyone have anything else?"

"I had a Hang-Around express his interest in being considered for prospect status. Mike Renner," Maverick said.

Hang-Arounds were friends of the club who were sizing up whether they were interested in applying for membership while the club evaluated the guy's likely fit for the club in return. Some guys hung around and never applied. Some hung around and either they or the club realized the fit wasn't there, especially if they weren't on board for whatever reason with the club's mission. Once they were out, they were out. Some guys went on to become prospects and later fully patched members.

Every single man around the table had gone through the latter process. A lot of guys who gravitated toward the Ravens were looking for a place to belong, like maybe they didn't have a lot of that other places in their lives. Some were hard-core bike enthusiasts looking for like-minded friends. Others were specifically attracted by the Ravens' protective mission for reasons of their own. It took all types.

"Discussion?" Dare asked. Taking on a new prospect was serious business. It meant they became a lifetime member of the family, could expect the club to have their back, and could be counted on to have their brothers' backs, too. It also gave them an in on sensitive information and brought them into the fold of the club's businesses and income streams.

Caine fingered the gauge in his right ear. "We already have two prospects. Is Renner someone we definitely want?" Blake Green and Jeb Fowler were prospects who'd come in at about the same time, nearly six months before.

"He's given time and money to the club the past few months, and even helped on one of our protection details when we were understaffed on a double-run night," Phoenix said. "Seems serious, reliable."

"He can be a sloppy fucking drunk, though," Bear groused as he tapped his pen against the table. A low rumble of laughter ran around the table, and a few guys shared stories. Given his father's drinking problem, Dare didn't have much tolerance for guys who couldn't handle their liquor, but as club president he only got a vote when there was a tie, which wasn't often. Didn't mean he couldn't work to influence that vote, though, which he did when he needed to.

"Hell," Phoenix said, "if that's a determining factor, more than one of us would be in trouble." His comment met with more laughter, and Dare was glad to see the guy joking around.

"Let's put it to a vote," Dare said. The yays won the

question, eighteen to six. "Let him know, Mav." Sitting at Dare's right, his cousin nodded. "Anything else?" Dare asked. When no one said anything, the meeting adjourned.

Guys spilled out of the meeting room at the back of the clubhouse and made their way into the rec room and front lounge to play pool or shoot the shit.

Bunny found Rodeo hanging at the bar in the rec room and gave him a kiss on the cheek. With his deep dimples, Rodeo always looked like he was about to break into a grin, but never more than when he was in Bunny's presence. The two had been together for the better part of fifteen years. Dare couldn't imagine what that kind of commitment would be like, and was more and more sure he wouldn't be finding out, either.

"Hey, Sugar. What's up?" Rodeo asked.

She put her arm around her man's waist. "I have something you all are really gonna like," she said, looking from Rodeo and Doc to Dare and Maverick, all gathered around the bar with glasses of whiskey in their hands.

"I know you do," Rodeo said with a wicked grin. "But I hope you don't think you're sharing it with these sorry fuckers."

Bunny elbowed him in the side, and Maverick shook his head at the older couple's antics just like he always did. He'd long ago given up on being embarrassed by his mother and Rodeo's public displays of affection. He was too happy that she'd escaped from his abusive prick of a father to begrudge her any happiness now. "Trust me," she said, nodding her head and encouraging them to follow her.

Rodeo shrugged, and they all followed her through the lounge and into the mess hall—where one of the tables was covered with four big trays of cookies. "Well, hell,

Bunny. You're outdoing yourself lately," Rodeo said, grabbing a big chocolate chip cookie.

"Yeah," Doc said. "What's with all the treats? You trying to sweeten us up for something?" The question met with laughter as more guys caught word that there was food and made their way into the mess hall.

"Can't a woman just do something nice for the men in her life?" she asked, looking way too innocent.

A loud, collective "no" followed by a round of raucous laughter filled the room. God, it felt good to laugh. And Dare really liked seeing his brothers have a reason to laugh, too.

"Well, screw y'all, then," she said, grabbing one of the trays and making like she'd take it back into the kitchen.

Dare got in front of his great-aunt—the only mother figure Dare had known since the day he fled his house—and lifted it out of her hands. She gave him plenty of shit, and he loved her for it. "That won't be necessary, Bunny," he said with a wink. "You know we're just giving you hell."

"I know you are," she said. "And you know I *know* what a giant sweet tooth you have, Dare Kenyon. So you better be nice to me."

Grinning, Dare nodded and returned the tray to the table. Peanut butter cookies with peanut butter chips, complete with the lines caused by mashing a fork into the top before baking. Shit if that didn't resurrect a long-buried memory.

Him and Kyle and Mom in their kitchen back in Arizona, making Christmas cookies. Dare couldn't have been more than six or seven. And not only had they made his mom's famous iced sugar cookies for the Diablos' big party, but she'd made a batch of peanut butter cookies—with chips like these had—just for Dare. Because they were his favorite. As he took a bite, the rich salty-sweet of the peanut butter flavor sucked him back to the moment when she'd surprised him with the dough and then let him have the fun of rolling it into balls and mashing the fork tines into it to make the design.

Stupid fucking thing to remember, wasn't it? Getting all sentimental over a goddamned cookie. Dare finished the one in his hand.

Fucking good cookie, though. And he wasn't the only one who thought so, judging by how fast they were flying off the trays. If it was one thing they could do in this club, it was pack away some food. A crazy big part of their monthly expenses went to food bills for the clubhouse— not that Dare minded. Sitting down to meals together made them feel even more like a family, and some of the guys didn't really have anyone to be going home to at dinnertime anyway.

Like, for example, you, Kenyon?

For fuck's sake.

Shaking away the thought, Dare elbowed his way to the table. "Y'all are a bunch of goddamned vultures," he said, diving in for another and taking two more for good measure.

"Asshole!" Maverick yelled to another round of laughter and name calling and cookie grabbing. Put a tray of cookies out and the Ravens were like a bunch of eight-year-olds, not a clubhouse full of hard-ass bikers.

But Dare liked seeing his brothers like this—happy and just kicking back. What did he need with a family of his own to go home to, when he had these motherfuckers to hang with and worry about?

He didn't. Not at all. Dare had everything he needed.

CHAPTER 6

Haven sat at the kitchen table with a small plate of cookies in front of her—the product of another restless night. Her sleeplessness had been less caused by anxiety than by excitement over the shopping spree for baking ingredients that Bunny had taken her on after they'd left the mall the day before. Haven had never been given such free rein in her life. And though a part of her felt guilty for spending money that wasn't hers, at least it was being used for the benefit of the club. She just got to have some fun along the way.

Peeking through the swinging door into the mess hall, Cora nibbled on a cookie. "They're a huge hit with the guys. Not that I ever doubted it," she said. "The trays are wiped clean. Annnd it's entirely possible Phoenix just picked up a crumb off the table and ate it. The ridiculously hot idiot."

"Wow," Haven said, a warm satisfaction curling

through her belly. "That was almost ten dozen cookies." Not counting the ones they'd kept in the kitchen for themselves.

"Well, there were a lot of guys here tonight," Cora said. "Not as many anymore though. It's starting to clear out." She ate another cookie and brushed her hands off. "I'll go grab the trays."

"I'll help," Haven said, butterflies doing a loop-the-loop inside her.

Cora smiled, but refrained from making a comment that probably would've had Haven second-guessing herself. They headed into the mess hall.

About a half dozen guys stood in a circle with Bunny, who gave Haven and Cora a wave and a smile. "You girls don't have to worry about that," she said.

"We got it, Bunny," Haven said.

Dare looked over his shoulder, then did a double take. His eyes went wide and his gaze ran a long, slow up-and-down over Haven's body, nearly pinning her in place. Heat filled her face. More than that, she felt hot everywhere. Part of her regretted wearing the new clothes—a second pair of jeans Bunny insisted they buy and a fitted pale-blue T-shirt—and part of her thrilled at the hungry look that suddenly came over Dare's face. That hunger scared her, too, so she turned on her heels and rushed into the kitchen with one of the trays.

"Did you see how Dare looked at you?" Cora whispered loudly.

"Sshh! Oh, my God, shut up," Haven whispered back. The tray clanged against the counter, sending both of them into a fit of giggles.

"You have to go back out there and get the others," Cora said, her expression full of challenge. "It's a roomful of people. Nothing's going to happen."

Heart racing, Haven planted her hands on her hips. "You think I won't."

Cora's eyebrows rose and she looked at her nails and sighed, a smile playing around her lips.

Haven turned around and went back into the mess hall. It was possible that there wasn't any oxygen in that room, though, because the minute she saw Dare again she got a little light-headed. What the heck was wrong with her? A single look should not throw a person into a complete freak-out. Then again, Haven wasn't normal. Or, at least, she hadn't been in a long time.

"You know you're not expected to"—Dare gestured at the table—"work around here, right? There's no quid pro quo."

She slid one tray on top of the other. "Okay," she said. "Keeping busy is good, though."

He gave a nod, and Haven felt his gaze running over her face as if he'd touched her with his fingers. Unsure what else to say, she ducked her head and made her way back to the kitchen again. She used her back to push the door open and found Dare still watching her, those intense brown eyes following her every move.

Why was he looking at her like that? Or maybe it was just her imagination?

The swinging door cut off Haven's view of him, and she turned and set the trays on the counter by the sink.

"Suddenly, you're the lion after they visited the wizard!" Cora said, a big grin on her face.

"Hardly," Haven said, filling the sink with water. Although it *did* feel good to do something all her instincts were warning her against doing, even if it was something totally small and unimpressive. At least, to other people it would seem that way. For Haven, being in a roomful of strangers was nearly the equivalent of going skydiving or bungee jumping. Actually, she'd probably be *fine* doing those things. It was people who scared her more than anything, because it was people who could do you the most harm.

In fact, now that she thought about it, she'd *love* to try skydiving someday. Imagine the thrill of the jump, the rush of the air, the once-in-a-lifetime view of the world, and the incredible pride you'd feel at having taken that chance when it was all done. So, yeah, a big kitchen of her own and skydiving. Look at her making plans, however crazy they might be.

Bunny came in just as they were drying the last of the trays. "Another hit, Haven." She helped them put away the last of the dishes. "You know, they say the way to a man's heart is through his stomach. You realize you're about to make forty bikers fall madly in love with you, right?"

It was a joke, of course, but the comment still whipped a shiver of nervousness across Haven's skin. "Nope," she said. "They'll all be in love with you."

Bunny grabbed her purse from a cabinet near the back door. "Ah, the old case of mistaken identity. How tragic for them." She gave Haven a wink. "Rodeo and I are heading out for the night. Call me if you need anything. Or just ask Dare. The man never leaves." She waved over her shoulder and disappeared back the way she came.

"You know what?" Haven said, feeling better, lighter, more hopeful than she had in a long, long while.

"What?" Cora asked, grabbing a couple of bottles of water from the fridge.

"Today . . . today was a good day." Not that anything big had really happened, but Haven's threshold for good days was sadly low.

Cora handed Haven a bottle and slung her arm around

her neck. "I can't even tell you how ecstatic it makes me to see you happy. Or, at least, happier."

"How about you?" Haven asked. "Are you happy? I know all this was way more than we ever—"

"I'm happy, too, Haven. Really," Cora said. "I'm with my best friend, who for the first time in years I don't have to worry about being mistreated by her father and his goons. Leaving Georgia was no sacrifice for me, you know this. I left a waitressing job at the truck stop and a drunk-ass father who—" She bit back the words and shook her head. "You know what? I'm not even dwelling on the past, because what makes me happy is that for the first time, we have a shot at a good, safe future. Together. Whatever it is has to be better than what we left, right?"

Haven nodded, Cora's words echoing some of Haven's own thoughts. But that didn't keep her mind from sticking on whatever it was Cora had been about to say about her father.

"So I propose a toast," Cora said, tilting out her water bottle. "To the future."

"To the future," Haven said with a smile. They tapped their water bottles. "Though I guess toasting with water is pretty lame."

Laughing, Cora shrugged. "One big adventure at a time. Ha! You know what you should do? You should make a list."

Haven sipped her water. "For what?"

"Of all the things you want to do and experience. All the adventures you want to have. Now that you're finally free to have them." Cora looked at her like she'd just invented sliced bread.

"And toasting with something more than water should be on this list?" Haven asked. How sad was it that she'd led such a sheltered life that something so boring would be new to her?

Then again, she'd seen and overheard and experienced things in her father's house that she hoped the average person never did even once. She'd seen men stabbed, shot, drugged. She'd walked in on more sex acts than she wanted to recall—not all of them consensual. She'd overheard plans to commit crimes and seek revenge and bribe officials. All of this was done in front of her like she was furniture, or like they believed she was such a doormat that she was incapable of posing a threat. But she'd also fought off unwanted advances, which the men usually got in trouble for, since she "belonged" to her father, but inevitably he would also punish her— for tempting them, for flirting with them, for causing trouble.

"You gotta start somewhere, Haven." Cora's words pulled her from the bad memories.

They knocked bottles again, Cora's idea becoming less and less harebrained the more Haven thought about it. She'd already mentally started a list anyway, hadn't she? Having her own kitchen, a place someday where she could bake to her heart's content? Skydiving, because what would feel more free than that? So, what could it hurt?

Haven linked arms with Cora as they made for the door. "You know what? Maybe I will."

"HAVE YOU SEEN Haven and Cora?" Dare asked Bunny as he and a few other guys helped her clear the break-fast table the next morning. Despite the generally macho culture of the club, they weren't too good to clean up after themselves. Besides, Bunny had made it clear long ago that there'd be no home-cooked meals around there unless there was help cleaning up after the fact. Bunny might've been Dare's great-aunt, but they all pretty much did what Bunny said rather than face her wrath, or her stubborn streak, which was legendary.

"Not sure where Cora went, but Haven's out on the back porch, I think," Bunny said as he followed her into the kitchen with an armful of dirties.

"Why doesn't Haven eat with everyone?" he asked. Even when Cora did, Haven usually didn't. Dare wasn't sure why he noticed that, or why it bothered him.

Turning on the faucet, Bunny shrugged. "She's a shy one. I expect she has good reason to be. She'll come out of her shell, though."

Dare nodded, his mind replaying his brief encounter with Haven from the evening before—her comment about wanting to keep busy was part of what convinced him he should talk to her today. Time to start figuring out how to help her and Cora. Though that hadn't been the only thing that stood out to him about last night—because Haven in clothes that actually fit her was a total stunner. "Were you responsible for the new clothes?"

"Uh-huh," Bunny said, rinsing off a plate. "All charged to the client fund per usual." *Clients* being a nice way of referring to the domestic abuse victims who made up the bulk of the clientele for their protective services. Bunny's first marriage had been an abusive shit show of epic proportions, so she had all kinds of firsthand experience with what was likely to make those they worked with feel most comfortable. Together, Dare's and Bunny's experiences with domestic violence had been big motivators behind the club's mission.

"Good, thanks, Bunny," he said, walking around the counter to the door. "And, uh, wouldn't be upset at all if there were more peanut butter cookies today." He winked.

Bunny gave him a funny look, but just laughed.

Outside, Dare found Haven sitting in a lounge chair in

the sun, her knees drawn up to provide support for something she was writing in a small notebook. Damn, she was a pretty thing.

"Haven, you got a minute?" he asked.

She slapped the notebook closed, her eyes going wide. "Uh, yeah. Yeah, of course." She swung her feet to the floor, sitting up straight to face him as he sat on the edge of the chair beside her.

Dare eyeballed the way she was clutching onto the pad of paper, but he didn't want to make her any more uncomfortable than she already seemed around him by asking about it. She wore jeans and a white V-neck shirt, and she looked like summer personified with her sun-kissed skin and all that long, wavy blond hair. His appreciation of her bothered him—Dare didn't get involved with their clients, partly because most of them were in the middle of or trying to escape bad relationships and partly because that wasn't why they were under Ravens' protection. But he couldn't seem to stop noticing Haven Randall.

"I need to talk to you about what happened to land you here," he said. The question wasn't based in idle curiosity—he needed to know to help her and to assess what kind of danger she might still be in. Because she and Cora had been rescued in the middle of the crisis with the Hard Ink team, Dare hadn't had a chance to speak with them before this.

"Where should I start?" she asked, her gaze part weary and wary.

He braced his elbows on his knees and nailed her with a stare. "At the beginning of whatever story will tell me what kind of trouble you're in and how to keep you safe going forward."

She dropped her chin, her gaze going somewhere in between them. "Right." For a long moment, she fidgeted with the notebook and pen in her lap. "Well, the short version is that, with Cora's help, I ran away from my father, who's a really bad man, and when we got to Baltimore our truck broke down. The tow truck driver apparently wasn't who we thought he was, because instead of taking us to a repair shop, he took us to a storage facility and forced us at gunpoint to go in." Her gaze flickered to Dare's, but she wouldn't really look him in the eye. "He was part of a gang, I guess, and they put us in a cell in the basement. And then those soldier guys rescued us and Ike brought us here, and along the way we lost everything we had."

Dare kept his expression neutral, but her story set off all kinds of alarm bells in his head. The bad father. The discomfort with eye contact. The involvement with the Church Gang—despite being torn apart on an organizational level, there could still be some guys around who could identify Haven and Cora, and therefore might be able to offer someone a lead that would point at the Ravens. "I think I better have the long version," he said, his brain racing through all the possible complications. "Starting with who your father is."

She shifted on the chair, her hand spinning the pen round and round. Dare observed all the little movements and already knew there was something that she thought was important that she wasn't telling him. Why, was the real question. "He's involved in all kinds of things, and probably some things I don't even know. Selling drugs, stealing and stripping cars, stealing various kinds of cargo and selling it off, intimidating business owners into paying him protection money . . ." She shrugged. "I'm pretty sure he pays off the local sheriffs so they're in on it with him."

As concern settled into Dare's gut, he heard what she hadn't said as loudly as what she had. "His name, Haven."

She licked her lips and quickly glanced at him and away again. "Randall, like me."

He tried to rein in the impatience that wanted to claw up his spine—because as long as she was there, a threat against her was a threat against *everyone* there, but he didn't want to make her clam up by coming on too strong. "Haven."

When she finally met his gaze, her eyes were filled with such fear that it kicked Dare in the stomach.

"You don't have to be scared, that's why I'm asking these questions. My people can't protect you if they don't know from which direction the threats might come."

Just when he was sure she wasn't gonna spill, she said, "His name's Rhett Randall, from Hall County, Georgia." Even after the words were out of her mouth, she wore a conflicted expression, like she wasn't sure she'd done the right thing in sharing the information with him.

The name didn't ring any immediate bells for Dare, but Georgia was far enough away that they had no regular business there. Which was one positive in all this. "Okay, and why did you have to run away?" he asked, not liking any of the reasons he could imagine.

She hugged herself. "My father was very controlling. He looked at me as his property, property that only he could decide what to do with. When that didn't end when I turned eighteen, I worried it might never end. The more time that passed, that seemed more and more likely."

"Wait, just how old are you?" he asked.

"I turn twenty-three in July," she said, finally looking him in the eye.

Multiple reactions warred inside Dare, and most of them turned his blood hot with anger. "Are you saying he held you prisoner in your own home?"

"Pretty much, yeah," she said in a soft voice. "I mean,

I could leave the house sometimes, but never alone. I had a guard at all times."

The ramifications of her admission stunned him. That likely meant Haven had very little experience out in the world, and the first time she'd gone out on her own she'd ended up in the hands of the Church Gang. Which shined a whole new light on her trust issues, didn't it?

"For what purpose?" he asked, still trying to get a handle on the father's motivation.

Haven rose and paced to the railing a few feet away. Notebook still in hand, she leaned against the railing and stared out at the view. Dare followed the direction of her gaze, finding the same solace in the dark green of the Blue Ridge that he always did. He rose and leaned his hip against the railing a few feet away from her, dread snaking through him the longer she didn't talk.

"At first I really didn't know," she finally said, her gaze still distant. "Part of it was just because he wanted to control me, which was a big reason why he pulled me out of school. Once I was eighteen, I thought maybe he just needed someone to cook and clean for him, which had been my job for years. But I think it was also because my mother had run away from him when I was a baby, and he wanted to make sure I didn't, too."

Dare didn't know what to react to first. "He pulled you out of school?" Her father was a real piece of work.

"Yeah. Awesome, huh?" She peered up at him.

"Not even a little, Haven. Why the hell did he think he needed to yank you from school?" Dare asked. This part of her history struck a real nerve with him, since being on the run from his father for his latter teen years meant he hadn't had a typical education either. It wasn't until he got settled with his grandfather at the age of seventeen that he buckled down to get his GED, even though by then he already had a fucking PhD in life experience. And, damnit, he suspected Haven did, too.

She dropped her gaze as her cheeks went pink. "I don't know."

Her reactions said that wasn't true, but Dare had a lot more he needed to get from her that was likely more pertinent to her recent circumstances. He shook his head and forced his fisted hand to relax on the railing. "Okay, skip that for now. Why did Cora run with you? What kind of trouble was she in?"

"She wasn't in trouble," Haven said. "I mean, her dad sometimes worked for mine, so he wasn't all on the up and up, but he just did things on the side. She came because she knew I wouldn't be able to do this on my own."

Dare nodded and thanked God that they weren't dealing with two times the threats, at least. And he found himself feeling grateful to Cora, too—he respected the kind of loyalty and friendship the other woman had demonstrated. Without Cora, Dare never might've met Haven. Although, why that should matter . . . Dare shook the thought away. "Okay. So if things had been like that for all these years, why did you and Cora decide to run now?" Because no way was it as simple as she'd just woken up one morning and decided she'd had enough.

Her throat bobbed once, twice, as if she was trying to force the words up and out. "He was going to make me marry someone," she finally said. "Told me he'd been saving me for just the right deal to take his empire to the next level."

Make her marry . . . ? Aw, what the actual fuck. "So, what, it was to cement some business alliance with another crook?" Dare asked, his hackles all the way up.

She cut her gaze to his. "Yep."

"Jesus Christ," Dare bit out, raking a hand through his

hair. As bad as that all sounded, Dare knew she was painting the picture of her life using the broadest strokes. The details of her day-to-day would probably make him want to smash things with his bare hands. And given how the father viewed her and his desire to use her that way, he was probably pretty damn motivated to get her back and save face with the would-be groom, whoever the hell that was. "What was the other guy's name? The one you were supposed to marry?"

"Ray Landry," she said, her voice thin, her tone sad. "God, I sound even more pathetic when I say all that out loud."

On instinct, Dare stepped right into her space. He saw a lot of things when he looked at this woman, and none of them were pathetic. "Don't say that, Haven. You hear me? From what I can tell, you survived, you escaped, and you persevered in a bad situation. That must've taken an incredible amount of fortitude and courage, so don't discount yourself like that. I won't stand for it," he said.

Eyes wide, chest rising and falling fast, mouth open in surprise, Haven peered up at him like she was afraid to move. "Okay," she whispered, her gaze flickering over his face, lingering on his lips.

That little show of interest speared white-hot lust through Dare's body. He was hard in an instant, his mouth suddenly ravenous for a taste of her. Which meant it was time to get the fuck out of there before he did something they'd both regret. He reared back, nodding. "That's good for now. I'll let you know if I have any more questions," he said, and then he took off without waiting for her to respond.

Anyway, he had much more important things to be doing than sniffing around a woman—a *much younger,* way-too-innocent-for-him woman. He had two Southern criminals to track down. Before they found Haven first.

CHAPTER 7

You're going to be mad at me," Haven said as they sat side by side on the bed in Cora's room, watching an addictive cooking competition show. Shows about cooking had been among Haven's favorites for as long as she could remember, and television had been her main source of entertainment growing up. The one nice thing she could ever remember her father doing was buying her a small flat-screen TV for the kitchen so that she could try new recipes along with the chefs on TV—and that was only because her cooking benefited him.

Cora sat the bowl of popcorn down on the bed between them. "I doubt it," she said. "About what?"

Haven clicked off the TV and shifted to face her friend. Her conversation with Dare that morning had been weighing on her all day, but Haven couldn't put off telling Cora any longer. Better to find out from Haven than from Dare, in case he cornered Cora, too. "Dare asked me a bunch of questions this morning."

"I figured that was coming at some point. Did you stick to what we agreed to say?" she asked.

Haven fingered a pulled thread in the bedspread. "Not entirely." She just hadn't been able to lie or hold back all the key pieces of information when Dare's concern for her seemed so genuine.

"Oh, Haven, what did you tell him?" Cora asked.

"Not everything," Haven rushed to say. "I didn't tell him about the reward." From the minute they'd been rescued by the soldiers at the storage facility, she and Cora had agreed not to tell anyone about the reward. They hadn't known who to trust and didn't want to give anyone financial motivation to say they'd help them while all along they were planning to use them to cash in. The one thing they didn't know was how much the reward was for, but Haven had no doubt that her father would want her badly enough to pay—or do—whatever it took to get her.

Cora sighed. "Well, that's good, but what is it you did tell him?"

"My dad's name, where we're from, and that I was going to be forced to marry," she said.

"Geez, Haven. If they can find your father, they can find out about the reward," Cora said, her tone more worried than angry.

"I know, and I'm sorry. But I think we can trust Dare, don't you? He says that everyone here wants to protect us, and we've been here for over two weeks and no one's done anything to make that seem untrue, don't you think?" God, she really needed Cora to feel the same way.

After a long moment, Cora released a deep breath and nodded. "Yeah, I think that's right. But we can't be too careful with you, Haven. You can't go back there for any reason. Ever."

"Neither can you," Haven said.

A shadow passed over Cora's expression, but it disappeared so quickly that Haven wasn't sure she'd seen it at all. "No, I don't want to go back either. But you . . . you're the one who would be in real danger. I'm not mad at you, I'm just worried for you." Cora reached across the bed and squeezed her hand. "I could never be mad at you. You're a good person. Of course you'd want to tell the truth to someone who's helping you."

Relief flooded through her. "Right. Thanks."

"But can we keep the reward to ourselves for a little longer? Just until we get to know the people here more and see what our plan is going to be?" Cora asked.

"Of course," Haven said, pretty much willing to follow Cora to the ends of the earth. After all, Haven would still be in Georgia and probably married to a horrible, disgusting middle-aged man by now without her.

"Okay, then," Cora said, settling back against the pillows again. "Don't worry. Okay?"

Haven took a handful of popcorn. "Before I agree to that, can I ask you something?"

"What?" Cora asked.

"Are you . . . is everything okay?"

"I'm fine. Why?" Cora frowned as she took a bite.

"I don't know. Sometimes I get the sense that something's bothering you. I know I've asked before, but I want to make sure I'm not being so self-involved over here that I'm not there for you, too." It wasn't the first time Haven had asked in the weeks since they'd run away. Though Cora was almost always upbeat and funny, there were moments when Haven's gut said it was an act. Just like it had been when she'd told jokes about her empty lunch boxes when they were little.

"Something *is* bothering me, Haven. Making sure you stay safe. I know you're here for me, too. I promise. So don't worry. Really."

"Okay," Haven finally said.

But that night as she lay in the quiet darkness of her bedroom, worrying was *all* Haven could do. God, if she wasn't the oldest twenty-two-year-old on the face of the planet. Sometimes she felt absolutely ancient. Finally, she gave up on sleep, slipped into her clothes, and crept down to the kitchen. The clubhouse was dead quiet, which Haven appreciated, since it meant she could get elbows-deep in baked goods without worrying about disturbing anyone or being found out.

She gathered everything she needed for lemon-almond bars, which were great for breakfast or as a treat all day in case there weren't a lot of guys here in the morning. As she added the dry ingredients to the butter mixture, her mind calmed enough to drift. Soon, she was thinking of the list she'd been working on when Dare joined her on the porch. As if their conversation hadn't been awkward enough, Haven had been hyperaware of the fact that she'd been standing two feet from him holding a notebook full of firsts she wanted to experience, adventures she wanted to have, and goals she wanted to achieve.

Mortified wouldn't begin to describe how she'd feel if anyone besides Cora read it. And she wasn't even thrilled with Cora reading it. Not only did it make her feel really exposed, but it felt a lot like saying your birthday wish out loud. If Haven admitted her dreams to someone else, maybe they wouldn't come true.

Haven put the crust in the oven to bake, then set about cleaning up and preparing to make the filling, her thoughts spinning around how Dare had talked to her before he'd stormed off the porch. The way he'd gotten up in her face should've scared her, but it hadn't. Haven had liked it. That was hard to believe, but true. Besides Cora, Haven didn't think she'd ever had another person so passionately defend her. And it had done strange things to her. For a heartbeat, she'd wanted to kiss him. Just thinking about it made her pulse race even now.

What would it be like for that harsh mouth to kiss her? For that gravelly voice to whisper into her ear in the dark? For those rough hands to touch her, skin on skin?

And what the heck would she do if Dare ever tried to do any of those things?

She wasn't a virgin, but she wasn't exactly experienced, either. She and Zach, her first real boyfriend, had loved each other. They'd been together for four months when they'd gotten caught in his truck at one of the river overlooks. She never learned how her father knew where they were, but the memory of him ripping open the driver's door and finding her straddling Zach's lap remained crystal clear in her head. That night had been the last she'd ever seen Zach, and it had been the real beginning of her father's twisted need to control everything about her life—by whatever means it took to bend her to his will. First, by punishing her. Second, by forbidding her return to school. And third, by threatening to harm Zach if she ever saw him again. That had been nearly eight years ago. Eight years without a man's touch—or, at least, without the touch of men she actually wanted.

Haven shook the whole train of thought away as she pulled the warm crust from the oven and poured the lemony filling into it.

It was a moot argument, of course, since there was no way Dare would think of her that way. He was older and world-wise and the leader of this club where all these people looked up to him—she saw it in how they interacted with him every day. Still, thinking about Dare was enough fun that he'd inspired a whole section of her list. After all, being inexperienced and sheltered didn't mean she was an angel. She *wanted* to experience all kinds of things. She wanted to feel something good. And maybe now that she was free she could.

Finally, it was time for the third and final layer of the bars—the crumbly almond topping. She sprinkled the crumbles over the whole baking dish and slid it back in the oven one last time. The kitchen smelled sugary sweet and just a little tart. It made her mouth water.

By the time the bars were done, cooled, and ready to be cut into squares, it was close to dawn. Haven took one for herself and moaned as the creamy-and-crunchy sweetness of the bar filled her mouth. So dang good.

She enjoyed the Ravens' kitchen so much she almost regretted that at some point she and Cora would have to leave. Hopefully that wouldn't be for some time. Her gaze ran over the room for a moment. Number one on her list remained having an amazing kitchen of her own someday. That wouldn't excite a lot of people and it sure as heck wouldn't make most people's must-do/must-have lists, but Haven would gladly forego the rest of the house to have a killer kitchen of her own.

She flicked the light switch, plunging the room into darkness.

If they were really safe, maybe she could finally start believing her dreams might come true.

By FRIDAY MORNING, Haven felt stupid for ever contemplating kissing Dare. He'd avoided her all week, and she didn't think she was imagining it. One day he'd come onto the back porch while she was sitting out there and promptly turned around without a word. Another time he'd come into the kitchen while she and Cora were helping Bunny with something, and he'd never acknowledged or even looked at Haven the whole time he was there.

And when she'd belatedly come down to dinner the night before, Dare excused himself from the table not long after she sat down. Granted, it wasn't like they were friends or anything, but it had seemed from the couple of interactions they'd had that he at least cared about her, so it didn't feel like she was blowing any of this out of proportion.

Not that it mattered, she guessed. Obviously, he didn't owe her anything. Just the opposite, in fact—she owed him and the Ravens everything.

Like the full truth about the reward?

Lying on her bed with her notebook open in front of her, Haven tapped her pen against her lips. Yeah, probably.

Just then, Cora knocked on the door and came in. "I'm here on serious business," she said, stretching out beside Haven, who scooted over to make room.

"I'm all ears," Haven said, folding her hands over the open pages.

"There's gonna be a party here tonight. I really want you to come down with me." Cora gave her a hopeful look.

Butterflies whipped through Haven's belly, but it was time to put something on her list into action, and attending a party was definitely on there. "Okay," she said simply.

"Wait, what? Really?" Cora's eyes went wide.

Laughing, Haven nodded. "Really."

"Aw, you rock," Cora said, throwing an arm over her shoulder in a move that nearly tackled her.

"Well, let's save the proclamations until we see if I end up freaking out." Haven tapped the notebook. "But I'm serious about this. I don't want to waste any more time. I feel like I've missed so much. I just want to live."

"You will. You *are*," Cora said. "It will all get easier when you realize not everyone's like our dads and their goons." She peered at Haven's notebook with a mischievous glint in her eye. "So what else can you check off tonight?"

"Well, if it's a party, I was thinking I could try some drinks." At almost twenty-three, she'd never had a single glass of wine, beer, or anything else. She might hate it, but she'd never know unless she tried.

Cora tapped her finger against her lips and nodded. "Okay. I like it. We need to make sure you eat before-hand, then. What else?"

"More?" Haven asked, laughing.

"Yes, more. Live dangerously, within reason, of course." Cora winked.

Haven scanned the first of four pages she already had filled up. Some of the items were silly and frivolous, while others were serious and big and Haven had no idea how she'd make them come true. But there was *so much* she'd never done or been allowed to do.

> *Have your own kitchen*
> *Have your own home*
> *Go skydiving*
> *Get GED (go to college?)*
> *Get a pet*
> *Get a job (what do I want to be?)*
> *Thank the teachers who tried to reach out to me*
> *Put the past behind me*
> *Conquer fear and anxiety*
> *Volunteer to help people (a soup kitchen?!)*
> *Find a way to repay Cora*
> *Make a mess and don't care!*
> *Go skinny dipping*
> *Fly in an airplane*
> *Visit another country*
> *See a castle*

Haven flipped to the page of Dare-inspired items.

> *Kiss a guy*
> *Kiss a lot of guys!*
> *Have fun at a party for once*
> *Wear makeup*
> *Drink*
> *Ride a motorcycle*
> *Learn to drive a motorcycle*

"Kiss a guy?" she asked, looking at Cora.

"I was hoping you were going to pick that one. Why not? It could just be a kiss on the cheek. Or maybe it'll be more, who knows?" Cora waggled her eyebrows.

Haven closed the notebook and flopped flat on the bed. "This list is juvenile." Not to mention impossible. The idea of checking things off the list was fun, but how heartbreaking would it be for some things—maybe a lot of things—to never get done? Maybe it would be better not to dream, not to want. Maybe she was wanting too much.

"No, it's not," Cora said. "This list is about you thinking about what you want out of a life you're just now being allowed to lead."

Haven sighed and let Cora's words sink in. "Okay, well. Then kissing a guy is a ridiculous idea," she mumbled into the pillow. After a moment, she rolled her head to peer up at Cora. "Who would I even kiss? And what would I do, just walk up to someone and be like, I'm gonna kiss you now?"

Cora laughed. "Just see if an opportunity presents itself. Being open to it happening is half the battle. So now the question is what you're going to wear."

Haven lifted her head and pushed her hair behind her ears. "I want to look pretty."

"Well, that's easy, since you're gorgeous anyway." Cora ran her fingers through the end of Haven's hair.

Haven rolled her eyes, uncomfortable with compliments no matter who they came from. In her experience, compliments had almost always stemmed from unwanted attention and came with a price tag—like you owed the guy something because he thought you were pretty. "I mean, I want to look good. Really good." Her stomach did more loop-the-loops.

"You want to look *hot*," Cora said. "Also easy. Does that mean I get free rein on putting you together for tonight, then?" she asked, her face alive with anticipation.

"Don't make me regret it," Haven said. For the next forty minutes, Haven wore and did and went along with everything Cora suggested. She ended up in her new tight jeans and clingy black shirt, with her hair styled in big loose curls that Cora pinned up on the sides to create a cascade of curls down her back. Haven didn't have anything more adventurous than the black sandals Bunny had bought for her feet, but Cora did her makeup so beautifully— another check for her list—that she looked like someone else altogether. "Oh, my God. Is it too much?"

Cora looked over her shoulder into the mirror. "Not at all. Man, you look stunning. I do good work."

"You do great work. It's like it's not even me." Haven turned her head back and forth, trying to look at the back of her hair.

"It's totally you, Haven. Just you, glammed up." Cora grabbed her shoulders. "We're gonna have so much fun tonight! Let me do my hair real quick and then we'll go down for dinner."

"Okay," Haven said, moving away from the mirror so Cora could do her thing.

While she waited, she sat on the edge of her bed and

picked up her notebook. She flipped through the pages of items on her list and chose to see it Cora's way. Because it was time for her to live her life and stop being scared of everything. At least, it was time to try. With a grin, she grabbed the pen and flipped to the first page. Inspired by Cora, she wrote two words at the top, and underlined them for good measure:

Live Dangerously!

CHAPTER 8

The loud rumbles of their motorcycles told Dare that his brothers were back from the day's run. He made his way through his cabin on the outskirts of the Ravens' compound to the front porch in time to see Maverick, Phoenix, and Caine dismounting their bikes.

"How'd it go?" Dare asked, bracing his hands on the rough-hewn log railing. With the help of some of the other Ravens, especially Bandit, who could do just about anything with his hands, Dare had built the two-bedroom cabin more than a dozen years before. While Doc had been more than happy to have Dare live with him, Dare's demons had taken up even more space when he was a younger man than they did now, so he'd wanted his own place.

The light from the porch stretched to where the men stood in his driveway. They turned to look at Dare.

"By the book," Caine said, adjusting the cap on his

head. Today's run had been a protective detail to escort a woman and her two teen daughters to western Pennsylvania. The family had been under Raven protection for half a year since the mother learned that her longtime boyfriend had been abusing the older of the girls. When the girl finally came forward, the scumbag boyfriend threatened and intimidated all of them until the Ravens had finally gotten involved, providing a protective shield that enabled them to live their lives, seek justice via the often glacially slow legal system, and stand up to the abuser. The guy had been convicted and only awaited his sentencing hearing now, which gave the family the ability to make a clean break and a fresh start out of the area. The Ravens were only too glad to help, since the law often didn't, couldn't, or wouldn't.

"No issues," Phoenix agreed as they moved toward the house. The black doo-rag wrapped around his head made the jagged scar running from his eye into his hairline appear more pronounced. "We got them settled in and checked that the security setup in their new place was online."

"Good," Dare said, "that's real good." The goal of the Ravens' protective services wasn't just to create a human shield between the innocent and the evil, but to help their clients feel safe again in the wake of whatever jeopardized that feeling in the first place. That meant they often put resources into securing their homes, especially when there were children involved. Dare knew what it was to be a kid who lived in fear and stayed awake at night to be ready for what seemed like an inevitable boogie man to jump him when he least expected it. He didn't mind going the extra mile to try to give other kids the security he never found until he was an adult. Because fears developed in your most formative years died hard, slow deaths. Dare would know. "Come on in," he said.

His friends followed him in and crashed on the brown couches in his living room. The first floor was decorated in earthy hues—browns, dark greens, warm beiges, and fiery clays. "Decorated" was probably too strong a word for it, though. While the house was furnished, Dare had never spent any time hanging pictures or curtains or doing much else to give the place any personality beyond *a cabin where a guy probably lives*. He'd put more time into outfitting the detached garage where he worked on his bikes than he had to the interior of the house. He grabbed a couple of beers from the fridge and passed the bottles out to the guys as he joined Maverick on one of the couches.

"Everything was quiet along the route," Phoenix said. "Put out some feelers like we talked about. My contacts aren't hearing anything involving us, so we're good for now."

Dare nodded. "Ike said the same thing about the situation in Baltimore. The biggest issue there right now is that the Church Gang's demise left a power vacuum that several groups are hoping to fill. It's apparently open season on the remaining Churchmen."

"Maybe that works to our favor," Maverick said, raking a hand through his blond hair. "The fewer of them who survive this, the fewer people in Baltimore who ever knew Cora and Haven existed."

"Amen," Dare said, clinking bottles with Mav. The mention of the women made Dare realize he had news of his own to share. After the way his body had reacted to Haven earlier in the week, he'd stayed the hell away from her, but that didn't mean he could keep his nose out of her business—not until he better understood what kind of threat her father might pose to her and the Ravens as a whole.

"We need to keep an eye on Baltimore," Caine said in a quiet voice. "Power plays are filled with their own problem. We have skin in that game whether we want to or not."

"Roger that," Phoenix said, peeling the label from his bottle.

Nodding, Dare took a long pull on his beer. "I finally got some intel today on Haven Randall's father," he said, gaze scanning over each of the men. "Midlevel criminal with regional contacts in important places and expansionist ambitions. Right now he's pretty much an equal-opportunity thug, meaning he's into a little bit of everything. Fact that he's known as far north of some of our contacts in southern Virginia says we gotta keep our eyes on him. I'm digging for more." Hard to imagine someone as sweet and innocent as Haven emerging from that background, and it made her seem even stronger to him that she'd escaped it—just like Dare had once done, now that he thought of it. Like Butch Kenyon, Rhett Randall wasn't someone to underestimate or fuck around with.

"Well, shit," Maverick said. "Sounds messier than I hoped."

"Yeah," Dare said. "Especially since Haven believes her father has the local cops in his pocket." What he didn't say was that his gut told him there was more to the story, something else that was relevant that Haven hadn't told him. And talking to Cora hadn't yielded him anything more either, which just proved they'd well coordinated their stories. All of which meant he was going to have to confront both of them again, whether he thought he ought to keep his distance from Haven or not.

He and the guys shot the shit for another half hour, and then Maverick stretched out his big-ass body and yawned obnoxiously. "We headed over to the clubhouse tonight or what?"

Dare nodded. "Yeah, let's do it. Party's no doubt in full swing by now." The LED clock on his cable box read 10:20 P.M. The club was tight-knit enough to want to kick back together on a regular basis, and that closeness was something Dare was proud of—he wasn't the only one who thought of the Ravens as a family. So things tended to get rowdy on weekend nights at the clubhouse because it was a time when a lot of the brothers were available to hang socially. Dare maintained an open-door policy to any and all brothers at all times. He wanted them to think of the compound as a second home the same way he did, as a place where they'd always be welcomed and always belong.

Outside, they each took to their bikes, all four of them riding Harleys—though the shared brand belied the significance of the differences between the specific models, engines, paint jobs, and other custom design features. Bikes were more than modes of transportation—they were extensions of each rider's identity, personality, and even mood, which was why some guys had more than one.

Maverick was on a blacked-out Night Rod Special, which meant elements that were often chrome on other bikes had been painted a matte pitch black, giving the bike a sinister look, further enhanced by the aggressive riding position the driver had to take. Caine was on a Dyna Fat Bob, a bike with a hard-hitting street presence and kick-ass speed performance. Phoenix rode a Dyna Super Glide, black with sharp orange accents—something with a little show and flash, just like him.

As for Dare, he had a hard-core Dyna Street Bob, all clean lines and minimalist styling. Matte black paint made the bike look like the grim reaper coming down the road, and it was Dare's favorite. Among other custom badges, all four of them had Ravens' graphics airbrushed onto their bike tanks.

The trip to the clubhouse only took ten minutes from Dare's place at the edge of the three-hundred-plus-acre compound. Doc had inherited the land decades before from the uncle who'd founded the speedway and associated resort. As a show of support, Doc had put his name on the deed, making Dare half owner of the land and everything on it. Damn hard to believe for a kid whose father jealously guarded everything they had and made the smallest generosity feel like a fucking gift you should get on your knees and grovel for.

They came in through the gated, private Raven Riders' entrance that cut through the woods closest to the main part of the compound. The lot was packed with the bikes of club members and the cars of their guests. The clubhouse was a big two-story brown building with a covered front porch that stretched from one end of the building to the other. Across the parking lot sat the club's chop shop, and off to the side of the clubhouse sat the first of six cottages left over from the resort era. They used them now to house race drivers or brothers or clients in need. On a typical Friday night, most of the action would be down the mountain at the racetrack, but it would be another week before they got their operations there up and running again.

Inside, the place was jumping—music jamming, and people talking, laughing, and making out in every possible corner. A crowd around the pool tables was decent proof that there was some serious betting going on. Another crowd gathered around one end of the bar, but Dare couldn't figure out what the attraction was there. The vibe was nearly frenetic, proof that everybody needed a night without reminders of their recent losses to just let go.

Dare talked and laughed and flirted as he cut through the crowd, feeling lighter than he had in a while. It was moments like these when he knew finding his grandfather and building a life here with the Ravens had made him who he was as a man and very likely saved his life to boot. This place was his home. These men were his family. This was his community. And he'd defend all three against every and any threat.

Finally, he made it over to the bar and managed to catch a prospect's attention. Dare ordered his usual whiskey and peered down the bar, trying to see what the raucous crowd down there was all about. Finally he asked Blake, "What's the deal?" He gestured toward the far end.

Blake swept the long strands of dark blond out of his eyes and smiled. "There's a girl doing a taste test."

Dare frowned. What the hell did that mean? And then a thread of discomfort curled into his gut. *What girl?*

Probably Cora, given how shy Haven was. She hadn't even been able to come into the room at their last party, and tonight was rowdier by far. Still, the idea of Cora getting drunk as a public spectacle didn't sit right with him. He at least wanted to make sure someone was looking out for her.

He pushed through the crowd of onlookers until he made it to the far end of the bar, and there was Cora—except she was sitting sideways on her bar stool, seemingly looking at someone else. He tapped a couple of younger guys on the shoulder, and they stepped back for him the minute they realized who it was.

And that's when Dare saw Haven.

Standing at the bar in a pair of killer tight jeans, heeled

black sandals, and a clingy, form-fitting black shirt that emphasized her curves. Her hair was stunning—pulled back in some sort of complicated arrangement and tumbling in soft waves all the way down her back. The crowd immediately around her quieted for a moment, and she must've noticed, because she laughed and glanced over her shoulder, a puzzled expression on her face.

And that's when she saw him. "Dare," she breathed, her voice high and light, clearly the effect of alcohol, like the pretty pink flush on her cheeks.

But what he noticed even more was the makeup on her face. She didn't need it—in fact, he preferred her without it—but he couldn't deny that she looked like a model done up to such perfection.

Jesus Christ.

Dare was rock hard in an instant, his effort to rein in his body by avoiding her all week undone with just one glance, just one word.

"What are you doing?" he bit out.

"Trying new things," she said, swaying a little on her low heels. "Join me?" One eyebrow went up just the littlest amount, and the challenge implicit in that tiny gesture was like waving a red flag in front of an angry bull.

He sidled in next to her, so that when she turned to face Cora, her back was at his front. "Exactly what is it you're trying?" he asked over her shoulder.

She spun to face him. "For right now, different kinds of drinks. I never had anything before tonight. Can you believe it?"

Uh, yeah. He could. Though it was hard to resist her obvious pleasure in trying something new, even apart from the growing inebriation. She wasn't drunk yet, but she was a few sips past tipsy for sure. It made her body fluid and loose, all of her usual timidity and tenseness gone.

The confidence she wore might've been all the liquor talking, but it was still sexy as fuck.

Why did she affect him this way? She was too young and too innocent and too in trouble for him. And did he mention too young?

"And what have you tried so far?" he asked, his gaze dragging over the line of bottles and shot glasses arrayed in front of her.

She chuckled. "I don't remember what all their names were," she said, looking to Jeb, the club's other current prospect. "Except for the Buttery Nipple. That one's kinda hard to forget."

Jeb braced his hands on the bar top, his brown hair covered by a black doo-rag knotted around his head. Dare must've been throwing off some hard-core displeasure, because the kid looked at him like he knew he needed to tread carefully. "She's had very small sips of red and white wine, vodka, tequila, whiskey, and rum—just enough to taste them, and mini-shots of a Buttery Nipple, Alabama Slammer, and Lemon Drop. So far." A mostly empty glass of water also sat in front of her, so at least the kid had been doing that much for her.

Haven grinned at him. "Vodka and tequila are not good by themselves. Though you probably know that. But whiskey is pretty good, and I really liked the Alabama Slammer and Buttery Nipple." She wobbled, her hand gripping the edge of the bar largely responsible for holding her steady. "What should I try next?" she asked Dare.

"A Blow Job!" someone behind them yelled. The crowd laughed and cheered.

Despite the fact that Haven's cheeks filled with a dark pink, she met Dare's gaze and licked her lips, making them shiny. "Should I? Try a Blow Job?"

Dare's cock throbbed as a dull ache settled into his balls.

She stepped closer. "Dare?"

He leaned his head close to hers so that his lips brushed against her ear. As he spoke, she shuddered, and the reaction did nothing to cool his blood. "Do you know what you're doing right now?"

One of her hands gripped his shoulder. "I'm trying to live, to be a normal girl, to have fun." She pulled away enough to peer into his eyes, and the desire in hers was so fucking blatant that he wasn't sure how he resisted tossing her over his shoulder, taking her to one of a half dozen places he could get to in under a minute, and burying himself deep inside her sweet little body. Hell if he wasn't a dirty old man. Her hand dragged from his shoulder down his chest, where it rested. "That's all," she said. "You should join me."

He raised an eyebrow and gave her a small nod. "Have whatever you want, Haven," he said, meaning the words in all kinds of ways he had no business meaning them.

"I want a Blow Job, Jeb," she said, grinning at the prospect.

"That's what he said!" someone called to the group's amusement.

"You want a regular one or a mini?" Jeb asked, his gaze cutting between her and Dare. But Dare wasn't paying the bartender any mind. His eyes were all for Haven—he studied her expressions, the makeup painting her face, her smiles. Her delight was a physical presence all around her, and was likely what had drawn the crowd in the first place. Her pleasure was raw, honest, pure. And it was like she was the flame and they were all moths, drawn to her, unable to resist her light, her beauty, her heat.

Cora leaned closer, a big smile on her face. "You should do a regular one, because you drink this one without any hands."

A confused expression swam over Haven's features. "How the heck does that work?"

"Make it two," Cora said, winking at Jeb. "I'll show you."

Jeb topped off the Baileys and Kahlua with a big dollop of whipped cream on each shot. "Here you go, ladies. Two Blow Jobs."

"Okay," Cora said, making a show of lacing her hands behind her back. "This is how you do it." She bent over, wrapped her mouth around the top of the glass, and then stood upright and tilted her head back until the small glass was empty. The crowd went nuts for the little show, and even more with the anticipation that Haven would be repeating the act.

"I don't know if I can do this," Haven said with a laugh. "But I'm definitely going to try." Her gaze cut to Dare, her smile parts mischievous and uncertain. Then she shrugged and laced her hands behind her back. "Here goes nothing."

Dare's gaze was glued to Haven—how her lips swallowed the whipped cream and wrapped around the glass, how her eyes fell closed as if in pleasure, how her throat worked around the long swallow of the liquor. He threw back the rest of his whiskey, the bite taking the sharpest edges off his arousal—which wasn't fucking saying much. When Haven was done, she slammed the little glass on the counter and threw her arms up in victory. Everyone around her cheered and clapped her on the back, but all Dare could see was the flat, firm surface of her bared stomach from how her shirt rode up.

Haven Randall was maddening. Sweet yet sexy. Innocent yet provocative. Beautiful yet seemingly unaware of what she was doing to him. Hell, him and probably every other man around the bar.

She hugged Cora.

Dare laid his fingers on the bare skin of her side, and Haven jumped a little as she turned to see who was touching her. His intensions had been honorable—to encourage her to drink some water before she ended up learning about the not-fun side of drinking, the side that put you on your knees and made you promise to any god who would listen that you'd never drink again if only they would end your suffering.

But the way Haven's dark pink lips dropped open and the way her eyes went hooded and soft when she realized Dare's hand cupped her skin momentarily short-circuited his brain. "That was so much fun," she said, closing the distance between them. "What should I do next?" She stood just shy of pressing her front against his, and the sliver of distance was pure hell.

The name of every innuendo-filled cocktail Dare could imagine flitted through his head, but the last thing he wanted was any of those words coming out of her lips in front of a bunch of his brothers.

"How about a Sloe Comfortable Screw?" Jeb asked. "Do you know what that one is?"

She shook her head but kept her eyes glued to Dare's. "No, but it sounds good," she said, that eyebrow quirking up just a little again. "Really good. Tell me."

Dare's heart was suddenly a jackhammer in his chest, because he didn't think he was reading too much into her words and the way she was looking at him to think that she was talking about the real thing, not the innuendo-filled drink by the same name.

"It has sloe gin, Southern Comfort, orange juice, and vodka," Jeb said, already pulling the bottles he needed in front of him. "You in?"

"Yeah," she said with a nod, eyes still on Dare. "I definitely want one of those."

"One of what?" Jeb said, leaning forward with his hand cupped behind his ear like he didn't know what she wanted.

Haven grinned and looked to the prospect. "I want a Sloe Comfortable Screw," she said a little louder. More laughter and cheering. Jeb made her a mini version of the cocktail, and she drank it in a few eager sips, her eyes smiling at Dare over the rim of her glass.

She shook her head and blinked her eyes, the alcohol clearly hitting her harder now. She pressed her fingertips into her cheeks, then dragged them down over her lips. "I'm tingly," she said, obviously enjoying the feeling.

Cora pushed a full glass of water in front of her. "Drink some of this, sweetie."

Haven did as she was told, and then she waved her arms to indicate she was done. "Thank you, Jeb," she said, hooking her finger to invite him closer. When he leaned over the bar, she pushed herself up and kissed him on the cheek. "Thanks for making that fun for me."

"You got it, beautiful. Any time," he said, giving her an eager smile full of invitation.

Dare glared at him, and the guy was suddenly really fucking busy cleaning up the bar top.

"Ooh, it's kinda warm in here," Haven said, chuckling.

"Why don't you get some air on the back porch?" Dare suggested, knowing she liked it out there.

She turned to Cora. "Wanna go outside?" she asked.

Cora was in such deep conversation with Phoenix, the two of them arguing about something, that Haven had to tap her shoulder and ask her again.

"Sure, I'll come if you want," Cora said, looking back at Phoenix beside her.

Haven glanced between her friend and his Road Captain. "No, you stay. I'll be right back," she said.

"Are you sure?" Cora asked.

Haven smiled. "Yes, don't worry." She turned and walked into Dare. He caught her with an arm around her shoulders, steadying her.

The way she leaned into him about made him insane, especially when she lifted that electric blue gaze to his. "Will you take me?" she asked.

She didn't mean it the way his body wanted to hear it, Dare knew that much for sure. But that didn't keep his arousal from ramping up even further, his cock like steel, his need near ravenous.

Fifteen years, Kenyon. She's fifteen years younger than you. Keep a lid on it.

"I don't mind," he managed, keeping her tucked close to him as he guided her across the room. He hadn't intended this when he suggested she go get some air, he really hadn't. Which meant he needed to rein himself in. Hard. Right fucking now. "Come on."

CHAPTER 9

S o much better out here," Haven said, the night air cool against the tingling warmth of her skin. Although she was pretty sure that not all of the heat burning through her insides was from the alcohol—her unusual flirtatiousness and closeness to Dare over the past half hour had made her desperate with a heat that had nothing to do with her drinking game.

She walked to the railing and leaned against it, chuckling a little at herself for needing the support it offered. She felt so damn free, and it was a heady, exhilarating thing.

"What's funny?" Dare asked, settling a hip against the railing right beside her. Arms crossed, jaw ticking with tension, dark eyes blazing, he was staring at her like he wanted to reprimand her or devour her. Oddly, neither alarmed her the way she would've expected it to.

Haven shook her head, leaning it back and letting her

gaze float over the night sky. Blurry points of light swam in the moonlit heavens. It was beautiful and peaceful despite the pounding bass beat of music thumping from inside the clubhouse. "Not funny, just good. Happy, you know? Being able to do something a little . . . scary, but knowing I'd be safe doing it." When Dare's gaze narrowed, she shrugged. "I don't know."

A long moment passed before Dare finally spoke. "You are safe here, Haven. Never doubt it."

Peering up at him, she nodded, all kinds of words sitting on the tip of her tongue, challenging her to let them fly. "It's weird feeling safe—or at least safer—after a lifetime of not. It makes me want to try things I could never let myself try before. It makes me . . ." She shook her head and dipped her chin.

Dare stepped closer, his thighs coming up against her hip. He lifted her chin and made her look at him. The contact combined with the command in the gesture lanced white-hot desire through her veins. "Makes you what?"

"Want to feel alive," she whispered, her heart suddenly racing in her chest.

Dare's jaw ticked again as his gaze swept over her face. She didn't think she was imagining the raw emotion pouring off of him and wrapping around her, but she wasn't sure if she was reading that emotion right or projecting her own desire onto him.

"Do you feel alive, Dare?" she asked, the alcohol flowing through her and the night spinning around her like she was walking through a dream.

"Jesus Christ," he bit out.

The rough desperation in his voice made her wet between her legs. "Just once," she whispered, not sure what she was asking him for.

But he seemed to know. Because his hand was suddenly

tangled in her hair and his mouth was suddenly on hers, claiming, probing, tasting. Haven moaned and parted her lips, inviting him deeper.

Dare jerked back from her, his fingers rubbing roughly over his lips. "Fuck, I'm sorry."

On instinct, Haven's body pursued his, pinning his back to the railing. "Please don't stop," she said as her hands gripped his shoulders. She had the strongest urge to climb him, to wrap her legs around him, to grind against the hard bulge pressing electrically against her belly. "Please," she whispered, tilting her mouth toward his. "I liked it."

Dare's hand cupped the back of her head. "You're killing me."

"Dare," she said, her body restless against his.

In a move that sent the world spinning, he flipped them around so that she was the one pinned against the railing. He pushed his legs between hers and leaned down over her, forcing her to arch her back, to yield, to open to him. "Tell me what you want from me. Say the words," he said, his eyes absolutely on fire.

Her heart was a runaway train in her chest, frantic and picking up speed. The thought of giving voice to her desires was terrifying and thrilling and dizzying all at once. "I want your mouth," she said. The words sounded odder out loud than they had in her head, but they were more accurate than asking him to kiss her—because *her* mouth wasn't the only place she wanted his.

"Jesus," he rasped again, his mouth coming down on hers once more.

The whimper she released was part relief, part anticipation. It had been so long since she'd kissed someone that she felt a little uncertain, but Dare's intensity barely allowed her the capacity to worry about it. He was like a dark storm bearing down on her, relentless, magnetic, all-consuming. Rough callouses from his hands scratched against her cheeks as he guided her. Hard breaths spilled over her lips, and the wet slide of his tongue tasted like whiskey and desire and man. Her hands found the soft length of his hair, and her breasts pushed against the hard plane of his chest.

Then her lips were freed as his mouth slid over her skin—exploring her cheek, her jaw, her ear, her neck. He hiked her up to sit on the wide railing, the move surprising a gasp out of her, especially as he crowded the space between her legs, pushing himself closer, bringing his erection against the place between her legs craving friction, hardness, so much more of him. Maybe even all of him.

One strong arm wrapped around her back and held her steady, while the other hand stroked her hair, her face, her breast. The soft groans and breathy grunts spilling out of him were delicious and thrilling, and bolstered her confidence that she wasn't the only one losing herself in this moment, in these touches. She almost couldn't believe this was happening, and part of her was certain she must be dreaming. Because Haven Randall didn't have beautiful things in her life. At least, never before.

DARE HAD TO stop. He had to stop this.

Except he couldn't. He couldn't force his hands off Haven's straining body, his tongue off her warm skin, his hard body from grinding against all her softness.

It didn't matter that Haven had offered this—no, more than that, *asked* for it. Or, at least, it shouldn't matter.

But it did. Dare didn't know everything about Haven, but he did know her life hadn't been easy, she'd been treated miserably by her father, if not outright abused, and that the trust she was demonstrating right now was a rare, precious gift. And her desperate need, the beautiful fucking honesty of it, was like a drug roaring through his veins, clouding his judgment, fueling his own need, turning his world upside down.

So Dare wanted to give her this. Hell, he wanted to give himself this.

He licked up her neck, and a needful moan spilled out of her as his tongue dragged over the spot below her ear. He sucked her there, and the sound got louder. Her hips thrust against his, bringing her core flush against his hard-on.

"Oh, Dare," she whispered.

Loving the sound of his name on her tongue, he grasped her face in his hands and claimed her mouth with a devouring kiss. It was probably too rough, too aggressive, the way he forced her lips open and penetrated her mouth with thick, sweeping, dominating thrusts of his tongue, but she took everything he gave her, her small hands fisting and gripping at the lengths of his hair.

Haven scooted forward on the railing so that her body pressed harder against his. Her hips rocked and jerked against his cock, pulling shuddering, gasping breaths from her throat that ricocheted to his balls, making them heavy and hot with need.

"That's it, Haven," he said, gripping her ass in his palm. Despite the mess this could cause once the harsh light of daytime cast some glaring common sense on the situation of him screwing around with a client he was supposed to be protecting, with a young woman too innocent for all his demons, he wanted nothing more in that moment than for her to find pleasure using his body. He couldn't remember the last time he felt this kind of urgent arousal, and certainly not just from kissing. And he didn't know whether to chase that feeling into oblivion or resent the hell out of it for making his usual fucks seem dull and ordinary by comparison.

And they weren't even fucking.

A whine spilled from her throat and her hips moved erratically. "I . . . I . . ." She shook her head.

"What?" he asked, his lips brushing hers, their faces eye to eye. "You gonna come for me?"

Hooded eyes stared back at him, full of pleading and need. "I don't know," she whispered, heat filling her cheeks.

Unfuckingacceptable.

"I do," Dare growled, tugging her off the railing to stand in the tight space before him. In an instant he had her jeans open and his hand down her panties, his rough fingers sliding into the slippery heat of her lips.

Her mouth dropped open on a surprised, desperate cry, and Dare forced her stance wider, his hand filling up the space between her thighs.

"Aw, Jesus, feel that," he said, his harsh breaths mingling with hers. He stroked fingers against her wet heat, petting, preparing. "You need this, don't you?"

"Oh, God. Yes," she said, her eyes falling closed.

His middle finger sank deep inside her, and Jesus she was tight, the walls of her pussy sucking at his flesh. He moved his finger inside her, making sure his forearm gave her clit a hard, steady friction. "Look at me. Look at me when I make you come." With his other hand he gripped her hair, tugging her head back so he could see all of her beautiful, painted face.

Her eyelids flipped open, and the abject need he saw there made his cock throb.

And then her brow furrowed and her mouth opened in a silent cry. She held her breath as her core fisted at his finger again and again, a moan finally spilling out of her.

He could only imagine how good that would feel if it were his dick. "Yeah, yeah, yeah," he gritted out as he watched and felt her shatter.

If he thought her face in ecstasy had been beautiful, it was nothing compared to the sated, adoring look she wore as she gazed up at him in the moments after. As much as the whole experience had speared a hard-core satisfaction through him, that adoration was also a problem. He slipped his finger free of her pussy, his hand out of her clothing.

Haven buried her face against his chest and gave her head a little shake.

"What?" he asked, his other hand petting the soft waves of her long hair.

She didn't respond for a long moment, and then said, "I've just . . . never . . ."

Dare hung on the edge of her words. He stepped back and tipped her chin up, needing to know what she was going to say.

Suddenly, Haven frowned. "Oh, God." Panic filled her eyes, and then she spun, bent over the railing, and threw up so hard her back arched at the force of it.

"Fuck," Dare said as he held her hair out of her way. As she puked again and again, guilt and self-loathing gathered in his chest until it was a river rushing through his veins. He should never have let things go so far when she was this drunk. He knew better. She didn't.

"I'm sorry," she rushed out between wretches.

The words made him feel that much worse. "You have nothing to be sorry for," he said.

When it seemed her body had finally emptied itself, she pushed upright, shaky hands braced on the railing. Haven slowly turned to face him, and then her eyes went unfocused and she stumbled.

On a curse, Dare caught her in his arms, and then he lifted her into a carry.

Her eyes fluttered up at him. "Everything's spinning," she whispered.

"I've got you," he said. Though she wouldn't be in this position if he'd taken control of the situation the way he should've—starting in at the bar. Goddamnit.

He went in through the kitchen door and carried her through the dining room and lounge and up the central steps. Given that the party was still raging, there was no help for others seeing them, and Dare got a few cat-calls and amused looks that only made him kick himself harder. Upstairs, he found her room door locked, so he awkwardly fished the master key out of his pocket and let himself in. He crossed the dark room and lay Haven on her bed, then reached to flick on the bedside lamp.

She barely responded to any of it, which pissed him the hell off—what if he hadn't been the one standing here right now? What if she'd exposed this kind of vulnerability to someone else, someone willing to take advantage of it?

Like you just did?

Fuck.

Dare slipped off her sandals and pushed the door shut harder than he meant to, but not even the slamming of it disturbed her.

Given how violently she'd thrown up, Dare wasn't sure he should leave her. So he planted his ass in the corner chair and reconciled himself to watching over her. Like he should've done from the start.

Her face at rest, her body so small in the queen-sized bed, she looked really young lying there. And, of course, she *was* really fucking young. Twenty-two. Twenty-two versus his thirty-seven. Twenty-two and on the run from bad men who'd taken advantage of her.

And damn if he didn't feel like he'd just done the same thing.

Huffing out his frustration, he shifted in the chair, bringing his ankle up to rest on the opposite knee. His foot bounced and a tense restlessness surged through him—from his anger, from his guilt, from the unfulfilled need still simmering below the surface. And didn't that make him an even bigger asshole.

He forced his gaze away from Haven and scanned it over the room. But there was really nothing distracting enough to look at. All the guest rooms were the same, and he'd been in them countless times over the years.

On a soft moan, Haven curled onto her side, facing him. She drew her knees up so she lay in a ball, and the movement knocked something to the floor.

Her notebook. The one she'd been writing in the day he'd asked about her past. The one she'd been so protective of.

Dare studied the book for a long moment. Finally, he scooped it off the floor. He examined the plain cover, and curiosity urged him to open it. Maybe it was a diary, and he'd find in its pages whatever it was she was holding back. Because his gut told him there was mostly definitely still something.

His gaze flickered to her beautiful face, just feet away from him. He remembered the look she'd worn as she'd come down from the high of her orgasm. All filled with blissful satisfaction and worshipful adoration.

Sonofabitch.

After all the other ways he'd wronged her tonight, he couldn't bring himself to flip the book open. He tossed it onto the table beside the bed.

Dare blew out a long breath, figuring he might as well get comfortable. He rested his head on his fisted hand and closed his eyes, but then he caught the faint scent of her arousal still clinging to his fingers. As if he needed the additional reminder of what he'd done.

"Jesus," he bit out. He shoved up from the chair and crossed to the bathroom. As he washed his hands, he met his own disapproving gaze in the dark mirror. *She was so drunk that she puked and passed out, asshole.*

He threw the towel onto the counter and braced his hands on the edge, his head hanging down on his shoulders. How the hell was she supposed to trust him when he'd taken such advantage?

Dare didn't know. He only hoped she could forgive him. And it would start by his promising it would never happen again.

CHAPTER 10

Haven awoke on a groan. Her stomach was sour and unsteady, and a dull ache pulsed behind her temples. Her mouth tasted like a wasteland, and opening her eyes revealed that the world was still a little spinny around her.

A hand stroked over her hair. "Take this, sweetie."

"Cora?" Haven croaked.

"Yep."

Haven forced herself to look at her friend sitting on the edge of the bed. "What time is it?" And how had she gotten in bed? She didn't remember coming up there last night.

"Nine," Cora said. "Not too late. Here." She held out a fizzing glass of water toward Haven. "It'll help your stomach and your head."

On another groan, Haven pushed herself into a sitting position and accepted the glass. She took a sip and grimaced. "Tastes so bad."

"I know," Cora said. "But in fifteen minutes, you'll thank me."

Haven sucked the fizzing water down in a couple big gulps, just wanting to be done with it. When she lowered the glass, she noticed she still wore her clothes from last night. From the party.

The party.

Drinking at the bar. Kissing Dare. Him making her come with his fingers. Getting sick.

"Oh, my God," she rasped, pressing her hand to her mouth.

Cora placed her hand on Haven's knee. "I'm so sorry I let you drink too much. I thought since Jeb made most of them so small, you'd be okay."

Haven shook her head and waved her hand. "That's not your fault and not what I'm freaking out about."

Cora pressed her lips together, clearly trying to restrain a smile. "Freaking out about Dare then?"

Gasping, Haven nodded as the details started coming back to her. She didn't know what to be more humiliated about—throwing up in front of him right after having one of the most amazing experiences of her life, or not remembering what happened afterward. "Wait, how did you know that?"

"Well, first of all, you left the party with him," Cora said, her eyebrow arched. "And then you didn't come back. But mostly I suspected that was what it was about because when I came in to check on you after the party, I found him sitting in that chair." She nodded to the blue armchair in the corner.

Haven's gaze cut to the chair. Now empty, obviously. "He was here?"

"He said you got sick and asked if I'd keep an eye on you. And then he left. That was around two-thirty."

"What else did he say?" Haven asked, her mind struggling to process this information.

"Nothing," Cora said, eyeballing her. "But he seemed, I don't know, agitated. So I'm guessing there's a good story involving the time between when you left together and I found him in here."

Rubbing her lips, Haven nodded. And oh, what a story it was. The way he kissed her. The way he touched her. She'd never been so turned on in her life—and she'd never had an orgasm with a man before, either. It had been scary and thrilling and absolutely mind-blowing. If feeling like that was living dangerously, she was ready to sign up. Except without the puking and passing out, of course.

Cora grabbed her hand and gave her a little squeeze. "Um, dying over here."

Haven wrapped her arms around her knees and tried to find the words. Heat flooded into her face. *Screw being embarrassed, Haven! Just say it.* "We kissed. A lot. And he ended up making me, um . . ." She made a vague gesture with her hands that no one in their right mind would be able to decipher.

But Cora's whole face lit up. "He gave you an orgasm?" she yelled, not at all uncomfortable discussing sex—she had a lot more experience with guys and a lot fewer hang-ups.

"Yeah." Haven nodded, hiding a grin behind her knees.

"And?" Cora asked, possibly wearing an even bigger grin.

"And . . . it was amazing. I wasn't once scared he'd push me further than I wanted to go." Her mind replayed their stolen moments. "Honestly, I'm not sure how far I would've been willing to go with him. But then, of course, I puked and got really dizzy, so I never got to find out."

But just giving voice to the question had her gut giving her an answer. She would've slept with Dare. No, that wasn't strong enough. As aroused as he had her, she would've jumped all over sleeping with Dare. And that wasn't just the alcohol or her newly resurrected libido talking. Something about Dare lured her in—he was strong without being a bully, a leader without having a power trip, rough in all kinds of ways without being hurtful. She still found him intimidating sometimes, truth be told, but he also made her feel safe. So safe that she sometimes found herself telling him things she never volunteered to anyone else—some of it not even to Cora.

And she certainly couldn't forget about the way he'd praised and defended her that day out on the porch. Just thinking about that moment made a ripple of excited appreciation go through her chest.

"Forget about the throwing up part," Cora said with a wave of her hand. "I'm so freaking excited for you. Whatever is between you two, you deserve a night that makes you smile like this."

The words pulled Haven from her thoughts. "I'm pretty excited for me, too." Her smile sagged. "Although I guess I'm less excited when I hear that you thought he seemed agitated."

Cora shook her head. "I'm sure he was just worried about you." She gave Haven a reassuring smile. "Anyway, focus on the bright side, you checked a whole bunch of things off your list last night. You wanted to live, and you did."

"I did, didn't I?" Searching for her notebook, Haven found it on the nightstand. She opened it to the first page, scanned the list, and placed check marks next to everything she'd done. It was silly, she knew it was, but didn't she deserve a little silly? Because she'd never been allowed to have silly or frivolous or just for fun before. "Hmm, should I give myself credit for kissing a lot of guys, since I kissed Jeb on the cheek?"

Tapping a finger against her lips, Cora hummed. "Tough call."

Chuckling, Haven wrote a check mark next to it with a question mark, then she turned the page to the more Dare-inspired "to-do" items. None listed his name, but things like *have an orgasm with a man* had definitely popped into her head after she'd spent that night fantasizing about kissing him. Among other things. And that one got a check mark, too.

"Look at me go," she said with a wry laugh as she closed the book and tossed it onto her pillow.

"For real. We've been on our own for just a few weeks and look how I'm corrupting you. You taught me math and how to cook, and I teach you how to get drunk," Cora said with a wink. When Cora would come to visit after Haven had been forced to drop out of school, they'd work on Cora's homework together. Haven had always been good at math, so it allowed her to feel like she was contributing something to their friendship and still getting to learn.

Haven shook the memories away. She was tired of walking the straight and narrow, and absolutely fed up with being scared to take some chances—because as much as throwing up sucked, it wasn't anything like being backhanded, or locked in the shed out back, or forced to play waitress to her father's rowdy weekly poker games, groping and lurid commentary included. So she was done being afraid to live. "Well, Cora, if this is being corrupted, then I don't want to be good. Not anymore."

"SON OF A bitch," Dare growled, tossing his cell phone on his kitchen counter. He'd had a few people digging further into Haven and her father—and now Dare knew exactly what the fuck Haven had been hiding.

There was a reward out for her capture and return. A fucking reward. Initially set at fifty thousand dollars, it had been recently expanded to a hundred grand. A hundred grand that incentivized every lowlife scumbag from Georgia to God only knew how far to be looking for Haven Randall.

Which was likely why the Church Gang had picked her and Cora up in the first place. The description of the women and their truck, which thankfully was no longer in the picture as a possible point of identification, had been blasted far and wide. Some gangbanger probably thought he'd hit the jackpot.

Now the question was, had the Churchmen gotten in touch with Rhett Randall or his people? Were they, even now, in possession of information that could lead them to Baltimore? And, from there, to the Ravens themselves?

"Fuck," Dare bit out, pacing in the silence of his kitchen. Anger and worry roared through him in equal measure. Haven had been at the compound for more than three goddamned weeks. *If* Randall knew that the Church Gang had had the women in custody and lost them, three weeks was plenty long enough for all kinds of pieces to be moved into place. Which meant the net could be a lot smaller than Dare had believed.

That reward changed fucking everything.

He grabbed his cell and jabbed at the speed dial number for Maverick. He cursed when voice mail picked up, then waited for the beep and said, "Mav, we've got a problem. I need the officers at the clubhouse as soon as we can get everyone together. Hit me back when you get this." With every additional call he placed and voice mail he left, his frustration ramped up until he wanted to punch something.

He'd been out in the garage most of the morning trying to forget his fuckup from the night before by immersing himself in a rebuild he'd finally gotten some parts for, so he hopped in a quick shower, hoping it might take the edge off his mood. No such luck.

Problem was, there wasn't anything likely to chase away the black cloud hanging over his head as long as he needed to confront Haven—and that was exactly what he needed to do.

No sense putting off the inevitable. Besides, he'd do them both the one kindness of having this conversation in private.

Normally, riding cured a lot of what ailed Dare. Love of riding was the one good thing his father had given him, the one—and only—way Dare didn't mind resembling his old man. But today he felt like his bike was delivering him to the gallows.

Goddamnit.

Somehow he had to get his temper under control before he talked to her. He was pissed, and rightfully so, he thought. But that didn't give him the right to scare Haven, and it was the last thing he wanted to do anyway.

He took the long, long, way-the-hell-out-of-the-way route to the compound.

The chop shop was hopping, but otherwise, the lot was pretty empty, which meant his other board members weren't here yet. Just as well. It would give him time to talk to Haven and come up with the start of a plan to present to the others.

Inside the clubhouse, Dare was glad he didn't run into anyone as he crossed the lounge and beelined up to Haven's room. He gave her door a few hard thumps, and then repeated them against Cora's door when Haven didn't answer. Neither of them were there.

Where the hell were they? Dare spun on his heel and made for the stairs again when a thought crossed his mind.

Haven's notebook.

He hadn't read it last night because he hadn't wanted to violate her privacy on top of all the other ways he'd failed her. But all bets were off now that Dare had confirmed that she was withholding important information—important not just for protecting her and Cora but for keeping his brothers and everyone he cared about safe, too.

Dare unlocked her door and slipped inside. The notebook lay on the pillow of the unmade bed. With none of the hesitation of the night before, he picked it up and opened it.

And hoped the news didn't get any worse from there.

CHAPTER 11

Dare's eyes scanned down the page. A list of some sort. He flipped through to the end of it, not yet making sense of what it was for. At the top, Haven had written:

> ### To-Dos/To-Haves
> ### Live Dangerously!

The second line made him frown. Living dangerously got people hurt, or worse. Just like what could've happened if Haven had been with the wrong kind of man last night when she passed out. Just like could *still* happen if they didn't find effective ways to mitigate the risk this reward posed for all of them.

His eyes ran down the first few items, and then the first title of the list made more sense. This was a to-do list for

Haven's life. A bucket list. The thought set off an uncomfortable pressure in his chest. Her father had clearly denied
her so much. So Dare had to give her credit for having
dreams and goals. It had taken him a while after he'd come
to his grandfather's to feel safe, secure, and stable enough
to start making any plans for the future. But here was
Haven, a few weeks out from years of virtual captivity and
already figuring out what kind of life she wanted to lead.

> √Kiss a guy
> Kiss a lot of guys! (√ ?)
> √Have fun at a party for once
> √Wear makeup
> √Drink

Dare frowned as he took in that section of to-do items,
most of which were checked off—and had probably
been checked off last night, with him. Multiple reactions
warred through him. She'd told him she'd never drank
before, so did that mean *all* the things on this list were
first-time experiences for her? And, if so, did that mean
he was the first guy she ever kissed? And who the hell
else had she kissed?

"Christ," he bit out, sitting heavily on the edge of the
bed. For the first time, a thread of guilt curled into his
gut, because there wasn't anything here that would help
with this reward situation, which meant now Dare was
just snooping.

But her words had snared him, and he couldn't make
himself stop reading. Some of the things she wanted to
do were so . . . basic that Dare found himself shaking his
head in disgust at her father. What kind of life did you
have to have experienced to want to put making a mess
and not caring on a life to-do list?

He turned the page, and his eyes couldn't take in the words fast enough.

> *Ride a motorcycle*
> *Learn to drive a motorcycle*
> *Get a driver's license again*
> √*Have an orgasm with a man*
> *Have sex. All kinds of sex. Everywhere.*

"Holy shit," he said, scrubbing his hand over his face and feeling even guiltier for continuing to read. But how was he supposed to walk away from the apparent knowledge that the orgasm he'd given her last night had been her first—with a man? Which of course suggested she'd had others that she'd given herself, and the mental image *that* plastered all over the inside of his brain had him rock hard in an instant. Especially when followed up by list items that had him questioning if she was a virgin and wondering if last night was her first sexual experience. Ever.

Because that rushed some serious protectiveness through his veins. And not a little masculine satisfaction. Annnd throw in some self-loathing, too. *This* was the list of a young person, bright and shiny and new. And he was a moody, hard-edged, guilt-ridden biker with demons too numerous to count and responsibilities that *ought* to be getting his attention.

He raked a hand through his hair as his eyes continued to devour the list. She clearly wanted to see the world (*Go to the beach, See the Pacific, See a Broadway play, See the sun rise over the Atlantic*) and have new experiences (*Go to a dance, Go skinny dipping, Get a tattoo, Ride a horse, Go to a concert*). For a split second, Dare's brain started making plans, thinking of how easily he could make some of these come true for her.

"What are you doing, Dare?" he said to the empty room.

Because just last night he'd decided to put the brakes on anything else happening between him and Haven, and that wasn't very likely if he was going to spend a bunch of time with her making her dreams come true. For fuck's sake. Not to mention, despite the way reading this had softened his anger—and softened it when little else had, which hadn't escaped his notice—he was still angry. And disappointed that she'd felt she couldn't trust him with the information about the reward. And worried about his people.

He skimmed to the end of the list, and the last item punched him in the stomach: *Belong to someone, in a good way.*

He couldn't help but wonder when she'd written that. Or hope that she'd been thinking about him when she had. Fucking ridiculous, all things considered, but that didn't make it any less true.

Damn, this woman had him tied in knots. He hadn't felt this out of control in decades, and never before over a female. Not to mention, the first people he'd ever truly, deeply cared about had died, which meant he needed to keep his shit in check, because he wasn't going through that hurt again. Ever.

A motorcycle's engine revved right out front. Dare stepped to the window, hoping his brothers were starting to arrive. Instead, he found Jeb sitting on his bike, his body turned toward Haven and Cora, who were both laughing and talking animatedly. Haven grasped a helmet Jeb offered her and settled it over her long hair, braided down her back.

Ride a motorcycle

Aw, hell the fuck no.

Dare shot out of the room, nearly forgetting to put the notebook back where he found it. And then he was hauling ass through the clubhouse. The roar of Jeb's bike told Dare he wasn't moving fast enough, and sure enough, he made it out the front door in time to see Jeb and Haven shoot across the lot and toward the winding road that cut across Raven Riders land toward the racetrack.

As he straddled his bike and started the engine, he gave Cora a nod. "Cora."

"Hi Dare," she said, looking at him like he had three heads. Awesome.

He tore out after Jeb and Haven, across the lot, down the wooded driveway, and out onto the roadway that curved down the mountain to the track. Dare pushed the bike hard, leaning into the curves aggressively. It didn't take him long to catch up to Jeb, who clearly was riding easy so he didn't scare Haven.

Dare shot in front of them on a straightaway and skidded to a stop.

Jeb slowed to a roll and put his boots out to brace the bike. "What's wrong?"

"I need Haven," Dare said, not meaning the words the way he'd said them. Or maybe he had. Shit. "I'll take her from here." Over Jeb's shoulder, Haven peered at him through the flip-down shield of the black helmet, and Jesus if she wasn't sexy as fuck straddling a bike in a pair of jeans and that pale-blue T-shirt he'd seen her wear before.

"Uh, okay. Sure." Jeb reached a hand around and helped Haven off. She lifted the helmet off, but Jeb shook his head. "Keep it. I'll see ya back at the clubhouse later. Or you can just leave it on the bar."

"Okay, thanks," she said, tucking it under her arm.

Jeb looked between Dare and Haven like he wasn't sure what was going on. Well, hell. Make that two of them. Dare nailed the prospect with a pointed stare, and the guy finally got the hint, pulled a U-ey, and headed back the way they'd come.

Which left Dare sitting on his idling bike and Haven standing there like a deer in the headlights.

"What's the matter?" she asked. Sunlight spilled through the trees hanging over the road, and golden light made her hair and face even prettier. He wouldn't have thought that possible.

Dare should've said what needed saying right there. He knew he should've. But that feeling from back in her room still had its claws in his brain. It was stupid and maybe even reckless (*Live Dangerously!*), but he wanted to give her something from that list. Giving her a ride? That was easy. And if she was going to have that particular experience, it was going to be with him.

Like that wasn't fucking confusing. Because bikers attributed as much significance to who shared their ride as they did to who shared their bed. Maybe even more. What Dare couldn't stand was seeing her on another man's ride, arms around another man's waist, her thighs wrapped around another man's ass, her laugh spilling into another man's ear. It didn't matter how innocent it all was. Not when Dare had tasted her, been inside her, heard his name moaned in ecstasy from her lips.

So instead of manning up and confronting her, Dare just nodded his head. "Get on. If you want to ride, you can ride with me."

NERVOUS EXCITEMENT RIPPLED through Haven's belly as she approached Dare. His brow was furrowed and his eyes were narrowed, his whole expression painted with an intensity she couldn't read. But, oh my God, did he look hot sitting on that bike. Strong thighs straddled the motorcycle. Lean, cut arms stretched to the handlebars. Long hair all blown back from his face.

Wild. Hard. Raw.

As excited as she'd been to ride with Jeb, she was about a million times more ecstatic to ride with Dare. After last night, arousal flowed lazily through her just to look at him. So getting to be so close to him when she wasn't sure that would happen again? She couldn't have been happier.

"Okay," she said, slipping the helmet back on. Dare wasn't wearing one, and Jeb hadn't either. Weren't they supposed to wear helmets? Wasn't it dangerous not to? But his face was wearing that serious, shuttered look he sometimes got, the one that wasn't much open to answering questions, so Haven didn't ask.

He gave her a hand on, and then she had no choice but to wrap her thighs around the outside of his and press her front against his back. She rested her hands lightly on his hips, suddenly feeling awkward about holding on to him the way she'd done so innocently with Jeb. She was probably way overthinking it, but what had felt easy with Jeb felt more weighted, more significant with Dare.

"You ready?" he asked over his shoulder.

"As I'll ever be," she said.

Dare pulled her hands around him, making her embrace his chest. Their closeness shot butterflies through Haven, because he felt so good in her arms. "Hold on to me, Haven," he said, beckoning even more butterflies. And then he took off, slowly at first, like Jeb had done.

She couldn't believe she was touching Dare this way, but between their closeness, his hard heat, and the ride, Haven was grinning into her helmet. They rode down the mountain at an easy pace, Dare leaning them gently into the curves.

Haven loved the openness of the ride, the way the warm air rushed over her skin. It made her feel like she was flying, like she could go anywhere, like she was free. When the road flattened out into a straightaway, they passed a big parking lot and stadium—the race-track she'd heard people talking about. A huge mural filled one whole exterior wall—the words *Green Valley Racing* painted in green over a waving black-and-white checkered flag. She'd never seen a car race in person, but she would love to. Maybe that was another thing for her list.

And, oh man, the fact that she got to check another item off after having done it with Dare absolutely tickled her.

Which made her wonder again why Dare had come after her and Jeb.

I need Haven.

His words came back to her, making no more sense now than they had when he'd said them. What did that even mean? What did he need her for? Did it have anything to do with what happened last night? Haven didn't know whether to be excited about that possibility or scared—after all, Cora had said he'd seemed agitated. What if whatever had agitated him was why he wanted to talk?

Her shoulders sagged at the thought.

They came to a stop sign at the edge of the racetrack's long driveway, and Dare looked over his shoulder at her. "Wanna take it fast or slow? Your call."

Something in his eyes made her belly flip. "Fast," she said.

The corner of his eye crinkled. "Was hoping you'd say that. Hold on tight."

Dare pulled a left onto the country road that ran in front of the racetrack. They went up a rolling hill, around a big bend at the foot of the mountain, and then hit a long straightaway in the valley beyond. And that's when Dare took off like a shot.

Haven screamed and then laughed as the bike tore down the road, and she couldn't stop laughing. Holding on to Dare for everything she was worth, a feeling of elation rolled through her unlike anything she could ever remember experiencing. It was a light, buoyant, expansive feeling that filled her chest with a warm pressure.

And Dare was the one to make her feel this way.

"You okay?" he called over his shoulder.

"More than okay," she said, grinning. Then she hugged him tighter, her front now plastered against his hard, broad back. "Can you go faster?"

One of his big hands pressed hers more firmly to his chest in answer, and then the bike was roaring down the road, cutting through green, rolling farmlands. The setting was tranquil, peaceful, beautiful, but the ride was fast and loud and a little scary in the same way the roller coaster she'd once ridden was.

Good scary. Fun scary. Do-it-again scary.

The thrill of the whole experience bloomed into arousal for the man she was holding on to. Her nipples hardened against Dare's back, the friction of their bodies making her breasts achy and sensitive. Her core clenched and tingled from the vibration of the ride and the way her thighs were spread around his. She fought the urge to rub herself against him, to let her hands wander down his body, over his abs and his parted thighs, to that part of him that was most male.

The road became more hilly and curvy, and Dare slowed the bike as they started through the forest covering another mountain. A few minutes later, he turned onto a narrow road that was part of a park according to the wooden signs posted here and there. The surface turned to gravel and then opened up into a small empty parking area. Dare pulled the bike to a stop and cut the engine.

"Where are we?" Haven asked as Dare helped her off the bike.

He dismounted and stowed her helmet for her, his gaze running over her face, her hair. She probably looked a mess from the ride. Wisps of hair had been blown out of her braid and hung all around her face. But she didn't regret it for a minute.

"Someplace . . ." He shrugged with one shoulder, but she couldn't tell if the gesture was casual or uncomfortable. "Just someplace I thought you might like."

Well that was unexpected, and really sweet, too. Her heart thrummed against her breastbone, pulsing excitement and nervousness through her in equal measure. They walked side by side down a wide dirt path that opened after just a few minutes to reveal a big dark green lake. A long, narrow beach stretched down toward the left. Sun sparkled off the gently rippling surface, and trees rose up and up majestically to frame the whole scene.

"It's beautiful," she said, her gaze drinking in the site. She walked onto the sand, wishing she could feel its softness between her toes. "How did you find this place?"

Hands in his jeans pockets, Dare looked out over the water, his gaze almost distant. "I've explored every bit of the area at one time or another, and this is a nice place to be alone, to think."

And he shared it with her.

Haven nodded. "Do you mind if—"

His gaze swung to hers, intense and penetrating. The request died in her throat. "What?" he asked, voice tight.

She didn't understand the odd intensity rolling off of him, or the seriousness carving hard angles into his harshly attractive face. "Uh, I just wanted to take my shoes off."

His gaze flipped down her body and slowly dragged back up. He gave a single nod.

Haven toed off her ratty sneakers, one of the few things she'd left Georgia with, and then reached down and rolled up the denim. The sand was cool between her toes and made her smile. "You should take your boots off," she said, grinning up at him.

One eyebrow arched up in answer.

"Oh, come on," she said, planting her hands on her hips. She wasn't sure why she was poking at him, given the odd intensity he was projecting, except that maybe being playful would make him happier, too.

"I'll pass," he said.

Haven shrugged. "Suit yourself," she said, walking down to the water. At first, she let just the tips of her toes get wet. "When I was a kid there was a river near my house where everyone went swimming. Little schools of minnows would dart around your legs, and it was ticklish. God, I haven't thought of that in so long." She stepped in a little further, until the water danced cool and soft around her shins.

When Dare didn't say anything, Haven glanced over her shoulder at him and found him blatantly staring at her. Feet spread, shoulders tense, arms folded tightly over his chest in a way that made his biceps pop. Like he was there to protect her. And, in a way, she supposed he was.

Which, hmm, was kinda hot.

But a part of her really wanted to crack that hard-edged

façade. A mischievous thought flitted through her head, something she never would've done before. In her old life, in the life that really hadn't been living at all. Before she let herself think better of it, she turned on a heel and kicked a little spray of water right at him.

CHAPTER 12

One minute Dare was standing on the beach, trying to keep himself from giving in to Haven's innocent playfulness. The next he was wet from forehead to knees from Haven splashing him.

She actually splashed him.

His reaction was pure instinct. He took off like a shot, bolting toward her like a wild animal after its prey.

Haven's beautiful face went from uncertain to startled to amused, and on a scream and a laugh she turned and ran, her feet kicking up water as she cut through the shallows.

"I'm sorry, I'm sorry," she yelled between laughs.

Dare just ran faster, not even caring as his boots hit the water's edge. She didn't have a chance in hell of outrunning him, and he wasn't giving up the chase until he had her in his arms—and made her pay.

A burst of laughter exploded out of her as she veered

back and forth, pleading words spilling haltingly from her lips. And then Dare clasped his arms around her upper body, hauled her in against him, and took them both down to the sand right at the water's edge. He turned his body so that he took the brunt of the fall, bringing Haven down on top of him. The chase and the challenge and the closeness had him rock hard in an instant. Not surprising, since he'd been sporting a semi since she'd straddled his bike, spread her legs around him, and taken him into her arms.

"You splashed me," he said, eyebrow arched, hand fisted around the long braid in her hair.

Wearing a grin so open and carefree that it made his chest feel suddenly too small for his heart, Haven nodded. "Oops."

"You think that's funny?" he asking, growing harder as she shifted her weight, making her belly grind against his hard-on.

A small gasp of recognition, and she bit down on her lip as the cast of her eyes went from playful to aroused. "A little," she said in a breathy voice. She licked her lips.

Dare couldn't help but track the movement, and want to suck the trail of moisture she left there off the plump, pink skin.

What the fuck was he doing?

Haven's hands gripped his shoulders, and she subtly shifted her weight again, pulling herself up his body—just a little, but enough that her lower belly now pressed and thrust against his cock. And Jesus if the need blazing out of those bright blue eyes wasn't crystal clear.

For a split second, Dare thought of Haven's list, her lie of omission, the expression she'd worn on her face when he'd made her come. And what he *wanted* to do ran roughshod over what he *should* do.

Startling a high-pitched gasp from her, Dare flipped

their positions so that she lay in the soft sand and his body lay partially over hers. With his forehead against hers, he nailed her with a stare. "You sure you want to provoke me?" His left hand dragged down her body, over the small mounds of her breasts and the flat plane of her stomach. His fingers settled on the button to her jeans. "Because you realize now I have to exact my revenge." He paused there, giving her the chance to tell him to back off.

She shivered beneath him. "I guess fair's only fair," she whispered.

That's my girl, he thought, even though the sentiment was really problematic. On all kinds of levels. "You want me to stop, Haven, you just say the word."

"Don't stop," she said, her lips parting, her breathing coming faster.

On a groan, Dare claimed her mouth with his. He tugged the button to her jeans free, yanked down the zipper, and pushed his hand beneath the snug material to find her hot and so damn slick.

Her tongue stroked against his, and he swallowed her moans as his fingers stroked her folds. She rocked her hips and parted her legs without him having to ask, pulling a growl of approval from low in his throat—and making him know that fingering her wasn't going to be enough. Not for him.

Not this time. And not that it had really been last time, either.

Dare wanted more of Haven. He wanted to taste her, drink her down, wear her on his skin. On his mouth.

Kissing her long and hard and deep, he gently withdrew his hand from between her legs and pushed at the denim around her waist. Haven clued in to what he was doing and helped him push down the material until she was naked to her knees.

And then Dare shoved down her body, gripped her hips in his hands, and planted his face against the triangle of blond hair at the junction of her thighs. His tongue pushed between her slick lips, and she nearly bowed up off the sand beneath him. Jesus she was magnificent and honest and responsive in ways that made him want more, want everything.

He held her hips to his mouth as she thrashed and jerked and thrust beneath him. He flicked his tongue against her clit, relentless and demanding. Her taste was all sweet female musk, and he relished every drop he drew from her. Haven's body strained and her knees parted as much as they could, given the way he was holding and pinning her.

"Oh my God, oh my God," she moaned again and again, her hand lightly falling atop his head.

"That's it, Haven," he groaned before plunging his tongue between her folds again.

"Dare," she rasped, her thighs shaking, her fingers winding into his hair.

The sound of his name from her mouth made his balls heavy and full. Christ, he wanted to bury himself inside her little body and ride her hard, fast, deep.

An urge that got about a million times stronger when she bucked into his mouth, pulled his hair, and screamed his name in an orgasm that sounded so good it nearly made him come, too.

Fucking beautiful.

Shaking and breathing hard, several long moments passed before Haven's muscles relaxed and her hold on his hair loosened. His scalp burned from the pull, but he loved every second of the way she'd both let go and held on tight. Held on tight to him.

That she'd let him expose her, that she'd trusted him to

do right by her, that she'd given herself over so freely to him—it all blew his goddamned mind.

Haven pushed against Dare's shoulders, and he let her force him up onto an elbow. Looking him in the eye, she scooted down and trailed her hand over his abdomen to his groin. With a shaky touch that said she wasn't sure he'd like it, she palmed his cock through his jeans, rubbing and squeezing in a way that made him a little crazy.

He liked it, all right.

God, how he wanted to let her have her way, how he wanted to see exactly what she wanted to do, how he wanted her hands and her mouth and her body all over him.

Except there was that damn looming confrontation to consider, wasn't there?

He stilled her hand. Pushed it away. Shook his head, hating the shadows of confusion and rejection that passed behind her eyes. But he couldn't let her give him pleasure—well, any more than he'd already received from pleasuring her. Not when *he* was the one now withholding information.

What a fucking epic mess. One he'd just made messier, no doubt.

Way to go, Kenyon.

So instead of doing what he wanted, he did what he had to. Rose to his feet, helped her up, and turned his back while she righted her clothes. He heard her hand rubbing over her skin, and peeked over his shoulder enough to see that she was trying to brush the sand off her legs and ass. Jesus, he really hadn't given that much thought, had he? Which made him an even bigger prick.

"Sorry I got you all sandy," he gritted out, regret at his thoughtlessness pushing its way to the fore.

"It's just sand," she said in a small voice. A voice that

made him want to tell her how much he'd loved eating her to orgasm, that made him want to explain why he'd kept them from going further, that made him want to show her some tenderness instead of reinserting the distance between them he should've left there in the first place. "I'll, uh, just get my shoes."

Looking to his right, Dare watched her trail down the beach, feeling like he'd wrecked the beautiful thing that'd happened between them—and knowing that his lack of willpower where she was concerned posed a problem he couldn't let go unaddressed for very much longer.

HAVEN'S HEAD WAS spinning, and not just from the most amazing orgasm she'd ever had—although that was certainly part of it. Even now, she couldn't believe that Dare had shattered her to pieces with just his lips and his tongue. But he had, and it had been without question the most intimate moment of her life.

But then, somehow, it had all gone wrong. And Haven didn't know what she felt most—embarrassment at what she'd let him do and how easily she'd given in to her desire to have him do it, hurt that he wouldn't let her return the favor, or confusion about why his mood had changed so suddenly. Her heart rate had barely evened out before the shutters had come down over his eyes and face, hiding the hot, fierce desire he'd worn and taking him away from her.

And if all that wasn't bad enough, she had sand in places you didn't really want sand. It turned out that sex on a beach sounded more romantic than perhaps it was. Mark that one down as lesson learned.

Although Haven would've let herself be buried in sand from neck to toes if Dare would've let her explore him, please him, take him in her mouth. That was at least something she had a little experience with, as she'd done it with Zach a few times before her father had forced them apart.

She shook her head as she brushed the sand off her feet and slipped them back into her sneakers. Finished, she turned to find Dare standing behind her, a strange expression on his face.

"Is something the matter?" she asked.

For a split second, she saw the answer in his eyes, and then he glanced to the trail that led down to the parking lot. "We should head back."

"Just tell me." She crossed her arms, hugging herself against the feeling of dread settling over her body.

He stepped toward the trail, and she thought he wasn't going to answer, but then he turned on his heel and stalked up to her. "You know what? Yeah. Something's wrong. You lied to me."

"What? When?" she asked, her mind racing, panic lancing through her veins.

"The fucking reward, Haven. Did you really think I wouldn't find out? Jesus."

The words sucked all the oxygen out of the air. Instinctively, she stepped back, her chin down. "I was going to tell you," she said, her response sounding as pathetic as it was.

"Oh, so you did know, then. How?" he asked, words clipped, tone full of disappointment.

Tears pricked at the backs of her eyes. But no way was she letting them fall. "We heard the guys who held us talk about it."

"You mean the ones who held you in the storage facility, the Church Gang?" he asked, and then he chuffed out a humorless laugh. "And this didn't seem like information that you should maybe share with the people trying to keep you safe? Like, say, when I specifically asked you to tell me everything I needed to know?"

Suddenly, all the stress of the past weeks welled up inside her. The escape. The kidnapping. The rescuers they hadn't known whether they could really trust. The uncertainty of it all. Haven forced her eyes to meet his, anger straightening her spine and making her stand taller. "It did. But it seemed equally like information that could be used against us. As that gang did. It seemed like information," she said, taking a step forward to close the gap between them again, "that should be guarded until we knew for sure who we could trust." Standing chest to chest with him, adrenaline shivered through her. "When we talked, I didn't know if I could trust you, and—"

"And now?" he asked.

"You have to ask?" After everything she *had* told him, was it possible he didn't realize how huge it was that she'd opened herself up to him the way she had? That making herself so vulnerable to him could only have happened if she trusted him—in a way she hadn't trusted anyone in years?

"Yeah, I have to fucking ask." He nailed her with a stare.

Which meant that despite how bare she'd laid herself open to him, Dare didn't trust her. And that really freaking hurt, because of everything he and the Ravens were doing for her and Cora. Because she understood why he was mad, even if she thought she'd been justified—at least initially. And because Haven liked him. *Really* liked him. And wanted him to like her back. "Yeah, I trust you," she said, forcing her eyes to stay up, to drink in the disappointment he was throwing off.

His jaw ticked like he was clenching his teeth, but finally he gave a tight nod. "Then I need you to not keep anything else from me."

"Okay," she said. Part of her wanted to say more—to explain, to defend, to fight—but she didn't want to make things worse.

After a long moment, he cursed on a sigh and raked his hands through his hair. He paced away, then turned, his eyes flat, expression resigned. "You need to know that I've called a meeting of the club's board to strategize how to deal with the existence of this reward."

Her stomach dropped to the ground. "What does that mean?"

"It means we have to operate under the assumption that the Church Gang had time to contact your father and let him know you were in Baltimore," he said, a hard edge slipping back into his tone. "And if that's true, it means we have to assume that it's possible for your father to learn what happened to you after the Churchmen lost possession of you."

Fear had her heart racing and goose bumps rising over her skin. She pressed shaky fingers to her lips, her thoughts racing. Why had she never put it together like that? Why had she stayed put with the Ravens? What if her father or his goons were close, or closing in? "I can't go back," she whispered. But then her financial reality closed in on her—she'd stayed because she had absolutely no means of leaving, of running, of starting a new life somewhere far, far away.

"You're not going back," Dare said. "Ever."

The conviction behind his words cut off the sharpest edges of her panic. "But I can't stay here either. Can I?"

Oh, how a part of her longed for him to respond with the same fierce conviction. But he only said, "Well, that's part of what we need to discuss."

It made sense, but it also made her feel like she was losing the one safe place she'd ever found. She'd always known the Ravens wouldn't let her and Cora just live there forever, but she hadn't thought her time there would be over so fast, either.

She heaved a deep breath, stuffing all the hurt and regret and sadness down. Burying it deep. Pretending it wasn't there at all. She had a lot of experience doing that, after all—when you'd lived the life she had, willfully ignoring all the things that could most hurt you became a survival skill. Something that you needed in order to pull yourself out of bed in the morning, to put one step in front of the other through the day, to not go crazy as the darkness of another night closed in on you.

"Then I guess you're right," she said. "We should get back. I don't want to make things any worse than they already are."

CHAPTER 13

Dare didn't know which was worse—the desolation that had put out the light in Haven's eyes during his conversation with her back at the lake, or the expressions on his brothers' faces as he'd brought them up to speed regarding Haven and the reward. Both left him feeling like somehow he'd fucked things up and, no matter what, was letting someone down.

And the fact that *not* letting Haven down ranked anywhere close to not letting his fellow Ravens down? That said something. What, exactly, he wasn't sure. Or maybe he just didn't want to probe it too closely.

"This changes a helluva lot," Maverick said, concern furrowing his brow. "I think we gotta assume that the threat is imminent. Which means we can either sit here and wait for it to come to us, or we can neutralize it by going on the offense or setting up the women with new lives far away from here. Which protects them and us."

"Going on the offense isn't really our style," Doc said, concern deepening the lines on his weathered face. "And do we really think the club is up for waging war on some far-off crime family within weeks of what went down in Baltimore?"

Dare heaved a deep breath. Doc was right on both counts—the Ravens didn't object to violence and even lethal intent in the name of defending their own, but they tried like hell not to be the ones to start shit or to create unnecessary enemies. It was part of what made them different from the Diablos.

Caine's eyes narrowed as he looked at his brothers seated around the big meeting table. "Procuring quality documents and making all the necessary arrangements will take the better part of two weeks. Ten days at best. So it's not really an either-or scenario. We need to plan for the threat *and* figure out what comes next for Cora and Haven."

Nods and low words of agreement rumbled around the table.

Purchasing new identities wasn't something they did often, but they had done it a handful of times over the years in the most dire cases, when the system failed a client altogether and their safety couldn't be secured any other way. The thought of this as one solution had crossed Dare's mind, too. But he'd be lying to himself if he didn't admit it fucking hurt in unexpected places to think of Haven becoming someone new, someone he couldn't know or see or touch. Ever again.

Probably made him a selfish bastard, especially after the way he'd jumped all over her back at the lake, but that didn't make it any less true. Not to mention, a new burr had settled itself under his saddle on the torturous ride back to the compound—he'd gone on the attack over her lie of omission, and he still felt some justification in that, despite the fact that part of him had understood her rationale for holding out on him. But at the same time, he was keeping something from her now, too. That he knew about her notebook. That he'd read it. That part of his behavior today had been about wanting to help her check things off her list—wanting it to be *him,* specifically, to give her those experiences.

Yet he hadn't admitted any of that. Which made him a goddamned hypocrite, didn't it?

All the more reason it was probably better for Haven— and for all the people he was supposed to be taking care of—if she was gone and Dare got his head screwed back on right again.

Because right now, he was *fucked.*

"In the meantime, the two of them shouldn't go out in public without at least two of us with them," Phoenix said, his hand scrubbing over the scar from a knife fight that had nearly taken his eye. "Actually, trips into public should be limited period. Oh, and I hate to say it, but Haven's hair is too fucking unique. You should probably have her change it." Phoenix directed those words to Dare, as if he held some special sway over the woman—which meant his brothers were probably keyed in that something was going on between him and their client. Fantastic.

Dare worked to keep his expression a careful neutral at the thought of making her change one of his favorite things about her, of making her change at all. Given how she'd lived these past years, how she'd been forced to play a role for so long, he hated that he was going to have to ask her to do it again.

Dare just nodded, knowing the precautions Phoenix suggested made good sense. "I should have images of Randall and some of his known associates tonight or tomorrow," he said. "As soon as I do, I'll shoot them around. Phoenix, let's get them into the hands of our contacts to see if anyone's seen these assholes in our backyard."

"You got it," Phoenix said.

Thoughts of the photos brought a new idea to mind. "Meanwhile, I'll put in a call to the guys over at Hard Ink and see what help they might be able to offer." During the weeks they'd worked together, Dare had seen enough of the former Special Forces soldiers' investigational techniques, computer savvy, and willingness to stray to the wrong side of the law if it meant achieving a greater good to know their help might be invaluable. Anyway, they owed the Ravens. And this was as good a reason as any to call in some favors.

"We're not thinking this sitch should cancel next Friday's race, are we?" Jagger asked, his fingers tapping out a rhythm on the table.

"Shit," Dare said. He really didn't want them going without their racing income for yet another week. They'd already lost a month's worth of betting and other racing revenues, and they faced expensive identity, relocation, and setup expenses for Haven and Cora, on top of the relocation and setup expenses they'd just absorbed for the client they'd moved to Pennsylvania. The Ravens made good bank from their various businesses, and they weren't hurting for money. But that stemmed in part from the fact that they were judicious in managing everything they brought in. They might wear leather and denim and care fuck-all for authority, but that didn't mean they weren't good businessmen. "Not unless we have specific intelligence that necessitates doing so."

Jagger nodded. "Well maybe you should ask Nick and his guys to come provide extra security at the event while you're at it. If we're gonna open the compound up to the public, it wouldn't hurt to have more boots and guns on the ground. And they obviously know how to handle themselves."

"Will do," Dare said. "Otherwise, the threat level is officially set at high, which means we're instituting watch rotations beginning immediately." Over the years, they'd put routines and protocols into place whenever high-profile targets resided on the compound—to keep their clients and themselves safe. A high threat level meant constant manning of their security camera feeds, concealed carry of weapons by all club members, and twenty-four/seven on-compound watch rotations, among other things. "Anyone gets any news, get in touch with me day or night. I don't care what time it is. All in favor of this plan?"

Every hand around the table rose.

Dare nodded, his gut knowing sending Haven and Cora away was for the best for everyone involved, but his heart regretting the decision more than he wanted to admit. "Let's get it done, then."

Having been quiet for most of the meeting, Doc sat forward in his chair, a serious, contemplative expression on his aging face. "This right here is why we do what we do," he said, meeting each of the men's eyes. "Because there are people who imprison their kids, treat them as if they're no more than assets in a business deal, and put rewards out on their heads that make them vulnerable to every kind of low-life scum. You make me proud of what we do here, of each and every one of you."

Doc's gaze met and held Dare's, and he knew that the older man was thinking in part of his own son, Dare's father. Doc hadn't said anything about it in years, but Dare knew it weighed on his grandfather that Butch Kenyon had become so corrupt, so morally bankrupt, so selfish and arrogant and downright fucking evil. Doc felt responsible for the way his son had turned out, and, alongside the shit Bunny had gone through in her first marriage to Maverick's father, it had long ago cemented his grandfather's commitment to their protective mission.

Dare's, too.

The meeting broke up after that, although most of the guys hung around to brainstorm or put plans into place or just shoot the shit.

Two bangs on the door, and then it flew open. Blake stood in the breach, turning Dare's already dark mood black. Prospects didn't belong in Church. Ever. "What the fuck do you think you're doing?"

"I'm sorry," Blake said. "But we've got a situation." The guy's serious gaze cut to Maverick. "Alexa's here. It's bad."

Oh, shit. Alexa Harmon, the only woman Maverick had ever been serious about. Who chose another man over him.

His easygoing demeanor immediately gone, Maverick bolted across the room. "Where is she?"

Dare and a few others followed Blake and Maverick as they rushed through the clubhouse to the kitchen, where they found a bruised, bloodied, and very shaken-up Alexa sitting at the kitchen table. Haven crouched down next to her, embracing the other woman in her arms.

"It'll be okay now," Haven said. "The Ravens will take care of you. I promise."

If the picture of Haven offering a total stranger such compassion didn't reach into Dare's chest and fuck with his heart, her words certainly did. And they also made him feel like an even bigger pile of shit for doubting her trust back at the lake, because he'd seen how his doubt had cut her deep.

Alexa and Haven both looked up at the same time at the group of men pushing into the kitchen.

Oh, hell, Dare thought, scanning Alexa's battered face. Maverick had been a teenager when his parents' marriage imploded, which meant he'd been old enough to see Bunny's face look like that more than once, so Dare knew what this must be doing to the guy.

"Jesus," Maverick bit out, taking a knee in front of where Alexa sat. "What the hell happened?" he asked. He reached out as if to touch the cut on her lip but stopped just shy of doing so. Haven stood, giving Mav room to get right up into his woman's space. Well, in his mind she was his, anyway. Alexa had always seemed to resist the chemistry clearly brewing between them, and the way that cut at his cousin had often left Dare feeling a flicker of resentment toward her, truth be told.

Alexa dipped her chin, bringing long brown waves down to shield her face. Dare turned to the men behind him and jerked his chin toward the door. Phoenix, Jagger, Doc, and Blake backed out of the room, leaving him, Mav, and the women. Whatever had happened here, Alexa didn't need a big audience for it.

"I just overreacted," Alexa finally said, her voice high and tight. She shook her head and wiped her fingers under her eyes. "I shouldn't have come."

Dare frowned, his attention divided between trying to make sense of what Alexa was saying and watching Haven move about the room—wetting some paper towels, grabbing a bag of peas from the freezer, filling a glass of water, and spilling a couple of pain pills into her hand from the cabinet over the sink, which had developed over the years to the one-stop shop for all their medicinal needs.

"Look here," Maverick said, gently tipping Alexa's chin up with a nudge of his fingers. In addition to the split on the right side of her lips, she had a bruising cut on her right cheekbone and eyebrow, too. "Coming here was exactly what you should've done."

A quick shake of her head as panic filled Alexa's hazel eyes. "No, I'm sorry," she said, pushing up from the table. Almost immediately, she lost her balance and nearly fell against Maverick, who caught her in his arms. "Please," Alexa said, desperation lacing through her voice. "Let me go."

Haven rushed across the room and placed a hand on Maverick's shoulder. He initially braced as he looked up at Haven, but then his gaze went to the things she carried in her hands. "No one's keeping you here, Alexa. Don't worry," Haven said. "But let's get you feeling a little better before you go anywhere, okay? Let's start there." She put the towels, frozen peas, water, and pills down on the table in front of Alexa.

Maverick heaved to his feet on a troubled sigh, backing up just enough to let Haven tend to Alexa but staying close enough to be there for her, too. Should she let him?

"Okay," Alexa said, giving Haven a small, tentative smile. "Okay." Alexa swallowed the ibuprofen and tilted her head back to allow Haven to clean up her face.

"I'm sorry if I'm making it hurt worse," Haven said, leaning over to gently swipe at Alexa's bleeding injuries. Watching her work was when Dare realized she'd changed clothes, and the damp waves of her hair revealed she'd showered, too. Which of course made Dare think about *why* she'd needed to shower in the middle of the day. For fuck's sake.

"You're not hurting me," Alexa said, wincing as Haven dabbed at her cheekbone. "And thank you."

Haven smiled, a smile so compassionate and sincere that Dare would've given just about anything to see something so beautiful and honest directed at him.

Even more than that, Dare was absolutely floored—and not a little awed—at how *good* Haven Randall was in a crisis. Gone was the shy, introverted woman she usually was. Instead, she was taking charge, doing what needed to be done, and putting Alexa at ease the way no one else could. The only other person they had around to play that role was Bunny, but she wasn't always there and was old enough that they couldn't just expect her to be at their beck and call at all hours of the day and night.

"You have the prettiest hair I've ever seen," Alexa said. Dare couldn't disagree. Which was why the compliment dropped a rock of guilt and regret into his gut. Since he was going to tell her she had to change it and all . . .

Haven's cheeks flushed pink on another smile. "Thank you," she said, and then she looked up at Dare. "Any chance you have something like butterfly stitches around here?"

"Yeah," Maverick said, already moving toward the medicine cabinet. How had Haven become so competent at providing first aid? And why did it always seem like those who had lost the most or had the least were always among the most generous, the most giving, the first to put themselves out for others?

Haven's default in this situation had clearly been to do what needed to be done, and that resonated so fundamentally with Dare that it had his chest feeling tight with need, with want, with appreciation. For her.

"Here you go," Maverick said, eyeballing Haven's every move where Alexa was concerned.

Nodding, Haven accepted the little packages into her hands and set about applying a few of the adhesive strips to Alexa's cheek and eyebrow. "Okay," Haven said. "I think that's as much as I can do. You should probably go to the ER to get—"

"No doctors," Alexa said on a rushed exhale, her eyes going wide with what looked like fear.

What the hell had happened to her?

Haven gave her hand a squeeze, and then passed her the bag of peas. "No doctors, then," Haven said. "Don't worry. Okay?"

Alexa nodded and shivered as she gingerly pressed the cold package to her face.

Finally, there was nothing to do but to ask again. "Why don't you tell us what happened, Alexa?" Dare asked. "We want to help however we can."

Maverick glanced at him, a look of appreciation clear on his face.

Alexa's gaze darted between the three of them, and you could almost see the wheels turning in her head. Earlier she'd said she shouldn't have come, so clearly she was second-guessing herself or talking herself out of thinking the situation was as serious as it was. They saw that so often—how women in abusive relationships internalized the criticism and twisted worldviews of their abusers, how they explained away abuse or blamed themselves. Dare really hoped that wasn't what was happening here, because that would mean Alexa was in trouble. And that realization would torment the fuck out of Maverick, especially if she wouldn't let him help.

Pulling a chair in front of her, Maverick took a seat and grasped her hand. "Al, talk to me."

The look they exchanged suddenly felt loaded, intimate, and Dare wasn't the only one who thought so, judging by the way Haven shifted her feet and ducked her chin.

"Hey Haven," he said in a quiet voice. "Why don't we give them a minute?"

A quick nod, and then Haven was following him toward the doorway to the mess hall. "I'm not going far if you need me," she said, looking between Alexa and Maverick. They both nodded.

"Thanks, Haven," Alexa said.

Dare hadn't suggested they leave to get Haven alone, but the minute they stepped into the mess hall—and in front of the observing eyes of his brothers and grandfather—he wanted her all to himself. More than that, he needed to let her know what they'd discussed in Church, before she heard it from somebody else.

"What's the deal?" Jagger asked, jutting his chin toward the kitchen. Maverick's unreturned interest in Alexa wasn't exactly a secret around the club.

"Don't know all the details yet," Dare said, clasping his brother on the shoulder. "But see that nobody bothers them in there, will ya?" Phoenix and Jagger nodded. "I'll be in my office." He turned to Haven. "Come with me."

"Okay," she said in a quiet voice.

A rock parked itself in Dare's gut as he led the way to the back of the clubhouse. He wasn't looking forward to this conversation, not one damn bit. But it wouldn't be fair to her to put it off, either.

Rock, meeting fucking hard place. For both of them.

He pushed into his office and gestured to the chair in front of his desk. "Close the door and have a seat, Haven. We need to talk."

CHAPTER 14

Haven closed the door and leaned back against it, too keyed up to sit, too anxious to be still. Between the adrenaline coursing through her while helping Alexa and the dread weighing her down from knowing the Ravens had essentially been discussing her fate, Haven felt a little like she might come out of her skin.

Arms folded over her chest, she stared at Dare, her gaze running over the hard angles of his face, the way his club cut emphasized the breadth and bulk of his shoulders, how the old denim of his jeans hugged his thighs.

"Haven," he said.

Her gaze cut to his. And, oh, man, she was so busted, wasn't she?

"You gonna sit?" he asked, lowering himself into the ancient black leather office chair.

She shook her head. "I'd rather stand," she said. Nervously, she glanced around the room. Files, papers, and odd dog-on-motorcycle knickknacks cluttered his desk, while bike-related signs and posters filled the walls. The window over his shoulder looked out onto the clubhouse's back porch and let in the warm breeze and the birdcalls she enjoyed so much when she sat outside.

Just another thing she would miss.

"Okay," he said, rising again and coming around to the near side of the desk. He rested his butt against its edge and crossed his arms over his chest, his position mirroring hers. "So, the club's come up with a plan to keep you safe."

Obviously, that was a good thing, except then why did it make her stomach drop to the floor? "Which is?" she asked, meeting Dare's serious gaze.

"For the long term, we think it probably makes sense to relocate you and Cora and set the both of you up with brand-new, foolproof identities. That includes everything—birth certificates, Social Security numbers, driver's licenses, and the like."

Haven's brain raced at all the implications—living somewhere new, having a new name, stepping into a whole new life. Given the likelihood that her father would never stop looking for her, it made sense. But it also settled a dull ache in the center of her chest. Because it meant she'd never really be able to stop watching and waiting and worrying that he might only be a half step behind her.

Changing her name also meant losing her only real connection to her mother, who Haven knew had picked it because her father told her that every time he told her how stupid it was. Because her mother had left while Haven had still been in diapers, Haven had no firsthand memories of the woman. But even though it had hurt for a long time that her mother had abandoned her, Haven also couldn't help but feel some small sympathy for a woman who had maybe hoped her baby would provide a safe haven in an otherwise bad life. Apparently, it hadn't worked.

Blinking out of her thoughts, Haven said, "Um, maybe I should go get Cora for this." What would her reaction to all this be? Haven already felt bad that her problems came with such enormous consequences for the best friend she ever had.

Dare reached out a hand as if to stop her, even though she hadn't actually moved. "I'll talk to her, too. But there's more I need to tell you."

"Okay," she said, head spinning. And then something occurred to her that made her totally nauseous. "Dare, I don't have any way to pay for something like that. Like, I literally have nothing." A shiver of panic raced over her skin, and the words rushed out of her. "I don't even know how I—"

"No," he said. Dare was in front of her in an instant, his hands gently grasping her by the arms. Heat shot from his touch into her face, her breasts, her belly. "I know that, Haven, and this is on us, not you."

She blinked, overwhelmed by his words, his closeness, the longing she felt for him. "Why?"

Shadows passed behind his eyes, shadows that Haven didn't understand. "It's what we do."

"But why?" she asked again. Without knowing, it was so much harder to believe that he and the Ravens would do so much for someone they knew so little and owed even less.

Dare released her and stepped back, and there was that distance again. Physical and emotional. He crossed his arms over his chest and shook his head. "It's just what we do," he said. "I told you that from the very start."

He was right. Haven remembered the conversation they'd had in the lounge the night she'd first met Dare. Intellectually, she knew that had only taken place a week before, but for some reason it felt like she'd lived a whole lifetime since first meeting Dare Kenyon.

"Okay," she said. "What else do you need to tell me then?" She wasn't sure how anything else could possibly be as big as pretending to be someone you weren't—for the rest of your life. But something about the way Dare wasn't quite meeting her eyes made her instincts jangle. Whatever it was might not be as big as all that, but it was still big enough.

"While you're still here, you can't go out in public. At least, not without having a few of us with you."

That news made her nausea even worse. She'd gotten free of her father's house, only to . . . what? Be imprisoned elsewhere? Be imprisoned by her past? Be imprisoned by fear, forever?

"It's not what you think," Dare said, his brow furrowing as he peered down at her. "It's just for your safety."

"Sure," she said, trying to fend off the irrational feelings of defeat and resignation threatening to swamp her. It was all for her own good, after all. Right?

"And one more thing," he said. "Just to be on the safe side, we think . . . well . . . you gotta change the hair. The length makes you stand out, and it's identifiable from a distance. It might be overkill, but we have to assume the worst—that your father knows you're in the greater Baltimore area and that you were taken by the team operating out of Hard Ink. It wouldn't take too much digging for someone with the right skills and motivation to tease that trail in this direction, and we've got a race open to the public next weekend, so . . ."

Her hair? She had to change her hair? Tears pricked

at the backs of her eyes, and she ducked her chin to her chest. After everything else he'd said, her reaction to the idea of cutting her hair was probably ridiculous. It was a little thing in the greater scheme of things. And it would grow back, of course. But then why did it make her stomach hurt and her shoulders sag?

It's for your own good, it's for your own good.

She repeated the mantra in her mind and shook her head. "Okay," she said. "How should I, uh, go about that?"

"Oh, uh," he said, looking uncomfortable. "I'll take you somewhere. Or something. Let me figure that out."

A fast nod and lots of blinking. When she was sure her voice wasn't going to crack, she said, "Thank you, for all of this. It's pretty amazing that you'd help complete strangers." Although, she didn't feel like a stranger to Dare. Not even a little, and that made that hollow space inside her chest ache even more. "And I'm sorry that I didn't tell you about the reward sooner. I just . . . it wasn't . . ." She shook her head again. "Just, I'm sorry."

Dare stepped closer and bent down so he could look at her eye to eye. "I get why you did what you did. Okay? I'm not pissed about that. Not anymore," he said.

His closeness stole her breath, and suddenly Haven found herself trembling for reasons that had nothing to do with how overwhelmed she felt. As her gaze scanned over his darkly handsome face, she licked her lips, hungry for a taste of him. Hungry for everything, with him. And that feeling beckoned words she didn't mean to say out loud.

"Will I get to see you . . . after?" Heat flooded into her cheeks at everything the question potentially revealed. But she probably didn't have time to play games or be subtle or wait to see how things worked out, did she?

His eyes narrowed. "After you're relocated?"

She nodded.

"No," he said, neither his eyes nor his expression revealing anything about how that made him feel. "It would be sorta like the witness protection program. New name. New home. No contact with anyone or anywhere from your old life."

"Oh, of course," she said, her tone sounding a heck of a lot more normal than she felt. Because she would be giving up not only the one place she'd ever felt safe but the one man who had ever made her feel safe, too. And, of course, safe was only just one of the things Dare made Haven feel. And maybe not even the most important— which was saying something for someone who'd lived the way she had for so very long. "And when would we leave?"

"Could take as much as two weeks to get everything ready," he said on a sigh. "Or it could be sooner. But I'll keep you posted."

Two weeks. *Two weeks.* She wanted to be happy about that. She wanted to feel like, *oh yay, in two weeks I can finally have the life I've always wanted.* Except she didn't feel that way at all. Instead, it felt like the clock was ticking down all around her, marking the minutes and seconds until she'd have to give up some of the best things she'd ever found.

"Two weeks," she said out loud. "Well, that sounds, uh, great." The last thing she wanted was for him to think she wasn't grateful, because she was. "Anything else?" she asked, suddenly wanting to flee, to be out from underneath the intensity of his too-observant gaze.

"No, but Haven—"

Two knocks against the door.

Haven startled at the sound coming from right behind her. She jumped out of the way as the door opened.

Maverick poked his head in. "Oh, sorry."

"Don't be," Haven said. "We were all done. I think. Right?" She looked to Dare.

He frowned. "Yeah, about done."

"Well, then, can I talk to you?" Maverick asked, looking to Dare.

"I'll go," Haven said, not even waiting for Dare to respond. She pulled the door open further and then slipped by Maverick. He seemed nice, which made her feel bad for him and Alexa, because it seemed like there was something between them. "Is Alexa okay?" she asked.

Maverick peered over his shoulder at her. With his blond hair and blue eyes, he was a cute guy, more traditionally handsome than Dare, she supposed. "She will be," he said. "Thank you for what you did for her."

"Of course," Haven said, nodding and needing to get away from the way Dare was staring at her over the other man's shoulder. "It was nothing."

"No, Haven," Maverick said, turning all the way toward her. "You taking care of someone I care about will never be nothing."

"Okay," she said, unsure how else to respond. "I really hope things work out for her." With a nod, Haven turned and rushed down the hall, hoping against hope that things worked out for herself, too.

WELL, THAT SUCKED ass, Dare thought. He blew out a breath and waved Maverick in. "What's up?" he asked Maverick as the two of them settled into the chairs on either side of the desk. "How's Alexa?"

Maverick braced his elbows on his knees and dropped his face into his hands. He ground the heels of his palms into his eyes and heaved a troubled breath. "Fuck," he bit out, and then he looked up at Dare. "She won't tell me what happened, just insists it was a misunderstanding. Like we haven't heard that before."

"Yeah," Dare said. "A misunderstanding that involved her face getting slammed against some immovable object?"

"Right." Mav shoved to his feet and paced. "I don't know what to do."

Fuck if this conversation wasn't going to suck, too. "You're not gonna like what I have to say."

Maverick pointed at him. "No, I'm not. So don't say it."

"Maverick—"

"I fucking mean it, D," he gritted out.

Dare stood and braced his fists on the desk. "You can't help someone who refuses to be helped. You know that, maybe more than anyone. And Alexa Harmon is possibly the most stubborn woman on the face of the earth."

His cousin chuffed out a humorless laugh. "Ain't that the truth." He paced along the short space in front of the desk, and then raked his hands into his blond hair. "But then what do I *do*? I have to do something. I can't just sit here waiting for the next time."

"Shit, Mav. Whatever's going on for her, she's gotta want out of it before you can do anything. That fucking sucks, I know—"

"No, you don't goddamn know," Maverick yelled, glaring at him.

Dare didn't take offense. He could only imagine how he'd feel to see Haven bruised and bloodied like that—

The thought nearly stole his breath, because he didn't have many days left to see Haven *at all*. A vague sense of dread coursed through his veins. How did he know she'd be safe without him, even if they took every precaution in setting up a new life for her? How did he know if he wasn't there?

And why did the prospect of not being there make him

want to pound his fist into a wall? Why did it feel like he was the one running away—again? Like he'd done the day Kyle and his mom had died, instead of staying and fighting . . .

Dare shook the thoughts away. Or he tried to. "You could set up some low-key surveillance of her house for a few days," he managed, wanting to solve just *one* person's problem today.

Mav's eyes went wide. "But what about the manpower we need here? Until we can make arrangements for Haven and Cora?"

"We'll make it work," Dare said, and then he nailed Maverick with a stare. "But do not fucking engage. Not while you're by yourself."

"Yeah, yeah. Of course not." Maverick sagged into the chair behind him. "Thanks."

"Is she still here?" Dare said, taking a seat himself.

"Yeah. Bunny came and she was talking to her. I hoped maybe Alexa would open up more to a woman." Even though Bunny was Maverick's mother, he'd used her nickname for as long as Dare could remember. Everyone did. "Speaking of which, Haven was great with her."

Dare nodded, working hard to school his features. "She was."

Maverick tilted his head and eyeballed Dare. "What's going on between the two of you, anyway?"

Pulling his cell out of his jeans pocket, Dare shook his head. "Nothing." The word tasted sour on his tongue. If it was nothing, then why was he so tied up in knots?

"She sure doesn't look at you like it's nothing."

"Is that so?" Dare asked, checking his texts and e-mails to see if the pics of her father and his men had come through yet. What kind of pathetic was he that he took pleasure from hearing Maverick say Haven looked at him like she was interested?

"Don't tell me you don't see it," Mav said.

Eyes still down, Dare shrugged. He saw it. He saw *her*. "Doesn't really matter, does it?" Something hit him in the forehead. He flinched as a pencil tumbled down his front and fell to the floor. "Ow, you fucker. Coulda taken my damn eye out."

"Uh-huh. Stop shitting me for a minute," Maverick said.

Dare sat forward in his chair and threw the cell to the desk. "What do you want from me, Maverick?"

Maverick's eyes went wide, and then narrowed as they studied Dare. "You like her."

"Mav—"

"You fucking like her." The big idiot grinned. Like there was anything good about Dare's errant feelings. For fuck's sake.

"Good-bye, Maverick. Don't let the door hit ya in the ass on the way out." Dare gave him a pointed look.

Maverick settled back in the chair and crossed his hands and fingers over his stomach. Goddamned pain in the ass. "You're totally feeling her."

"I'm not fucking around, Maverick. We're not talking about this." No sense in trying to deny it, because his cousin could get like a dog with a damn bone. Better just to cut the whole conversation off at the knees.

"Not going anywhere, D. For five years you've known about how I crashed and burned with Alexa. If you think I'm backing off of the first time you went and got the feels for a woman, you're crazier than I thought you were." Maverick's expression said he was having way too much fun with this topic. The bastard.

"Any chance you could rub a few more brain cells together and remember what the hell we talked about in Church not a damn hour ago?" Dare asked.

For a moment, Maverick looked almost comically confused, and then his mouth dropped open. "Oh. Oh, shit, D."

"Now, can we be done?"

All the humor bled out of Maverick's expression. "Yeah, I'll, uh"—he thumbed toward the door—"go check on Alexa and Bunny."

"Good plan," Dare said, feeling like an asshole.

Maverick left without saying anything else, leaving Dare sitting all alone in the quiet of his office. All alone. He hadn't ever really had a steady relationship, not in all the years he'd lived in Frederick. Plenty of fucks, and a few friends with benefits, but no one he ever wanted for longer, for keeps, for his. Still, he had women when he wanted them. He had his brothers. He had his grandfather and great-aunt. He'd been alone, but he hadn't ever felt lonely.

Until now. And there was only one thing different about his life.

Haven.

CHAPTER 15

■ have something to tell you," Cora said as she knocked
■ on the door to Haven's room and walked in.

"I probably know what it is," Haven said from where she
sat on the bed, back against the headboard. She was under
the covers despite being fully dressed and it not even being
dinnertime yet. Ever since her talk with Dare, she'd been
mindlessly watching cooking shows, although she couldn't
actually have said what kind of food they'd been making.
"Where were you?" She pulled her gaze from the TV.

"I was hanging with Jeb over in the chop shop watching him work on his bike. And then Phoenix came and
found me," Cora said, crawling onto the bed and getting
in under the covers next to her.

Sitting shoulder to shoulder, Haven looked at her best
friend. "So you know we're going to be leaving soon?
Getting new names and identities and being set up somewhere else?"

Cora nodded, but Haven couldn't read any reaction in her expression. "Yeah. What do you think?" Cora asked.

"I mean, yeah. It's great," Haven said, nodding. And working really hard to be positive.

Frowning, Cora tilted her head. "Why don't I believe you?"

"You should," Haven said. "Starting a whole new life is exactly what we wanted." It was. But a funny thing had happened. Haven felt like she'd already started living that new life. Right here. With the Ravens. That was probably stupid, considering that no one had ever once suggested this as anything more than a way station until they figured out what was next, but she couldn't help how she felt.

"You do remember that I am your best and longest friend, right?" Cora arched an eyebrow.

"Uh, yeah, of course," Haven said.

"Here, give me that." Cora grabbed the remote and turned off the TV. She shifted to sit facing Haven. "So be honest with me. Because I can hear in your voice that you're not thrilled. It's Dare, isn't it? What the heck happened to the two of you this afternoon anyway? He took off after you and Jeb like he was pissed or something."

Haven liked how Cora didn't even wait for the answer to her question. She knew Haven too well. "He stopped Jeb, said he needed me, and took me for a really awesome ride up to this beautiful lake . . ." She stopped there out of both embarrassment over the thought of describing what'd happened afterward and fear that trying to describe it would beckon the tears she'd been fighting since she left Dare's office.

Cora squeezed her knee over the blanket. "And then?"

"And then, stuff happened," she said in a quiet voice.

"Well, you know that isn't gonna fly, my dear." Cora scooted closer. "Spill."

Heat crept into Haven's cheeks as she searched for the words.

"Oh, *good* stuff," Cora said, laughter in her voice.

"I splashed him," Haven said, remembering the look of surprise he'd worn, and how he'd chased her. Caught her. "Next thing I knew, he tackled me onto the beach, and then . . . we were kissing and he was touching me with his hands and, uh, his mouth." God, her cheeks were on actual fire. At least, that's how they felt.

Cora gasped. "He went down on you? Aw, lucky you. Did you like it? Was he good?"

Haven opened her mouth to answer, and burst out crying. Yes, she liked it. Yes, it was good. And, yes, she wasn't thrilled about leaving the Ravens because she didn't want to leave Dare. And it felt like someone was ripping out her heart.

"Oh, sweetie," Cora said, embracing her.

It took Haven the better part of a half hour to rein in her emotions and finish recounting her afternoon with Dare—right through the conversation in his office.

"I didn't mean for it to happen," she said, scrubbing the last of the wetness from her face, "but I like him. And I like it here. And now we have to leave."

"Maybe you should just tell him that," Cora said, giving her a small, sad smile.

"It wouldn't matter," Haven said. "Dare said the Ravens decided this was what they wanted to do—they think it's what's best for us, and the reward puts everyone here in danger, too. How could I stay here if it meant my father might hurt the people trying to help us? All because I have a crush on a man who has no problem sending me away?" She shook her head.

"I think it's more than a crush," Cora said in a quiet voice. "Don't you?"

Haven wasn't exactly sure what she felt. All she knew was that her chest ached and her stomach hurt and everything inside her rebelled at the thought of leaving. "It doesn't really matter though, does it? Because he wants me to go. And I *have* to go." Closing her eyes, she took a deep breath. She didn't want to talk about herself anymore. "I'm just sorry that you're caught up in all this, too."

"Don't be crazy, Haven. I'm here because I want to be. And I wouldn't be anywhere else."

Haven forced her eyelids open and looked at her friend—and saw nothing but sincerity on her pretty face. "I am glad you're here."

"Of course you are," Cora said. "Because I'm awesome."

Chuckling, Haven nodded. "You are."

"You know what? Don't worry, okay?" Cora clasped her hand. "Whatever happens, we'll be together. Let's trust that for now."

"Yeah," Haven said, working at a smile.

"I have an idea." Cora swung her legs off the bed. "I'm going to go downstairs and whip us up some dinner and snacks, and then you and I are going to get crumbs all in the bed and watch movies until we fall asleep."

Exactly the kind of thing Cora used to do back in Georgia to cheer Haven up and distract her from the rest of her life. And it proved how well Cora knew her. Because Haven felt too shaky inside to go downstairs and be among a big group of people, and, truth be told, she felt bad for not once thinking about the kind of trouble she might be bringing to the Ravens' door. "Sounds great," Haven said. "I'll look for some movies."

Fifteen minutes later, Cora knocked on the door, and then came into the room followed by Phoenix.

"Hey, Haven," he said with a small smile. He was carrying a big tray loaded down with food and drinks.

"Hi," she said, chuckling. "Cora has you doing her heavy lifting, I see."

Grinning, he nodded. "I'm sure I'll get a favor back in return some time." He settled the tray on the nightstand next to Haven.

"Don't hold your breath," Cora said, more than a little amusement painting her expression. "Here's your tip. Don't eat the yellow snow."

Phoenix folded his hands over his heart like he was wounded. "Aw, why ya gotta do me like that?" Haven watched the two of them as they exchanged banter, and it became clear as the back and forth escalated that it was more than that. They were flirting. And Haven could totally see why. Phoenix was funny and outgoing and overflowing with confidence, a lot like Cora. "Fine, fine," he finally said as he backed toward the door. "I'll go nurse my wounded ego elsewhere."

"Thank you, Phoenix," Cora said in a singsong voice.

For a moment, Phoenix hung at the door, and then he looked at Haven. "For what it's worth, I'm really sorry everything has to go down like this. You all fit in great around here. I wish you could stay."

The sentiment poked at the ache that had been lingering in Haven's chest. "Thank you, Phoenix."

He nodded, then pulled the door closed behind him.

"Well, look at him being all sweet," Cora said, her expression more than a little moved.

"You like him," Haven said. "I'm not the only one crushing on a Raven. You like him, too."

Cora rolled her eyes and busied her hands with the food. "He's easy to look at and fun to tease," Cora said. "But I'm not interested in him. Really. Besides, they say he's a total player. No, thank you." Haven eyeballed her, but nothing about Cora's expression or behavior belied her words. "Now, what movies did you find? Because girls' night in is officially on."

THE KNOCK WOKE Haven from a dead sleep. "Was that the movie?" she asked, looking to Cora.

Her friend was already sliding off the bed. "Nope, but I'll get it."

"What time is it?" Haven asked, yawning and stretching on the bed.

"After ten." Cora pulled open the door. "Oh, hi, Dare."

"Cora," he said, stepping into the room. "I'm sorry to bother you all." His gaze cut to Haven and moved over her body, and she felt it like it was his fingers, not his eyes, that had caressed her skin.

She pushed herself into a sitting position, suddenly self-conscious about her appearance. After they'd eaten, she and Cora had slipped into pajamas, which for Haven meant an oversized T-shirt Bunny had given her. Cora at least had on a pair of men's boxers rolled at the waist.

"Dare," Haven breathed.

"I should've given you more notice," he said, shifting on his boots. God, he was hot standing there in his cut, tattoos running over his biceps, his hair looking like he'd been running his hand through it.

"For what?" she asked.

He looked from Cora to Haven. "Bunny has a friend who runs a beauty shop, and she agreed to come over after she closed up tonight to do your hair."

Cora's eyes went wide. "You're getting your hair done? Wait. Why are you having it done here and not at the shop?" She frowned at Dare. "What's going on?"

"Oh, uh," he said, clearly uncomfortable to be put on the spot.

"The Ravens thought it would be a good idea for me to change my hair. Too unique given the length. And it's perfect timing, because you know I've been wanting a change." She gave Cora a pointed look and hoped her friend got the message. *Don't contradict me.*

"Uh-huh," Cora said, not sounding very convincing at all.

But it must've done the trick for Dare, because he nodded and turned for the door. "Well, she's getting set up down in the kitchen, so, if you want to get dressed and come on down?" His gaze lingered on her bare legs for a moment, and then cut back to her face.

"Yup. Be right down," she said.

He nodded and closed the door behind him.

Waiting no more than five seconds, Cora turned and planted her hands on her hips. "What the hell, Haven?"

Haven flew off the bed. "I don't want to do it, okay? But they think it's too noticeable, and Dare's pretty convinced there's a good chance my dad or his men are nearby. They think I need a disguise, just until we leave here."

Cora shook her head, her mouth opening and closing like she wasn't sure what to say.

"I don't think I've ever seen you speechless before," Haven said, crossing to the chair and stepping into her jeans. She changed into a tank top so that her sleep shirt didn't get all hairy.

"I want you to cut your hair when you're ready to do it, not because you have to do it. Why didn't you tell me?" Cora asked.

Haven hugged herself. "I didn't want to be a baby about it."

"Stop that right now," Cora said, coming right up to her and fingering the loose blond wisps hanging around Haven's face. "I know how much you love your hair. I'm sorry you have to do this."

Haven waved a hand. "It's just hair, right? It'll grow out." The words were for herself as much as they were for Cora.

"That's right. And you would be gorgeous if you were bald." She squeezed Haven's shoulder.

Haven grimaced. "Let's not test that theory."

Chuckling, Cora nodded and headed for the door. "Give me a minute to throw on some clothes and I'll come down with you."

"I'd like that," Haven said. Besides, Cora could talk a mile a minute and would provide the perfect distraction from the fact that Haven wasn't really ready to do this. Her father hadn't given her money or approval to go out to do things like getting a haircut because it didn't serve him in any way, so the last time she'd had one she'd been sixteen. Or maybe it was fifteen? She couldn't even remember.

Cora popped back in wearing jeans and a tee not a minute later. "Okay, I'm ready. Are you?"

"SHE'LL BE RIGHT down," Dare said, walking back into the kitchen. Bunny stood at the counter, pouring a cup of coffee, while her friend Joan set up a makeshift shop on the kitchen table. Two towels lay over the back of a chair pulled out into the middle of the floor.

"Don't worry, Dare. Joan's great. So good she's usually booked weeks ahead of time. She'll take care of Haven," Bunny said.

Dare nodded, though he didn't care if Joan was the best hair stylist who ever lived. None of that would make a difference to Haven if she really didn't want this done. Despite how much sense Phoenix's words made back in Church, for right that moment, Dare didn't feel that much different from her father. Or, at least, he feared that she'd feel that way. And he wouldn't blame her.

A few minutes later, Haven and Cora came in. Haven's face was scrubbed clean and her hair was a little messy from sleep, but she was showing the most skin he'd ever seen in a skimpy pink tank top—well, except for when he'd found her in bed wearing nothing but a men's white T-shirt. Without even trying, she'd looked sexy as fuck, making him wish he'd been there for a totally different reason.

"Ah, Haven, this is my friend Joan." Bunny made introductions and the women exchanged greetings, Haven shaking the older lady's hand.

"Have a seat, hon," Joan said, tucking the side of what Dare supposed was a stylish cut behind her ear. "And tell me what you're thinking."

"Oh, well." Haven slid into the chair, looking small and even a bit fragile. She had a way of doing that, suddenly shrinking into herself as if to make a smaller target, or to blend into the background. "Mostly, just different," she said. And that was the moment Dare knew she wanted no part of this. Because what woman didn't know exactly what she wanted done to her hair?

"Stop," Dare said. "You don't have to do this."

Frowning, Haven peered up at him. "Yes, I do." She turned to Joan. "Shorter. Maybe up to here," she said, holding her hand flat against the top of her biceps to mark an invisible line.

Joan unwound the band holding the length of Haven's hair in a braid. "Do you want any color?"

"Uh." She glanced to Cora. "Maybe . . . maybe I do. But I don't know much about it."

Haven was doing exactly what he told her to do, and he hated it. He shoved off the counter and stalked out of the kitchen, through the clubhouse, and into the rec room. A few guys playing pool called out a greeting, but Dare only had eyes for the bar, where he grabbed a glass and poured himself some whiskey. He tossed it back, savoring the burn, and then poured some more.

Fuck, what was he doing? If she was going to suffer through having the change made, then he sure as shit could man up and sit with her while it happened. Whiskey in hand, he returned to the kitchen.

"I don't think we should go too dark because of how fair you are," Joan was saying. "But a light brown would give you a change without washing you out. We could even do some low lights to give it more depth. And brown would be so pretty with those gorgeous blue eyes."

Gorgeous blue eyes which held so much uncertainty. But Haven pushed through whatever doubts she had, because she agreed to Joan's suggestions and watched as the woman set about mixing solutions in small bowls with brushes. Finally, Joan wrapped a towel around Haven's shoulders and clipped it together in front of her throat.

"All ready, hon?" she asked Haven with a smile.

Haven's gaze went to Cora again, and the other woman gave her a small nod. Licking her lips, Haven glanced to him. "Wait. Can I have a drink of that?"

"The whiskey?" Dare asked, lifting the glass.

She nodded and accepted the tumbler into her hand. Tipping the crystal to her lips, she took a long enough drink that she almost emptied the glass. "Okay," she said, passing it back to Dare. "Let's do this."

Fucking hell. He emptied the glass and tried not to think about the fact that it'd just been between her lips.

"You're cutting off so much length, you should consider donating the hair to one of the organizations that uses it to make wigs for cancer patients. I could take care of that for you if you like," Joan said, sectioning the long lengths into small ponytails and wrapping them in rubber bands.

"People do that?" Haven asked, her eyes going wide. "Because I would love to do that."

"Oh, yeah," Joan said. "You're a great candidate for that with all this beautiful hair."

Dare feared that the words might make Haven hesitate, but instead, she smiled genuinely for the first time since she'd come downstairs, like she wasn't just resigned about getting her hair cut, but interested in doing it. "I love that idea so much," she said.

Well, what do you know? When the cut was about protecting herself, she seemed to regret doing it, but now that the cut could help someone else, Haven was suddenly more enthusiastic. As if he didn't already admire enough about her. Because he really did.

One by one, Joan chopped each of the ponytails off, showing Haven as each one came free.

"No going back now," Haven said, smiling at Cora.

"It's gonna be great," Cora said. "Just you wait."

For the next hour, Haven sat and chatted with the other women while Joan painted a solution onto Haven's hair and wrapped chunks of it in foil.

"Maybe I'll just go with this look," Haven said when her whole head was covered in aluminum. "What do you all think?" The women all laughed and joked.

Bunny kept giving Dare odd looks, probably wondering why he was hanging around for what was clearly a female bonding ritual, but he didn't want to leave Haven, even though he wasn't really contributing a damn thing or helping in any substantive way. He stood against the counter, arms crossed, and every once in a while he'd respond to a text message or check his e-mail to see if the photo of her father had come in yet.

As the foil came off, Dare got the first glimpse of her new dark hair. He'd found the blond striking from the very first time they met, but Jesus if she wasn't gorgeous with brown hair, too, and not lacking a single iota of the brightness and lightness that he associated with her.

Joan spent more time cutting, and then finally blow-drying, until she was asking Haven, "Well, what do you think?" She handed her a mirror.

A total fucking knockout. That's what Dare thought. Maybe a little edgier and definitely a lot sexier, but still very much the Haven he— Well, the Haven he'd come to know.

"It feels so much lighter," Haven said, turning her head back and forth to make it move. She played with the ends as she looked in the mirror. "And so much wavier now."

"You were long overdue, my dear. It's so much healthier now," Joan said, wiping her hands on a towel.

Haven nodded as she continued to look at herself, an awed expression on her face.

"It's so much shinier now, too," Cora said. "God, you look freaking fantastic, Haven."

"I like it," she said, a big smile lighting up her face. "I like it a lot." She shot to her feet and gave Joan a hug. "Thank you so much."

"Oh," Joan said, caught off guard. The older woman laughed and patted Haven's back. "You are more than welcome. It's not every day that I get to give a complete makeover like this. I enjoyed myself."

"How come you never make me look that good?" Bunny asked, winking at Haven as she brought over a broom.

"Oh, Bunny, you and me both," Joan said as the women laughed.

The happiness on Haven's face was a sucker-punch to the gut—Dare was relieved and glad to see it, but also completely blindsided by how damn *important* it had become to him to see Haven happy. When the hell had that happened? And what did it even mean?

"What do you think, Dare? Do I look different enough?" Haven asked, smiling at him.

"You look good," he said, unable to hold back the compliment and play it cool. "Really good."

She grinned like he'd just given her the best present ever. "Well, thank you," she said. "If it wasn't for you, I never would've known how much I'd like this."

She was . . . thanking him? Beyond floored, Dare shifted his feet and nodded. "Yeah, of course." Just then, his cell phone rang. "Better get this," he said, and then he ducked out of the room—as much to keep his mouth from running away from him as to find out what news might be coming down the line.

HAVEN WASN'T THE least surprised she hadn't been able to fall back to sleep. Yesterday had been quite possibly the most eventful day of her life—between the motorcycle ride with Dare, what had happened between them at the beach, the club's decision on relocating them, and having her hair changed. Her brain was like a merry-go-round with no Off switch.

And she was just as happy to be up, because it gave her time she hadn't taken in a few days to do some baking—cinnamon buns and peanut butter cookies, because of how popular both had been the last time she'd made them.

Waiting for the dough for the buns to rise, Haven lined up balls of cookie dough on the baking sheet and flattened them with presses of a fork. Within minutes of putting the cookies in the oven, the kitchen smelled incredible—like rich peanut butter and sweet cinnamon. Mindlessly filling the minutes until the cookies would be done, she cleaned up and wondered how many more things she could make here before they had to leave. Would her new place have a nice kitchen she could bake in?

A shiver of dread ran over her. Wherever they moved, how were they supposed to live? Cora had waitressing experience, but Haven had no skills at all. She'd never held a job in her life and didn't even have a high school diploma. The unknowns that lay before her were so numerous she could barely think on them all.

When she'd left Georgia, there'd been a lot of unknowns then, too, of course. But she'd believed to the depths of her soul that whatever happened, wherever she went, it would all be better than where she'd been—trapped in hell with her father.

Now that she'd lived with the Ravens for nearly a month, she wasn't sure she could believe the same. It was good here. How did she know whatever came next would be, too? Because now that she'd found safety and good people and a little sliver of happiness, the prospect of giving it up hurt in a way that her father's mean comments and treatment never had. Because she hadn't let that get under her skin. She'd refused.

But this place . . . oh, and Dare—he was so far under her skin she wasn't sure how she'd ever get him out. Or if she'd ever find another man who made her feel all the things he did.

The timer on the oven went off, pulling Haven from her thoughts. She scooped the cookies onto a flat expanse of aluminum foil to cool, having made six dozen total. When the ovens reached the correct temperature, she put the buns in to bake next.

Waiting again, sleepiness finally hit her, so Haven busied herself with cleaning up to keep awake. A little before five in the morning, the buns were done and iced, giving Haven just enough time to grab a few hours' sleep before breakfast—which she planned to attend.

If they only had a few more days here before they had to go, Haven didn't want to spend another second of it hiding out in her room. Because who knew if she'd ever feel as safe again as she did with the Ravens.

And with Dare.

CHAPTER 16

Haven came down to breakfast late to find at least twenty people already digging in. She'd been so nervous to walk into a big group of mostly strangers that she'd delayed in her room forever, fussing over her clothes and her new hair, which she loved even more in the light of day. But she was done with letting her fear keep her from doing things, trying things, living life to the fullest.

All of which led her to walk into a room of mostly seated people, and not a few heads turned her way—and did double takes.

"Whoa, Haven. Is that you?" Phoenix asked from where he sat across from Cora, who waved her over, wearing a big smile.

"I'd tell you but then I'd have to kill you," Haven said as she rounded the table and scooted between the chairs until she got to her own. Laughter filled the room, which eased some of her anxiousness until she noticed Dare staring at her from where he sat at the head of her table, dark eyes hot and intense.

"Please tell him then," one of the Ravens she didn't know said to more laughter. Phoenix flashed his middle finger at the guy.

By the time she sat, her face was on fire, but she felt good for having come.

"You came," Cora said in a low, excited voice. "I'm so glad."

"I'm here," Haven said, her gaze flicking to Dare, who was still looking at her. "And I'm kinda starving."

"Well, we have the perfect cure for that," the big guy next to her said. He passed her a platter filled with scrambled eggs and bacon. "I'm Joker, by the way."

The guy who'd tried to talk to her at the party that first night. She should've recognized those friendly green eyes and the dark beard. "Hi Joker, I'm Haven." As she scooped some food onto her plate, other words threatened, and then she decided to throw caution to the wind and just say them. "I'm sorry I freaked out at the party when you tried to introduce yourself. I'm kinda ridiculously shy, and big groups like this . . ." She shrugged. ". . . well, they're usually too overwhelming for me."

"Don't worry about it, darlin'," he said with a wink. "We have a knack for being intimidating."

"You do," she said with a little laugh.

"Here, you gotta have one of these, too," he said, passing her the plate with her cinnamon buns.

"I'd love to," she said, biting down on her lip to try not to smile. She took one and then passed the plate to Phoenix, who was waggling his fingers for it.

Cora elbowed Haven in the ribs, and Haven threw her a look.

"Too bad you're already taken, Bunny," Phoenix said. "Because I'd marry you in a heartbeat for making these buns." Raucous exclamations and agreements circled the room.

"You'd break those vows in five minutes," Bunny's husband, Rodeo, said with a wicked grin.

"Yeah, probably," Phoenix said, not seeming to mind the ribbing at all. "But I'd be deep in love for all five of them."

Shaking her head, Bunny laughed. "Well, I'm just glad you're all enjoying them. Now stop all the yammering and eat."

It didn't take long for all the platters and plates to be licked clean, and then Cora and Haven helped Bunny and a few of the guys clear the table.

When they came back out for another haul of dirties, Dare waved Haven and Cora over. "Can I talk to you two for a minute?"

"Uh, sure," Haven said, following him into the lounge with Cora.

"A contact sent us some photos, and I want to confirm identities with you two before sending them out to our people." He punched a code into his cell phone.

"Okay," Haven said, standing next to him. God, he smelled good. Like Ivory soap and leather and something all Dare.

He tilted the phone toward them. "Is this your father?"

"Yes." Haven stared at a photo taken of him when he was out in public somewhere. He wore the same angry-at-the-world expression he always did, and just seeing it rushed a shiver that was part dread and part relief that she'd escaped him over her skin. "Did you have someone take these?"

Dare nodded, and thumbed to the next photograph. "All

I know of some of these men is that they're in his organization. Any names you can add would be helpful." He
showed them three pictures, and Haven was able to identify them all as people who worked closely for or with her
father. "How about this one?"

Cora gasped. "That's my father, Hank Campbell."

Haven nodded, though something in Cora's tone made
Haven study her friend's face. Cora gave her a small smile
when she noticed, but Haven felt like she'd just watched
her friend don a mask.

"Okay," Dare said. "Are we missing images of anyone
you think we should know about?"

Haven and Cora exchanged glances. "The men you
showed us are my father's right-hand men, so I don't think
so. Do you, Cora?"

She shook her head. "Those are the most obvious guys."

"Good," Dare said. "Thanks. I'm gonna send these out
to the club and a broader circle of contacts we have, just
to get some other eyes on this."

"Okay," Haven said, the precautions Dare was taking
making her nervous about just how much her father might
know about her whereabouts.

Dare frowned and, for a moment, looked like he was
going to say something more. Then he shook his head
and backed away. It was almost like he'd had a whole
little conversation—with himself. "Catch ya later, then,"
he said.

Haven nodded, and, when Dare was gone, she turned
to Cora.

"He is so into you," Cora said, eyebrow arched.

"You got that from that weirdness just now?" Haven
rolled her eyes, even though everything inside her wished
it was true.

"No," Cora said. "I got that from watching him watch

you looking at his cell phone. His eyes were on you the whole time."

Butterflies whipped through Haven's belly. "Well, who knows what that means."

"Only one way to find out," Cora said, pointing toward the hallway down which Dare just disappeared. "And he just went that way."

Haven shook her head. "I'm not following him. Come on, we have to help Bunny finish cleaning up."

"If you say so," Cora said, giving her an amused, challenging look.

"I do." They made their way back into the mess hall, which was all cleaned up, but they were in plenty of time to help with the dishes.

When they were putting away the last of the dishes they'd hand-washed and dried, Bunny turned to Haven. "You realize that when you two leave, the guys are going to wonder why they're not getting any more amazing baked goods. All my marriage proposals are going to dry up overnight." The older woman was wearing an amused smile and a vintage Harley Davidson T-shirt with a pair of jeans.

And that was when Haven realized that she was going to miss Bunny almost as much as Dare, maybe more, since she'd never had a mother figure in her life before. Her own mom had fled from Haven's father when Haven was still in diapers. Guess he'd treated her badly, too. There'd been a time when Haven resented the heck out of her mother for leaving her behind, but after a while it had felt pointless to hold a grudge against someone she didn't remember and would never again see.

But Bunny, in just a few short weeks, had offered her friendship, advice, guidance, protectiveness. Haven wasn't going to forget her any time soon, and it made her ache.

"I didn't think of that," Haven said. "Though I hadn't actually expected to leave so soon, I guess. What should I do?"

"I hadn't expected y'all to leave so soon, either," Bunny said, her expression sympathetic, almost sad. "But on the baked goods"—she reached behind her and grabbed the plate of peanut butter cookies—"I think you gotta start with telling Dare."

Haven stared at the plate like it might bite her. "Really?" The thought of revealing something else she'd been keeping from him made her big breakfast sit like a rock in her stomach.

"Really," Bunny said, exchanging a look with Cora that Haven couldn't read.

Cora nodded. "Probably a good idea."

Haven accepted the cookies into her hands. "He's going to be mad at me."

Bunny shook her head. "I doubt that, honey. You just go see. You two will both feel better after you talk."

"Fine," Haven said, deciding to get this over with sooner rather than later. "But when he's mad at me, I get to say I told you so."

"Deal," Bunny said, giving her a wink.

Haven crossed through the clubhouse doling out cookies along the way to guys who saw what she was carrying. The more Ravens she talked to, the less intimidating she found them. They were just guys, guys who were really loyal to one another, as far as she could see. Maybe they wore the badges of their club on their backs and had lots of ink on their skin, but they also took in and helped people like her. And that counted for a lot in her book, because she knew that brand of kindness and generosity wasn't universal. Not by a long shot.

By the time she got to Dare's office, the pile of cook-

ies wasn't as high as it had been, but she still had plenty
to offer up as an olive branch. Taking a deep breath, she
knocked on the door.

"Come in," came his voice through the door. His gaze
cut up when she opened it. "Haven. What's up?"

"Can I talk to you for a minute?" she asked, slipping in
and shutting the door behind her.

"Of course. Is everything okay?" he asked, getting up
and coming to her.

"Yeah," she said, thrusting the plate into his chest
out of nervousness. "Bunny said I should bring these
to you."

He chuckled and grasped the plate. "That's because
Bunny knows these are my favorite cookies in the
world."

A wave of satisfaction rolled through Haven's body at
the thought. "Really?"

Popping one in his mouth, Dare nodded. "So damn
good," he said around a bite. When he swallowed, he
added, "I told Bunny she was officially my favorite person
ever for making these again."

Haven hugged herself and nodded, and something
Bunny said came back to her—that it would make both
her and Dare feel better to talk. What the heck was that
supposed to mean? And why was Haven thinking of it
now?

Dare placed the plate on the corner of his desk and
grabbed another cookie. "And you're my second-favorite
person for bringing them to me," he said with a wink. He
took a bite.

Heat filled Haven's cheeks, and she shook her head.

"What is it?" he asked, stepping closer. He ran his
knuckles over her cheek, clearly noticing her blush.

"Um," she said, fortifying herself with a deep breath

to make her admission. She looked up at him, ready to tell him.

"I didn't think I could like your hair more than I did before," he said, stroking his fingers through it at the side of her face. "But you look beautiful, Haven."

The words stole her breath and kicked her heart into a sprint. Did he just call her beautiful? "I do?"

He nodded. "Could barely keep my eyes off of you at breakfast. I know you noticed."

And she'd thought her blush couldn't get any hotter. She shrugged. "I guess so."

He broke a piece off his cookie and handed it to her. "Want some?"

She let him put it in her mouth, her stomach fluttering because the look in his eyes suggested those words might not be about just the cookie. Although he could be so hard to read, and she wanted him so much she was always half sure she was projecting her desire onto him.

"Good, right?" he asked. His gaze ran down her face and stopped at her lips.

"Yeah," she said, swallowing the last of the cookie. *Now tell him.* Right.

"Shit, I have to . . ." His hand threaded into her hair and grasped the back of her head. And then his mouth found hers and his tongue slid in deep, stroking, twirling, penetrating. She surrendered to the kiss and pressed her body against his, loving how big and hard and strong he was against her. His erection dug into her belly, and she loved that, too, the evidence that she wasn't the only one feeling so out of control.

By the time he pulled back from the kiss, Haven was breathing hard and a little dizzy and totally aroused.

"Had to taste you with that flavor in your mouth," he said in a gritty voice. "Just as good as I thought it'd be."

His words did nothing to cool her off, but still she managed, "Dare, I have a confession."

His expression darkened, and he tried to step back, to put that old distance between them again.

But Haven grabbed the lapel of his club cut. "Don't go. Please."

He glanced down to how she was holding on to him, and it took everything Haven had not to shy away from the intensity of his gaze. "What's your confession?"

"I made the cookies," she rushed out. "And the cinnamon buns."

The darkness bled out of his eyes and off his face, only to be replaced by confusion. "You made the cookies? You're the one who's been making all the cookies and bars and buns?"

She nodded.

"You?" His eyebrow arched as he stared at her, and then his eyes went wide with what looked like surprise. "Jesus, Haven, you're really fucking good at baking. You know that, right?"

She shrugged. "I like to do it."

"You *should* be doing it. It's your thing." An arm around her waist, he reached for another cookie. Ate it. Closed his eyes and hummed as he chewed it. "So fucking good. And you made it." He shook his head.

The whole thing made Haven smile. "So you're not mad?"

His eyelids flipped open. "Why the hell would I be mad?"

God, she loved the feeling of his arm thrown so casually around her, her body still pressed all up against his. "Because I kept something from you again."

He shook his head. "I don't care about that, but why did you? Just out of curiosity."

"I bake when I can't sleep. It calms me, and I really enjoy it. But I didn't want any attention for it, especially when I didn't know any of you," she said, looking down at his chest.

Fingers gently tipped her chin back up. "I get it," he said, and then he was quiet for a long moment. Suddenly, he frowned and his brow furrowed. "I'm glad you told me. And, well, I have something to tell you, too. A confession of my own."

"You do? About what?" she asked, unable to imagine what he could need to reveal to her.

Sighing, he stroked his fingers through the side of her hair again, his eyes tracking the movement. "So, the other day—"

Bang, bang. The door flew open, and Phoenix and a man Haven thought was called Caine stepped in. Where Phoenix could be a playful screwball, Caine seemed quiet and severely serious to the point of being kinda scary. But she'd thought that about Dare once, too, hadn't she? "Oh, shit. Sorry, Dare, Haven," Phoenix said. Both men seemed upset. Or, at least, Phoenix didn't seem like his usual smart-alecky, laid-back self. "We got something."

Dare looked down at her, and that was the moment she realized that he hadn't let her go when the men had let themselves into his office. His arm still wrapped around her lower back, holding her to him. "Can we finish this later?" he asked her. "I'm sorry."

"Of course. I hope everything's okay," she said. She pulled away, only to have him grab her hand and tug her back again.

He kissed her long and deep and hard, and Haven thought her heart would beat out of her chest from the intensity of it, from the fact that he'd done it in front of his brothers—and that she'd *liked* that he'd done that. "Later."

"Later," she whispered, her lips still tingling from the kiss. She slipped out—or floated out, more like it—and wondered how she was going to avoid going crazy until she saw him again and heard whatever it was that he needed to confess.

CHAPTER 17

"N ot a word," Dare said, glaring at his brothers. He shouldn't have kissed her in front of them, but they'd already seen them all up against each other and Dare hadn't been able to resist having just one more taste. It turned out having a little bit of something good in your life just made you want more. "What's going on?" Dare asked as Phoenix held up his hands as if in surrender and Caine closed the door behind Haven. Now Dare understood the first item on her list a helluva lot better, didn't he? *Have your own kitchen.*

Jesus. She shouldn't have to wish for something that talent demanded be nurtured.

"We put out the word about the hardware we want to get rid of like we talked about," Phoenix said, meaning the guns they'd acquired from the Church Gang a few weeks before.

"Yeah," Dare said, the thought of Haven's list making

him regret that they'd been interrupted before he could confess to knowing about it. Maybe it was just as well he hadn't opened his mouth any more than he already had, though. Because that woman extracted all of his self-control every time they were within five feet of each other. "Any word?"

"Unfortunately, yes," Phoenix said, exchanging dark looks with Caine.

"Shit, what is it?" Dare asked, shaking off all thoughts of Haven and getting his mind back in the game.

"We have an interested buyer in Baltimore," Phoenix said. "A gang called the Iron Cross, one of the top contenders to fill the Church Gang's shoes in the city. I need to know how to respond here, because if I tell them they're no longer available, that may impact our ability to sell elsewhere. But if I ignore or say we won't sell to them, then we risk making an enemy." Caine nodded, a scowl on his face.

"Fuck," Dare said, leaning his hip against the desk. "What do we know about them?"

"Not a lot yet," Caine said, "but the guys at Hard Ink might be able to find out more. Didn't they have some sort of gang contact?"

Dare nodded. "They do. And I think it's time to call in some favors." He rounded the desk and took a seat, and Phoenix and Caine sat in the chairs on the other side of the desk.

From weeks of working together, Dare had Nick Rixey, the informal leader of the team of elite Army vets, on speed dial. "This is Rixey," came a voice through the speakerphone.

"Nick, it's Dare. How are you?"

"Dare," Nick said, his tone indicating he was pleased. "Things are good. Thanks in part to you and your men."

"Glad to hear it. Speaking of which, I've got Phoenix and Caine here with me. You're on speaker." The three of them exchanged greetings.

"So I take it this isn't a social call," Nick said.

"Wish it was," Dare said. "But we find ourselves in need of your help."

"Name it." The words were spoken without hesitation, and Dare found himself respecting Nick even more than he already did. Any man who kept his word so unequivocally was a good friend to have in his book.

"The rest of your guys around?" Dare asked. "If so, it might be easier to put me on speaker on your end, too."

"Give me five and I'll call you right back," Nick said. They hung up.

"Good to see they're keeping their word," Phoenix said, a dark shadow crossing his normally carefree face. But given that his cousin had died protecting the folks at Hard Ink not even a month before, Dare totally understood why that would be so important to Phoenix.

Dare's phone rang, and Nick explained he had everyone present. "What's going on?"

"A couple of things," Dare said. "First, I've got some photographs I was hoping Marz could run through his various programs for further identification and information."

Marz was their computer tech and had capabilities acquiring information from the web that Dare couldn't hope to replicate. The guy's voice came down the line. "That's not a problem. Send me whatever you want me to search."

"If you have their names, can you also find out things like what kinds of vehicles they own?" Dare asked.

"Probably," Marz said. "DMV records are likely a piece of cake next to the shit we've had to access the past few weeks. I'll give it a shot."

"Thanks," Dare said. Having that kind of information would give them other ways to be on the lookout for Haven's father and associates. "We also have a developing situation that might complicate things in the city. We're in the midst of finding a buyer for the hardware we acquired, and we've got interest from a gang called the Iron Cross in Baltimore. We were hoping you could look into them. We're not interested in dropping that kinda heat so close to home, but we need to know more about them before we respond."

"We've got a contact at the city's gang task force and some resources on hand about known Maryland gangs. That's not a problem," Nick said. "Do you expect to do an in-person meeting with them?"

Dare met his brothers' gazes across the table. "Haven't gotten that far," Phoenix said.

"Well, let us know if you need backup if you do. Things are volatile with the Church Gang out of the picture, so we want to keep our finger on the pulse of that situation anyway."

Dare nodded, this conversation confirming it'd been the right call to bring the Hard Ink team in on all of this. "I appreciate that, Nick. I'll keep you posted."

"Good," Nick said. "Now I have a question for you. Ike said the races were starting back up next weekend. We wondered if you might be up for a visit. Be nice to get out of the city for a few hours."

"Funny you should ask," Dare said. "Since I planned to invite you myself. Though I was hoping you might provide undercover security for the event. Turns out the two women you rescued, Haven and Cora, have a reward out on their heads for a hundred Gs. So we could use the extra eyes to make sure no one's in the crowd we don't want there. We've got space for all of you to stay the night."

There was some murmuring in the background of the call, and then Nick's voice came through loud and clear. "Consider it done."

When the call ended, Dare shot off the photographs to Marz.

"Well, that went about as good as could've been expected," Caine said, his pale eyes like ice.

"Agreed," Dare said. "Now we wait to see what information they're able to find."

HAVEN HAD PROMISED herself no more holing away in her room, so when her full belly left her sleepy in the late morning, she changed into a tank top and a pair of shorts and took a blanket out into the backyard while Cora headed over to the chop shop to hang with Phoenix, Jeb, and Blake. Haven didn't mind being alone, since she knew she was likely to fall asleep. It was a gorgeous, warm May day, and the views of the mountains and the valley were stunning from the Raven clubhouse. The perfect recipe for a nap that would pass the time until she and Dare could finally talk.

She found a flat spot with a particularly good view under the long, swaying branches of a weeping willow tree to spread out her blanket, and then she did something that not too long ago would've been unthinkable—she lay down and closed her eyes right there in the grass. Her father's house had a big built-in pool in the backyard, but Haven hadn't used it since she'd been a kid. No way could she wear a swimsuit and bare that much of her body in that house. Ever. Here, though? She didn't have a single concern that she wouldn't be safe.

With the breeze blowing and the birds singing and the distant strains of music coming from somewhere, Haven fell asleep quickly. When she woke up, she wasn't sure how long she'd slept, but she was absolutely ecstatic about having done something so simple as laying out in the sun to take a nap. Stretching pulled a long, moaning yawn out of her and—

"Good nap?" came a man's voice from behind her.

She whirled onto her elbows. Dare. Sitting in his jeans, black T-shirt, and cut with his knees up and his back against the willow's trunk.

"What are you doing?" she asked.

The look he gave her turned the sleepy warmth flowing through her body into something darker, something needier, something hotter. "Watching you sleep," he said. He gave his bottom lip a long, slow flick of his tongue.

Haven was suddenly ravenous for a taste of that tongue, that lip, that harsh, masculine mouth. "Why?" she breathed.

"'Cause I don't seem to be able to stay away from you, no matter how hard I try." His blunt honesty did nothing to rein in her arousal. Instead, his declarations made her heart race and her hips press instinctively toward the ground, seeking a friction that wasn't there but that she wanted desperately.

What would it be like to give such blunt honesty in return? Goose bumps erupted over her warm skin the moment she decided to find out. "What if I don't want you to stay away?"

He looked away for a long moment, and Haven worried she'd said the wrong thing, but when he looked back, the battle playing out on his expression told her he'd liked what she'd said. A lot.

"There's a lake on the compound not too far from here," he said, his voice like gravel, his gaze running over her body. Then his eyes returned to hers. "Any chance you'd like to go for a swim?"

She grinned. "Really? That would be awesome." She

pushed up to sit on folded legs. "Oh, except I don't have a swimsuit."

"You could wear what you have on," he said, his gaze dragging over her again. "And take other clothes to change into."

"Okay, I'll do that," Haven said. "Let me just grab some things." Up in her room, her gaze snagged on her notebook while she grabbed other clothes. Going skinny dipping was on her list, but no way she could do that in broad daylight with Dare. Could she? No. No, she wasn't *that* brave. Not yet. Maybe never. She grabbed some clothes and a towel from the bathroom and met Dare out in front, where he was waiting for her on his bike.

He stuffed her things in a compartment on the side of his bike and gave her a hand on. "Put this on," he said, handing her a helmet.

"Why don't you wear one?" she asked as she slipped it on and put down the visor.

He grinned over his shoulder. "I do on longer trips, but, you know, I like to flaunt the rules and live dangerously, too."

The words were innocent enough, but the echo of what she'd written in her notebook made her stomach flip-flop.

"Ready?" he asked.

She wrapped her arms around his stomach and rested her head on his shoulder. "Yes."

Haven hadn't been sure she'd get to ride with Dare again, so being on the back of his bike made her almost giddy with happiness. They left the clubhouse heading in a different direction than they'd ridden the other day, and within a few minutes arrived at an appealingly rugged cabin nestled in the woods. Clouds blocked the sun, casting the house in shade, but it didn't detract from the secluded peacefulness of the wooded lot.

Dare eased the bike to a stop in the driveway and kicked out his boots to steady them. "Just need to grab some things," he said, helping her off the bike. "Come on in."

"This is your place?" she asked, her eyes drinking in the almost picturesque setting, the rustic log façade, the separate garage that sat at the back of the lot.

"Yeah," he said, leading them up onto the small porch. He unlocked the door and gestured for her to go first.

Haven wasn't sure what to expect of the place where Dare lived. She so associated him with the clubhouse that she'd never imagined him in his own space. The interior was all warm, rough-hewn wood, limestone accents, and earth tones. It was masculine but inviting, even though there wasn't a lot that personalized the space. "This is really nice," she said. Much of the first floor was open, and her gaze went right to the kitchen. Drawn by the granite counters, she headed there, her hands smoothing over the cool surface.

Turning, she found Dare watching her take in his place, and it brought heat to her cheeks.

"Make yourself at home," he said, pointing to the stairs. "I'll just be a minute."

She nodded and watched him jog up the steps. And good God did he do all kinds of justice to a pair of jeans.

With furniture situated around the big stone fireplace, the living room drew her in next. An overstuffed recliner sat next to the front window, an old fleece throw draped over the back. It looked like the kind of thing you could curl up in with a book or for a nap, and Haven couldn't help but try it out.

Sitting down, she reached for the reclining mechanism that had her laying back and stretching out. Despite the fact that it wasn't much to look at, it was quite possibly the most comfortable chair she'd ever sat on in her life. She burrowed into the soft fabric and turned her body to peer out the window, the position giving her the most relaxing view of swaying trees and graying sky.

God, why did she feel so comfortable here? And why couldn't she have found this fundamental sense of rightness with someone she could keep—or who would keep her?

The question made her think of her list, and that made her wonder if she'd find another man with whom she could imagine making all those experiences come true. What if she never found someone like Dare again? What if this—*he*—was her chance to really live?

Lying there in his home, Haven had the wildest notion to grab onto Dare while she had him, even if she couldn't keep him, even if she had to leave him behind.

Maybe she could have him *now*. And it seemed to her that sometimes now was all that mattered.

Footsteps sounded out from the staircase, drawing her from her thoughts.

"You look comfortable," Dare said, humor playing around his mouth. He carried a rolled-up bundle of clothing in his hand.

"I am," she said. "I don't know if I'd ever leave this chair if I lived here."

That drew a real smile out of him as he crossed the room. Bracing his hands on both armrests, he leaned over her. "Would you rather stay here?" His dark brown gaze was intense and observing, making her feel like he could see inside her. Where once the thought of that scared her, now she almost wished he could see her darkest desires. Then he'd know, and maybe he'd act on them, too. It would save her from having to say all kinds of impossible words, wouldn't it? Even if that was the chicken's way out . . .

Haven shook her head. No way was she giving up the

chance to see more of Dare's body. "Nope. I'm still happy to go."

Boxing her in, Dare leaned down and got right up in her space. "Whatever you want," he said, his lips just inches from hers.

I want you. Her brain taunted her to say it, to just put it out there and see how he'd react. To maybe even tell him she'd like him to help her make a whole list of to-dos come true before she had to go. While she knew she was safe and that he would treat her right. The thought made goose bumps spring up all over her skin.

She tipped up her chin, offering her lips. "You sure about that?" she asked, the brazenness of the question nearly stealing her breath.

"Oh, Haven," he said, "you have no idea what I'd be willing to do for you if you wanted me to."

Her heart was suddenly flying, his words filled with so much seductive promise that Haven could barely believe she'd heard him right. She grappled for how to respond and wondered if this was her moment to just lay everything out there.

"Do you want my confession now, or do you want to just hang for now and talk later?" he asked.

The question threatened to ground her in reality, and she didn't want that yet. She didn't want problems or reasons why wanting Dare was a risk she shouldn't—couldn't—take. She still wanted the fantasy, the heady promise she felt when she was with him, the feeling that being with him was so right there was no way it could ever end. "Talk later," she said.

Dare nodded. "Then let's ride."

CHAPTER 18

Dare wasn't sure what he was doing right now, only that he didn't want to be doing anything else.

Giving in to this attraction for Haven was probably going to make things even harder when it was time for her to leave—harder for both of them. But she didn't seem to be resisting, either. In fact, her *lack* of resistance was fucking with his head—making him think, making him want, making him regret. Toss into the mix the sexual tension that always seemed to be crackling in the air between them, and Dare felt like he was holding on to the end of a rope that was fraying at the middle and sure to give way.

With Haven wrapped tight around his back on his ride—something that felt more goddamned right than it should—Dare pulled out of his driveway and headed toward the lake. Luckily it was a warm afternoon, because the sky had grown overcast while they'd been in the house. It was probably good that she still wanted to swim, though, because watching her make herself comfortable in his space did things to him he didn't want to think too closely about.

He'd liked seeing her there.

Somehow, her presence had brought the house to life, had made it feel less solitary. Dare didn't think that was because she was one of the few women he'd ever brought there—and the *only* one whom he had any personal interest in. It was something about Haven herself, and the way she made him feel.

Fuck, you are so screwed. Dare pulled a right onto the road that headed out by Ike's place and the lake. As he leaned into the turn, Haven's arms tightened around him, and he reveled in the touch.

"Faster?" he yelled over his shoulder.

"Yes!" she shouted back, her arms tightening even more.

His girl liked it fast, and he loved the hell out of that. Refusing to analyze the thought too closely, Dare twisted the throttle. They roared up the mountain road, freedom and wind rushing over their skin. He liked it fast, too. It was easier to forget your problems with your knees and fists in the breeze.

By the time they reached the lake, the sky was spitting raindrops at them. Dare pulled into the dirt parking lot nearest the little beach everybody in the club used for swimming. He killed the engine and turned in his seat to face her. "What d'ya think about—"

The question died in his throat.

Because under the helmet's clear visor, Haven wore the most beautiful smile he'd ever seen in his life.

"God, I love riding," she said. She lifted the helmet from her head, shaking out her new brown hair. The movement made him hard. "What do I think about what?" She grinned up at the sky as a few fat drops landed on her face.

"The weather," Dare said distractedly, just struck stupid by her declaration, her beauty, the knowledge that riding with him made her so damn happy.

She shrugged, her expression entirely untroubled. "I'm gonna get wet anyway."

He swallowed around the desire stalking through his body. "Are you now?" he asked, purposely playing on the innuendo of her words when he knew she hadn't meant anything by them. Just to see if she'd take the bait.

Lips pressed together in a mischievous smirk, she looked him right in the eyes. "Sure hope so."

Game. Fucking. On.

He took the helmet from her and hung it on a handlebar. Then he turned back to her and ran his fingers teasingly over her lips. Rain droplets came a little more frequently, not enough to be a shower, but enough to promise that one was on the way. "I do love you wet," he said, his cock jerking in his jeans as her mouth dropped open and her tongue tentatively licked the tip of his middle finger.

"Well, that's good," she said, the words breathy.

He couldn't fucking believe she was playing along with this. Damn if she hadn't come a long way since they first met. It made him proud of her. It made him protective of her. It made him want to see how much braver she could be if she felt safe enough to really let herself go. "Why's that?" he asked, leaning in and stroking his nose along the bridge of hers.

Her head tilted back, offering her mouth up for a kiss. "Because . . . I'm . . ." She swallowed thickly. ". . . getting wet now." She'd spoken the words so quietly that it was clear they'd been hard for her to admit, but she'd still found the courage to say them.

And, man, hearing her admit that she was wet slayed him.

"Fuck, Haven," he said, his mouth coming down hard on hers.

She moaned into the kiss, her hands grasping his neck, his hair. The kiss was immediately urgent, frenzied, and the arousal slingshotting through Dare's body had his imagination running away with him. He pictured himself pulling her off the bike, shoving her jeans down, bending her over the seat . . .

A long, low rumble of thunder, and the skies opened up for real.

Haven gasped and flinched, pulling her lips away from the kiss. Her gaze flickered to the sky as all the playfulness bled from her expression. She tried to mask the anxiety the storm caused her, but it was crystal clear in her eyes when she looked at him again.

He wanted nothing more in that moment than to make her feel safe.

"Let's save swimming for another day," he said, stroking his fingers down her wet face. Even as it soaked her hair, the rain did nothing to detract from how fucking gorgeous she was.

"I'm sorry," she said.

He kissed her. "No need for that," he said. "Now hold on tight."

Between the wet roads, the force of the downpour, and having a novice rider in his saddle, the ride home took a little longer than the way there. He regretted that only because every time it thundered, Haven flinched against him, her face burrowing against his shoulders, her embrace tightening around his chest. She'd done the same thing that night he'd found her asleep on the porch, and it made a place deep inside of him ache with satisfaction that she sought solace in his body—and it equally made him need to know what had caused her fear of storms in the first place.

Home again, they ran up to the front porch, absolutely soaked to the bone. "Let me grab some towels," Dare said, turning to her after he shut the door and flicked on the light. And that was when he noticed that her pale pink tank top had gone totally sheer in the rain, the white lace pattern on her bra completely visible through the fabric, and the dark pink of her erect nipples apparent, too. Jesus.

"Okay," she said, shivering.

"Right." He made for the second-floor full bath.

Thunder crashed loud enough to make the windows rattle.

Haven's gasp reached him on the stairs, and he turned on a dime and went back to her. Taking her hand, he said, "Come on."

"I'll drip water everywhere," she said, following him despite the protest.

He turned just before the bottom step. "You think I care about getting the floor wet over taking care of you?"

Her eyes went wide. "I . . . I don't . . ."

Dare silenced her with a kiss, needing her to know, needing her to believe. "The answer's no, Haven." He led her upstairs to the bathroom that sat in the center of the hall between the house's two bedrooms.

"Wow," she said, taking in the room. "This bathroom is amazing."

Dare handed her a towel from the corner linen closet and grabbed one for himself. He followed her gaze around the room, over the large all-glass stall shower, over the spa tub beneath the big picture window overlooking the woods, over all the marble, granite, and steel surfaces. When he'd built the place, he'd wanted to do the kitchen and bathroom right, even if he wasn't sure he'd use all the bells and whistles.

"Thanks," Dare said, watching her run the towel over her face, her hair, her arms. She shivered again. "Let me find you some dry clothes."

"Oh," she said, looking down at herself. "I brought extra clothes. Are they still out in the bike?"

"Yeah," Dare said, looking at the hard rain blurring his view of the trees out the window. "You can borrow something of mine, though. Save me from getting wet again."

When she nodded, he disappeared into his bedroom, debating what to give her. He settled quickly on an old, soft, black Harley T-shirt. Unsure what she'd be most comfortable in for bottoms, he took a pair of old blue sweatpants that would likely be miles too big on her and a pair of gray boxers. The thought of seeing her in any of this—any of *his clothes*—flooded all kinds of satisfaction through his blood. Because despite the myriad reasons why it wasn't gonna happen, with every moment he spent with Haven an increasingly bigger part of him wanted to claim her for himself—in every and any way he could.

Back in the bathroom, he found Haven sitting on the tub's wide edge, staring out at the rain, the towel tight around her shoulders. "Hey," he said.

She whipped around and rose, like he'd caught her doing something she shouldn't. "Hey."

He wasn't having that. Walking up to her, he held out the clothes, but he didn't release them when she grabbed for them. "We might as well wait out the rain here, so make yourself at home, Haven. Sit where you want. Open doors and cabinets. Help yourself to anything I have. Got it?"

A small smile. "Okay."

Finally, he let go of the clothing, but he didn't back away—because he *couldn't* back away. Arousal still surged through his blood from their flirtation at the lake, from her looking so fucking perfect in his space, from the way her soaked shirt revealed just a hint of the porcelain of her skin beneath.

A low, drawn-out rumble of thunder, and Haven's eyes widened, just a little.

He cupped his hand around her neck and adored the way she leaned into the touch. "Tell me why you're scared of storms," Dare said, protectiveness rising up inside him. If he understood her fears, maybe he could help her battle them. For however long they had together.

Haven's eyes skittered away from his, and her cheeks paled. "I used to love them," she said, her voice going distant. "The raw power and sound of them. But when I was fifteen, I had my first serious boyfriend. His name was Zach, and he . . . he was my first," she said quietly, "and only."

Something deep inside Dare disliked hearing about another man having known her in ways Dare didn't, but the admission that she hadn't been with anyone since sucker-punched him with such raw sadness for her that it outweighed the jealousy that threatened.

"I don't know how, but my father found us together"— she made a face that made it clear exactly what kind of together that'd been—"and he . . . he was furious. Said I'd ruined myself, and that if I wanted to act like a b-bitch in heat, he'd treat me like one." Her shoulders curled in as her chin dropped, and it reminded Dare so much of the way she'd acted during their first conversation that it just about broke his fucking heart—and made him want to *rage*.

His hand slid up to cup her cheek, his thumb lazily stroking the soft skin under her eye. "You don't have to tell me more if you don't want to."

A little shake of her head, and for the first time in long minutes, she lifted her gaze to meet his. "I want to. This is me, you know? And I guess . . . I don't know why, but . . . I guess I'd really just like to let you know me."

Jesus if those words didn't reach right into his chest and *own* him. The sentiment resonated so deep inside him that the world rocked a little around his feet, shaking him to the core. Because there weren't many people who knew about his mom and Kyle, and Dare's role in their deaths. For the most part, their murders were a secret shame he carried, one that left him feeling like almost no one knew the real depth of his pain—or his failings. And sometimes he felt like such a goddamned fraud that he could barely look at his reflection in a mirror.

"What did he do?" Dare asked, his growing anger coming through in the gritty tone of his voice.

The cast of her eyes went bleak. "We had two Rotties, Roxy and Xena. He chained me to the dog run in the backyard with them for two days. He put my food in their food dishes, and though the dogs were never mean to me, I wasn't able to compete with them for it, either. The second night, it stormed. One of the worst storms I'd ever seen in my life—or maybe it only seemed that way because I was out in it. I think the only thing that kept me from going crazy was that the dogs laid right with me all night. They were scared, too. I'm not sure who comforted who more."

White-hot fury ripped through Dare's veins. He'd chained her up like a fucking dog? Dare's imagination unhelpfully provided a picture of what she must've looked like, lying on the ground soaking wet, a chain around her neck, dogs huddled up against her shivering body. The revenge fantasies instantly tearing through his mind were gruesomely satisfying. There was little Dare hated more than a cowardly bully who got off on torturing those weaker than him. And Rhett Randall was clearly that in spades. "Haven—"

"I've never liked storms since," she said, as if she hadn't heard him say her name.

Little fucking wonder. He scrubbed his hand over his lips, the gesture making him realize that his fury had him trembling, had him right on the edge of getting on his motorcycle and road tripping it down to Georgia to put an end to her bastard of a father once and for fucking all.

"Are you okay?" she asked, her eyes searching his.

"Am *I* okay?" he rasped. "Jesus, Haven—"

She ducked her chin as if he'd reprimanded her.

"No," he said, forcing her to look at him again. "I will *never* be okay hearing about all the ways you've been wronged. I want to hear them, because I want to know you. I *want* that, Haven. But right now I would squeeze the life out of your father with my bare hands if I had the opportunity, and watching awareness bleed from his eyes would be one of the most satisfying moments of *my* life. I would revel in it."

Her mouth dropped open, and he immediately worried that the violence of his words would scare her, would make her think that her father and he were cut from the same evil cloth. Fuck, Dare had often worried that was true about him and his own father—and it was clear that Butch Kenyon and Rhett Randall had a goddamned scary amount in common.

"You're the only man I've ever known who wanted to stand up for me," she said, tears making her eyes glassy for the first time. "The only man I've ever really known who didn't want to hurt me."

The words unleashed a chaos of thoughts inside his mind. He wanted to promise to *always* protect her. He wanted to rebuild her trust in men one day, one kiss, one touch at a time. And he was terrified that circumstances were about to keep him from being there to do any of it—and that she'd find somebody else instead. Because how could she not? Gorgeous, kind, brave, talented—any man would be privileged to have her.

"I would protect you with my life," he bit out, surprised by the vehemence of the declaration, but meaning it deep down into his soul. When had her happiness and safety become so fundamentally important to him? How had that happened?

Haven blinked until she reined in the threatening tears. Slowly, tentatively, she cupped her palm around his hand where it still held her face. And then, with a deep breath and in a trembling voice, she said, "I appreciate that more than you'll ever know, but I wonder . . . I wonder if there's any way . . ."

The words hung there until Dare thought he'd lose his fucking mind. "What, Haven? Say it. You can say anything to me."

Those fierce blue eyes looked straight into his, full of a need that reached inside his chest and squeezed. "I wonder if you'd have any interest in helping me live the life your protection has finally given me," she rushed out.

"Meaning what?"

Heat poured into her cheek under his hand. "Well, you see, I've been making this list."

CHAPTER 19

Haven could hardly believe she'd uttered the words, and a really big part of her wanted to take them back or tell him to forget she'd said anything. *Oh, God, why did I say that? He's going to think I'm ridiculous. He could have anyone, and probably does. He—*

"A list," he said, his tone odd, intense but also wary.

It was enough to make her lose whatever moment of crazy-reckless bravery she'd managed to call forth. "Never mind," she said, pulling away and trying to step around him.

He caught her easily, his big, calloused hands grasping her arms.

"Please forget I said anything," she said, panic rising up inside her and making her want to flee. She twisted out of his grasp and stepped to his side.

"Stop," Dare said, catching her by the hips and pulling her in tight against him. His arms banded around her front—one around her belly and the other snug against the bottom of her breasts. Her breath caught in her throat, as much from the quickness of his movements as from their position. Clearly, Dare could overpower her if he wanted, but she knew in her heart he wouldn't. Maybe it was reckless and naïve, but she trusted him. "Haven," he said, the word caressing her ear.

She shook her head, but she didn't try to get away.

"Tell me about the list," he said.

She shivered. Could she really tell him? Going through with this was ridiculous, wasn't it? She gave a little shrug, and adrenaline and fear made her tremble against him. "It's . . . it's probably stupid."

His arms tightened around her, plastering her back to his front. "What did I tell you about saying that? Stop cutting yourself down. Every time you do, it's actually your father talking anyway. And hasn't he said efucking-nough?"

"So much yes," she whispered. God, Dare could read her, and he always seemed to know exactly what she needed to hear—like how he'd reacted to what happened after the night her father had caught her with Zach. Dare's anger, his outrage, his desire to get vengeance for her all filled her with such a sense of understanding, acceptance, and more than a little affection, too. "Okay," she finally said.

"Tell me about the list." His voice was gruff in her ear, and she couldn't help but lean her face against his. His skin was so warm, his cheek scratchy from stubble. It was thrilling.

"It's a to-do list of things I want to experience now that I finally can," she said. Okay, that wasn't so hard, and that realization made the words come faster. "I'm so tired of being scared, Dare. And being taken in by the Ravens has let me believe I can actually want things, and have a chance of having them, for the first time ever."

"Look at me." He loosened his hold on her so she could turn, and then his arms went right back around her, hauling her up tight against his front. Jaw hard, eyes guarded, brow furrowed, tension rolled off him.

"I guess it sounds pretty silly—"

"Knowing what you want and going after it is fucking brave, Haven." One beat passed, and another, and he heaved a deep breath. "I know about the list."

For a moment, Haven couldn't make sense of the words, and then they crashed over her like a breaking wave. "Oh, God." Instinctively, she pushed against his chest, needing to escape, to hide, to run. With each second he resisted her efforts, the full ramifications of his admission pounded through her. Embarrassment turned into humiliation that morphed into gut-wrenching mortification. "Your confession." She gasped the realization. That's what he'd been trying to tell her?

"Yeah," he said, letting her go.

She reeled back until her spine hit the wall, and then she slid down into a ball and buried her face in her knees. "I can't believe . . . oh God." Right about now would be a great time for the floor to open up and swallow her whole.

"It was the day I found out about the reward. I knew you'd been keeping something from me, and the reward, the reward was pretty fucking big. I came to confront you about it, but you weren't in your room. And then I remembered seeing you write in that notebook, and I thought maybe it was a diary that would tell me if there was anything else I needed to know," he said, his voice gravelly, and maybe a little . . . sad?

Haven lifted her face enough to see him standing in the middle of the room, feet spread, arms folded across his chest. Lifting her gaze higher revealed that Dare's head hung down, his eyes to the floor. He looked almost defeated, and it struck her as so wrong. "Go on," she said, mind reeling but needing to hear it all.

A single tight nod. "At first, I couldn't figure out what it was, but then I realized that there was nothing there that could help me. But I was so moved by the things you wanted that I couldn't make myself stop reading. More than that, I wanted to help you make the list come true. Every fucking thing. I wanted it to be me, Haven. But then, I already knew that new identities were one possibility for you and Cora, and that would mean you'd have to go, so I . . ."

She looked up at his face, her mind and body a confused mix of embarrassed, angry, grudgingly understanding, and, impossibly, even a little intrigued. And then she gasped. "The motorcycle ride."

"Yeah," he said, gaze still down.

Slowly, Haven rose to her feet, her back still against the wall because this whole conversation was making the room spin. "The . . . beach?"

Dare finally looked up, and his dark eyes absolutely blazed with need and regret. "I didn't plan that. And I wasn't thinking about the list when I put my mouth on you either."

The blunt mention of what'd happened made Haven's belly clench. She swallowed, hard.

"I just needed my mouth on you like I needed my next breath. And I loved it—your taste, your come on my tongue, your hand pulling my fucking hair. I shouldn't have done it knowing I needed to confront you, but I sure as shit couldn't let anything more happen, which is why I pushed you away."

His recollection of what they shared, and his raw,

honest description of it did strange things to her. Oddly, the worst of her embarrassment cooled. Much of her anger yielded to a feeling of regret about how circumstances had forced both of them to questionable decisions. But most pronounced was how hearing him say these things out loud had her core suddenly aching with arousal and need. "You tried to tell me," Haven said, the room still a little spinny around her.

"I did," Dare said. "But I more than anyone know that trying ain't worth shit. Doing is what counts, and by that score I fucked up pretty much every way I could."

Hugging herself, Haven forced a long, deep breath, trying to figure out what all of this should mean to her. And then something occurred to her—Dare knew what was on the list. He knew and said he wanted to make it come true for her—make *everything* come true for her. Which meant . . . the hard part of maybe telling him what she wanted had already happened. And Dare wanted to experience with her all the things she'd dreamt of experiencing with him. "You wanted it to be you?"

His eyes narrowed, and the look he gave her was so hungry it made her wet. "I still want it to be me."

Haven's pulse was suddenly a runaway freight train pounding through her veins. She could feel it beating against her skin everywhere—against her breasts, her nipples, the slick place between her legs. She felt like the two of them stood on a cliff's edge and she didn't know whether to move or hold absolutely still.

And then Dare made the decision for her.

He was on her in an instant, his hands in her hair, his tongue in her mouth, his body trapping hers hard and insistent against the bathroom wall. Haven moaned at the contact and surrendered to him, her mouth sucking hard on his tongue, her hands pulling his still-wet hair in return, her hips thrusting against his. Willingly. Eagerly. Wantonly.

"Tell me you want this," he rasped around the edge of the kiss.

"I do," she said, plowing her hands underneath the damp fabric of his cut.

"Tell me you want me," he growled, his mouth sucking at her jaw, her ear, her throat.

"Want you, Dare," she whispered loudly, the sound morphing into a moan when he bit along the tendon sloping down toward her shoulder.

"How?" he asked, his hands going roughly to the hem of her shirt. A million competing answers rushed forth, leaving Haven momentarily unable to answer. He jerked his face back into her line of vision. "*How* do you want me?"

Breathing hard, Haven spoke the only words she could. "Every way I can have you." She could barely believe she'd said it, but Dare didn't give her even a moment to worry about it. He had her shirt off and then her bra, and her nakedness made Haven *need* his. "Off," she said as she tugged at the denim vest he wore over a black shirt, her voice almost embarrassingly breathy.

He leaned back enough to remove the cut, which he tossed onto the closed toilet seat, and then he tugged off his shirt for good measure.

Haven's eyes went wide, because Dare . . . Dare was the sexiest man she'd ever seen in her life. Tattoos covered his chest, his neck, his biceps, his ribs. She didn't have time to take them in before his tongue was in her mouth again, demanding and intoxicating. His chest hair was ticklish against her hands but was thrilling, too. Masculine and rough. His palms were calloused against her breasts, and the sensation made her gasp and moan and writhe against him, especially as his fingers plucked and twisted at her nipples.

"Oh, God," she whispered, gasping for a breath. Her brain could barely keep up with her body, and part of her hardly believed this was real. But then Dare reminded her touch by touch. His teeth tugging her bottom lip. His rough callouses dragging against all her sensitive softness. His hard erection grinding so deliciously into her lower belly that she wanted to wrap her legs around his hips and ride him. Hard.

Dare's hands settled on the button of her shorts. Breathing hard, he rested his forehead heavily against hers, his dark brown eyes piercingly clear. "You want to stop, just say the word."

She shook her head. "I'm not going to want you to stop."

"I'm just sayin'—"

Eyes still open, she kissed him. And the look he gave her back was almost ferocious. "Don't stop," she said when she released his lips.

And then he was tugging down her shorts and she was stepping out of her shoes and he was pulling down her panties so hard she thought she heard them rip. It was exciting and breath-stealing and made her heart pound so fast she was a little dizzy. Naked against the wall, Haven held on to Dare's shoulders as he pushed his thigh between her knees and his fingers between her thighs, right where she was wet and hungry and almost desperate to have him.

"Aw, feel that fucking pussy," he rasped, his face right up against hers. He kissed her hard, his tongue mimicking the act they were barreling toward, his fingers circling and stroking and pushing inside her one at a time. "So ready for me."

"Yes," she said, rocking against his hand, faster, harder,

searching, needing. She grasped his neck and hauled his mouth to hers. Their teeth knocked, but she didn't care. She just knew she might die if she didn't have him touching her everywhere he could and penetrating her every way he could. His tongue filled her mouth and his fingers filled the aching place between her legs, and the hard heel of his hand rubbed against her again and again where she was most sensitive and most desperate and suddenly about to come apart in his arms.

The orgasm was shattering, the most powerful thing she'd ever felt in her life. She nearly screamed into Dare's mouth and he grasped the side of her face, holding her through it, almost praising her in the gentleness of the touch.

"Fuck, yeah," he rasped, easing his hand from between her legs. He brought his fingers to his mouth, and, looking her right in the eye, he slowly licked at the wetness on his skin.

Haven's mouth dropped open as she watched him savor what he'd just brought out of her. Without even thinking, she grasped his wrist and licked the back of his middle finger.

Dare's eyes flared. "Jesus Christ, Haven, I need in you," he said, tugging his hand free so he could unbutton his jeans. He shoved the denim and a pair of boxers down over his hips until they were hanging on his thighs, and then his fist circled his erection and stroked it hard, once, twice.

Haven watched hungrily, finding what he was doing incredibly erotic but a little intimidating, too. Dare was much bigger than Zach had been—his whole body and that particular part of him. A man where Zach had been a boy. She wasn't a virgin, but it had been a long time, and it suddenly made her nervous.

"Tell me what you want," he said, stepping in close again, the hanging denim heavy against her legs, his moving hand bumping his knuckles and the head of his erection against her belly.

"You," she whispered. Despite the nerves, she was utterly sure. "I want you."

He shuddered out a breath. "What am I . . ." He shook his head. "I should slow this down, lay you out, do this right." He grasped her hand and made to pull her toward the door.

"No," she said, tugging against his hold. "Here. Now." Part of her was afraid she'd freak out in the time it took to go wherever he wanted to take her, but a part of her *liked* the idea of it here. In the bathroom. Standing up. Against the wall.

His eyebrow lifted, and he gave her a slow up-and-down look that set her body on fire.

"Now, Dare," she said, her voice shaky but her mind made up.

The approval that slid into his expression lit her up inside. He stepped out of his boots and the rest of his clothes until he stood gloriously naked in front of her. Tattoos—some pictures, some words—ran the length of his lean body, along with more than a few scars. His body was rugged, strong, utterly masculine.

He retrieved something from the wallet in the back pocket of his jeans. And then he ripped open the little square wrapper and placed the rubber against his tip. As he rolled it on, he watched her watching him until she thought she might die of anticipation. And the fact that he'd thought of it—when her brain had barreled right past the consideration for protection—proved that she was entrusting this moment to the right man.

God, Dare really was the right man. For her. Except—

"Here?" he rasped, boxing her up against the wall again. The contact chased away her thoughts, especially as he pushed his erection between her legs and rubbed the thick head against her clit.

She nodded and grasped his shoulder. Instinct had her sliding her leg up the outside of his until her thigh hooked on his hip. With one hand, he grasped her leg and helped hold it there, and with the other, he guided his blunt tip deeper between her legs until he was probing her entrance.

"Now?" he asked, his eyes absolutely on fire.

"Now," she breathed, tilting her hips, aligning her need with his promise.

"It's been a long fucking time for you, Haven. Don't let me hurt you," he said.

The words made her smile. "Just the fact that you said that makes me know you won't."

"Jesus." His hips thrust forward, just a little, but enough to impale her on his tip.

She moaned and arched, her head falling back and her hips angling toward him. Wanting more. Needing all of him.

"Fuck," Dare bit out, the raw desperation of the curse making her wetter, allowing her to take more of him. And, finally, all of him.

Dare was big, and it had been a long time, and the feeling of fullness and stretching was a little uncomfortable. But it was something more than that, too—it was . . . it was freedom. She was free, free to choose this, to choose him. "Oh, God," she cried. "Move. Please move."

A big hand grasped her other thigh and hauled her up the wall, until Dare was all that held her up—his hands under her legs, his hips against hers, his cock deep inside her. A long withdraw and a slow, deep thrust had them both moaning.

Haven wrapped her arms around Dare's neck and held on as his strokes picked up pace, his hips withdrawing and returning faster, his breaths coming harder, a stream of groans and curses spilling out of that harsh, beautiful mouth.

"Christ, Haven," he ground out. He kissed her deeply— her mouth, her lips, her neck, and back to her mouth again. As he moved faster, they couldn't hold the kiss. Instead, he leaned his forehead against hers and their hair made a curtain around their faces, his dark brown, hers lighter. And it made her feel like they were together against the world and no one could hurt her ever again.

"Don't stop," she said. "Don't stop. Never stop."

Dare pulled her off the wall and carried her to the vanity. "Not a chance," he said, sitting her down on the granite between the double sinks.

Haven braced her hands behind her, her head reclining back against the mirror.

"Not a fucking chance," he said, leaning in to kiss her.

The new angle had his pubic bone grinding against her clit again and again. She gasped into the kiss.

He pulled his lips away from hers and stared down to where his body penetrated hers. "Look how good we look," he rasped, watching her watch him disappearing inside her. Again and again.

Heat filled Haven's cheeks even as she was absolutely fascinated by his movements, her slickness on his length, the wet sounds they made together. "It's really . . . freaking . . . hot," she said.

One side of his mouth quirked up into a wicked grin. "It's really *fucking* hot." He arched a brow, as if challenging her.

She looked down again just as he sank deep and his sack rocked against her butt cheeks.

He planted his hand against her lower belly and stroked his thumb over her clit. Fast and firm. "Say it. Tell me how hot it is."

Haven's mouth dropped open on a moan. "It's really fucking hot," she whispered, her gaze flashing back to his.

"That's right," he growled, leaning in again to claim her mouth. His thumb continued to strum at her clit until she felt entirely overwhelmed by him—his mouth stealing her breath, his body pressing her down, his cock deep inside her. "You coming all over my cock would be even hotter," he said, nailing her with a stare.

Those words out of that mouth was like someone had taken a blowtorch to her skin. She flashed hot and felt herself get wetter, her heart ready to explode from her chest. His hips moved faster, his thrusts deeper, more pointed, rocking her whole body. All the while his thumb stroked her. And then he grabbed her ass in his hands, leaned over her, and lifted her up into his strokes so that his pubic bone ground into her clit on every mind-blowing thrust.

"Come on me, Haven," he rasped against her mouth. "Fucking come on me."

It was the hottest, wildest, headiest thing anyone had ever said to her. Sensation wound up inside her tighter and tighter until she was holding her breath and reaching and finally, finally coming all over him, her body fisting around his again and again. Her cry sounded tortured to her own ears, but then Dare was shouting and straining against her and holding her so tight it almost hurt. But it was the best thing she'd ever felt in her whole life.

Everything she'd never even known she wanted. Something she already knew she would never be able to live without.

"Beautiful, everything about you," he whispered

roughly against her cheek. Dark eyes flashed at her when he pulled away. "Stay right there." He eased out of her and discarded the condom in the trash can, then he stepped to the big glass shower and reached inside to turn on the water.

Haven missed his heat immediately but found herself absolutely fascinated by the huge tattoo covering most of his back—the same raven perched on a knife sticking out of a skull's eye socket that appeared on all of the Ravens' logos. An arch of capital letters sat above the image— RAVEN RIDERS. The ink covered a large scar that ran all down the right side of his back.

He turned to her and helped her down from the counter. "You doin' okay?" He pressed his lips against her temple.

"Better than okay," she said, oddly self-conscious given what they'd just done as he walked her to the shower. She gave him a shy smile, loving the tenderness softening the harsh angles of his face, but not sure whether she was reading too much into it. "Way better."

"Want to take care of you," he said. "Come on."

CHAPTER 20

Dare was fucking shell-shocked. There was no other way to put it. With her honesty, her bravery, her guileless pursuit of pleasure, Haven Randall had knocked him on his metaphorical ass. And he didn't know what to do about any of it. Given that he was planning to send her away and all.

He pulled Haven into the shower with him and moved her under the warm rushing water. He didn't know what he was doing, or even exactly why he was doing it. Every bit of what was happening here fell into the category of firsts. Bringing a woman to his home instead of to the club. Seducing her in his private space. Wanting to take care of her, and maybe even be taken care of in return. Taking the risk of opening himself up, when he knew all the ways that could go wrong.

Which was when it occurred to him that Haven wasn't the only one with a list of things she wanted in her life—

though of the two of them, she'd been the one brave enough to figure that shit out and go after it, whereas Dare felt a whole lot like he'd been stumbling around in the dark his whole life.

Until now.

Until Haven.

"It's still raining," she said, her gaze on the dark gray afternoon visible through the window as the water cascaded over her head. "I hadn't even realized."

Dare arched a brow. "That's good. Because I would've been doing a piss poor job of pleasing you if you still had brain cells left to think about the weather."

A shy grin rose up on her pretty face, and her eyes cut back to his. "I'd say I was well pleased."

The comment made him feel ten feet tall. After all the wrong that'd been done to her, Dare wanted to do right by Haven. In every way he could. Maybe he wasn't good enough for her, or even good for her at all, given how screwed in the head he was about his past. But she seemed to want him, and as long as she did, he'd take care of her right.

He stroked his hands over her wet hair, and she tilted her head back, exposing her throat. He couldn't help but taste her there, to taste the water from her skin. She released a contented sigh that reached into his chest and poked at things not used to being poked at.

His cock stirred against her belly. From the closeness. From her satisfaction. From everything she was making him feel and think and want.

Tentatively, her hands grasped his sides. And slowly slid down until they paused on his hips. She brought her head upright, those beautiful blue eyes assessing and observing him.

Dare grasped her right hand and slid it to his now erect

cock, circling his hand around hers on his rigid length. Haven's mouth dropped open. "You can touch me," he said. "Any way, anything you want."

Her tightening grip ripped through him like an electrical current, hot and fast.

"That's it," he said, bracing one hand on the shower wall over her shoulder.

She licked her lips and looked down, watching herself pump him. Dare released her hand to let her set the pace, his arousal ratcheting up hard and fast despite the powerful orgasm she'd just pulled out of him. Haven might've been inexperienced, but she wasn't prudish, and she wasn't bashful when it came to sex and pleasure. And the combination of curious and eager was a fucking killer to his self-control.

"I want to put my mouth on you," she said.

Case in point. Jesus. He tipped her face up and bored his eyes into hers. "Say that again."

Eyes hooded, lips glossy wet, her expression was filled with desire. "I want to put my mouth on you. Here." She squeezed his cock at the base, sending a jolt of arousal through him. "I want to make you feel the same way you made me feel."

Hand in her hair, Dare kissed her hard. "Then suck me with that pretty little mouth."

Slowly, Haven sank to her knees onto the shower floor, her face coming up even with his jutting cock. She peered up at him through wet eyelashes, not even aware of how beautiful and brave and sensual she was. She grasped his cock by the base and bathed his head in a long, slow lick.

"Fuck," he rasped, one hand still braced on the wall, the other cupping the side of her head.

She licked him until he was ready to beg for her to suck,

but she beat him to it, wrapping her lips around his length and sliding down, sliding deep. The moan she unleashed shot right to his balls, making him want to rut and rock into her mouth. But he kept his hips still, letting her explore him and torture him with pleasure.

Taking hold of his ass, Haven brought her face up tight, sucking him down, keeping him deep. Nothing about her approach was shy or reserved, which made him think she'd done this before. And he didn't fucking care one bit as long as she kept burying his head in the back of her throat.

For a long moment, she set a pace that had him fisting his hand in her hair, and then she pulled off, gasping for air and looking up at him with the most pleading expression. "Tell me what feels good to you."

"Just keep doing what you're doing. It's fucking phenomenal." He dragged his thumb over her lips, and she caught it with her teeth. He pushed it into her mouth and she immediately sucked at his flesh, her eyes making it clear how turned on she was. By pleasing him.

She took his cock deep again and got into a rhythm that alternated between fast and shallow and slow and deep. His thighs shook and his hand kept fisting and he could no longer keep his hips from pushing for more. Always more.

"Gonna come," he rasped, tugging at her hair.

She popped free long enough to say, "I want it." And then she took him deep and sucked him off until Dare was grasping her head and coming down her throat with a shout and a groan.

When she finally eased off of him, he pulled her up and kissed her hard, his tongue sweeping into her mouth and stealing her breath. Like she'd stolen his. "You're fucking good at that, you know it?"

The smile that crept up her face was ridiculously cute. "Yeah?"

"Yeah. Do it absolutely any time you want," he said with a wink.

She threw her head back and laughed. "I'll keep that in mind."

They finally got down to getting clean. She did her thing and he did his, but in trading kisses and small touches and heated glances, it felt intimate, loaded, full of promise for something more. And Dare was down for that, because as long as the storm raged outside his house, he was keeping Haven here. In his sights, in his arms, and in his bed.

Because when the rain cleared, the time they might have together would be counted in days at best. And that was hardly enough when he'd finally found a woman he wanted for longer, for more, and maybe even for everything.

"YOU HUNGRY?" DARE asked when they were dried and dressed and downstairs again. He wasn't sure how long any of those were going to last, given how sexy Haven looked wearing a pair of his boxers and his old Harley shirt knotted at her waist so it didn't hang halfway down her legs.

"Actually, I'm kinda starving." She leaned her elbows on his kitchen counter. And damn if she didn't look perfect there, hanging out with him in his house doing a whole lot of nothing in particular.

Dare opened his wasteland of a fridge. Given how often Bunny cooked up at the clubhouse, he'd gotten into a routine of eating there with whoever showed up, or making himself the odd bowl of cold cereal here on the fly. Otherwise, his fridge was filled with beer, milk, condiments, and a package of hot dogs. "How 'bout I order a pizza?" he asked, turning to her. "You like that?"

Haven nodded. "Yeah."

"What kind?" he asked, grabbing his cell.

"I like just about anything, so whatever you want." Her expression was totally open and honest, but something about the words still rubbed him wrong.

"I want to know what you *want,* not what you'll accept," he said, giving her a pointed look.

"Oh. Uh. I really like pepperoni and sausage," she said, uncertainty slipping into her gaze.

Dare leaned in for a deep, lingering kiss. "I really like when you tell me what you want." He pulled away, arched his brow at her until she smiled and nodded, and dialed the phone. "Be here in thirty," he said when he hung up.

"Do you use your kitchen much?" she asked, her gaze taking in the room.

He came up behind her and braced his hands on either side of her body. Leaned in and kissed the side of her neck. "Not nearly as much as I should."

She tilted her head, opening to him. "That's a shame," she whispered distractedly.

"What would you make?" he asked, sucking on her earlobe.

On a soft moan, she said, "Oh, everything. Fluffy pancakes and waffles for breakfast and grilled sandwiches for lunch and hearty pastas and grilled steaks for dinner."

He tugged the too-big neck of her shirt to the side, exposing her whole shoulder, and ran nipping bites all along the skin there. "And for dessert?"

Haven shivered and leaned into him. "Chocolate cake made with real fudge and a layer of raspberry filling with mini chocolate chips in between. I'd cover it with a buttercream icing and decorate it with big, thick shavings of chocolate." She turned her face to his. "And peanut butter cookies, too, of course."

"Man, I'm hard just thinking about all that," he said. And, truth be told, a little sad thinking about it, too. Because he'd lived alone so long he could hardly imagine what it would be like to live in a house that was actually alive. Hell, even the house he grew up in was weighed down by fear and tension more than lit up with anything that approximated life.

"Is that so?" She pressed her ass more firmly against his crotch. "Oh, yes, I see."

Dare chuckled at her playfulness, loving to see it, given where she'd been a few weeks before.

Looking over her shoulder, she smiled. "If just talking about what I could make causes all this, maybe we should see what happens if I actually made you a meal here sometime."

The idea did funny things to Dare's chest. Suddenly, he could see Haven there in his kitchen. Wearing one of his big T-shirts over a pair of panties and nothing else as she cooked breakfast. Pulling a big tray of cookies out of the oven, and making the whole house smell like fucking heaven. He could see them there together. Eating. Living. Loving. "Yeah," Dare said, getting caught up in his head. "We should definitely see about that."

Her smile sagged a little. "Maybe a farewell dinner before I go. Or something. To say thank you."

The cold, hard reality of her words pulled him out of his pointless thoughts. "Yeah." He stepped away from her and grabbed a beer from the fridge. And was glad when the delivery guy showed up a few minutes earlier than expected.

He paid the guy and turned toward the table to find Haven grabbing plates from a cabinet, as if she'd done it a hundred times before. And it lured more of those thoughts into his head. What was wrong with him? She had to leave. It was safest for her. Safest for his people, too. *That's* where his head should be.

"That smells good," she said, sliding into a seat at the table.

Dare set the box down and flipped open the lid. "It does. Dig in." He waited for her to grab a slice before he took two for himself.

For a long moment, they ate in silence, and then Haven said, "Can I ask you a question?"

"Always," he said. Part of him was curious to learn what she wanted to know. Most of the time they'd spent talking over the past few weeks had been about her background and situation, and Dare half wondered what a sheltered twenty-two-year-old and he could have in common to talk about—part of him hoped it wasn't much. Although he'd already been surprised more than once about the experiences they'd shared—their abusive, megalomaniac fathers, missing out on school and the typical teenage experience, running away from home and knowing they were being pursued. And finding shelter with the Ravens—he certainly couldn't forget that.

She swallowed a bite and took a long sip of water. "Why did you join the Raven Riders?"

He almost laughed. The question seemed simple on its face but was actually the single thing she could've asked that would unravel lots of strands of his life. And there was almost no way to answer without either sharing the way he'd failed Mom and Kyle or omitting the way he'd failed the two most important people in his life—and hadn't there already been enough lies and omissions between them?

"Well, it's a bit of a long story," he said, taking a bite. "The short version is that I ran away from my father's house in Arizona when I was fifteen. After a few years of being homeless and floating around on my own, I worked up the courage to approach my grandfather. I hadn't come here right away because my father had said for years that Doc was a mean, selfish bastard who wanted nothing to do with me or any of us. But life on the road alone wasn't easy . . ." Which, given the things he'd done and sacrificed to survive, was a major fucking understatement. But whatever. ". . . and I wasn't sure I wanted to keep living at all if I had to keep living like that. So I figured, what the hell, it was worth the try. Doc knew who I was with one glance and took me in without even a question. I should've known my father had lied and come here sooner. But after escaping two bad situations, I just hadn't wanted to risk a third until I got desperate. The Ravens already existed then, but they were small and the members were mostly older or aging out. I'd grown up around my father's club, and I liked the loyalty and brotherhood, the family, that a good club could be. So Doc and I agreed that I could stay on and earn my keep rebuilding the club and running the compound. On one condition."

Haven's expression was nearly rapt as she listened to him. "Which was?"

"That I never make the Ravens into the kind of club my father's Diablos were." He finished his first slice and wiped his fingers on a napkin. "A lot of bikers are drawn to clubs not only because they want to share in the motorcycle lifestyle with others who know and appreciate it, but because they also want to live life on their own terms. Some clubs, like the Diablos, take that a step further and want to live life without the restraints and oversights of rules and laws and authority. Instead, they want to make the rules and be the authority, which often leads to territorial disputes and conflicts with other clubs or gangs or criminal organizations. They go on the offense to secure territory and have no problem using violence—in some places, your number of kills or prison terms is often a way of proving your loyalty and moving up in the organization."

Haven nodded as she grabbed a second slice of pizza. "Okay," she said.

"Doc didn't want that for us, and having lived it in my father's club, I agreed. We believe in live and let live. We'll resort to violence in the interest of self-defense if we have to—we're not going to let anyone push us around. But we specifically chose business interests for the club that would create the least likelihood for treading on anyone else's toes."

"The racing?" she asked, her tone still interested and not at all disapproving.

Dare nodded. "And the betting that takes place around it, yeah. That's our primary asset. We also do some trucking escorts in the region—we're hired to provide additional security for sensitive or high-value transports. Basically, we make sure things get where they're going unmolested. I'm not going to sit here and tell you all this is on the up-and-up by the feds' book, but we try to keep out of guns and drugs as much as possible, because that's where the biggest contentions arise." Given her background and her father's criminal activities, Dare wasn't sure how she'd react to a frank admission that they weren't a hundred percent aboveboard.

"And how did protecting people come into it all?" She took another big bite of her pizza, her seeming acceptance of what he was sharing encouraging him to dig into another slice himself. He hadn't realized that he'd care what she thought of him and the Ravens, but talking to her like this made him realize he did. It mattered to him for reasons that weren't entirely clear and probably didn't make a shitload of sense. But it mattered all the same.

"It really started with Bunny," Dare said, his memories easily taking him back to when her first marriage unraveled in the most violent of ways, the law doing almost nothing to protect her.

Haven's mouth dropped open, surprise shaping her pretty face.

Bunny's history was pretty widely known by the club, so Dare wasn't talking out of turn by telling Haven, and Bunny had been known to tell some of the women that landed here herself when it seemed like it could help. "Her first husband—Maverick's father—had always had a controlling streak none of us liked, but Bunny seemed happy with him, and as long as she was, we didn't make too much of it," Dare said. "But then he lost his job and Bunny was bringing in most of their money working for me and Doc at the racetrack, which caused all kinds of problems, especially as his paranoia grew that she was running around on him with a Raven. She wasn't, but of course that didn't matter. There was no convincing him. When the abuse started, we closed ranks around her until he agreed to a divorce and a restraining order we were willing to enforce however necessary. That whole experience changed a lot of things for me and Doc and Maverick. Made it personal. Made it something we wanted to be able to do for others like her if we could."

"It's hard to imagine Bunny . . ." Haven shook her head. "She's so amazing."

The affection in her voice for his aunt reached inside his chest and squeezed. "She's the best." A long pause, and then, "What we were able to do to help Bunny also struck home with me for another reason."

The pizza was suddenly a rock in his gut, but while the

idea of telling Haven about his worst failure was about as appealing as going ass-over-ears on his bike, it was also kinda freeing, too. To be wholly known was not something Dare permitted often. But Haven had shared some of her deepest and darkest with him, and he felt like he needed to return the gesture. Anyway, she'd be gone soon. And if it changed the way she looked at him—for which he wouldn't blame her—little would be lost. A major gut check belied the thought, but Dare ignored it like a motherfucker.

"I ran from my father's house as he was murdering my mother and older brother. I didn't do a damn thing to help, which I will regret for as long as I live. So protecting others, it's me trying to make right that first wrong. No matter how impossible it might be." He heard the note of belligerence in his tone, almost daring her to judge him.

As if she could do it more harshly than he did it himself.

No matter how fast she blinked, Haven couldn't hold off the threatening tears. For Dare. For the boy he'd been. For all he'd lost. For the pain in his voice and that haunted look in his eyes she'd seen time and time again and never understood. Until now. "Oh, Dare."

"So, yeah. That's how it came about," he said, shoving his plate away and crossing his arms over his chest.

Haven didn't have the right words—assuming any even existed. All she knew was that she couldn't be so far away from him. Nerves fluttered through her belly, but she pushed through it, got up from her seat, and rounded the table to him. And then she went to her knees on the floor, laid her head against his stomach, and wrapped her arms around his waist as best she could. "I'm so sorry."

For a long moment, his body was rigid and unyielding, totally unmoved or maybe even put off by her touch. But then his muscles went loose, and it was like he was surrendering to her compassion, maybe even accepting it. A big, calloused hand stroked the hair off the side of her face. "I am, too," he said in a tight voice.

"You were fifteen," she said, the horror of his story washing over her. "You were lucky to survive yourself." She peered up at him. "Imagine all the people who might never have gotten the Ravens' help if your father had killed you, too."

His lips pressed into a tight line and his eyes narrowed. He swallowed hard.

"Was Kyle your brother?" she asked. One of the tattoos on his chest included the name.

A tight nod, but nothing more.

Haven wasn't sure if his silence was regret for telling her or difficulty telling her any more. But he wasn't pushing her away, and he wasn't telling her to drop it. So she didn't. "What was he like?"

Dare's expression softened, and she felt it deep in her chest. "He was a tough guy with a killer sense of humor who would give you the shirt off his back. He was a terrible student who got away with murder at school because he could charm the hell out of the teachers. And he was loyal and protective of his family and took care of my mom and me when things got bad. Which they did often. He taught me a lot of what I knew about how to be a man, or at least, the right kind of man, despite the fact that we were only two years apart. And he saved my life."

"He sounds amazing," she said.

"He was," Dare said. "Come here."

Haven rose and let Dare guide her until she straddled his lap. His hands ran up the outsides of her thighs as her arms went around his neck. "At least you're doing something with your life," she said. "At least you're making what Kyle did for you mean something. That's a form of fighting back, too. You know?" She shook her head. "Unlike me. The crap I let my father get away with for so long. I just took it. And I can't see how I'll ever manage to do anything half as meaningful as what you've done for so many others. And for me."

"I'm no hero, Haven," Dare said, his expression agitated.

"You are, Dare," she said, meeting his gaze. "You are to me. And I bet you are to Bunny, too, because she adores you."

Dare's hands stroked her back, his eyes suddenly softer, unshuttered, uncertain. He pulled her closer until their foreheads touched. "What are you doing to me?" he whispered.

Haven's heart tripped into a sprint, because the words held so much emotion that it made her heart ache with something a whole lot stronger than affection for him. "I don't know," she whispered back. "But you're doing it to me, too."

The admissions sparked heat between them until it seemed like the air itself was alive with electricity and desire. Between her legs, he hardened, and it shot a thrill of need through her body so hard and fast that her heart raced and her breathing shallowed and quickened.

"Fuck, Haven," he rasped, his hands tangling in her hair.

"Yes, please," she whispered, her whole body throbbing with arousal.

Dare had her shirt off in an instant. And then he was standing her up, stripping her down, and spinning her around. The chair he'd sat in screeched against the floor and his palm fell on her back. "Hands on the table." Haven had barely complied when he gripped her butt cheeks in his fingers and spread them apart. And then he buried his mouth right where she needed him most.

Haven nearly screamed. She went up on her toes in pleasure, her arms bowing, her legs shaking. Dare ate her like a man possessed, hard licks, deep plunging penetration, using his whole face to drive her wild. And she was. Babbling, crying, trembling, pressing. She was nearly as mad to come as he seemed to be to make her come.

The orgasm was like a bomb exploding her world apart and putting her back together in whole new ways—of which Dare would always be a part. Like he'd imprinted himself on her very DNA.

Head still spinning, Haven wasn't sure what was happening as Dare hauled her off the table and backward. And then he sat her down on his bare lap, his jeans hanging around his calves. "Ride me, Haven. Fucking ride me so damn hard." He lifted her over him, and Haven centered herself over his cock until she was taking him in, taking him deep, taking him all.

"Oh, God," she said with a gasp as she looked down and watched her body swallow him whole. She felt full and stretched and powerful and absolutely crazed with the need to shatter him the way he'd just shattered her. Feet together on the floor, she braced her hands on his thighs, and then she rode him fast, lifting and lowering her body over his again and again and again. Dare was cursing and grunting and digging his fingers into her ass. Haven was gloriously wet and breathing hard and sweating with the exertion of taking him.

"Fuck, Haven. *Fuck*. So good," Dare growled. And then he grabbed her around the waist and stood them up, his body curled around hers. Arms banded tight around her, he held her in place while his hips flew, the sound of their clashing skin and panting breaths loud in the room.

It was such a frenzy of movement and emotion that Haven felt totally overwhelmed, totally out of control, but she knew that Dare had her in his arms—and that nothing could happen to her as long as that was true.

The realization wound sensation tight within her body. It spiraled inside her until it was concentrated within the tight channel Dare's cock filled until Haven was moaning nonstop and trying to push herself back against him.

The groan that ripped out of Dare was the single sexiest thing Haven had ever heard, but then he pulled out of her, leaving her dizzy and confused—until she felt the hot lashes of his come against her butt and her back. Knowing that he'd spilled himself on her skin—that he'd thought to protect her in the heat of the moment, *again*—was a complete turn-on, and did absolutely nothing to detract from the arousal still whipped tight inside her.

"Dare," she whimpered.

"Jesus, Haven," he said, hugging her until she stood up straight, her back still against his front. He was still a little hard behind her, and she couldn't help the way she ground her hips against him. "Fuck, baby, you need to come again, don't you?"

Her head reclined on his shoulder just as his right hand slid down her body. "Please," she whispered.

His fingers were relentless, centering and circling on her clit in a firm, fast, slick grind. Almost desperate, Haven thrust her hips forward into his touch, chasing, needing, wound tighter than she'd ever been in her life.

"Come on, Haven. Come on," Dare ground out.

The orgasm stole her breath and bowed every muscle in her body. Her nails dug into Dare's arms as her breath finally exploded from her chest in a shaking cry. Her knees went soft, but Dare caught her. Of course he did. And he sat them back down on the chair.

On instinct, Haven spun in his lap and wrapped her arms around his neck. She buried her face against his throat and curled up against him.

And she didn't care if it seemed needy or revealed too much about how she was feeling, or even about the fact that they were both wet with Dare's come. Because Dare . . . Dare just held her right back.

CHAPTER 21

Dare's thoughts didn't get more settled as they watched movies together the rest of the night, the rain still constant, the thunder occasionally rumbling. Haven was just easy to be with, a quiet, soft comfort to a man who'd had very little solace in his life. She was a great listener, and she had a knack for honing in on the most important questions. The sound of her laughter tempted his smile every damn time. And she took pleasure in absolutely everything. Dare had to admire that.

Finally, he made a deal with himself—enjoy her while you have her. Which started with tonight. After that, he could spend time sitting and spinning on all the bullshit in his head.

Which was why he'd already decided: "You're sleeping with me," he said to Haven at bedtime. She looked up from where she reclined against his chest on the couch. "Upstairs to the left. Use whatever you need in the bathroom."

"Okay," she said, turning against his body and stretching to kiss him. "I'm not a very good sleeper, though."

"Don't you worry about it," he said, tucking a light brown wave behind her ear. "I'll lock up and be right there."

She stretched, revealing the soft skin of her stomach—and bringing his cock to life for possibly the thousandth time today. Not that he minded.

As she made for the steps, Dare hauled his ass off the couch, turned off the lights, and checked the doors. Her sounds echoed from upstairs—footsteps on the floorboards, the bathroom door shutting, the water running at the sink. The noises of someone else in his space were so unusual it was like his house was new to him all over again. He liked it. Too much.

He was on her the second she walked out of the bathroom door. Pressing her against the wall and kissing her deeply. Just because he could. She tasted like his mouthwash, and there was something really nice about that. And the smile she gave him when he released her? It lit him up inside like he hadn't ever felt before.

When he finally made it to his room, he found her sitting stiffly on the edge of the bed. And that wasn't going to do at all.

Walking toward the bed, he shed his shirt and unbuttoned his jeans. Haven's eyes on him were like fire in his blood. When he reached her, he tugged her shirt over her head. Because there was no way he could put her in his bed and not bury himself inside her. "I'm gonna reach for you, Haven. All night long." He tossed a handful of condoms on the bed.

She lifted her hips and let him pull off the borrowed boxers. "Good," she said around the edge of a kiss. "I hope you do."

Dare stepped out of his jeans until they were both nude. He didn't know what tomorrow might bring, so he wanted nothing between them tonight. His fingers dipped between her legs. "Aw, you're always so ready for me, aren't you?"

"Yes," she rasped, thrusting against his hand.

"I'm laying you out this time," he said, pushing her back onto the dark gray covers. He helped her scoot up the bed until his body hovered over hers. "Nice and slow," he said, staring into her eyes as he rolled on a condom, settled his weight on top of her, and pushed his cock into her pussy. "Nice and fucking deep."

As he penetrated her inch by hot inch, he could've come from the expression on her face alone. Rapt, almost anguished, and with something that looked a whole helluva lot like affection in her beautiful eyes. Forehead to forehead, his fingers knotted in her hair while hers dug into his shoulders like he was the anchor in her storm. Fuck, he wanted to be that, too. Like he hadn't wanted anything in a long time. Maybe ever.

His hips snapped against her, driving his cock hard and deep on a series of demanding, punctuated thrusts. She gasped and moaned his name on each stroke, her eyes falling closed and her mouth falling open so that they breathed each other's air.

"Look at me," he said, sucking her bottom lip into his mouth. "Look at me while I take you."

"Yes," she whispered. "You make me feel . . . *oh God* . . . better than I've ever felt in my whole life."

Which made him realize he felt the same way.

It was, without question, the first time that fucking became laden with emotion for him. Despite all his lays, fucking had always been about the physical release, and maybe an hour or two of companionship, too. Not about emotion. *Never* about emotion. Maybe that wasn't surprising, given the way he'd lost his virginity a million years ago, but a part of him had figured his wiring had just gotten crossed somewhere along the way. And he was fine with that. More than, actually. Because emotions were nothing if not messy. Losing his mother and brother had taught him that.

Haven's hands grasped at his back, her movements becoming desperate, needy. He could feel her core tightening around him, clamping down. He ground himself against her clit, moving faster, harder, needing her to come.

"Oh, oh, God, Dare," she cried as the orgasm rocked through her.

The minute it did, Dare let himself off the leash. He grasped her arms, pushed them against the mattress next to her head, and held her down as his hips swung hard and fast and rough against her, their skin slapping, the bed groaning, the wetness from her orgasm slicking his way. He worried he was holding her too tight but couldn't let go, couldn't back off, until finally he was coming inside her, coming hard, seeing fucking stars.

Seeing fucking everything.

HAVEN LEARNED WHAT peace was that night. She found it in Dare Kenyon's arms. It quieted her mind, eased her worries, and gave her some of the best sleep she'd had in years—despite the fact that Dare made good on his promise to want her, and take her, again and again. Or maybe even because of it.

Her body was sore and her muscles were tired and her skin felt a little tender from his hands and his mouth and his hips and the burn of his stubble. And she would cherish the feeling for the rest of her life.

Because she couldn't imagine finding someone like

Dare again. Someone who she could trust without question, someone who she could reveal her darkest parts and deepest desires to, someone who made her feel beautiful for wanting things. And who gave those things to her with such incredible generosity and passion.

Not to mention someone who'd grown up in some of the same hell she·had. Maybe even more. She'd been absolutely blown away by what he'd shared with her as they'd talked yesterday, and everything he'd gone through only made her respect and admire him more. And care, too.

Oh God, who was she kidding? She was falling in love with him.

Maybe had already fallen in love with him.

No doubt she'd been beyond naïve to think she could open herself up this way to a man and just keep it about the physical experience—an item or ten she checked off her life to-do list.

His arm around her stomach, a big hand cupping her bare breast, Dare stirred behind her. The clock on the nightstand read five-fifteen as the dim light of morning spilled through the window next to his big bed. It had stopped raining a few hours ago. "Why are you awake?" he said with a voice full of gravel. A really sexy voice, especially accompanied as it was by the erection growing against her butt.

"Just thinking," she said, her voice quiet.

"'Bout what?"

"How did you get by after you ran away from home? Before you got here? How did you make it on your own like that?" He'd glossed over that part of the story, only saying that times had been hard, hard enough that they'd forced him to seek help in a place he'd been told he'd never find it.

He heaved a deep breath behind her. "I lived in a cave

for a week, waiting for Kyle to come like he'd promised he would. I'd heard the gunshots, but I was just a stupid kid. And I'd held out hope."

Haven moved to turn in his arms, but his grip tightened, holding her right where she was.

Dare cleared his throat. "When I finally faced facts, I started hitchhiking. I had about seventy dollars to my name, and I made it last as long as I could. In New Mexico, I found a restaurant that would save me their evening leftovers, so I stayed there for a while. But that was too close to home to settle. So I kept moving. Going nowhere in particular. Stealing when I had to. Sleeping on park benches. And then I got picked up by this middle-aged couple, Lisa and her husband, Brant. They had an RV, and they were just traveling, going nowhere in particular, too. They were nice. It seemed good. It was better than being dirty and homeless and hungry, for sure."

She could hear the *but* hanging on the end of his words, and her heart kicked up in her chest. She linked her fingers between his where he still palmed her breast.

"After being with them for a while, one night they gave me an ultimatum. If I wanted to keep traveling with them and sharing their food, Lisa wanted to have sex with me. And Brant wanted to watch."

Haven couldn't hold in the gasp. He was fifteen. Fifteen! "Did they know how old you were?"

"From the first day," he said.

Oh, God. Her belly squeezed with dread and sadness. Especially because she knew what it was for people to push you for things you didn't want to give. Despite having been "spoiled" by Zach—her father's word—her dad made it clear to the men who hung around that Haven wasn't on the menu unless he put her there. He never did. Not officially at least.

But the guys took liberties when they thought they could get away with it. Pawing her butt and breasts. Grabbing her face and stealing a kiss. Forcing her hand against their erections—one guy had gone so far as to push her hand into his pants and use it to jerk off. Her arm had been bruised for days after. It had only taken one time for someone to drunkenly come into her room at night and molest her while she slept before she started bracing her desk chair against the back of the door. Of course, the lewd comments, innuendos, and threats were par for the course.

And there were never not a bunch of guys around her father's house.

As for her father? He looked the other way every time, and punished *her* for causing the trouble in the first place sometimes. One time he even beat her with his belt for fighting back and managing to give the guy a black eye. She knew that had been about proving who was boss, but it had taught her a lesson, too. Don't draw attention. Stick to the shadows whenever possible. Hide the parts of her they all seemed so desperate to claim.

Finally, Dare continued. "We were in the middle of nowhere Nevada during a brutal heat wave. Miles from the next town. I think they planned it that way. Knew I couldn't walk anywhere from there. Not safely." Haven felt him shrug. "So I agreed."

Part of her wanted to pour out all the words of sympathy and outrage she felt welling up inside her, but Haven's gut told her he wouldn't want that, wouldn't appreciate it, and might even stop talking if she did. So she forced herself to be still and quiet until he started talking again.

"Brant watched. Jerked himself off to me screwing his wife. It became a thing after that, and it became more and more tied to paying my way. I hated it, but I didn't have many options. I was already making an exit plan when they announced one night that Brant wanted his turn with me. I had to fight him off. And I ran that night."

Haven swallowed, the sound thick to her own ears. "How long were you with them?"

"All told? About six months. After that, it took me most of another year before I made it here."

In her horror over his situation, something absolutely sickening occurred to Haven, and she whipped around to face him. "Oh, God. Is that what I'm doing? Using you?" That he might think so made her so nauseous that she had to wrap her arms around her stomach.

"No," he said, the word loud and fierce, a scowl darkening his whole face. He pressed her back into the bed, hovering over her, his hair casting shadows over his harsh features. "Fuck, no, Haven. I've wanted every second I've had with you. What happened back then—that was exploitation and survival. What's happening now, right here, between us—"

She hung on the edge of a cliff, desperate to know how he'd characterize it. He dragged his fingertips down her cheek.

"It's the first real connection I've had in my whole goddamned life."

No one had ever said something so beautiful to her, all the more so because she felt the exact same way.

"I hate them for hurting you," she said, anger mixing with her affection for him to create a dangerous, restless cocktail in her blood.

His gaze dropped from hers as his eyes followed his fingers down her throat to her collarbone. "Yeah, well, ancient history."

Haven didn't call him on it, but the restrained emotion in his voice belied his words. She knew enough to know that there was a difference between moving past something and forgetting it altogether, between not letting something control you and being able to excise it from being a part of you at all. Some things cut too deep.

Her thoughts tangled, her little slice of hell mixing with his, until she was angrier than she'd probably ever been— probably ever let herself feel—in her life. Her body felt like she might explode with it, like she couldn't possibly hold it in without detonating and taking everything around her down, too. Suddenly, tears pooled and leaked from the corners of her eyes. She tried to turn her head away, to hide them.

"Aw, Haven, don't be sad. Not for me," he said, swiping at the wetness with his thumb.

"I'm not," she said, her voice raw with emotion. "Well, I am, a little. But I'm more . . . I'm pissed off for you." She turned her head back to him, adrenaline sending a shiver through her. "I could kill someone I'm so mad. Why are there so many people who think they can just take what they want from you? Or think you exist to do something for them? It's so . . . so . . . so *fucking* unfair," she said, the words coming faster, spilling out of her. The cuss word she'd never once said before Dare coaxed it out of her yesterday feeling like the only thing that could really capture the scope of her rage. "That's why what you do is so important, Dare. You stand against all that for people who can't do it for themselves. Somebody has to, because, because—"

He kissed her. So hard and so deep that she couldn't breathe, but with so much passion that it momentarily made oxygen seem completely unimportant. The kiss shot heat through her blood, and his erection against her thigh was proof that she wasn't the only one affected. "I just want to be with you," Dare said around the edge of the kiss. "I just want to touch you and talk with you and lay with you. Just like this."

As aroused as she was, she was so moved by his words that her heart pounded out a hard beat against her chest. She pulled him down beside her, and they lay completely entangled with one another. Their foreheads close enough to kiss, their arms embracing, their legs entwined.

He stroked his hand against her hair, his fingers softly combing against her scalp. "I can't seem to get enough of you, Haven."

"I hope you don't," she whispered, absolutely melting at his words. Skin against skin, body against body, it was the most intimate moment of her whole life, not just because they were naked, but because they were so exposed. "I know I won't ever have enough of you." She closed her eyes to keep him from seeing her sadness. But, *God,* she never wanted this to end. This crazy, impossible thing she had with him.

He kissed her forehead, and his thumb stroked her cheek. "Pretty girl," he whispered, everything about the moment feeling like the life and connection he'd talked about before.

She felt it, too.

But now morning was here and the storm was over. Which meant he'd take her back to the clubhouse and continue making plans to send her and Cora away. She knew he had to. She did. But that didn't mean everything inside her wasn't screaming to stay, for this quiet, peaceful, perfect moment to last forever.

And then his cell phone rang, bringing them back to reality even faster than she'd feared.

CHAPTER 22

We've got a problem."

Phoenix's words were still ringing in Dare's ears as he led Haven into the clubhouse, their stolen night together feeling like way too distant a memory even though he could still smell her on his skin.

"I hope everything's okay," Haven said when they got inside.

"Me too," he said. He leaned in and kissed her on the cheek, when what he really wanted was to push her against the wall and devour her. One more time. "I'll see ya later."

She nodded, and he hated the uncertainty in her expression. But he couldn't blame her for it.

He found Maverick and Phoenix in his office waiting for him, both of them wearing troubled, agitated expressions. "Happy fucking Monday morning," Dare said as he pushed the door mostly shut and dropped into the chair at his desk.

"Yeah," Phoenix said. "That about sums this up. Got two calls this morning. One from Marz and one from the Iron Cross. The two confirmed one basic point—refugees from the Church Gang are not only being taken in by the Iron Cross, but the Iron Cross is recruiting them. Hard. Word on the street is that it's a join-or-die-type invitation, and it seems to be working. Because Dominic, the buyer who called from the Iron Cross, made a point of demonstrating that he knew the specifics of our inventory. He could only have gotten that intel from a Churchman who knew what the original arms deal—the one where we picked up the hardware—was supposed to entail."

"Shit," Dare said. "They're probably going after intel like that as much as building their ranks."

"My thoughts exactly," Phoenix said. "Hoping to defuse this, I told Dominic we were already in talks with another buyer but that we'd be happy to do business with them another time. He told me to walk away from the other deal."

That feeling of dread that Dare had been feeling the past few weeks ballooned inside his chest and weighed down on his shoulders. And not just because this group could be the source of new threats to the Ravens and their interests. If the Iron Cross could get that kind of specific intel on the arms inventory, they could certainly find out about Haven and the reward. Or maybe already had.

"Makes you wonder why he thinks he has the leverage to make that demand," Maverick said, those dark blue eyes flashing.

"Yeah," Dare said. "It sure does. So the question is, do we sell them all, part, or none, and let the shit fall where it may. Damnit, I don't want to give them anything, especially pulling this bullshit."

Phoenix shook his head. "Neither do I. We could always

call their bluff. They're clearly desperate for the guns. Maybe without them they're all bark and no bite."

"Did Marz have any other insight on them?" Dare asked, his mind racing through all the ways this could play out.

"Just that by all accounts, the Iron Cross is best situated to come out on top when the dust settles. They were already strong competitors of the Church Gang, so they've got market share and territory, and they seem to have stepped into the power vacuum the fastest to grab up everything the Churchmen had."

"So there's gotta be some bite there," Dare said, his gut telling him they were going to have to do some kind of business with these jackholes. And *this* was why the Ravens stayed out of guns and drugs as much as they could.

Knee bouncing, Maverick sighed. "I think we gotta meet them halfway. I hate it, especially pulling this punk-ass bullshit. But if we give them nothing, we risk another war we want no part of. If we give them everything, we let them think they can walk all over us. We give them part of the inventory and it's a good-faith gesture, one that's on our own terms, one that says we made an effort despite being in talks with someone else."

"Yeah. That's where I'm landing, too," Dare said. "Which means we need to set up some terms and find a drop spot. Nowhere near here. I want it done as soon as possible. Get these fuckers off our backs."

Phoenix nodded. "Goddamned Churchmen just won't die."

"No shit. You know what? When you talk to this Dominic asshole, make the deal contingent on their agreement that they hold no sway over our betting activities in the city. No doubt they know about them at this point. Ike op-

erates unmolested or they can go fuck themselves," Dare
said. Years ago, that had been one of the points of con-
tention between the Raven Riders and the Church Gang,
one that had taken a few knock-down fights before they'd
reached an uneasy détente.

"Yeah, that's right," Maverick said. "That right there
actually makes the deal make sense for us. We don't want
to fight that fight all over again."

"Agreed. We don't want to fight at all." Dare sighed,
thoughts racing. "They don't get any of the sniper rifles.
Make it clear those are gone. They can have the AKs and
the Glocks. Remind them that our shit is high quality,
courtesy of Uncle Sam, and push them on price. Tell them
it's a convenience fee for walking on the other deal," Dare
said, scratching at the scruff on his jaw.

"Got it," Phoenix said.

"Good. Then make the call, Phoenix. And play it cool."
Dare had total faith that his Road Captain could handle
this. Phoenix could be smooth as glass and charming as
all fuck when he wanted, winning him guys who wanted
to be his friend and girls who wanted to be his lay in
equal measure.

"I told him I'd call him back around nine. So consider
it done," Phoenix said.

Dare woke up the screen on his cell. 8:35 A.M. It was
too early for all this bullshit. He ought to rain some hell
down on these Iron Cross bastards just for making him
leave his bed the first time he'd ever brought Haven to it.
"Okay," Dare said, blowing out a breath. Then Phoenix
got a funny expression on his face Dare couldn't figure
out. "What's with the face?"

Phoenix's lips slid into a smirking grin. "Cora said
Haven spent the night at your house."

"What is this, fucking high school?" Dare asked. Last

night, he'd called Bunny to let her know Haven was staying at his place so that no one worried, so he knew at least some of these idiots would find out.

"You really have to ask?" Maverick said, doing a piss-poor job of restraining his own amusement. "Come on, spill."

"Nothing to spill. I was going to take her swimming. We got caught in the storm, so we holed up at my place and just ended up staying there." Dare booted up his computer, wanting to see if Marz had shot him any other information this morning while he'd been so busy digging up intel on the Iron Cross.

"Uh-huh," Maverick said. "And the last time a woman spent the night at your place was . . ." He leaned forward, as if hanging on the edge of Dare's words. Words Dare had no intentions of giving him.

"None of your damn business," Dare said, eyes on the computer monitor, his fingers moving over the keys.

"Look, don't get your panties in a bunch," Maverick said, his tone suddenly more reserved. "We were just thinking that if you're serious about this girl, maybe we find a plan B that doesn't involve sending her away."

Fuck if that didn't cut too close to where his own thoughts kept straying. But all the plan Bs were shit compared to the certainty of safety—for both the women and his club—that would come from new identities and relocation. Especially if the Iron Cross knew the details about Haven and the reward, the way they'd learned about the Ravens' gun inventory.

"I don't need you all playing what-ifs with my life or worrying about who gets my dick wet," he said, his voice rising with the pent-up frustration he felt. "I'm not fucking serious about Haven, okay? She's just a client like every other client. Nothing more. So drop it. She's leaving, just like we planned, just like the club voted. It'll be better for everyone when she's gone." Better for her, better for the club—or, safer, at least. And safe was the bare minimum he owed everybody. Still, his words were filled with half-truths and outright lies, each and every one of which tasted like ash on his tongue. But maybe if he said them out loud, he'd have a chance in hell of believing them himself. Last thing he wanted was his brothers thinking he was distracted by a woman just as the club was facing off against a new threat.

A creak on the hall floorboards and a quiet knock on the door.

"What?" Dare yelled, annoyance clear in his voice.

The door eased open. And there stood Haven with a plate in her hand. Wearing another Harley T-shirt she'd borrowed from him this morning with that pair of jeans he loved on her so much. Her face absolutely ashen. "Bunny saved you some breakfast," she said, her voice small.

Dare wanted to smash the plate over his own head. Because everything about her demeanor right now suggested she'd overheard what he'd just said. "Thanks," he said, willing her to meet his gaze as she settled the plate on the corner of his desk. She wouldn't.

"Sorry to interrupt," she said, quickly backing out of the room.

Dare rose. "Haven—"

"It's okay," she said, closing the door. All the way this time.

"Fuck," Dare said. He stepped toward the door, torn between the business they needed to get done and going after the woman he'd just wronged in a fucking horrible way. And that was when he noticed the plate—along with the bacon, scrambled eggs, and toast sat two peanut butter cookies. He sagged against the wall and dug his hand into his hair.

"Go make that shit right," Mav said.

He wanted to. *Fuck* how he wanted to. But Phoenix needed to place his call in less than ten minutes. And this arms deal was the most important thing right now. Or it should be. No, it was. For all the Ravens' sake, this shit needed to go down perfectly. Which meant Dare needed to get his priorities straight and his head screwed on right.

Gut in a goddamned knot, he threw the entire plate in the trash. "Eyes on the prize, Maverick. Got it? Now, Phoenix, place the fucking call."

DARE DIDN'T THINK they'd be here again so soon—at the Hard Ink Tattoo building in downtown Baltimore. It was a big, red-brick monster of a building that had clearly been some kind of old warehouse or factory back when Baltimore still had a decent industrial sector. Once L-shaped, only the long side of the L remained, the short side having been destroyed when the Hard Ink team's enemies had attacked them a few weeks before, killing two of the Ravens' own.

The chain-link gate swung open, letting Dare, eight other Ravens on bikes, and a truck full of product into the gravel lot behind the building. The moment gave him a whole lot of déjà vu.

But it couldn't be helped. Phoenix's call with the Iron Cross had gone about as well as they could've expected. Dominic had pushed back against their demands but finally acceded to their ultimatum on their betting activities and a competitive price on the guns. They'd thrown in more ammo than they'd planned, in order to maintain the appearance that they were meeting them halfway. And both parties wanted it done quickly—the deal was going down at nine o'clock tonight. In just three hours. All that remained was letting the Iron Cross know where the exchange would take place, which was part of why they'd come to Baltimore, and to Hard Ink, early.

As they parked and dismounted their bikes, men spilled out the back door of the building. Dare gave a wave as he hooked his helmet on the handlebars, and then he and his guys closed the distance to where their new allies and friends stood to greet them.

"Welcome back," Nick said, extending a hand to Dare.

"Just wish it was purely a social call," Dare said, shaking the other man's hand. Tall with dark hair and pale green eyes, Nick was the team's leader and the guy Dare had gotten to know the best when they'd been here a few weeks before.

One by one, Dare shook hands with Nick's teammates, his guys following suit. There was Shane McCallan, with his Southern accent and pretty-boy good looks; Edward Cantrell, who went by the nickname Easy, a tall, built African-American man who was probably the guy Dare knew least of all; Derek "Marz" DiMarzio, their tech guy, who had provided them with all kinds of useful information about the Iron Cross and Haven's father's organization today; Beckett Murda, a big mountain of a guy with a badly scarred eye and an always-serious expression. Nick's brother, Jeremy, and Jeremy's boyfriend, Charlie, hung back from the group. They weren't part of Nick's Special Forces team, but from everything Dare could tell, they'd been integral to the fight the vets had waged. Jeremy gave Dare a wave.

"Good to see you doing better, Jeremy," Dare said. The guy had been through brain surgery a few weeks before when he was injured during a fight with the team's enemies—an injury that was still apparent in the form of a scar visible through his recently shaved brown hair.

"Thanks," Jeremy said, his expression reserved. Dare knew Jeremy felt some responsibility for the deaths of Harvey and Creed when the building collapsed, but Dare had put that blame where it belonged—on the lowlifes who bombed the building in the first place. And that score had been settled as far as Dare and the Ravens were concerned.

Ike stepped through the crowd and held out his hand. "Didn't think I'd get to see your ugly mug again so soon," he said.

Dare clasped his hand. "Shut up, ya bald motherfucker." A rumble of laughter went through the group.

"Come on in," Nick said. "We've been working on a plan for tonight."

"Lead the way," Dare said, even though he and his guys knew the building like the backs of their hands after having helped protect it. Their footsteps echoed loudly in the industrial metal-and-cement stairwell, and then they poured into a huge room on the second level. With cement floors, exposed beams, and brick walls, the big rectangular space looked like the warehouse it had probably once been, though now it was filled with exercise equipment, a giant makeshift table around which Dare and his guys had eaten numerous meals, and a big computer setup in the back corner—the team's nerve center, where Marz could usually be found clacking away.

They formed a big circle around Marz's desk, some guys sitting on metal folding chairs and others standing. Who'd have thought that the Ravens would find themselves standing side by side with a bunch of highly decorated Army vets once, let alone twice? But Nick and his men were good guys—guys who understood the values that the Ravens prized. And that was more than enough for Dare.

Nick pointed to an enlarged map tacked to the wall. "We're advocating using the same garage location where the original deal went down. We know it and have planned ops in that location before. Your men know it. And as usefully, it's in territory that the Iron Cross doesn't control right now, which means they're not going to want to spend any more time there than they have to and are going to want to keep a low profile."

"Whose territory is it?" Dare asked.

Marz pulled out a sheaf of papers. "A group called the Black Soldiers. They're small, but they're on good terms with a few other gangs around the city, which gives them friends if they need them. Official thinking is that the Iron Cross isn't going to want to give their rivals a reason to band against them, not before their position is more secure. Things are too volatile right now for anyone to get too cocky."

"One can hope," Dare said, nodding. "The garage makes sense, and the fact that we know it gives us a tactical advantage." His gaze went to his guys, and Maverick, Caine, and Phoenix all nodded their agreement. "So let's play this thing out."

The group of them spent the next hour brainstorming strategy, personnel placement, and contingency plans should plan A go fubar on them, as plan As were wont to do. Maybe it was overkill, but Dare didn't want to take any more chances with his guys than he had to. And that went for the Hard Ink team as well. They all had too much to lose, a point that was driven home when a group of women poured in through the door on the far side of the room carrying trays of food and drinks to the big table.

Nick clapped Dare on the shoulder. "Figured y'all

might want a quick bite before we get this show on the road. Becca's idea."

"She's a good woman, Nick," Dare said.

"The fucking best," the guy said, a look of contentment on his face that Dare would pay good money to feel himself. Just once.

Around the table, a new round of greetings took place. Becca Merritt was Nick's girlfriend and an ER nurse who'd helped patch guys up more than once during the recent fights. With her blond hair and blue eyes, she looked a lot like the girl next door, but from everything Dare knew, she'd proven herself a fierce ally of Nick's over and over again. Sara and Jenna Dean were red-haired sisters who all the Ravens had gotten to know pretty well after they'd played a role rescuing Jenna from one of the Churchmen who'd apparently gone a little fucking crazy over her. Marz's lady, Emilie Garza, was probably the woman among them Dare knew least of all—though he'd heard tale of the gut-wrenching scene that'd played out when she'd found her brother's slain body dumped outside Hard Ink the same day Dare's guys had been killed. And then there was Nick's sister, Kat, a bad-ass chick Dare had gotten to know decently well because she'd taken more than one shift in the sniper's roosts they'd operated during the height of the crisis.

Everyone dug into the food, and Shane and Sara made their way over to him. "We were wondering how Haven and Cora are doing," Shane said.

Dare wasn't surprised that Shane and Sara would want to know—from what Dare understood, Shane had been the one to find the two women locked in the basement of the Church Gang's storage facility. Once the women had been rescued, Sara had taken them under her wing until the plan for the Ravens to grant them shelter had come to fruition. "They're still at our compound," Dare said. "We're working on a plan to get them set up someplace new as we speak. A whole new life, where Haven can be safe from her father and his whole organization."

"So that's who she was running from," Sara said, leaning against Shane.

"Yeah," Dare said. "But we'll make sure he can't find her. Don't you worry."

"I have been," Sara said with a small smile and a little shrug. "They reminded me so much of me and Jenna. I just want them to be happy like we are now." She looked up at Shane with so much affection on her face that it sucker-punched Dare. Because he wanted that. He wanted that with Haven. Who he'd let believe all damn day that she wasn't important to him. In the chaos of planning for the arms exchange, there just hadn't been time to pull her aside and do the conversation justice, especially when Haven had made herself scarce. No doubt purposely.

"They will be," Dare said, meaning that down into his very marrow. No matter what, he would take care of Haven Randall just like she deserved. "You've got my word on that."

"Thanks, man," Shane said. "We appreciate it."

Luckily there wasn't much time for more small talk about Haven, because before long they'd all filled their stomachs and were back in business mode. The Hard Ink guys were going in wearing tactical gear that would hide their faces, because the last thing any of them needed was the Iron Cross putting two and two together, especially if that equation hadn't already been solved. They'd be hidden on the outskirts unless the Ravens needed them front and center. Hopefully it wouldn't come to that.

At seven-thirty, Nick and his teammates left for the location, wanting to get in place before the other side had time to arrive. As promised, at eight, Phoenix placed the call alerting the Iron Cross to the nine o'clock meeting place, and then the Ravens were back in the saddle and heading there themselves.

Hoping to be done with this city and its fucking gangs once and for all.

CHAPTER 23

At exactly nine o'clock, ten men from the Iron Cross spilled from four black Humvees that had just entered the big, abandoned parking garage in a derelict part of the city. The Ravens had been waiting for fifteen minutes, their positions well chosen, their escape routes well protected, and their rides parked facing handlebars out so they could get out fast if they had to. Nick's team couldn't be seen, and hopefully wouldn't have to be. But it was gold knowing they were there and that they were listening—Beckett and Marz had some kind of equipment that would enable that from a safe distance.

Feet spread, arms crossed, jaw set, Dare stood in front of several nondescript wooden crates filled with wood shavings, guns, and ammunition, Maverick and Phoenix at his sides, the rest of his men at his back.

The men from the Iron Cross had one obvious feature in common—most of them had shaved white heads. Which made their recruitment of the mostly black Church Gang members even more interesting, didn't it? Not all gangs were racially exclusive, but Baltimore's racial lines were generally pretty deeply drawn. Had been for as long as Dare had known the city, at least.

Wearing some kind of black military getup that didn't look too different from the gear Nick's guys had worn, the tallest of the men stepped forward. "I'm Dominic," he said in a deep voice, soulless blue eyes like ice. "Who's Phoenix?"

"That's me," Phoenix said with a nod, then he pointed to Dare. "This is our president, Dare. He'll be handling the deal from here."

Dominic's gaze sliced to Dare, and he repeated the name as if it was something distasteful. The guy might've had a few inches on Dare, but Dare sure as shit didn't scare easily, and he didn't do intimidated at all. Not the way he'd grown up, and not the way he lived his life now. "I want your word, man to man, in front of all our combined people, that you'll keep clear of our betting activity in the city," Dare said.

"Which of your men is in charge of that here?" Dominic asked.

"That's me," Ike said, stepping up beside Maverick. Ike Young was pretty well known around the Baltimore underground for sports betting, so no doubt the Iron Cross already had a decent idea who he was. "I'll do my job and stay out of your business if you give me the same respect."

The two men eyeballed each other for a long moment, and then Dominic nodded. "You have our agreement. The Iron Cross isn't interested in making enemies." An agreement between outlaws might not seem like much, but reputation and your word mattered a fucking lot if you wanted to get deals done and keep other groups from stabbing you in the back.

"We're glad to hear it. Then if you have our money, we assume you'd like to inspect the product," Dare said.

Dominic held out a hand behind him, and one of the other guys slapped a thick envelope into his hand. "It's the amount we agreed." Dominic handed the package over, and Dare gave Phoenix a nod. The Road Captain got busy with a crowbar, popping the nailed lids off the crates—two of guns and one of ammo.

Dare then handed the envelope off, letting Phoenix double-check the amount, which should've been on the order of about fifteen grand. They could get a couple times retail on the Glocks, but the AKs didn't go for more than five hundred on the street, and that was on a very good day. They'd been able to get these fuckers up to four hundred per. Tension hung in the air like a fog as Dominic and two of his men stepped to the crate and withdrew some of the unloaded weapons to inspect them.

"The Glocks are excellent quality. Not much used if ever," one of Dominic's men said.

"The AKs are good quality, too. Everything's in good shape. And the promised ammo is all here," another man said.

"We're good," Phoenix said from behind Dare, who gave a nod to confirm he'd heard.

"The crates are all yours," Dare said. The man crouching near the ammo gave a nod and began resetting the lids. With a single tilt of his head, Dominic called a few other men forward. Two by two, they carted the crates to their waiting vehicles, packing them away in trunks as everyone watched.

Dominic turned to Dare. "We appreciate your making this happen."

"We don't want to make enemies either. With you or anyone in the city. We hope you and your people will take it as the good-faith gesture it is," Dare said, nailing the guy with a stare. They were so close to being done with this that Dare could nearly taste it.

"We do, though it strikes me that there's something else you could offer that would achieve that even more," Dominic said.

Dare didn't outwardly react as whatever this other shoe was potentially dropped on them. "Can't imagine why you'd need any more proof than I've just given you."

"Because I've got men to take care of, just like you do. And I assume as new friends you'd be willing to help me do that." One eyebrow raised over Dominic's lifeless eyes. Inwardly, Dare reveled in the fact that this guy had a fucking sniper rifle trained on his big white forehead right now and didn't even know it.

Humoring him, Dare asked, "And what exactly is it you think I could offer that would help?"

"The identity of the men you worked with to take this hardware from the Church Gang in the first place." Dominic crossed his arms over his chest and looked down his nose, waiting, challenging.

The one thing Dare had no intention of giving. Ever. "That's a nonstarter, Dominic. You're not just asking me to give up a business partner, you're encouraging me to make an enemy. What happened with the Churchmen doesn't have to have anything to do with you if you don't let it. Start fresh and let the past lie."

The tall asshole shrugged. "We'll find out with or without you. I was just hoping you'd be smart enough to be on the right side of the decision."

"Keeping your word to another is *always* the right decision," Dare said, taking satisfaction that they apparently didn't know about Nick's team yet, which should mean that even if they knew about Haven and the reward, they didn't know what had happened to the women after the Church Gang lost them. "So we're done here."

"Appears that way," Dominic said with a nod. And then he turned and crossed toward one of the cars, his men falling in line behind him as he passed. They packed back into the Humvees and tore out of the lot, tires squealing against the concrete. And then they were gone.

"Let's ride," Dare said, already in motion. "Routes home just like we discussed. No stops, no detours. Anyone gets in trouble or picks up a tail, give the signal." Everyone hustled toward the line of motorcycles waiting at the entrance behind them.

Engines roaring, the ten of them shot out into the night, riding off in groups of two and three in different directions to head out of the city. They'd preplanned their exit strategy ahead of time to combat against being followed. With Maverick at his right and Joker behind them in the truck, Dare worked his way out of the run-down neighborhood and onto one of the main arteries that led past the stadiums and out to Interstate 695. Their sixes were clear all the way, allowing Dare to take a deep breath for the first time in a couple hours, especially as *all clear* messages came in from the other groups of riders.

Sometimes it took a whole tankful of fuel before you could screw your head on straight. And as Dare rode home, he felt like it was one of those nights. Fists in the wind, he was glad for the time and space to himself, to replay the night in his head on his own before he and the guys were together and blowing off steam.

A couple things rose to the surface of his thoughts right away. First, he didn't trust the Iron Cross or that creepy Dominic fucker for an instant. Second, that deal hadn't done jack shit to cement any kind of decent relationship between the two—Dare felt that down into his very blood. Third, the Iron Cross didn't yet know Haven's where-abouts, which meant things were urgent but not critical on that front. Yet. Thank God for small favors, assuming that could be counted as one.

Shit, yeah, he'd take the good news where he could.

When they got home, his guys were all kinds of in the mood to celebrate, and Dare totally understood why. He did his best to join in, to not be the moody motherfucker Maverick always accused him of being. But despite the fact that the night had gone about as smoothly as could've been expected, doing the deal with the Iron Cross hadn't done a thing to alleviate the feeling of dread Dare had been shouldering the past few weeks.

Instead, he felt more certain than ever that a shit storm was heading their way.

And that meant he needed to get Haven out of the line of fire while he still had time—and probably faster than he'd even originally planned.

WHO DO YOU want to be?

Haven had been thinking about that question for most of the past twenty-four hours. Yesterday afternoon, as the Ravens had fallen into a frenzy of activity preparing for some meeting that had unexpectedly taken a bunch of them to Baltimore, Caine had found Haven and Cora and asked them that question. He hadn't meant it metaphori-cally, he'd meant it literally. They had to pick their new names by lunchtime today, which was when he needed to let his contact working up their new identities know.

Lying on her bed still in her pajamas, the morning sun-light spilling in through her window, Haven had never been more grateful for something to think about in her life, since it kept her from replaying Dare's words over and over in her head.

I'm not fucking serious about Haven, okay? She's just a client like every other client. Nothing more. So drop it. She's leaving, just like we planned, just like the club voted. It'll be better for everyone when she's gone.

Better for everyone when she's gone. He wanted her gone. Because she wasn't anyone special—not to him.

Oh, who was she kidding? She hadn't been able to think about anything except his words. She just couldn't figure out how her instincts had been so damn wrong. Haven wasn't so naïve that she equated sex with love, but Dare had said and done things, too. Things that made it seem like she wasn't the only one getting in deep—holding her, taking care of her, saying he couldn't get enough of her. Just the memories they'd shared with one another about their lives would've made their time together emotional, even if nothing physical had passed between them.

But it had.

It had, and it had meant everything to Haven.

And nothing at all to Dare.

God, she was really going to have to get a whole lot tougher if she was going to make it in this world, wasn't she? Because if someone she believed to be fundamentally good could hurt her so bad, she'd have to be a whole lot stronger to withstand someone who intended her harm.

And that all started with a new name. At least they got a choice in the matter.

Haven stared down at the blank page in her notebook. Cora lay beside her, scribbling away. They were supposed to be comparing lists. Of course, that was assuming Haven could think about anything except Dare. And her stupid, naïve broken heart.

"You're not writing anything," Cora said.

"I know. I'm thinking." She pressed her pen to the page and wrote the first thing that came to her mind. Alice. Not because she particularly liked it but because Haven felt like she had a heck of a lot in common with the fairy tale character by the same name. She'd certainly fallen down the rabbit hole, hadn't she?

Cora peered over her arm. "Be serious. Alice is too old for you."

Haven collapsed facedown on her notebook.

Shoving her to the side, Cora frowned down at her. "Okay, that's it. Tell me what's going on right now. I could tell you were upset yesterday, so I tried to give you some space to come to me when you were ready, but now I'm too worried to play it cool, so just tell me what happened. Did Dare hurt you?" Something close to panic slid through Cora's green eyes. "Because if he did—"

"No, no," Haven said, grasping at Cora's wildly gesticulating hand. "Well, he did, but not the way you're thinking."

"Haven, so help me—"

"We had sex. And then I overheard him telling Maverick and Phoenix he didn't care about me and would be glad when I was gone. Okay?" She flopped onto her back and blew out the breath she felt like she'd been holding since that awful moment before she'd walked into Dare's office.

Cora stared at her, her brow furrowing into a sharp frown. "Oh, Haven. What happened?"

Why had she thought she could keep all this bottled up from Cora? The time with Dare had just been so amazingly overwhelming that she'd needed to process it and get her emotions under control so she didn't end up sounding like a love-struck idiot. And then he'd gone and proven she was exactly that. And it had just been too much to share—with anyone.

Blinking fast to hold back the tears that she'd so far refused to let fall, Haven pushed herself into a sitting position against the wall. "I don't even know where to start. But I know where it ends—with a freaking broken heart. And it's my own fault." She shook her head.

"Did he . . . did you want him to—"

"Yes, I wanted it. I wanted it all seven times, depending on whether you include oral sex as *it*." Heat rushed into her cheeks.

Cora's mouth dropped open, and her expression was almost comical. "Seven? Seven? Holy crap, Haven. He holed you away at his place for an overnight sex fest and then tells his guys you're not important to him? That's bullshit."

Haven shrugged. It didn't feel right to her either, but she'd heard the words. Plain as day.

"What did you say?"

"When?" Haven asked, confused.

"When he said that," Cora said, anger making her cheeks pink.

"I didn't say anything. Bunny had asked me to take him a plate of breakfast she'd saved, and I totally walked into his conversation. Phoenix and Maverick were there. It was clear that they all knew I'd overheard, so I just left as fast as I could." God, just thinking back on it made Haven's stomach turn.

"And he didn't come after you?" Cora asked. Haven shook her head. "That asshole."

Shaking her head, Haven's thoughts whirled. "It's not all his fault—"

"Haven," Cora said, voice full of disapproval.

"No, listen. Hear me out. I told him about my list, and I asked him if he'd help me make parts of it come true. You know, the sex parts." God, her face was on fire. "I've never felt safer with another man than I have with Dare.

And I like him. So I just . . . kinda . . . went for it. And he agreed," she said, leaving out the part about Dare having read her list already. As it was, Cora might never forgive Dare, and Haven didn't want to be unfair to him in all this. Not after everything he'd done for them. And not when she was the one who'd let her emotions run away. He'd never promised her a thing. Heck, she knew he was sending her away when she asked him to take her. And that part of it? The sex parts? She didn't regret that one bit. In fact, heartbreak aside, they were some of the best memories she had in her entire life.

Because Haven knew the difference between a touch that cherished and one that was indifferent or, worse, hurtful. Dare's touch had cherished her. For a few short hours, she had been cherished.

Cora huffed out a breath. "I'm so sorry, Haven."

"Me too. I don't regret it, though. You know?" She peered up at her best friend.

"Well, I'm glad for that. Once we're settled somewhere, you're going to find your happy ending. You know it?" Cora's smile was small but hopeful.

But Haven couldn't see past leaving something she didn't want to leave to feeling hopeful about the future. At least, not yet. Still, she managed "We both will."

Nodding, Cora handed her the discarded pen and notebook. "But first we need names."

"Okay," Haven said, forcing herself to focus more this time. She thought about it. Really thought about it. Pushed through the sadness at having to give up her own name. Because she hadn't realized how much a part of her own identity her name was—the only thing she had that her mother had given her—until she faced losing it. Although hadn't she felt that way about her hair? And look how much she loved it now.

So. Right. Suck it up.

She tapped her pencil against the blank page.

"So, was it good?" Cora asked, eyes on her own list.

"Amazing," Haven said, chest suddenly so full of emotion that it was hard to breathe. "The most amazing day and night of my life." Something to be grateful for, even if it hurt like hell.

Which was when the idea came to her.

Gratitude. It was just one of the emotions she felt for Dare, and it was one he felt toward someone, too. His brother. Kyle.

So what about . . . Kylie?

Goose bumps broke out over her skin.

Dare had described him as tough, funny, generous, charming, loyal, and protective. Haven could do a whole lot worse than to name herself after someone like Kyle. And, in a way, she'd always carry a piece of Dare with her. That was kind of nice, too. And it wasn't like she had a family of her own to memorialize in any way.

She wrote the name down on the page.

Kylie

The more she thought about it, the more she liked it. It was young and fun, and sounded like it should belong to a woman who hadn't a care in the world. Haven would like to be those things, too.

She wrote it down again. Bigger this time.

Kylie

"I'm done," Haven said, certainty easing a little of that tender discomfort in her chest.

"How can you be done already?" Cora asked, leaning over.

Haven showed her the page.

"Kylie." Cora pressed her lips together as if considering, and then finally nodded. "That's cute. That's really cute. Like you. Totally fits." An eyebrow arched at her. "How'd you come up with something so perfect so fast?"

"It just came to me," Haven said. "And it feels right. Let's see your list. What are you thinking?"

"I'm thinking it's time to ditch the old-lady name," Cora said, staring at her paper.

"What, Cora? I've always loved your name. Pretty but tough. Like you." Haven shifted to sit closer.

Cora rolled her eyes. "What do you think?"

Scanning the list of names—Jessie, Tessa, Eve, Quinn, Nina, Cassidy, Alex/Alexandra, Kara—Haven tried to imagine using each one for Cora for the rest of their lives.

"I was trying to go for tougher names," Cora said with a shrug. "Names for a girl no one would push around."

The words drew Haven's gaze from the page. For a moment, she would've sworn that a troubled look shadowed Cora's eyes. "Are you worried about what's going to happen to us?"

With one blink, Cora's expression changed, and she smiled. "No, I'm not. It's gonna be good. I know it."

Haven nodded, taking strength from Cora like she always did. "I really like Quinn and Cassidy, though they're all really cool."

Cora quietly repeated the names to herself a few times. "You know what? I'm going with Cassidy. A Cassidy would be tough, fun, and sassy. That chick would know how to get shit done. Plus Cass is kinda cute."

"It really is. And I think you're totally right." Haven held out her hand. "Well, hi there. I'm Kylie."

Laughing, Cora played along and shook hands. "Hi, Kylie. I'm Cassidy, but everyone calls me Cass. Nice to meet you."

"Nice to meet you, too," Haven said, feeling lighter with the decision made—for both of them. "I think you and I are going to be good friends."

Cora winked. "The best. Now, let's go find Mr. Tall, Goth, and a Little Creepy and tell him who the hell we are."

CHAPTER 24

Hey, Bunny? You in here?" came a male voice from the kitchen doorway.

Haven looked up from where she and Cora were cutting a big tray of warm corn bread for dinner to see a Raven she wasn't sure she'd met before standing there with two boys. "Uh, hi," she said. "Bunny left a little while ago. Rodeo is sick, and she had to go get his prescription."

"Shit," the man said under his breath. With shoulder-length light brown hair, light hazel eyes, and a killer square jaw, the guy might've been handsome if those eyes didn't look so utterly lifeless. And Haven thought *she* carried the weight of the world.

"That's a quarter for the cuss jar, Dad," the younger boy said, peering up at his father. Haven guessed he was maybe six or seven.

The man tousled the boy's hair. "Sorry," he said with a long sigh.

"Maybe we can help you? I'm Haven and this is Cora," she said, a shot of nerves zinging through her belly at inserting herself where she hadn't been invited. But the guy looked at his wit's end. She finally noticed a name on his denim vest—Slider.

He dragged a hand through his hair. "I need a babysitter," he said, looking from Haven to Cora. "I'm on call overnight and I have a tow I need to do as soon as I can. My regular lady's not available, and Bunny sometimes helps me—"

"Dad," the older one said, "we can just ride along with you." Probably about ten, there was no denying that this boy was Slider's son, because he was his father's mirror image.

"Not on a school night, Sam. Besides, you know the company doesn't like that." Slider pulled out his cell.

"Oh, well," Haven said, looking at her friend, who gave a nod. "Do you want to leave them with us? Whoever is around will be having dinner soon, and then the boys can hang out until you come back."

"I appreciate that, but if it ends up busy, I don't know what time that would be. And Ben can't really sleep if he's not in his own bed." Slider gave the littler boy a squeeze on the shoulder, like he was letting him know he understood and it wasn't a problem. In just that one gesture, Slider offered his son more love and affection than Haven had received from her father her whole life. And it made her want to help.

"So you need someone to spend the night at your place with them?" Haven asked.

"Yeah," Slider said.

"Well, maybe we could do that, too." She looked at Cora, not wanting to volunteer her friend for something she didn't want to do.

"It's not like we're doing anything else," Cora said. Haven smiled, knowing she'd be game for it. "Do you live nearby?"

"'Bout ten minutes from here," Slider said, some of the concern bleeding from his expression.

Maverick came into the room behind Slider and the boys. "Yo, my main men," Mav said, doing some kind of funny handshake with Ben, who gave him a big grin. He turned to Sam next and held out his hand. "Don't hold out on me now."

Sam did the handshake, too, although it was clear the kid was humoring him. Both boys looked at Maverick like they idolized him, and it made Haven realize what a community all these people were to each other. A community she would've loved to have been a part of.

"How you been, Slider?" Maverick asked, moving to the refrigerator and grabbing a bottle of water.

"Same old," the other man said. His gaze shifted back to Haven. "So, uh, you two would really do this?"

Haven nodded. "If you're comfortable with it, I'd be happy to. We'd just need to grab some stuff for the night." Beside her, Cora nodded.

Maverick frowned. "Do what?"

"Watch the boys at my place tonight," Slider said. "I'm in a jam."

"Would that be okay?" Haven asked, looking at Maverick. "We won't go anywhere else." She knew the Ravens didn't want her and Cora going out in public, but they would hardly be doing that staying at Slider's house for a night.

"I don't see why not," Maverick said after a moment. "Let me just grab you some phone numbers in case you need any of us." He leaned toward the counter and snagged a crumb of corn bread off the platter with a wink, and then he left.

Haven walked over to the boys. "I'm Haven. Do you guys like chili? Should I pack us up some dinner to take to your place?" She glanced up at their father, who was watching her with a strange expression on his face.

"I love chili," Ben said, grinning up at her. "I'm Ben. I'm six."

"I'm Sam," the older boy said. "Chili would be great."

Cora stepped up beside them and introduced herself, too. "Why don't you pack the food and I'll throw an overnight bag together for us?"

"Sounds good," Haven said. "Should I pack some for you, Slider?"

"No," the man said, an air of impatience hanging around him.

"Okay. I'll be quick and then we can go." Haven busied herself by spooning chili from the massive Crock-Pot on the counter into plastic bowls, and then she wrapped up four pieces of her corn bread for them, too. Though Haven had made it, the chili had been Bunny's idea, because it was apparently Rodeo's favorite dish. Cora returned just as Haven found a brown paper bag in which to carry the food.

"Ready?" Slider asked.

"Yes, all done," Haven said, scooping the bag into her arms. "I should just find Maverick for that list of phone numbers." She didn't have to look far. Maverick found them in the big front lounge. And then they were heading out to Slider's pickup truck.

"Climb in the back, guys," he said to the boys. "Sorry the ride isn't nicer."

"It's no problem," Haven said, wanting to put him at ease. There was just such an aura of heaviness around the man. She hated to think what might've put it there. She and Cora rounded the back of the truck.

"You guys have any games?" Cora asked the boys.

"We have lots of games," Ben said, grinning at her as he climbed in the truck bed, Sam helping him.

"And do you mind getting beat by a girl?" she asked, smiling at them.

Both boys broke into a stream of taunts and laughter as Cora took the middle seat in the cab and Haven hopped in after her. The boys tapped on the glass, clearly still reacting to Cora's throw-down, though Haven couldn't hear what they were saying.

"Now we gotta make good on that threat," Haven said, elbowing Cora.

"I know, right?" Cora said.

"The boys love to play games," Slider said in a quiet voice as he backed out of the space. "So, thank you."

"You're welcome," Cora said. "Really, we've just been hanging around for a couple weeks, so this will be a nice change of pace."

He nodded and headed out of the parking lot. And Haven decided that Cora was right. It would be good to get away from the clubhouse for a little while. At least she'd have a night when she wouldn't have to worry about steering clear of Dare, although it wasn't like he'd come looking for her, either. Which was just as well, because she couldn't decide what would be worse—him trying to explain what he'd said or offering no explanation at all.

Now maybe she wouldn't have to find out.

TIRED FROM A day of doing maintenance down at the track, Dare and Jagger came into the clubhouse to find a handful of people around one of the tables in the mess hall.

"Aw, something smells fantastic," Dare said, clapping Maverick on the shoulder where he sat. "What's cooking?"

"Chili and corn bread," Maverick said. "Good, too. Better hurry before there's none left."

"You bastards better have saved us some," Jagger said to a round of laughter and gibes.

In the kitchen, Dare loaded his bowl up with chili, sour cream, tomatoes, and cheese, then grabbed himself two big squares of corn bread—which he couldn't help but wonder if Haven had made. Where was she, anyway? He'd barely seen her since she'd brought him breakfast the morning before. And like a fucking coward, he hadn't been particularly searching her out, either. Anything he might say at this point would just cause even more of a problem. He could tell her he hadn't meant it, but then he was admitting he did have feelings, which made no sense when he was sending her away. Or he could tell her he'd meant it but was sorry she'd heard him say it, which just made him an asshole all over again.

Lose-lose all the way around.

For fuck's sake.

"Think this new dust suppressant will be worth it?" Jagger asked, piling up his own bowl next to him.

They'd invested in a new treatment for the surface of their racetrack, one that promised to control dust, which made things safer for the drivers and more enjoyable for the fans. Some days, Dare could hardly believe how much he'd learned about racing and racetracks over the years. "We'll know Friday night," he said. "But it looks like it has potential, and if it works, it's gonna save us a shit-ton of money. So good on you for finding it."

"Thanks," Jagger said. "You know that track's my baby." Responsible for managing the maintenance and operation of the track, Jagger was one of a handful of Ravens who the club paid full-time for their services. The guy lived and breathed that racetrack and did a helluva job for the club.

Out in the mess hall, they dropped into seats at the table. "I'm surprised you aren't staking out Alexa's place," Dare said to Maverick.

"She has a class on Tuesday nights," he said. "I'll head there later."

Dare didn't comment on how well Maverick knew her schedule. "You been seeing anything when you've been over there?" he asked, knowing Mav had been spending all the time he could keeping an eye on her place the past few days.

"No," Maverick said, his expression dark.

"Well, no news is good news." Dare dug into his chili, which was spicy, thick, and full of flavor.

"Or it's just no news," his cousin said, shoving up from the table, empty bowl in his hand. He returned a few minutes later with a second helping. "Gonna miss Haven's cooking when she's gone."

The comment lodged a big ball of regret in the center of Dare's chest. Because he was going to miss a helluva lot more than that about her. For that matter, all the Ravens were going to miss her. Word had gotten out that all the sweets and some of the meals they'd been raving over the past few weeks were hers, and she had more than a few die-hard fans as a result. The Ravens might be hard asses, but they weren't complicated. Loyalty. Good lovin'. Good food. All of these were direct routes to a man's heart around here.

Certainly to his.

Which, *fuck*.

"Where is she, anyway?" Dare asked, hating the idea that what he'd said had driven her back to the solitariness of her room again. Just when she'd been coming out of her shell.

"At Slider's." Maverick ate a big spoonful.

Dare's gaze snapped up. "What?"

"She's at Slider's house," Maverick said.

"What the fuck is she doing at Slider's house?" Dare asked, something dark and needy rising up in his chest.

Maverick's brow arched in an expression full of *chill the fuck out*. "She's babysitting Sam and Ben. Cora's with her. Slider was in a bind, and I told them they could go. They'll spend the night there and be back tomorrow."

Dare didn't like it. He didn't like it one bit. He didn't like that she was out there on her own. He didn't like that she was at another man's house. And he didn't like the useless feelings of protectiveness and possessiveness welling up inside him. Because if he felt like this when she was temporarily ten minutes away, how the hell was he gonna feel when she and Cora were permanently relocated—and out of touch—seven states away?

And he sure as fuck didn't like how Maverick was looking at him, like he knew exactly where Dare's head was right now.

Four hours later, every one of those feelings had grown stronger until Dare was a ball of goddamned restlessness sitting at his desk. Despite the fact that he'd been parked there for a while, the pile of contracts he was supposed to be reading and signing hadn't gotten any smaller, because he couldn't concentrate worth shit.

Missouri. That's where Caine's contact would be setting up Haven and Cora with a whole new life. The logistics message had come in after dinner and distracted the hell out of Dare ever since.

All of which was why, within another hour, he found himself standing sentinel in the darkness outside of Slider's two-story white house, Dare's bike parked along the side of the road in the shadows of a big tree. Out of sight but close enough that he could see silhouettes move past the lit windows. Everything was quiet and peaceful. Including his damn head, now that he knew Haven was just fine. Thank you very much.

Christ, he was fucked six ways from Sunday, wasn't he?

The porch lights cast a golden glow over the barren flowerbeds that lined the front of the house and the badly faded wreath that hung on the front door. Both spoke to the loss this house, this family, had suffered. After Slider's wife had died, that once colorful garden never saw another flower, and the springtime wreath she'd hung had never been changed. It was like the house was frozen in time, or slowly but surely decaying under the weight of that loss—a description that equally fit the man who lived inside, too.

Standing there in the dark, Dare realized for the first time how much Slider's grief weighed on his own shoulders. Because he loved the guy like a brother and couldn't do a goddamned thing to make it better, to fix what was broken, or to help ease the guy's burden. Even if just a little.

And yet here was Haven, helping Slider. Finding a way to lighten his load. Helping someone she barely knew just because she could. Helping *his brother* in a moment of need, when she wasn't in the best of places herself. And the thing was, she wouldn't even know how meaningful helping Slider was. But Dare did, and the generosity and selflessness of her actions reached inside his chest and made things ache like a motherfuck. Gratitude, admiration, respect—he felt all of these for her. But that wasn't all, not by a long shot.

Around one o'clock, the house went dark. Dare kept telling himself he'd go in another five minutes, but he couldn't make himself do it. Which was why he was still there when the living room lights came on a little after three. Instinct told him that it was Haven who was in there awake and moving around. She'd told him she wasn't a very good sleeper, and he knew enough about what her life had been now to know exactly why. And hell if he didn't want to be the one who helped her finally find enough peace and security to give in to the pull and vulnerability of sleep.

That thought in his head, it took everything he had not to go knock on the door, but the last thing he wanted to do was scare her—or say something that would just make everything that much more complicated. And given how many times he'd taken her the night they'd stayed at his house, it was also crystal clear that he couldn't keep his hands off of her either. So he kept his ass planted in the shadows, just standing watch because his mind wouldn't let him do anything else.

And, truth be told, neither would his heart.

CHAPTER 25

Dare cleared out of Slider's place before the guy came home from the towing company's night shift. He didn't want Slider to think there was any reason he couldn't count on the women to take care of the boys on their own, nor did he want to explain to anyone why he felt the need to watch over them. Or, at least, over one of them.

Not having slept, the morning air rushing over his skin helped revive him, but what he really needed was a major infusion of caffeine and a belly full of sugar to jump-start his day. So he passed by the fast-food joints and the chichi coffeehouses on the strip leading into Frederick and made his way to his favorite local hole-in-the-wall—Dutch's. Renowned for its breakfasts, it was only open for breakfast and lunch, mostly because Dutch said he was too old to stand on his feet through a dinner service, too.

Dare found a parking spot on one of Frederick's quaint

downtown streets and made his way to the corner shop. Dutch's was a long, narrow place in the first floor of an old brick building. From the long Formica counter with its spinning stools to the big red-and-white booths to the jukebox on the wall, the interior was all old-time diner, though the restaurant had been there so long that it had probably seemed modern at some point.

"Dare Kenyon," came a booming voice. Dutch Henderson was already settling a mug and pouring a cup of coffee at one of the stools. "I haven't seen you in weeks."

Dare shook the older man's brown hand. Despite the fact that he tasted everything he made, Dutch was tall and thin, and the only thing that had changed on him in all the years Dare had known him was the color of his hair, from black to gray. "Been a crazy couple weeks, too," Dare said. "How's business?"

"Good, good. I'm just trying to keep up," Dutch said. "Getting my hip replaced next month. Can't put it off no more."

"Damn, I'm sorry to hear that. But you'll be good as new in no time," Dare said, taking a sip of the strong, hot coffee. Fucking perfect.

"The usual?" Dutch asked. He knew pretty much everyone in town and remembered what they liked to order, too.

"You know it," Dare said. While he waited for his food, he flipped through some e-mails and was pleasantly surprised to find a message from Marz detailing the vehicle registrations for Rhett Randall and all his men. Today was looking up already. He forwarded the info on to the club with a note to be on the lookout.

Then his gaze snagged on the dessert case. Dare slid off his stool and perused the small selection of sweets, thinking about all the things that Haven had made or talked about making. *This* was the kind of thing she needed to do with her life. Wherever they set her up, maybe he could look into finding her a place to open up a shop of her own.

"See something you want to try, hon?" one of the waitresses asked.

No was right on the tip of his tongue. "You know what, give me a chocolate chip and a peanut butter cookie," he said, making his way back to his seat.

"Here you go," the woman said, settling a plate in front of him.

Dare gave her a nod and picked up the peanut butter. Took a bite. It was decent. Before today, he might've thought it was good. Except Haven's fucking cookies were better. Richer in flavor, moister, and hers had chips, too. Same with the chocolate chip cookie. These were okay, but given how Haven's treats tasted, these could be better. Her talent made Dare proud of her, it really did.

It also cemented in Dare's mind that she had to have a chance to do this thing she was so good at. And if he helped her get started at it, maybe she would remember him for something more than the shit she'd overheard him saying the other morning. It shouldn't matter to him, but it did.

Because Haven mattered to him.

Dutch placed a plate of scrambled eggs, toast, bacon, and home fries in front of him. "Here you go."

"Thanks, Dutch." Dare dug into the grub, every bite making him feel a little more human. At some point, that night of no sleep was going to catch up to him, but for now, this would see him through.

"Green Valley opens back up this week, right?" Dutch asked, refilling coffee for a couple of customers farther down the counter.

"That's right," Dare said.

"Good. You know we missed it," Dutch said. The Ravens' races put money into other parts of Frederick—out-of-towners booked hotel rooms, ate in the restaurants, and did some sightseeing while they were here. The club hired locals to work the races, too—parking, concessions, and janitorial were all farmed out. Put all that together with the Ravens' mission to protect, and it was easy to see why the club got on well with the town and had the support of the business community most of the time. Dare made it a point for the Raven Riders to get along whenever he possibly could. It was good for business all the way around, particularly given that some of their business was a few shades shy of legal.

"I know," Dare said. "Hated to close down, but it was unavoidable. Shouldn't happen again." The three weeks most of the club had been in Baltimore had made holding the races impossible, and then it had taken them two more to get the schedule up and running again. Dare couldn't think of a time in all his years when they'd had to close down for so long before. He sure as hell hoped they never had cause for it to happen again.

Dutch nodded as he put the coffeepot back on its warmer. "I was hoping to make it out, but I don't do so good walking on uneven surfaces right now. Damn hip."

"Tell you what. You come out, you call me and let me know," Dare said as he pulled a card from his wallet and pushed it across the counter. "I'll have someone meet you at your car with a golf cart and escort you up to the track. I'll have VIP seating waiting for you and Shirley. On the house."

The man's face went almost comically surprised for a moment. "That's a helluva offer," Dutch said, pocketing the card. "I just might take you up on that."

"I hope you do," Dare said, giving the old man a smile. Dutch was good fucking people.

An older couple got up from the far end of the bar, and Dare happened to glance to his right in time to see the look of disapproval on the woman's face as she eyed him—or, more likely, his colors—the patch and insignia on his cut. It didn't bother Dare none. Not everyone understood what motorcycle clubs were about, and even a lot of people who *thought* they did had gotten a very particular view of them from television shows and cable news. And, anyway, even in a town as small as Frederick, you couldn't expect everyone to like you, now could ya?

Dare cleaned his plate and threw a twenty down on the counter. "I'm heading out, Dutch. Hope to see you Friday night."

From where he stood clearing dishes at the end of the bar, Dutch waved. "Me too. Ride safe."

Dare smiled, because Dutch had offered that same farewell as long as Dare had known the man. "Always do." He stepped out into the morning feeling more ready to face the day. Which was good, because the days immediately before a race were always a blur of activity and unexpected fires that needed to be put out. Jagger handled the lion's share of it, but Dare helped however he could and whenever he was needed.

After all, race night running like clockwork equaled money pouring in, and after taking a month off, the club needed Friday night to run like a well-oiled machine. And it was Dare's job as president to make sure it was fucking so.

HAVEN WAS GLAD she was going to be here to experience one of the Raven Riders' races. It would be just one more thing she would have to carry with her from this place that she'd come to love. And apparently one part of race day was food. Lots and lots of it. Food for the Ravens preparing for the race and working race day, food for their guests, food for the after-party. Which meant Haven was right in her element as she and Cora rolled up their sleeves and pitched in however Bunny needed them to.

She and Cora had seen Sam and Ben off on the school bus, and then Slider had come home and brought the women back to the clubhouse first thing this morning. The boys were ornery and funny and sweet beyond belief, and they'd all had a total ball hanging out. Back in Georgia, some of her father's men had been in the habit of dropping their kids off for her to watch, so she'd spent a surprising amount of time around kids. And she'd loved it. She'd loved their innocence and their joy and their playfulness. Being around them felt hopeful, like anything was possible. And though the assumption that Haven was there to be used annoyed her, she didn't mind watching the kids—because in addition to the fun distraction they provided, she knew she was keeping them from being left alone or put in positions kids shouldn't be put in. Sam and Ben had reminded Haven how much she enjoyed kids— and made her actually contemplate having her own for the first time, now that she was free from that environment. So Slider's boys would be another part of the big puzzle that made up the Ravens, which Haven already knew she was going to miss.

Gah. She was being a total sap. It wasn't like she was ever meant to be a part of these people's lives. She'd *always* just been passing through.

A client, Dare had called her. A client like every other.

Whatever. She threw herself into the work, glad for the distraction from how fast the days seemed to be flying by.

And from the fact that she hadn't seen Dare more than in passing in almost three days.

By the time dinner rolled around, Haven was achy from standing on her feet all day, but she'd also had a ton of fun hanging in the kitchen with Bunny and Cora, a few Raven wives who stopped by to help or drop off dishes and platters, and the occasional Raven who dared to try to sneak a bite and risked the smack of Bunny's wooden spoon. That lady was *tough*. And awesome. The kind of woman Haven wanted to be. Which was why Haven loved her.

Haven loved . . . so much about the Ravens.

The three of them took their dinners in the kitchen to keep an eye on the variety of dishes they had going—the trays of lasagna Bunny was baking, the cinnamon roll dough Haven was preparing, the meatballs simmering in the giant Crock-Pot. Cora had prepared huge vegetable and fruit platters, and followed Haven's quickly dashed-off recipes for several types of cookie dough, also waiting to be baked. The big kitchen was like an assembly line, and they still had a lot to do.

A bunch of guys brought dirty dishes into the kitchen, signaling that dinner out in the mess hall had come to an end. Done with her own meal, Haven went out into the mess hall to help clean up. Dare sat at the head of one of the tables, head thrown back in laughter, Maverick, Phoenix, and Jagger next to him laughing just as hard.

God, Dare was freaking hot.

Really fucking hot. Say it. Tell me how hot it is.

The memory of his words licked over her skin and made her suck in a breath.

And then Dare's gaze landed on Haven, hot and direct, and she felt it like he'd reached across the room and touched her. And, God, how she wished he had. Because, yeah. With his darkly handsome face, that mess of brown hair she knew was so soft, and that harsh mouth that gave her so much pleasure, Dare Kenyon was really fucking hot. Even if his words had crushed her heart.

Ducking her head, Haven grabbed as much as she could off the table and retreated into the kitchen. The thing was, unlike weeks ago when being in his presence scared her, now she craved it, even knowing nothing would come of it—that *he* wouldn't let anything come of it. Not anymore.

She went back out for another load, and Cora followed, just in time to hear Phoenix shout into his cell phone, "Who the fuck is this?" He wasn't playing.

The room went deadly quiet, the words freezing the maybe ten remaining Ravens in place as every eye focused on the head of the table.

Phoenix mouthed something to Dare, then said into the phone, "What are you talking—"

Dare's expression was rank anger and outrage, and it knotted Haven's stomach for reasons she didn't understand. "Give me the phone," Dare bit out. He pressed a button and held the phone out in his hand. "This is Dare Kenyon, Raven Riders' president. Who the fuck is this?"

"Ah, Dare," came a man's voice through the speaker. "This is Dominic Hauer. We met on Monday. Turns out we have more business, just like I thought we would." The menace in the man's voice, the grim expressions on the Ravens' faces—all of it had Haven's heart racing and dread prickling across her skin.

"Our business is done," Dare said, ice in his tone. She'd never heard his voice sound so . . . deadly.

"Turns out, not so much. You see, we now find ourselves in possession of something I think you're going to be interested in."

Dare made eye contact with Phoenix, who shrugged and shook his head. "Fine. I'll bite. What would that be?"

Next to him, Maverick, Caine, and Jagger sat forward, jaws clenched, muscles tense.

"Information that the Churchmen held two women in their possession worth fifty grand in cold hard reward to some redneck down in Georgia. Well, a hundred thou now. And we've recently made acquaintance with this fine gentleman."

Haven slapped her hand over her mouth to smother her gasp as Dare's gaze collided with hers. *Oh, God. Ohgodohgod.* Her father . . . her father was nearby. And willing to pay . . . a hundred thousand dollars to get her back?

"And I care about this why?" Dare asked, the nonchalance and disinterest so convincing in his voice.

"Because you have them."

The words hung there, and Haven almost went wobbly on her feet. Except hands caught her, supported her. Cora on one side and Bunny on the other. When the older lady had come out from the kitchen, Haven didn't know.

"Hang in there," Bunny whispered into her ear.

"I don't traffic in women. That shit was all the Church Gang," Dare said. Tension and anticipation filled the room so thick you could've cut it with a knife. And Haven . . . guilt and embarrassment consumed her. That she'd brought this danger to them. That she'd ever withheld the information about the reward.

"Yes, and what *you* do is take in women in trouble. Like the two rescued out of the Churchmen's storage facility. Took me a little digging to find out that fact, but once I did, I no longer really needed to know who you were working with at that gun deal. Whoever it was, we know they also raided the storage facility. And you make the most sense for where those women went. Sound interesting yet?"

Dare heaved a breath and his face went serious, shuttered, emotionless, even the anger bled out of his expression. He was all do-or-die business. Eyes narrowed, jaw clenched, it was the most intimidating Haven had ever seen him look. She took a little comfort from it, because if anyone could handle this, Dare could.

Please, I can't go back.

"And if I am interested?" Dare asked.

A small chuckle came through the line. "Then you'll need to decide how interested you are. Because you've got forty-eight hours to beat the reward, or I send the redneck your way and collect the hundred K from him. Makes no difference to me. Though I suspect it does to you."

"And how do I know he and his crew aren't already on their way here?" Dare met Maverick's gaze, and the other man gave him a tight nod. Haven was quite possibly going to lose the dinner she'd just eaten.

"Because I'm telling you they're not. The deal on Monday went smooth and we did what we said we would. I'd hope that would buy me a little good faith."

"That would be easier if you weren't blackmailing me for six figures," Dare bit out.

"This isn't blackmail. This is business. We need cash. We have two sources to get it. Which one is entirely up to you," Dominic said.

Dare didn't flinch. "Fine. Make it seventy-two hours. I can't pull that kind of cash together in forty-eight."

Haven wrapped an arm around her stomach. *Dare* was going to have to pay a hundred thousand dollars for her freedom? On top of everything else he'd done and was doing to set up their new lives? The room spun around her.

"You'll need to make that extra day worth my while," Dominic said. "We're not the only one chasing down these skirts. Time is not on your side."

"Done. I'll have it by twelve noon on Saturday. You can name the drop spot," Dare said.

"That's a plan I can live with. Talk to you Friday with the details. Dare." The phone went dead.

Dare threw Phoenix's cell to the table in a clatter. He shoved up out of his chair, the legs screeching against the floor, and braced his hands on the table. And then he rose to his full height and scanned his gaze over the Ravens.

"Threat level is officially critical. Maverick, get everyone in and assign guard duty at all the usual locations. Everyone needs to ride hot." Nods all around the room. "Jagger, head down to the sheriff's office and share the intel on Randall, his crew, and their vehicle information. Tell them we've got protectees in imminent danger. Martin owes us for what went down with his niece, so I don't see any issue getting them on board."

As Jagger nodded, Haven was torn between terror and solace at Dare's calm, calculating command of the situation.

"Caine," Dare continued, "we need that documentation and the relocation arrangements in place by Friday." Friday? She'd have to leave on Friday?

"Shit, Dare," the guy said, stone-cold rage in his voice. "Monday was already pushing it."

"Do or pay whatever the fuck you have to." Dare raised an eyebrow.

"I hear you," Caine said with a nod.

"Want me to call in the Brothers' help for Friday?" Phoenix asked, though who he was referring to, Haven didn't know. What she did know was how much trouble they were going to. For her.

"Was thinking the same thing," Jagger said. "We need to be prepared for anything. More boots on the ground will help."

Dare nodded. "Good thinking. Do it."

Haven hung on every word, just trying to wrap her head around everything that was happening. Dare hadn't looked at her once, and all she could think was what an utter pain in the ass she'd become for him . . . and for all of the Ravens. "I don't want anything to happen to you," she forced herself to say. "To any of you. I'll just go tonight. If you could loan me bus money, I'll just go wherever the next bus heading far away takes me."

Dare finally looked at her, his gaze so hot she was surprised it didn't scorch her clothes. "The plan stays the same, just accelerated. Don't you worry about a thing."

Nods all around the room, which was when Haven noticed that every man there was looking at her with a fierce protectiveness in his eyes. She didn't see an ounce of irritation directed her way, and it made her heart feel too big for her chest. Finally, she gave a small nod.

"Church will meet at nine o'clock tomorrow morning," Dare said, looking at Maverick. "Spread the word."

"Will do," Maverick said.

"Good, then get to it." Dare's words sent the room into a flurry of motion. Jagger and Phoenix asked Dare questions, while Maverick gathered a group of guys in the corner, their heads bent together as he spoke. Caine stalked out of the room, his cell pressed to his ear. Haven thought she might be having an out-of-body experience, because though she was in the room, she felt apart from it, like she was floating somewhere and watching the whole thing from afar.

"Hey. Hey, Haven," came a voice from beside her.

She blinked and turned to find Bunny staring at her, a look of motherly concern on her face. "Don't you worry, hon. These guys have your back. Don't doubt it for a second."

"Yeah," Cora said. "If anyone can handle your dad, it's the Ravens." Though Cora's expression was quite possibly the most worried Haven ever remembered seeing.

"It's too much," Haven whispered, shaking her head. "This is all too much to expect anyone to do."

"Not for one of our own," Bunny said. "That's what this place is all about."

The words nearly broke Haven's heart. "But I'm not," she said with a small shrug. "I'm not one of you. I'm leaving."

Bunny pressed her lips together in a tight line. "Well, it makes no difference. Dare's gonna handle this no matter what."

As if her words drew him across the room, Dare appeared beside Bunny. He grasped Haven's hand. "She's right. Come with me," he said.

His skin against hers felt so perfect that Haven would've followed him anywhere, so she didn't ask a question or offer the slightest resistance as he pulled her through the kitchen and out onto the back porch illuminated by the very last light of day.

The screen door had no more slammed shut than Haven found herself pressed up against the wall. Dare was *all* over her. His hands in her hair, his hips pinning hers, his mouth coming down on hers hard. Given the things he'd said, maybe she should've pushed him away. But she couldn't. She didn't want to. In that moment, the threat against her freedom and her very life made everything else unimportant.

Claiming, devouring, penetrating, there was something so soothing in the roughness of his kiss. She couldn't breathe, she couldn't think, she couldn't move, and she didn't care at all. Because she felt like she hadn't had a deep breath since the last time their lips had met, and, once again, Dare had known exactly what she needed. As much as the deep demands of his kisses left her head spinning, they also made her feel stronger, more able to handle this new blow. So as her arms wrapped around his neck, she surrendered everything he wanted—and maybe some things he didn't. Because she'd never been more certain that she'd fallen in love with Dare Kenyon than she was right at that very moment.

"Christ, Haven," he rasped around the edge of a kiss. He was rock hard against her stomach. "I'm so fucking sorry."

"What for?" she asked, breathless and more turned on than she'd ever been in her life.

He shook his head. "Everything. Just fucking everything." He grasped the sides of her face in his big hands and rested his forehead against hers. His eyes absolutely blazed at her. "I will keep you safe. I will give you the life you deserve. I promise."

"I know," she said. She didn't doubt him. Not at all. If it was within his power, she knew he would.

"You do?" he asked.

"Of course," she said. "I believe in you, Dare. No matter what."

He stroked his hands down her hair, smoothing his palms over her neck and shoulders. Like he couldn't stop touching her. Like he *had* to touch her. As much as she needed to touch him.

"I've got shit I need to jump on, but I wanted to make sure you were okay."

She wasn't. Not really. "I really could go tonight," she said. "I hate that anyone here could get hurt, or that you'd be on the hook for so much. For me."

He cupped her face in his hand, and his thumb dragged across her cheekbone once, twice. "We got this."

"Okay," she said on a long exhale.

"Okay?" He arched a brow, exuding so much confidence that all she could do was agree.

"Yeah."

He kissed her again, a long, drawn-out meeting of lips and tongue that left her wanting more. Always more, with him. "Then I'll find you later."

CHAPTER 26

Dare found Maverick sitting at the desk in his office, his fingers flying over the keys. They had a 911 e-mail alert system that sent e-mail and text messages to every man in the club, and it was the easiest way to get urgent information out fast. Sitting in one of the chairs, Phoenix had his cell to his ear, deep in discussion with Walker Harrison, president of the Brothers of Steel MC, headquartered about two hours away in West Virginia.

Dropping into the wooden chair next to Phoenix, Dare braced his elbows on his knees and scrubbed at his face. What a clusterfuck this whole thing was, though on some level he wasn't surprised. He'd known for weeks now that Baltimore wasn't done with them and that shit was playing out right now, just like his gut had told him it would. Because sometimes the past just wouldn't fucking die.

The only thing he hadn't counted on was that Haven would be at the center of the danger.

Sonofabitch.

But now at least he knew exactly what the threat was. Dominic and these Iron Cross fuckers. And Rhett Randall and however many men he had at his side.

"Thanks, Walker. We'll see you Friday," Phoenix said, and then he hung up.

"They're in?" Dare asked.

"A hundred percent," Phoenix said. The Brothers were a newer, smaller MC that the Ravens occasionally crossed paths with, since they rode and lived in the same general region. Eager to build their reputation, the Brothers sometimes did business with the Ravens and had almost always followed the Ravens' lead when the chips were down.

And they were fucking down. Right now.

Maverick punched a key and turned toward them. "Word's out. I'll handle assigning people as they make their way in."

"Good," Dare said, looking his cousin in the eye. If he had to walk through hell, there was no one he'd rather do it with. "I need to catch Doc up on all this."

"Before you do," Maverick said, looking from Dare to Phoenix and back again, "we really paying this money?" Skepticism was plain in his voice.

That right there was the hundred-thousand-dollar question, wasn't it? Dare shook his head. "Fuck, no." It wasn't that he didn't have the money. And it wasn't that he wouldn't pay it for Haven if he had to, because he would. In a heartbeat. Hell, he'd do it for anyone they took under their wing, because they knew the risks involved with taking on the world's lowlifes.

"That's what I'm talking about," Phoenix said, nodding.

Maverick's expression took on a grim satisfaction, and not a little relief. "So what's your play?"

"Caine gets us the identity documentation and relocation logistics on Friday. We move the women as soon as we have it. Friday night, we cancel Saturday's exchange and tell Dominic—"

"He can go fuck himself," Phoenix interjected.

Dare nodded. "That, too. We tell him to send Randall our way if that's what he needs to do. And then we take care of the threat that's going to keep on coming whether we pay off the Iron Cross or not. Paying them not to talk isn't going to keep Haven's father from finding her if that's what he's intent on doing. He's too close as it is."

Maverick nodded. "That's right. The Iron Cross is a distraction in all this."

"Exactly," Dare said.

Phoenix shifted in his seat. "You think this Dominic fucker's just gonna take that?"

"No," Dare said. This whole train of thought had been spinning in his head since the phone call ended a half hour ago. "I think these assholes are gonna be a burr in our saddles from here on out. The question is whether we want to do something about them, too, because this sonofabitch is too fucking big for his skinhead britches. But I think we have a couple days' breather on deciding. We'll talk about it in Church tomorrow."

Both men nodded.

"How's Haven?" Maverick asked.

"She's tougher than she thinks she is," Dare said, swallowing hard. He'd hated the terror that paled her face as the call took place. And he hated Dominic for putting it there, for treating her like a pawn, and for trying to get him to do the same. It had taken everything he had not to go to her side as they'd strategized an immediate response. There'd been no way he could stay away after. Dare had needed to touch her, hold her, prove to himself that she was still there and unharmed.

Prove to himself that he hadn't failed her. And wouldn't. Because he couldn't handle failing someone else he loved, like he had before.

Loved? Yeah. Fuck.

He'd promised Haven safety, a fresh start, a new life away from violence and chaos. And he was going to keep his word. It didn't matter what it cost him—not his money, not his time, not his heart.

"You know," Maverick said, "if the plan is to take out her father, maybe there's no reason—"

"There's every reason," Dare said, knowing where Maverick was headed, because a part of his brain had been playing with the idea, too. If her father was out of the picture, maybe Haven didn't have to leave. Except it wasn't that goddamned simple, and Dare wasn't taking any chances of her falling into the wrong hands if things didn't go as planned. The consequences would be too dire for her. "Even assuming this thing with her father goes down like we want it, we are always involved in some shit here. Always. And now we've got the Iron Cross breathing down our necks, with her at the center of the conflict, which is going to lead to who knows what. That woman has been a prisoner of her father for the last eight years. He abused her and controlled her every way he could. She deserves a life free from violence, free from danger, free from all this bullshit," Dare said, raking at his hair. His gut gave a big old check that he ignored like a motherfucker.

Maverick held his hands up in a gesture of surrender. "I hear ya. I get it. Just wanted to make sure . . ."

Dare glared at his cousin. Like he wouldn't have thought about it. "All right. Lemme call Doc before it gets much later. I want him to hear the bulk of this from me." Because his grandfather wouldn't be happy about the way this was all going to go down. One way or the other, the Ravens were going to have to cross some lines.

But sometimes, that's just what you had to do.

HAVEN HADN'T EVEN tried to sleep. She knew there wasn't any chance of that happening, not when every little sound had her jumping with the possibility that it might be her father—there to take her prisoner again, there to force her back to a life she'd rather die than have to lead. Especially now that she'd had a taste of something more, of something free, of something that was even beautiful.

She couldn't go back.

Instead, Haven baked. Because that's what she did when her brain was too loud to let her rest. And it felt better to be useful than to be a burden. Which was exactly how she felt.

"Let's go to bed," Cora said, scooping fresh cookies off a baking sheet and laying them out to cool. Her eyes were bleary, her face pale. Unlike Haven, Cora was not a night owl, and it was nearly one in the morning.

Laying out balls of dough on a sheet of her own, Haven shook her head. "You go ahead."

Cora had been trying to talk her into taking a break for the past two hours, but Haven had promised Bunny she'd get some things done before the morning. And going upstairs was pointless anyway. Yawning loudly, Cora finished what she was doing and joined Haven at the counter. "It's gonna be okay, you know?"

"I hope so," Haven said. But did she know it? No. Because she knew her father too well. He was a man who didn't like to lose, to be disrespected, to be made to look the fool. And she'd done all three to him when she'd run away. He wouldn't stop until he had her.

"Haven—"

"You should go up," Haven said, dropping her spoon into the bowl of dough and forcing a smile. Cora had been trying to cheer her up since they'd overheard Dare's phone call. But Haven was so angry at the unfairness of the entire situation that she was afraid she'd take her friend's head off simply because she'd be a convenient target. Being alone to seethe would be best all the way around. "I'm not going to sleep feeling like this, and it makes me feel worse to know you're staying awake just to keep me company."

"That's what best friends do," Cora said, giving her a small smile.

"Which is why I'm telling you to go to sleep. Because you're my best friend, too. So let me take care of you, because unlike me, you don't do well without sleep. Staying busy makes me feel better. You know that. I'll be okay. Really."

Cora yawned again and her eyes watered. "Ugh, I'm sorry."

"Don't be," Haven said. "We got a lot done today. We made a good team. The two of us and Bunny."

"We did," Cora said. "Okay. But if you need me, wake me up. Any time. Promise?"

"I promise."

Holding out her arms, Cora said, "Come here."

Haven returned the hug. "I'm sorry I'm so moody."

"Oh my God, Haven," Cora said, pulling away. "You're entitled to be freaking pissed at this whole situation. You don't have to apologize to me. I'm pissed for you."

Tears pricked at the backs of Haven's eyes, and she blinked quickly to hold them back. "Thank you."

Cora nodded. "See you in the morning."

"Yeah."

Alone in the kitchen, Haven threw herself back into her

work with more banging and slamming than was strictly necessary. Cookies. *This is so unfair.* Cinnamon rolls. *I hate my father so much.* Muffins. *I can't believe this is happening.* A couple of pans of brownies. *I am so freaking angry I could scream.*

When she was done, she stared at the rolling pin for a long time, imagining the damage she could do with it if she ever got within swinging range of her father. Sick and twisted? Maybe. She didn't feel bad about it, though.

Finally, Haven loaded the dishwasher and washed what wouldn't fit until her fingers pruned. She was just loading a bunch of cooled cookies into a big plastic container when the door to the kitchen swung open behind her.

She turned on a gasp. "Dare. Hey," she said, hoping her voice didn't sound as startled as she felt.

"Didn't mean to scare you," he said. Tall, dark, and brooding, he was rough sex on legs, even if he seemed to have darker-than-usual circles under his eyes.

She blew out a breath, irritated at her fear. "It's okay." Although it didn't feel okay. None of this did. And she was so . . . freaking . . . pissed.

"No, it's not," Dare said, advancing on her like a lion on its prey. "None of this is okay." He got right up in her space, crowding her against the sink.

She stared at him a long moment, her insides nearly shaking with rage, and then she let the truth fly. "Okay, you're right. None of this is okay." She shook her head, trying to rein herself in. "What are you still doing up?"

He searched her face. "Could ask you the same thing."

Haven shrugged. "I can't sleep on a good day, let alone when I feel like this."

"Like what?" he asked.

She crossed her arms. "Scared. Pissed. No, so freaking mad it feels like I might explode apart."

"Haven—"

She pushed around him, restless and needing space. "I mean, shit, why does everyone in my life find me so hard to want and to love?" she asked, the question spilling out of her as she started pacing. "My mother just walked away when I was a baby and left me in what she knew was a bad situation, or she wouldn't have run away herself. And my father never looked at me as anything more than a nuisance or a possession, something he could use or sell to the highest bidder." The words represented her ancient, most fundamental hurts, and saying them was like purging a sickness from deep, deep inside.

Dare grasped her arm. "Haven, what your parents did has nothing to do with you being lovable—"

"Oh, really?" she said, yanking her arm free and spinning on him. "And this coming from the man who said it would be better for everyone when I'm gone, who said he wasn't serious about me and I wasn't anything special." She glared at him, the anger she'd been trying to beat back all night welling up inside her and finding a target.

Dare froze for a moment, and then his shoulders sagged. "Shit," he said, raking his hand through his hair. "I'm an asshole."

Strange laughter bubbled out of Haven. "Uh, yeah. A confusing asshole, at that. Kissing me one minute, pushing me away the next. Cuddling me one minute, telling your closest friends I'm nothing to you the next." In some distant part of her mind, Haven tried to tell herself to stop. Did she really want to spend her last hours fighting with him? When she had so few left? But now that her anger had escaped, she couldn't stuff it back down.

"Haven," he said, stepping closer.

"No," she yelled, moving back against the opposite

302 • Laura Kaye

counter. She pointed at him, a silent command for him to stay put.

He did. "You're right. I'm an asshole for all of that. And for lying to the guys about you."

"Lying," she repeated, weighing the word on her tongue. She scoffed.

Dare nodded, the circles under his eyes darker, his face a shade paler. Tired. "It's true. I didn't mean what I said to them. And I hated that you overheard me say it."

Shaking her head, Haven resisted the words. Believing them would just open her up again. Open her up for more hurt.

"I didn't mean it," he said again. He took a small step closer.

She threw her hands out in exasperation. "Then why did you say it? And why did you let the words stand until now if you didn't mean them? Why would you let me believe them?" Giving voice to the questions that had been weighing on her drained away some of her anger.

"I said it because I didn't want to admit that I cared," he said, coming closer. "Because then I'd have to admit that letting you go was going to fucking suck." Closer. "And I let you believe it because I hoped maybe, somehow, it would make it easier for you to leave and for me to watch you go." Closer still until he stood an arm's reach away.

She shook her head. "Don't tell me what you think I want to hear."

Suddenly he was right up in her face. "I didn't mean it. You are special to me. *Very* special. And I *am* interested, even more than I should be, given our age difference and my general moody disposition and your innocence and all the good things you deserve. And I don't fucking think it will be better for me for you to go, but it will be better for *you*. Safer. The fresh start I promised and you deserve after everything you've been through. That's not a line, that's the God's honest truth. On my mother's and brother's graves." His expression was fierce, his eyes blazing.

Haven's heart was a runaway train in her chest. His declarations were thrilling and healing. He'd never invoke his mother and brother that way if he didn't mean it—she believed that down into her very soul. Not that she knew what to do with what he'd said. It didn't change the fact that she was going away. Soon. She shook her head, exhaustion settling over her and calming the fight inside her. "Okay."

"Okay?" he asked, an eyebrow arched. "That's it?"

"I don't know what else to say," she said. "Thank you for telling me."

His whole face frowned. "Don't thank me. Not for that."

"Then what do you want?" she asked, meeting his intense gaze.

"You, Haven. Always you. I'm fucking *starving* for you. All the time. You think you're not wanted? *I* want you. I want you so much I don't know what I'm doing half the time. Every minute of every day, all I can think about is you." Breathing hard, eyes flashing, Dare loomed over her, the words hanging in the tight space between them.

And they were the most amazing, life-giving words anyone had ever said to her. Which made her know exactly what to say. "Then have me."

At first, he didn't react, but then Dare leaned in slow, so maddeningly slow that Haven thought she might die before his skin brushed hers. But for all that slowness, the instant their lips collided, a flashfire ignited. His mouth claimed hers, hard and urgent, and she gave back as good as she could—grasping his hair, pulling him deeper, sucking his tongue until he was groaning and rock hard against her belly.

"Can't go slow," he rasped, pinning her against the counter.

"Don't," she said. "Don't hold back." She wanted him just like this—raw and rough and real.

He jerked her jeans open and pushed them down until she could step out of them. "No one's around right now," he breathed harshly into her ear as he bared himself, shoving his jeans down his thighs. His cock fell heavy and hot against her belly.

"I don't care if they are," she said. And she didn't, not in that moment, maybe not ever. She was leaving, after all. In less than two days, now.

"Aw, feel that pussy." Two of his fingers slipped between her thighs, stroked at her clit, spread the wetness he drew out of her. Haven moaned and thrust her hips forward, so on edge from the fight and her anger and his words, and from wanting him and thinking she'd never have him again, that she felt close to exploding. "Gotta get in you," he said.

"Please," she whispered.

Dare found a condom in his wallet and rolled it on, and then he kissed her deeply while he pushed his cock between her legs. He grasped and lifted her thigh, hooking it on his hip. And then he bent his knees, angled his hips, and penetrated her inch by achingly good inch until he'd given her everything he had.

A groan ripped out of his throat when he bottomed out inside her, and then his hips were flying, the strokes fast and deep, his hold on her thigh and the back of her neck tight and almost bruising. Holding onto him, too, she wasn't complaining, because being needed, being claimed, being wanted—even if it was all temporary—was still the best thing she'd ever known. And she'd carry the memories of these stolen moments with Dare for the rest of her life.

Their foreheads together, their hair wild around their faces, their harsh breaths caressing one another's lips—it was all beautiful to her. Beautiful beyond anything she'd ever known—and Dare was the one who gave that to her. He'd told her once that she could find beauty in the world, and he'd been right.

It was him, all along.

His cock filled and stroked her so deliciously, and his pubic bone smacked against hers again and again and again until she was holding her breath and straining, straining for release.

The orgasm hit her like a shock wave, throwing her head back and knocking her knee out from under her so that Dare had to hold her full weight. Her breath exploded out of her on a long cry as her fingers dug into his shoulders, seeking an anchor in the storm of him.

"Fuck, yeah," he growled, his hard, grinding strokes crashing over her. "Fucking come all over me."

"Oh, God," she rasped, shaking and light-headed. "I wish you could come in me. I would die to feel that."

"Jesus Christ," he rasped, his mouth coming down hard on hers. And then he was groaning into the rough kiss as his cock jerked inside her. He moved through his release, his hips slowing, his body shaking, his face the most gorgeous thing she'd ever seen.

On a long exhale, he eased out of her and let go of her leg. But he didn't let go of her. Dare wrapped his arms around her shoulders and pulled her tight against him until they were touching from knees to forehead, her face buried in the crook of his neck, his hand stroking the back of her hair. His pulse raced against her cheek, and it was such a rush to know she wasn't the only one so affected by what they'd done. They stood like that for a long time, him just holding her, stroking her, soothing her.

Finally, he released her with a soft kiss and disposed of the condom, and then he helped her on with her jeans.

"Are you okay?" she asked, taking in the more-pronounced circles under his eyes.

"Sure. Why?" he asked, his voice even grittier than usual.

"You look tired, is all," she said with a shrug. "What are you doing now?"

"Not sure." He leaned down to look right in her eyes and stroked his fingers through the side of her hair, tucking it behind her ear. It made her chest balloon with emotion. She adored how he always got so close to her, like he couldn't stand the distance between them any more than she could. Like he craved being all over her. Like he couldn't breathe when they weren't touching.

Because that was how she felt.

"Lay down with me for a little while?" Something told her he needed it as much as she did.

Dare took her hand in his and pulled her from leaning against the counter. "That sounds like heaven."

CHAPTER 27

ists and knees in the afternoon breeze, Dare and Maverick rode the circuit of guards they'd put into place. Dare's thoughts raced as he and Mav checked on positioning, brainstormed contingency plans, and made sure their guys were ready for anything.

They were.

Still, dark anticipation hung over Thursday like a motherfucker, and the only thing that got Dare through was the five hours of peace he'd found in Haven's arms. Her soft, affectionate touch had given his tired body solace. The tightness with which she'd held him had quieted his mind like nothing else. The trust she'd placed in him after he'd messed up so badly humbled him and just leveled him to the ground.

But when he'd woken up, he'd still had only one thought in mind—he couldn't keep her.

He couldn't subject her to a constant run of danger and

conflict. The Ravens' protective mission made enemies out of the abusers they guarded their clients against. The longtime tensions with gangs in Baltimore over lucrative sports-betting territory clearly hadn't died with the Churchmen, and being involved in betting meant being involved in debt collection, too. And that could be a dirty fucking business. Sporadic scuffles with other MCs wanting to build their reps or expand their territory cropped up here and there. And even their trucking escort business occasionally earned them enemies out of those who coveted—or tried to steal—the cargoes they protected.

That was *his* life. He'd chosen to live with those risks. She hadn't. More important, she'd lived with danger and risk enough these past eight years. That was really all he needed to know.

Despite the fact that she gave him things no other person ever had. And made him feel things he didn't think he'd had in him. His head might've been settled on the right path forward for her, but his heart felt like it was caught in the middle of something he didn't understand. Frankly, maybe it was better if it stayed that way.

Coward.

Maybe.

But the last time he'd loved someone—unabashedly, unreservedly loved someone—he'd lost them. More than that, it'd been his fault. And every time he'd gotten too close to untangling the bullshit in his heart these past days, the pain of that loss jolted through him in reminder. So it was better this way. Better to *ensure* she was safe than chance her life so he might know love. If fighting the fall made him a fucking coward, so be it.

He'd left her still sleeping, a kiss on her hair his silent good-bye.

Dare heaved a deep breath as he and Maverick sped along a country road heading back toward the compound. The warm breeze rushed over his skin, but the ride didn't bring him the solace it normally did.

Thankfully, the day had been too damn busy to let him sit and spin on things that shouldn't matter, like whether he should've left a note to say good-bye, like whether she'd found the same comfort in him that he had in her, like whether she was wishing she could stay.

Sonofabitch.

He had more immediate things to think about anyway. Dare couldn't stop running through the events of the day in his mind, looking for things he'd forgotten, searching for other things he could yet do. This morning, Church had gone smooth as glass despite the buzz of adrenaline in the air. Everyone was on the same page where handling the Randall threat was concerned. Everyone was ready to do what they had to do—including to the Iron Cross, when that day came.

Jagger delivered the good news that the sheriff's office was on board, which was a relief given that the Ravens walked a very fine line in their relationship with them— sometimes helping them out under the table with things the law couldn't, and asking for a little looking the other way in return where the Ravens' business practices were concerned. And, after apparently applying some pressure where it counted, Caine had delivered the even better news that the paperwork would be ready before race time on Friday evening—later than they wanted, but still in time to put Dare's plan into place.

Just as they rolled back into the compound, Dare's cell rang. He parked and killed the engine. "Yeah?"

"Dare. Nick Rixey here."

"Nick, how's it hanging?" Dare said, swinging his tired

ass off his bike. He'd e-mailed the details of the new situation to the Hard Ink guys the night before.

"Better for me than for you, my man. Which is why I was calling. We wondered if you'd like us to come over tonight. Just to help strategize and put more men on the ground leading into tomorrow."

"Shit, yeah," Dare said, absolutely eager for anything that contributed to his people's safety. And with their skills and their willingness to do what needed to be done, the Hard Ink team was fucking gold where that was concerned. "I appreciate the hell out of the offer."

Maverick dismounted his bike and gave Dare a questioning look. Dare held up a hand, asking him to hang on.

"It's the least we could do. Just a heads-up—it's just the five of us from the team coming. We'll reschedule the social visit for another time," Nick said.

Dare nodded. He'd have made the same call. "Makes sense. We'll have eats when you get here."

"Sounds good," Nick said. "We'll shoot for six if the traffic's not too bad."

"That'll work. Ride safe," Dare said. They hung up.

"What was that about?" Maverick asked. The guy looked about as tired as Dare felt. Dare knew the deep lines on Maverick's face were worry for the club, but also worry for Alexa, too. Alexa, who Mav couldn't watch over the way he wanted, with all this chaos whirling around them. And didn't that hammer home Dare's own thoughts about Haven.

"Nick and his team are coming tonight," Dare said.

"Damn if it isn't nice to have a little good news." Maverick started up the steps into the clubhouse.

Dare followed, intent on throwing his boots up on his desk and catching a little shut-eye while he could. "Yes it is, brother. Yes, it is."

Two hours later, Nick was good to his word. The Hard Ink team rolled into the compound a little after six, and their arrival bolstered the spirits of the group rotating in for food at that moment—because you were always stronger fighting with someone at your back than going it alone. Which was the point of their MC in the first place, but that didn't mean it wasn't good to have friends on the outside, too.

Dare met the group of men as they got out of their cars and unloaded bags of gear. "Nick, good to see you," Dare said, hand extended.

Nick tugged off his dark sunglasses as they shook. "You, too. Been a while since I've been out."

"We'll do it up right another time," Dare said, moving on to shake the other guys' hands—Shane, Easy, Marz, and Beckett each offered words of support. Maverick and Phoenix made the rounds of greetings right behind him.

"What was this place?" Shane asked, looking up at the clubhouse.

"The Green Valley Inn and Resort, built when the race-track first went up," Dare said. "My grandfather inherited it and kept the land after the business folded. Made the perfect home for the club as it started to grow." He led them across the lot. "Come on in."

Inside, Dare led them from the front lounge into the mess hall, where a dozen Ravens sat around the table eating dinner on the fly before heading out to relieve others on guard duty. Having worked together for several long weeks in Baltimore, introductions weren't needed, but a hearty round of greetings went around the room as their friends settled in at the table.

"Dig in," Dare said, taking his seat at the end.

"And here I thought we've been packing away a lot

of food," Marz said, piling meatballs onto a roll. "You always have this many people here?"

"This clubhouse is every member's second home, so the door's always open at mealtime. Usually busier on the weekends than weekdays," Dare said.

Marz nodded. "I respect the hell out of that idea. Meals bring people together."

"You just fucking like to eat," Beckett said in a gruff voice, amusement clear in the crinkling around his eyes, even despite the scars he wore around one.

"You'll never hear me deny that," Marz said, grinning. No matter how much of a hard-ass Beckett had ever been, Dare had never seen Marz lose his cool with the guy. From what Dare understood, Beckett had saved Marz's life in Afghanistan, though Dare had never heard the full story.

Just then, Haven came out of the kitchen, a serving dish in her hands. "Thought we might need more lasagna out here." She leaned between Phoenix and Maverick to put it on the table, and Mav reached out to help her set it down.

"You are too good to us," Maverick said, smiling up at her.

The shy smile she gave him in return was full of satisfaction. "No such thing."

The words fucking slayed Dare. Just laid him out right there on the table. No such thing as treating his brothers too good.

"Haven?" Shane asked, looking over his shoulder.

"Hi, Shane," she said, her cheeks going pink.

He rose and stepped out from his chair. "Your hair's different," he said, his Southern accent coming through just a bit.

Haven fingered at the brown waves and smiled. "Yeah. It's good to see you."

It looked like Shane was holding himself back from hugging her, and though Dare didn't love the idea of the guy touching Haven—of *any* guy touching her—Shane was the one who'd found the women imprisoned in the basement of the Church Gang's storage facility, so he had a special interest in them that Dare couldn't fault. "You doing okay?"

"Thanks to you—well, all of you," she said, her gaze scanning over Dare's and Nick's men both, "I am. Can I get you anything? Something to drink?"

"No, I'm okay," Shane said. "Sara's going to be really glad to know you're doing good."

"Tell her I said hello. And thank her for how kind she was to us that day."

"You bet I will," he said, sitting again.

Hands on the backs of Phoenix's and Mav's chairs, she asked, "Anyone need anything?"

"No. Stop taking care of us," Phoenix said around a full mouth of lasagna. "You should come sit."

"I ate already," she said. "And I like taking care of you guys."

More than one man looked up at her with affection on his face. Like she was part of the family. Their family. *His* family.

That's when it really hit Dare—how comfortable she seemed with them. Or, at least, how much more comfortable. It was like he'd watched a butterfly come to life these past weeks—from cocooned chrysalis to learning to spread her wings to full-colored glory. And it fucking stole his breath.

She peered at him, a tentative smile playing around her lips. "You good?"

When I'm with you, hell yes. Not that he voiced that particular thought, especially as his mind spun on what that tentativeness was all about. "Yeah. Thanks."

With a nod, she disappeared into the kitchen.

"So, can you catch us up on the plan?" Nick asked, pulling Dare out of his head. His e-mail from the night before had detailed the nature of the threat, because Nick's people needed to know what these Iron Cross fuckers were all about, but Dare hadn't laid out the plan, since they'd still been nailing down all the pieces.

Nodding, Dare passed his plate down for some lasagna. "In terms of security, we've got lookouts stationed around the property at all the access points and along the major ways in and out of Frederick. Thanks to Marz," he said, giving the man a nod, "we have vehicle descriptions on all Randall's men's rides. We have the sheriff's office on board with this, too."

"You all work well with them?" Beckett asked, dark blue eyes maybe a little surprised. Sitting next to him, Easy's dark eyes were curious as he listened in on the conversation, which was when Dare noticed the guy wasn't really touching the little bit of food he'd put on his plate.

"Uh, most of the time, yeah," Dare said. "Long history there. We'll pull in some of those men and tighten the net around the property and track for Friday night, and we'll also have the help of another MC from West Virginia. How many Brothers did Walker say are coming?"

Phoenix nodded and swallowed a bite. "He's gonna try for a dozen."

"How many people typically attend the races?" Easy asked in a deep, quiet voice.

"Capacity is two thousand, but average is usually twelve to fifteen hundred, depending on the type of event and which drivers are appearing. We never know the full number until race time, because we sell tickets at the box office, but advance purchases usually give us a decent idea. Tomorrow night looks to be a big crowd already."

Dare wiped his mouth with a napkin and dropped it next to his empty plate.

Easy nodded. "Plus drivers, pit crews, employees, and all of us. That's a lot of bodies to police. We might want to divide the whole track area up into sectors and assign patrol teams."

"Good thinking," Nick said.

"I'll pull a schematic of the venue for that after we're done here," Dare said.

"Sounds like we might want some monitoring of the parking lot that night," Marz said. "Make sure no wheels get in that we don't want in. You have security cameras out at the track?"

"Not on the lot," Dare said. "But that's a good idea."

"I can get that up and running in the morning," Marz said. "Stream it into a control room set up in an interior space near the lot?" Dare nodded, already appreciating everything these men brought to the table. "I can also see what traffic cams exist in the area and patch into the feeds of any we think might be useful. Might give us a longer heads-up if trouble's en route."

"That's sweet," Maverick said.

Marz grinned. "Love my toys."

"What's the plan for Haven and Cora?" Shane asked, nailing Dare with a gray-eyed stare.

"We were able to move up the production of their identity documents," Dare said around a bite of lasagna. "Should have them Friday evening. We'll send a detail of Ravens to relocate them as soon as we have those assets in hand. Once they're clear, we call off the exchange with the Iron Cross. And prepare for whatever comes."

Dare's biggest regret in this plan was that there was no way *he* could be the one to see Haven to her new home. Not with so much going on here. Not with his people facing such a threat. And he felt the weight of the clock ticking down like an anvil on his shoulders. Less than twenty-four hours. Then Haven would be gone. For good.

As they talked, some of the Ravens finished up their meals and excused themselves from the table. Casual conversation broke out as some of his men said their good-byes, heading out to relieve others on guard duty.

When things quieted down, Nick braced his elbows on the table and asked, "So, how much do you trust that the Iron Cross hasn't already double-crossed you?"

"Or isn't yet going to," Beckett added.

Dare shook his head. "I don't trust them at all. That's why we're not entertaining the meet on Saturday. It's pointless every way I look at it."

"Agreed," Nick said. His gaze scanned over his own men. "We're gonna need to dig into these assholes, too." Nods all around.

"Just let us be the ones who cross any lines that might need to be crossed over the next two days," Dare said, meeting the gaze of each man from the Hard Ink team. He wanted their backup, but he didn't need them to do his dirty work. "I don't want that on any of you. You're doing enough."

"We'll let that be plan A," Nick said. "But you know as well as I do that plan A often gets fucked when it meets reality."

Some laughs from around the table. "Ain't that the truth," Dare said. But he was going to do everything in his power to make sure that didn't happen. Not this time. Not when so much that he loved was on the line.

CHAPTER 28

After last night, Haven had decided one thing: if she only had one night left there, she wasn't spending it alone. Not when Dare clearly wanted her the way she wanted him. Not when Dare held her in his arms and coaxed her to sleep with his touch. Not when Dare was everything she'd never known she'd always wanted.

Since the moment she'd felt him leave her bed this morning—giving her a silent good-bye in the form of a kiss on her hair—she'd been longing to be with him again. Circumstances being what they were, they'd been apart all day. Which was all the more reason to not waste a single moment now that they could be together.

All of which was why, after the kitchen had finally been cleaned up and with Cora's strong encouragement, she found herself interrupting the meeting in his office with a couple of the soldier guys from Baltimore.

"Haven? You okay?" Dare asked, his gaze cutting to hers where she stood in the doorway.

"Yeah. I just wanted . . ." She shrugged.

"Come in. We're almost finished," he said. A big architectural drawing of the racetrack lay rolled out on his desk, Dare, Shane, and a couple of others gathered around.

"So we can use this 911 system you have to communicate sector assignments with your people for tomorrow night?" a guy with dark brown hair and pale green eyes asked. Nick, she thought his name was. She and Cora had spent so little time at the Hard Ink building before Ike had brought them to the Ravens' compound that they hadn't gotten to know these guys. Though that didn't change how grateful Haven would always feel to them.

"Yeah," Dare said. "That's the best way."

"Then we're set for tonight," Nick said, looking to the other men.

"If you're ready for bed, I got spare rooms upstairs, or you can crash out on the couches pretty much anywhere down here. If not, there's beer, music, and a pool table in the rec room down the hall. I'll be right there." Dare rolled up the drawing and stashed it in the corner behind his desk.

"I'm wired, to be honest with you," Shane said, raking a hand through his dark blond hair.

"I'll hang," Nick said, extending a hand to Dare. "Thanks."

"That's my line," Dare said. "This is all above and beyond."

"Not after what you did for us," Nick said.

Dare nodded, and the guys left. Haven stepped aside to let them pass, and then she found herself alone with the man she wanted almost more than her next breath.

"Hi," she said.

He gave her the sexiest crooked smile. "Hi." He stepped into her space, both his hands going to her hair, pushing it back off her face, just running his fingers through it. Touching her like he always did. "What was it you wanted?" he asked, no rush or urgency to his voice.

"You." The word fell from her lips unbidden, but she didn't want to take it back. She didn't have time for anything but honesty. "Just you."

Laughter and conversation floated down the hall from the rec room, and then music started to play. An old rock ballad with a sexy, swaying beat. Something about the normalcy of the sounds made Haven smile.

"Well, that's the best thing I've heard all day," Dare said. "What's that smile for?"

"The song," she said. "I like it."

"Do you now?" he said, dark eyes peering straight into her. He reached down, grasped her hand, and lifted it against his chest. Her fingers curled against the name badge on his cut. But stupidly, she didn't realize what he was doing until he wrapped his other arm around her back, pulled her in tight, and started to rock them.

Dare Kenyon was dancing with her. In his office. To music playing on a jukebox in a motorcycle club's clubhouse. And it was so amazingly perfect that it brought tears to her eyes.

Haven clutched at his hand and his shoulder, but no matter how hard she tried, she couldn't keep all this emotion from overwhelming her. A tear spilled from the corner of one eye.

He kissed it away, still swaying with her to the strains of a soulful electric guitar. "Don't cry, pretty girl," he said in a low, rumbling voice. "I've got you."

She gave a quick nod and took a deep breath. And then she forced herself to be, to feel, to *live* in this moment she might never get again. Dancing with Dare, tight in his arms, bodies brushing together. Their faces were so close that the scruff on his jaw kept catching her cheek, but she wouldn't have changed that for anything. Not anything at all.

He had her.

Her hand slid up to the back of his hair, her fingers toying with the long, soft lengths of it. She tilted her head back—and the look on his face sent her heart into a sprint. Desire. Affection. Longing. It burned from his eyes and carved pained lines into his forehead. Haven didn't have a lot of experience, and she hadn't been around a lot of men this way, and she'd certainly never been in love. Well, not really. Not like this. But none of that kept her from *knowing* that the expression he wore was one of some kind of love. Because his face looked like her chest felt.

"Dare," she whispered.

"Haven," he said, leaning down and kissing her softly, slowly, deeply. The kiss went on and on as they danced in a slow, rocking circle. When he finally pulled away, he leaned his forehead against hers, his eyes closed. The next words that came out of his mouth . . . were sung. Gravelly, rasping, so damn sexy. "I say, my darling, you were wonderful tonight."

His eyelids flipped open, a note of uncertainty in their brown depths. And Haven kissed that away with everything she was worth.

And then the music changed. For a moment, he didn't stop even though the beat was entirely different. And when he did, that longing was back on his face again. "I . . . I wish things were different, Haven. Safer. For you."

"So do I," she whispered, and even though the words broke her heart, they also gave her something she'd never before had. The belief that someone wanted her. The knowledge that *Dare* wanted her. And if things were different . . .

No, she wasn't going to waste her last night with him on an endless circle of useless wishes. Not when she had him in her grasp right now.

She pulled out of his arms but kept hold of his hand. "Come to bed with me. I want as much of you as I can get before I have to go."

Humor slid into his eyes, though that longing was still there. "I love hearing what you want."

"Good. Get used to it. Because I plan to tell you all night long," she said, smiling even as heat filled her cheeks.

Dare winked and grinned. "Who is this brazen woman?"

Haven turned on him and threw her arms around his neck. "The woman I was always meant to be. Thanks to you."

Without missing a beat, Dare kissed her hard and deep, and then he hiked her into his arms, her thighs coming around his waist. He carried her through the clubhouse that way, and she imagined some of the other men must've seen, because they went right past the open rec room doors.

But Haven didn't care. Not about anyone or anything else in the whole wide world.

By FIVE O'CLOCK on Friday afternoon, Dare felt like a time bomb ready to explode. Dread hung over him like a shroud. No matter how hard he fought it off, his brain was tripping warning bells all over the place about tonight. He felt like he was missing something. And on top of everything, he'd been so busy setting up the security measures they'd brainstormed and dealing with normal race-day issues that he hadn't seen Haven once since he'd left her bed this morning. And now it was almost time for her to go.

Maybe it was better that way. Maybe they should let the incredible night they'd spent loving and talking and occasionally sleeping together be their good-bye. Because he wasn't sure how the fuck he was going to let her go if he saw her again anyway.

And now cars were pouring into the lot as race fans arrived early to eat dinner at the track or visit with the pit crews down on the field. From where Dare stood inside the control room they'd set up in the office next to the ticket window, his gaze scanned over three monitors playing feeds from various security cameras—one on each of the parking lot entrances recording vehicle information and one on the box office windows capturing faces. Randall's men's pictures and car descriptions were taped down on the table in front of the monitors. Joker and Blake were manning those feeds and had walkie-talkies to communicate incoming trouble if they saw it.

"Stay in touch." Dare clapped Joker on his mountainous shoulder.

"You know it, boss," the guy said.

Dare left the control room and passed through the back of the ticket and betting office, where four of his men were manning the windows, two of which would close once the races started at seven. For right now, though, all four guys were too busy to talk. Continuing outside, Dare checked the time on his cell again. Quarter after five. Caine, Tank, and Domino should be back any minute with everything they needed to start the road trip with Haven and Cora out to Missouri.

Dare hated how fucked their usual procedures were going to be on this relocation. Phoenix usually headed them up, but given that the Iron Cross might be in play here, everyone agreed he should stay local. So Caine was leading this trip, which was fine, though the guy wasn't particularly good at putting people at ease. And the last thing Dare wanted was for Haven to feel uncomfortable or scared. On top of it all, they'd never rushed through making relocation arrangements so fast, and that pissed him off on Haven's behalf. Because she deserved the best from them. Certainly, the best from him.

The late afternoon sun beat down warm and heavy, and an excited energy encompassed the whole venue as cars rolled into the lot and people streamed toward the track. Music played, announcements echoed over the loudspeakers, voices and laughter carried on the breeze, engines revved.

And all Dare wanted to do was head up to the club-house and steal a few final minutes with Haven. But it wasn't in the cards. Taking a deep breath pressed the guns in the holsters at the small of his back and under his left arm into his skin, and the feeling was one of comfort. He was ready for fucking anything.

Spotting Nick and Shane down by one of the entrances to the field, Dare headed that way. He gave a wave as he neared. "How goes it?"

"We're set," Nick said. He and his men were in regular street clothes tonight, not wanting to call any special attention to themselves. "Patrols are in place. Communications are up and running. Everything looks good."

The only thing keeping Dare sane was how smoothly the day had gone so far. The Brothers of Steel had arrived as promised, a dozen strong. Marz had had no difficulties getting the security cameras set up and had hacked into two potentially useful traffic cameras as well. And there'd been no major snafus on the racing side of things either. Even the weather had cooperated, giving them a gorgeous day sure to bring fans out in droves.

"All right," Dare said. "Stay in touch."

"Roger that," Nick said.

Before he'd taken two steps away, Dare's cell rang, and he looked to the screen, relieved to see Caine's name. Fucking finally. "Caine, what's the word?"

"We got a problem," Caine said.

"Don't tell me that," Dare said, that feeling of dread creeping up his spine. He covered his other ear with his hand as an announcement echoed through the loudspeakers.

"Nothing's ready. It may be later tonight. If not, definitely tomorrow, but good shit takes time." Frustration was plain in the guy's voice.

"That's the one thing we don't have," Dare said, his mind whirling on how to make this work.

"I know. Tank, Domino, and I are still in the city. We'll stay until we have everything in hand and then we'll hustle back," Caine said.

"Let me know the second you have it, brother," Dare said. They hung up.

"What's going on?" Nick asked.

"My relocation team's delayed with what we need for Haven and Cora." Dare sighed, thinking through the schedule.

"Fuck," Shane said. "What are you thinking?"

Dare shook his head. "The stuff might still come through tonight, which would be fine. We could get them out late and then get in touch with the Iron Cross about tomorrow as soon as we know they're clear." Maybe. Possibly. Sonofabitch.

"Or you could send them out of town now. Have your team catch up with the documentation," Nick said.

"Yeah. That's what I'll do if the paperwork isn't going to be done tonight," Dare said. He didn't want Haven anywhere around once the Iron Cross knew the Ravens weren't paying up.

"Play it by ear then?" Nick asked.

"For now," Dare said, keeping his mouth shut for a moment while a big, rowdy family with a bunch of kids moved toward the entrance. When they were out of earshot, he continued, "Though we didn't have a plan in place for protecting the women tonight."

"We can consolidate a few of the patrol sectors at the edges," Nick said. "That would free up people to create a protection detail to stay with them up at the clubhouse."

Nodding, Dare considered the idea. "Think that's better than bringing the women down here?" Part of him wanted Haven right by his fucking side, though the track was where any danger would most likely focus—assuming anything actually went down tonight. Man, was it too much to hope all this was overkill and the Iron Cross would be good on its word?

"If we get company, they're way more likely to show up here, don't you think?" Shane asked, echoing his thoughts.

"Yeah. All right, I'm going to consolidate sectors eleven and twelve," Dare said. "I'll take the former twelve team up to the clubhouse and let the women know what's going on. Be back in twenty to thirty unless you need me sooner."

The other men nodded. "We'll hold down the fort," Nick said.

Dare was already in motion and on the radio. His truck was parked in the service driveway farther down the lot, and Dare used it to pick up Jeb, Bandit, and Gunny, whose stint in the Marines and expertise with a gun made Dare particularly happy to put him on this assignment. It was the matter of a few short minutes until they walked into the clubhouse, where they found three duffel bags of the women's meager belongings waiting by the front door and Bunny, Doc, Bear, Haven, and Cora sitting at a table in the mess hall.

"What are you doing here?" Doc asked, his face sliding into a frown.

"We've got a slight delay," Dare said, his gaze going right to Haven. Fuck, she was beautiful. Beautiful and so damn innocent. Too innocent for all this bullshit. He hated it for her. "The package isn't ready. Caine, Tank, and Domino are waiting in the city for it and will be back as soon as they have it. Probably still tonight. If not, we'll go ahead and move the two of you a couple hours out and Caine's team will catch up."

A series of emotions passed over Haven's face—concern, fear, and something that looked a lot like relief. Dare didn't want to think too closely about why the delay might make her feel that way. "So, what do we do now?" she asked.

"Stay right here. Jeb, Bandit, and Gunny are your protection detail for the night, and they can get in touch with me at any point," he said, gesturing to the men behind him. "I'll check in when I can. The approach to the house is guarded, too, so you'll be safe here for a few more hours."

Dare's cell rang. Dutch's number registered on the screen. Dare put the device to his ear. "Dutch, how are you?" he asked, hoping he was doing a passable job of keeping the frustration out of his voice.

"I'm good. Shirley and I are taking you up on your offer. I'll be there in about ten minutes," came the old man's voice.

"Glad to hear it," Dare said, though he couldn't ignore the niggle in the back of his brain that didn't want Dutch in the middle of a possible storm. "What are you driving? I'll have someone keep an eye out for your car and follow you to your spot with the golf cart."

Dutch answered and they hung up, and then Dare radioed that information to Phoenix, who was stationed at the main entrance.

"I better get back down there," Dare said, wishing he had time to pull Haven into his office. Hold her. Love her. Claim her.

Fuck if her eyes weren't filled with the same longing he felt. "Right. Sure," she said. "Be careful."

He gave a nod. "Always am."

CHAPTER 29

Will the after-party still happen?" Haven asked after Dare and the three Ravens who'd come with him left the room. She looked from Bunny to Doc, concern plain as day on their faces. She wasn't sure how their staying longer might change things.

"I'll guess we'll have to wait and see," Doc said, his voice gruff but not unkind. He gave her a small smile as he stroked at his gray beard. "All this security might yet turn out to be unnecessary. Don't get me wrong," he said, gripping a coffee cup in his hand. "Taking the precautions was the right way to go—Dare's judgment was spot-on as far as that was concerned. But if nothing happens, then the rest of the night can be business as usual."

Bunny nodded and got up from the table. "Well, since you girls are staying for a while yet, what's say we get you some dinner?"

Haven looked at Cora and said, "I'm not very hungry, but I guess it's a good idea."

"Sustenance is always a good idea," Bunny said, her eyebrow arched in a gentle, motherly reprimand. "Gotta take care of yourself, Haven."

Haven and Cora followed Bunny into the kitchen, where there was a veritable smorgasbord of choices. They made plates of meatballs and lasagna and sat together at the table.

They made small talk for a while, but all Haven could think about was how large and unknown the future loomed before her. When she'd no longer be Haven Randall but Kylie Jameson. Thinking of her name made her think of her namesake—Dare's brother. "Were Dare and his brother much alike?" she asked quietly.

Bunny's eyes went wide. "He told you about Kyle?"

The awe in her voice made goose bumps break out on Haven's arms. Was it so unusual that Dare had talked about him? "Yeah, he did."

The older lady's expression went soft and affectionate. "I only got to see them together a few times when they were young because they lived so far away. But Kyle was the rabble-rouser. If there was trouble to find, he knew how to find it every time," she said with a smile in her voice. "And Dare and Maverick would follow. Now Dare, he was always the old soul, the one who weighed the consequences, the one who listened when others talked. All of which made Kyle and Dare a good team. And I guess they probably needed that with the way their father was."

That sounded very much like the Dare she knew today, too. Bunny's words made Haven wish she'd been able to meet Kyle, been able to see them together.

"Wait," Cora said, looking from Bunny to Haven. "Dare has a brother named Kyle?"

"He did," Bunny said. "Kyle died when Dare was fifteen."

Understanding dawned on Cora's face, and Haven felt a little bad for not revealing sooner where she'd gotten her new name. "Oh, my God. *That's* where you got it from?"

"Sshh," Haven said, giving her friend a look. Caine had told them not to reveal their names to anyone they knew now.

"Do I want to know?" Bunny asked, giving them both a suspicious look.

Haven shook her head. "No. Well, it's just, we can't tell you. It's about when we move."

"Oh, I see," Bunny said. "Yeah, I know how it works." She looked down at her coffee mug for a long moment. "Haven?"

"Yeah?"

"You love him?" Bunny asked, compassion and kindness in her tone and the way she looked at Haven.

"Yeah," Haven said, not at all ashamed to admit it. Not even to Dare's aunt. "I do." A knot lodged in her throat. She set her fork down on her plate. Her gaze flickered to Cora, who was looking at her with so much sympathy in her expression that it made the knot even bigger.

"Oh, hon," Bunny said. "Maybe something can work out yet. You'd be so good for him, and he's been alone too long."

The words built Haven up and tore her apart at the same time. Knowing Bunny would've approved of them meant the world because Haven respected her so much. But Dare had been very clear the night before. He didn't consider things safe for her here, which meant he didn't *want* her to stay. Despite what they'd come so close to admitting they felt for one another last night—with both their words and their bodies.

After they finished eating, there was nothing else to do but wait. As the sun got lower in the early summer sky and the shadows stretched out over the ground, Haven wished she could be down at the track. Watching the race. Knowing what was going on.

A little after seven, the roar of the race cars' engines made it more than clear that the races had started. It was amazing how loud it was across the almost mile distance separating the track from the clubhouse. The sound was a thrilling growl she could almost feel in her bones, and it spoke of speed and danger and maybe even a little reck-lessness. As it got darker, the glow of the stadium lights filled the evening sky out the front windows of the club-house, a beacon that let her know where Dare was. God, she hoped he was okay. She hoped *everyone* would be okay, because she wouldn't be able to take it if anyone got hurt on her behalf.

Suddenly Gunny rushed into the kitchen through the back door. "Get ready to move. Now," he said in a voice that was all business.

Haven looked to Cora as she rose from the table. "What's happened?"

"I don't have the details," he said, gesturing to her and Cora to get moving. "But Dare will be here in five to get you."

Maybe Caine was back with the documentation they needed? Haven took a step toward the mess hall door, but then turned and threw her arms around Bunny. "In case I don't see you, I just wanted to say that I'll never forget you, Bunny. Thank you so much for everything."

"The feeling is entirely mutual, honey," Bunny said as she wrapped her thin arms around Haven's back. "You take care of yourself and each other." Bunny hugged Cora next.

And then Gunny hustled them through the mess hall and into the front lounge, where Jeb and Bandit were waiting.

"What's happening?" Haven asked again. "Is Caine back?" But the guys just shook their heads and kept their gazes trained out the windows. Not knowing made Haven about ten times more anxious than if they'd just tell her.

Headlights swung into the parking lot and zoomed in on the front windows, the sound of tires crunching on gravel reaching her ears despite the roar of the races. The minute the truck came to a hard stop, the men were shepherding them outside and toward it, even as Dare hopped out of the driver's seat. He left his door hanging open as he rushed up the porch steps, where a small crowd had formed. Haven waited near the passenger door, wanting—no, *needing*—to hear what was going on.

"Randall and his men are here somewhere," Dare told Doc. "I can't spare enough people to secure this location, so I'm taking the women down to the control room and bringing the men back down to the track. We need all the bodies we can get down there."

He's here?

She grasped the edge of the door for support as the world spun around her. The reality of that statement was like a punch to the gut. He was here. So close. And maybe closing in.

Cora slid off the passenger seat and put her arm around Haven's shoulders. "I hope they kill him," she said. "I hope they kill them all." Never in their whole friendship had Haven heard such anger and hatred in her best friend's voice. Not that she disagreed with the sentiment. Not even a little.

"Count me in," Doc said, jogging down the steps toward the other Ravens who were climbing into the bed of Dare's truck. Bear followed suit.

"I'll lock up and head home," Bunny said. "Go. Do what you have to do." She placed a quick peck on Dare's cheek.

"Okay," Dare said, squeezing his aunt's shoulder. He returned to the truck and called out, "Jeb, stay here until Bunny's gone and then come down."

"You got it," Jeb said, hopping back down from the truck's bed.

Cora and Haven got in and shut the door as Dare climbed in through the other door, his expression filled with so much cold anger that it sharpened the angles on his already harsh face. He jerked the truck into reverse.

"How do you know he's here?" Haven asked, bracing her feet against the floorboard to keep herself steady on the large bench seat as the truck lurched.

Dare met her gaze for a brief moment, and there was so much emotion in the flash of his dark eyes that it made her heart race. "The sheriff found your father's and two of his crew's cars parked in a commuter lot off I-70. Traffic camera near that exit reveals they came into town late last night. Which has given them an entire day to get into place, and they've done it using vehicles we didn't know to fucking look for." His words absolutely seethed.

"Oh, God," Haven said. Her gaze darted from the trees along the side of the road to the lights radiating from farther down the mountain. With all that lead time, her father could be lurking anywhere, everywhere.

Dare's hand landed on her thigh. "We'll get through this," he said.

She grasped his hand tight in hers. "I know." She believed him. She *had* to, because the alternatives were totally unacceptable, which led her brain to unhelpfully conjure up all the possible worst-case scenarios—and made her consider what she'd be willing to do if any of them actually happened.

THE CONTROL ROOM was a long, narrow space with white-painted cinder-block walls, a big safe built into one of them, and two desks that had been pushed together to create a makeshift security station. Joker and Blake sat before a series of monitors that had her father's guys' photographs and cars taped in front of them, but the Ravens were only paying one of the screens much attention—the feed from the camera trained on the two open box office windows.

"Have a seat," Dare said to Haven and Cora, nodding to some chairs lined against the wall opposite the screens. At least she'd know more of what was going on from here.

"Marz is working on setting up a fourth camera," Joker said, turning in his seat. "On the main concourse hallway."

"Good," Dare said. "Because what we need right now is an eye on faces, not cars."

Joker nodded. "Can't believe these fuckers might've been here all along."

"Tell me about it," Dare bit out. He headed for the door, and just when Haven was sure he was going to leave without saying anything to her—after all, he had much bigger things to worry about—he looked back over his shoulder. And then he reversed directions, crossed the room to her, and leaned down until he was planting a long, deep kiss on her mouth. "Stay here. I'll be back. And don't worry." He kissed her on the forehead and rose, the movement revealing the holstered gun under his arm. It was one of two holsters she'd watched him put on this morning in her room, and it helped a little to know he was well armed as she watched him leave.

Cora took her hand but stayed uncharacteristically quiet.

Which was how Haven knew it was time to really worry. "It's gonna be okay," she found herself saying, as much for Cora as for herself.

A little while later, a new set of images flickered through one of the monitors, replacing the view of the mostly quiet driveway entrance.

"Now we're talking," Joker said.

"Maybe we can help," Haven said, moving to stand behind the men. Blake gave her a nod and a small smile over his shoulder.

Cora followed. "We'll probably recognize them even quicker than you."

"Help yourself," Joker said, keeping his gaze fixed on the screens. "The more eyes, the better."

Since the ticket windows in the room next door were quieter now that the races had started, Haven mostly trained her vision on the busier concourse feed, where people were coming and going to get food or go to the bathroom or buy souvenirs. She couldn't decide if she wanted to see her father's face among the crowd or not, but God, how she wanted this to be over.

So many people. It was like looking for a needle in a haystack. And it made her heart absolutely thunder in her chest, because God only knew what her father was willing to do to get her back.

The screen providing the view of the ticket windows revealed that it had finally gotten dark outside. The races went on and on, the sounds of the roaring engines so much louder down here, drowning out even much of the cheering of the crowd and calls of the announcers. Combined with the way she'd been focusing on the video feed for more than an hour now, Haven was starting to get a throbbing headache behind her eyes. But it didn't matter. Nothing mattered until they found her father—or he found her. At least she was safe here, in this windowless room that could've doubled as a bunker.

She'd no more had that thought than Blake froze, and then his right hand smacked Joker in the chest while his other pointed at the ticket window screen.

Haven gasped. Her father walked into the camera's view, gun drawn, and began a muted conversation with the Raven at the window. Two of his men stood behind him, guns also pointed inside. At the Ravens.

Cora clutched Haven's arm as the two men in front of them bolted from their seats, drew their weapons, and gathered on either side of the door that led out to the other room. Suddenly, her father's voice came through the walkie-talkies sitting on the desks, drawing the men's gazes as they debated the best way to approach the situation.

"I know you have her," her father drawled, eyes and gun fixed on a Raven she didn't know. "Want to know how I know?" It was a rhetorical question, of course. Her father liked nothing more than grandstanding and putting on a good show like the asshole that he was. He tossed something on the counter. What the heck? Haven walked toward the screen. Was that . . . a cookie?

All of a sudden the room sucked in on her. *It is. Does that mean . . . please say that doesn't mean—*

"You see, I paid a little visit up the mountain and found these. And since my daughter has cooked her whole life for me, I know her fucking food. So now that we've established that you assholes have what belongs to me, let's talk about how I'm going to incentivize you to give it back." His Southern accent was thick and strong, much thicker than hers had ever been.

It. He hadn't said *her,* but *it.* God, she hated him. She hated him so much that she could've strangled him with her bare hands and not felt an ounce of guilt.

He pulled out his phone and angled it toward the men, who visibly braced in the video feed.

"Why isn't someone taking him out?" Blake whispered.

And then her father angled the phone at the camera above him, allowing Haven to see something that nearly made her wretch.

Bunny. Duct tape over her mouth. Her cheekbone split and bleeding. *Oh, God!*

"I figure y'all probably like this little old lady, since one of you died defending her, but if I don't have my daughter back within one hour, she dies, too."

"Aw, fuck," Joker bit out. "That's why right there. She's his lifeline as long as he's on the property. Dare's not going to let them take Randall out until we know where they've got her."

Head spinning, floor falling out from underneath her feet, Haven walked toward the door. Oh, God, someone had died. And her father had Bunny. This was all her fault. "I have to go."

Joker caught her from behind and tugged her back, his voice harsh in her ear. "Not a fucking chance."

"He has Bunny," she said.

Joker slapped a meaty palm over her mouth. "Sshh. And he's not getting you. Now, can I let you go?"

Defeated, Haven nodded, and she stumbled toward Cora, whose face had gone pale white.

"And in case that's not enough incentive," her father's voice came through the radio, "you should know that my men are set up throughout the building, ready to take people out on my command. Let's say every ten minutes that pass without my having her back, I give the order and someone random dies. A mom, a dad, a kid, another old lady. Hell, even a driver. That could get real fucking interesting."

"Oh, God," Cora whispered shakily. Haven was too stunned by the magnitude of what her father was willing to do to speak.

"That's fucking bullshit," the Raven said.

"Think so?" A flash of light on the screen coincided with a loud bang in the room next door.

"Fuck," Blake said, dropping to his knees so he could peer around the lowest part of the door frame. "Fuck, Meat's down. He fucking shot him," he whispered loudly over his shoulder.

Now all three guns were trained on the remaining Raven at the ticket window. "Now that we've established that I mean what I say, you have ten minutes to either leave my daughter somewhere out in the open, where I can claim her and leave without any trouble. Your old lady will be left unharmed on the property before we go. Or I pick my next victim." He looked over his shoulder at Stuart Harring, one of her father's right-hand men. "Which car you like?"

The guy looked to the side, as if considering. "Eh, the number five car," Stuart said.

Her father spoke into his cell. "If you don't hear from me, take the driver of the number five car out in ten minutes. Set your timer." He pressed a button and started backing away. "We clear? Deliver the message to whoever you have to."

And then they disappeared from the screen and the walkie-talkies went momentarily silent before all hell broke loose.

Blake and Joker did a quick check around the door and then dashed to where a big guy was laid out on the floor, blood pooling around him.

"Meat, you with me, man? Hold on," Joker said as he started pulling at the guy's clothes, baring his bloody chest. From where she and Cora hovered in the doorway to the control room, Haven couldn't see exactly where the entry wound was.

"Calling nine-one-one," the man still sitting in his chair at the window said in a shaking, thin voice.

"Good," Joker said. "Blake, get on the horn and make sure Dare heard all that."

"He should've," the guy dialing an ambulance said. "I had the Send button pressed almost the whole time."

"It was good thinking," Joker said, pressing his hands over the wound. Meat's back arched, which Haven was going to take as a positive sign.

"I've got a gunshot victim at the Green Valley Race Track," the Raven said into his cell. "We need an ambulance . . ." He continued relating what happened and answering questions.

"Shit," Blake said, kneeling beside Meat. "Who do you think was killed defending Bunny?"

Haven's mind raced. "Oh, God. Jeb. Jeb stayed with her when we left."

"What?" Blake said, blanching. Haven had gotten to know the pair of them well enough to know they were good friends. "Jeb? Are you sure?"

A sob caught in her throat. "Dare asked him to stay until Bunny left."

"Oh, no," Cora said, silent tears spilling from her eyes. "Jeb. I can't believe this is happening."

"Why isn't anyone coming to see what the fuck happened here?" Blake asked.

Joker shook his head. "We don't know what they're dealing with out there. How many men Randall has. Where they even are. It's not like our guys can just stroll through the halls now. Now take your shirt off for me so I can use it here."

As if from a distance, Haven watched the men work to save Meat's life, Joker's words echoing in her ears. What *was* Dare dealing with out there? Was he safe?

Suddenly, those worst-case scenarios Haven had thought about on the ride down there didn't seem like she'd imagined quite bad enough. Which meant she needed to decide how many people she was going to allow to be sacrificed so that she might stay free.

CHAPTER 30

Dare had heard the entire fucking thing, and by his count, at least three of his own were already dead or in harm's way. Not to mention a driver and a stadium full of people. And the only woman he'd ever loved. Motherfucker.

And of course, Dare was about as far away as he could get—at the other end of the track checking in on patrol teams, as had been the plan. He should've known Nick would be right though, because the plan was so far fucked he could barely remember what it was.

Now, the trick was to make his way carefully in the direction of the front offices where the ticket window and control room were while not getting his ass shot, inciting a panic, or seeming otherwise suspicious to the fifteen hundred people they had in here tonight.

"We're taking up sniper positions around the top of the building's interior," Nick said through the walkie-talkie.

"We'll pick them off as we see them. Nice and quiet."
Three of his men had brought gear and left it up top. Just
in case. Hell, even with all Dare's dread, he hadn't thought
it would come to this.

"Roger that," Dare said, looking at the LED screen on
his cell. Two minutes tops, unless Randall was bluffing,
which Dare's gut said he wasn't. And, anyway, it wasn't
a chance he was willing to take. "Jagger, get that fucking
kid off the track." He walk-ran along a wall, stopping at
a hallway on the concourse to check that it was clear to
cross.

"I'm trying," Jagger said. He'd gotten word to the driver's pit crew that they needed to get their guy out of there.
He'd told them there'd been a threat against the driver
that they needed to take seriously, but so far, the ego-for-
brains twenty-one-year-old behind the wheel didn't want
to relinquish the high position he had in the field.

Haven. Dare had to get to Haven. He couldn't break his
promise to keep her safe. And he couldn't let her go back
to the horrors of her old life. It would kill him. Whatever
part of him had survived after allowing his mother and
brother to die without fighting for them would die knowing he'd failed Haven, too.

A loud crash from the field. And then another, and
another, as the number five car lost control and spun
out in the middle of a crowded field. "Fuck!" Dare said,
watching the nightmare unfurl before him as the fans
jumped to their feet in a collective gasp. Crashes happened all the time—they were prepared to deal with
them. But not because one of their drivers had been
fucking executed—and there was nothing else to think,
given that the car that started the pileup was the very
one Randall had threatened. And their block of ten minutes was up.

Dare took off at a run along the concourse, no longer worried about catching anyone's attention. When his cell rang, he was almost tempted to ignore it, but he didn't need any more unknowns in play right now. "This is Kenyon. Talk."

"Dare, it's Henry Martin. I've got some information for you."

"What is it, Sheriff? I've got a fucking situation. Randall and his men are here, and they've shot at least two of my guys, possibly shot a driver, and have taken Bunny hostage."

"I know. We've got state and local en route. One of your guys called nine-one-one. I'm going to text you new vehicle information on Randall's people. We were able to grab some shots off a traffic camera near that commuter lot. You're dealing with seven men total," Martin said.

Bad news, but useful, too. "Appreciate that. Send it now and I'll get some people on it. We're not gonna be able to keep this from turning into a goddamned Wild West shootout if your people don't get here." He continued down to the corner where the concourse joined with the next hallway.

"I hear ya. Sit tight." Martin hung up.

As if. A moment later, Dare's phone buzzed, and he turned the corner and rushed to the end of the next hallway while he forwarded the new car descriptions on through a group message. These fuckers might wreak havoc, but they weren't getting away scot-free. Not once the Ravens found and disabled their vehicles and set themselves up to lay in wait. This was ending. Tonight.

He'd no more pocketed his cell and pulled the pistol from his back holster again than he turned the next corner to go outside—and found himself staring at Rhett Randall. Standing about ten feet away under the glow of a streetlamp. In the flesh.

Randall got off a shot. And Dare did, too.

HE SHOT THE driver. He really shot the driver. He's not going to stop.

That's all Haven could think as she overheard the chatter on the radios and watched Joker and Blake try to keep Meat from bleeding out.

Her father wasn't going to stop. Bunny. Jeb. Meat. This driver. Four lives. Ruined, because of her. How many more was she going to allow?

None. Not even one more. She wouldn't be able to live with herself. Especially if anything happened to Dare.

Turning to Cora, Haven put her mouth up tight against her ear. "Don't say anything out loud. I can stop this. I have to stop this. So I'm going. But you stay and be happy. I love you." She threw her arms around her best friend and gave her every hug she'd ever wish she could give for the rest of their lives.

"No. No, Haven. No," Cora whispered, tears springing to her eyes.

"At least I got to do so many things I never imagined, you know? I fell in love, Cora. It's more than I ever hoped. Now I need you to let me do this," Haven whispered, her throat so tight it hurt. Because the things she'd gotten to experience would have to be enough to last her whole lifetime.

"Haven," Cora said on a shaky exhale, her expression shattered.

"Your friendship meant the world to me," Haven said, blinking back tears. She didn't have time for them. With a look over her shoulder to confirm that the men were too distracted to notice her movement, Haven took a few slow steps toward the door. And then she made a dash for it, shouts ringing out from behind her as the door closed.

Haven wasn't sure where to go to find her father. But as he was looking for her, she assumed she just needed to go somewhere out in the open and he or one of his men would find her. She ran along the main concourse hallway, dodging groups of people and looking over her shoulder to see if she was being followed. The roar of the race was so much louder outside. Apparently, the crash hadn't stopped the racing. When she got to midtrack, she stopped and stared down at the wrecks of three or four cars piled between the edge of the track and the center field, her stomach rolling. Because her own father had caused that. And, in a way, she had, too.

She walked up to the fence and stood there, willing someone to see her before anyone else got hurt. Almost everyone in the place was on their feet watching the pit crews and first responders pull people out of the crumpled cars. Then she turned in a slow circle, her gaze scanning for any faces she might recognize. Back to the field, Haven found herself looking down a hallway that cut out into the darkness of the lot beyond. She almost turned around to the field again before she realized she was seeing something on the ground out in the darkness.

Whatever it was moved.

On instinct, Haven took off, her gut telling her that was a person lying out there. No one else seemed to notice, because everyone was watching the race and the aftermath of the crash play out.

She was halfway down the hallway when she was close enough to make out what she was seeing. And it nearly killed her.

Dare. Lying on his back in the shadows. "Dare!"

His head rolled toward her, face painted with agony. He

gave a shake of his head she didn't take the time to process before she skidded to her knees at his side.

"Oh, God, Dare!" He was bleeding from his right shoulder and his left side, which he had his other arm curled around. His hand was shaking and bloody.

"And there's my fucking little princess," came a voice from her right.

Ice ran down Haven's spine as she turned to find her father standing a few feet away, gun pointed in a shaking hand at her and Dare. With short dark-blond hair and a face that looked too much like hers, he was bleeding from his thigh but still standing.

"Leave him alone," she said, noting that Dare's gun sat at least four feet from his boots. She'd never reach it. "I'll go with you willingly, but leave him alone."

Her father jerked the gun toward her, his leg and hand shaking worse. "That's right. You'll go willingly. Everything that's happening here, it's your fault. Including this prick's death. Now, get the fuck up."

Haven leaned her body further over Dare's, so far that she had to brace her hand on the other side of him, making sure her father didn't have a clear shot at his head or abdomen. She wasn't afraid of her father shooting her. She knew she was too valuable to him. "You're not killing him."

"Haven, don't." Dare's whisper was just loud enough for her to make out.

"You've done enough damage here," she pressed on. Sirens wailed in the distance. "So agree to leave him and tell your men right now not to harm anyone else, or I'll drag this out and those sirens will get here and you'll be trapped."

Chuffing out a humorless laugh, her father shook his head. "Aw, you're a big shot now, huh? Ran away and found your spine. I'm gonna have a good time beating that back out of you."

She didn't take the bait. "Do we have an agreement or not? Those sirens are getting louder."

"Fine. I'll leave him. Now get the fuck up."

"Call the shootings off now," she said.

Glaring, her father spoke into his phone. "I've got her. Pull back now. I repeat, pull back. We're moving out." He lowered his gun some and scanned his gaze around. "Now let's go before I lose my fucking patience with you." The words were a lie—she already knew she was going to pay for her defiance. But it would be worth it to keep anyone else from getting hurt.

Keeping one eye on her father, she looked down at Dare's face. He was pale. Scary pale. And his eyes were dazed, unfocused. "You hang on, you hear me?" She gently dragged her hand up his side, trying to avoid the wound, though she couldn't entirely. *Please, please, let that one be from his back holster.*

"Haven, I swear to Christ," her father bit out.

She leaned down and kissed Dare's forehead, and her fingers brushed the end of the grip of his second weapon still holstered under his cut. Oh, thank God. She'd never handled a gun before—her father had always kept her away from them—but she had to try. She had to fight. "I'm just saying good-bye," she said.

She shifted her legs like she was getting up and wrapped her fingers around the grip. As it pulled free, her eyes met Dare's. A moment of clarity spilled into those brown depths as he grimaced at the movement at his side.

Crouched on one knee, Haven whirled and pulled the trigger. The first shot caught her father in the shoulder, but the surprise of the hit sent him reeling even as he squeezed off a round that went wide. The second caught him low in the gut. The third, in the chest, and he went down on his back, blood bubbling out of the wounds. Every hit was the result of his low expectations of her, and she'd never been happier to be discounted in her entire life than she was just then.

She kept the weapon pointed at him, even as his hand went slack around his own gun. But he was still holding it.

From down the hallway, she was remotely aware of people screaming, but she couldn't pay attention to it. She couldn't pay attention to anything except Dare and her father. Not to the sweat pouring down her hairline and the center of her back. Or the way her heart raced so hard it was difficult to get a breath. Or the way her hand shook around the gun. Her own breathing loud in her ears, she stayed crouched over Dare's body, gun at the ready, finger still on the trigger. Just in case.

Footsteps came pounding toward her and she whirled. "I'll shoot!"

The men skidded to a halt in the darkness. "Haven, it's okay. It's Maverick."

She scrabbled to Dare's other side, putting her body between him and this new threat. "Stay right there or I'll shoot you," she said, her voice cracking, wetness on her face.

One of the men stepped slowly into the light, hands in the air. "Haven, it's Maverick. See? Put the gun down, sweetie."

Her brain couldn't process what she was hearing. "Mav . . . Mav . . . Dare . . ."

"I know." He came a little closer, and then Phoenix and Ike stepped into the light, too. "Put the gun down. Okay?"

But she couldn't. She couldn't make her muscles respond. She couldn't let herself believe the threat was over.

Maverick was within a few feet of her. "I'm gonna take it from you, Haven. Okay? Just real easy," he said, leaning in and wrapping his big hands around the barrel. He gently tugged it free.

Which was when Haven realized just how bad she was shaking. Her teeth chattered. Her bones hurt. It was suddenly like she was plugged back into her body, because all at once she heard a voice through the loudspeaker giving instructions and saw the colored whirl of emergency vehicle lights in the distance.

Maverick went to his knees beside Dare. "Dare?" he said, leaning over his cousin. But Dare was completely nonresponsive now. Mav pushed his cut open to reveal the full measure of his blood loss. "Get help. Now," he said, looking up to the other men.

"Oh, God, Dare," she said, her hand brushing his hair off his sweaty forehead. She curled over until her face touched his. "Don't leave me. You hear? Don't you leave me."

"I need a fucking ambulance at the west concourse hallway," Phoenix said into his radio. "Right now. It's Dare. And it's bad."

CHAPTER 31

Everything fucking hurt.
　　His head. His arm. His side.

As consciousness returned, Dare remembered the full horror of what happened. And that's when he realized that the thing that hurt worse than anything else was his heart. Because he'd failed Haven. Failed and let her father take her away.

On a groan, he forced his eyes open and licked dryly at his lips.

"Dare?" came a deep whisper.

Blinking up at the ceiling, he forced his eyes to the right to find Maverick sitting at his bedside. In a dimly lit hospital room. He tried to form his cousin's name, but his mouth wouldn't work.

"Don't try to talk, man." Maverick grabbed a white cup off a tray and held the straw to his lips. There was a joke in there somewhere. If Dare felt up to jokes, which he fucking didn't. But the water was like drinking the finest aged whiskey. Dare couldn't get enough.

"You look like hell," Dare rasped.

Maverick barked out a hushed laugh. "You ain't winning no beauty contests right now either, D."

Grimacing, Dare went to scrub at his face, but only his right hand would move. Forcing his head to look down his left side, Dare's chin dropped. Haven was sitting in a chair, her head and shoulders resting on the edge of his bed, her hand holding his. "Haven?" he said in a soft, disbelieving rasp. "Is that . . . I thought . . ."

"You should let her sleep," Maverick said. "I think it's the first time since everything went down that she finally managed to fall. And she won't eat anything either."

"I thought she was gone," Dare said, emotion clogging his throat. Emotion that the pain and the drugs and the wonder of her being here wouldn't let him hold in. He pressed his hand over his mouth and closed his eyes, holding his breath to staunch the fucking embarrassing sobs that wanted to break free.

"She saved your life, D. Saved your life and guarded you like a lioness guarding her cubs." The admiration was plain in Maverick's voice.

The words unlocked a door in Dare's memory, and he could see her hovering over him, shielding his body with hers, grasping the gun from his holster. "Her father? What happened?" He scrubbed a hand over his eyes, catching a bit of stray wetness.

Mav nodded. "She took care of him, though she's already been cleared by the police for self-defense. Nick's guys took care of a few others, including Cora's father. Our people took out the rest when they tried to come back to their cars, which is where we found Bunny, tied up in the backseat of one of them. She's doing okay," he said.

"I'm so damn sorry she got hurt in all of this," Dare said, knowing it must've killed Maverick to see his mother banged up again.

Maverick shook his head. "Don't worry. Doc, Rodeo, and Bear are with her at home. You know how tough she is. She's more upset that she can't be here with you. Meat's okay, too. He's down the hall. Jeb and the Winston kid driving number five didn't make it, though. The whole incident on Friday night is being pinned on Randall's crew and their attempted kidnapping of Haven."

Jesus, that was a lot to take in. Dare's chest ached for Jeb, a good kid who would've made a great brother. And he'd died trying to protect Bunny. "What time is it?" Dare's head felt like it was full of cotton, his thoughts all scattered.

"Uh, it's three o'clock Saturday afternoon. You were hit in the side and shoulder and were in surgery for five hours last night. You'll be all right, though."

Alarm shot through Dare's body, making him groan. "Fuck. The exchange."

"Cancelled," Maverick said. "Iron Cross is denying having told Randall anything. Said he found out on his own, and they didn't get paid shit from anyone. But let that be a worry for another day."

Dare sagged back into the bed. Another day sounded good to him.

"Listen, nearly the whole club's out in the waiting room, so I'm gonna go share the good news that your moody ass is awake and let you get some rest."

Damn, even smiling hurt. "Don't make me laugh."

Maverick rose from his chair. "Before I go, there's something I think you should see." He grabbed a thick envelope from the rolling tray and pulled something out of it. A card. He handed it to Dare.

"What's this?" Dare asked, trying to make his eyes

focus. Mav just waited, and finally Dare's brain caught up. A Missouri driver's license. Haven's new license. Except of course that wouldn't be her new name. His eyes scanned . . .

Kyle Grace Jameson.

Dare blinked. Kyle? She'd named herself Kyle?

He squinted and realized he'd read it wrong. Kylie, not Kyle.

Except having seen his brother's name in her newly chosen name, he couldn't unsee it. What were the chances the similarity in those names was a coincidence? His gut told him it was very little. His heart told him it was none at fucking all.

Haven had been planning to name herself after his brother? He squeezed the card in his hand. "Kylie," he whispered, emotion clogging his throat again.

"Yeah," Maverick said, placing the envelope on the tray. "Kylie."

The significance of that gesture sank into every fiber of Dare's being. On a cellular level, he felt the generosity, the sweetness, the incredible beauty of what she planned to do and who she planned to be.

Which was when he knew there was absolutely no way on God's green earth he was letting her become Kylie. Not when she was already his Haven.

Unless, of course, she wanted to go. Because after the horror show of Friday night and being forced to kill her own father, he wouldn't blame her one bit if she was chomping at the bit to leave, to finally find a place where she might be safe.

Dare wouldn't make her stay, even though she'd be taking his heart with her if she went.

HAVEN CAME AWAKE on a gasp, her gaze cutting immediately to Dare's face. Dark circles marred the skin beneath his eyes and lines cut deep into his skin, but his eyes were open and looking at her, and it made him the most gorgeous man she'd ever seen.

"You're awake," she said, sitting up. "Oh, God, you're really awake." She cupped his jaw in her hand, relief coursing through her.

"And you're still here," he said, voice scratchy. He'd been intubated during his surgery, and one of the nurses had mentioned he'd probably have a sore throat.

The words made Haven's belly sink, and she drew her hand away. "Uh, yeah. Well, they wanted to wait for you to decide what to do." From the moment Caine had returned with their paperwork and logistics, Haven had been nearly sick with dismay at the prospect of leaving.

Dare frowned. "I'm sorry, Haven." He pressed his lips into a grim line, and his eyes looked so bleak.

"For what?"

"For so much. For not protecting you. For not keeping my word. For putting you in the position of having to take a life." He shook his head, and the grimace proved that it was more movement than he was up for.

"In case you didn't notice," she said, fight stirring up in her belly, "I'm completely unharmed. You kept your promise. And killing my father was one of the most justified things I've ever done in my life. He killed people we cared about. He hurt Bunny. He was going to kill you and kidnap me. He was evil, pure and simple. So I'm not sorry. Not at all. And you shouldn't be either."

Dare studied her like he was searching for the truth in her words. "You're not upset?"

Taking his hand in hers, she shook her head. "Not about any of that."

"About something else?" he asked.

She dropped her gaze to the envelope on the tray next to him. "Caine got the paperwork."

"I know," he said, holding up her driver's license in his other hand. She hadn't noticed he had it. "You named yourself after my brother." He didn't phrase it as a question.

Heat filled her cheeks. "I wanted the name to mean something."

"My brother means something to you?" he asked, a strange expression she couldn't read playing over his face.

Discomfort rolled through her stomach. Did he disapprove? She dropped her chin and her gaze. "Yeah, because he means so much to you."

He squeezed her hand weakly. "Look at me." She forced her eyes to meet his, and he stared at her a long, long moment. "What do you want?"

Feeling like she was standing on the edge of the tallest cliff, Haven knew she had to jump. Her life depended on it. "I want to live. To really live—"

Pain flickered over his face, making her swallow her words. "Then we'll get you out of here as soon as we can. Because you deserve that, Haven."

Wait. What? "No," she said, shaking her head. "I want to live, Dare. And *you're* the one who showed me that I could. Who showed me how beautiful it could be—"

"Killing your father was beautiful?" he bit out.

"I'm free now. For real. And someone who made a life out of hurting others is gone. Maybe that's not beautiful, but it's good. And if that makes me a horrible person, then I'm okay with it."

"Should've been me," he said, grit in his voice.

"I don't need you to protect me, Dare. I appreciate it, but I can survive on my own. I've done it all my life. But I don't want to just survive. Not anymore. I want to live and experience all the beauty and power and chaos of life. And I want that . . . I want that with you."

Dare frowned, and then his eyes went wide. "Are you saying—"

"I don't want to go," she said. "Unless you don't want me to stay. Unless . . . unless I'm really not that special to you." Giving voice to those words was one of the scariest things she'd ever done. But she had to know. Once and for all.

She could barely breathe as she waited for him to reply.

On a groan, he reached for her with his good arm, and she leaned in to let him cup the back of her neck and pull her closer. "Come here," he whispered. She got as close as she could without putting any of her weight on him. His gaze went soft and unshuttered, and then words spilled from that harsh, beautiful mouth. "I love you," he said. "I fucking love you so much that I don't think I can exist without you. Not anymore. I don't want you to go. Not at all. You're the most special thing I've ever found. You've given me love and acceptance and peace and comfort and made me realize that I want things out of this life, too. Things I hadn't realized and certainly hadn't been pursuing. But the world I live in . . . fuck, this life isn't—"

Haven kissed him, happiness, relief, and overwhelming love making it impossible for her to speak. So she poured everything she felt into the way her lips caressed his, the way her hand stroked his hair. And then she looked down into his questioning eyes. "I love you, too," she rasped. "You own my heart and you always will, because you taught me what love was and you showed me what life could be. You gave me wings, Dare, and they brought me right back to you. And they always will."

"You love me?" he asked, raw wonder in his voice.

"Maybe from the very first time we spoke," she said,

happiness welling so big and warm inside her chest that she wasn't sure how she could hold it all in.

"Fuck," he said, his face crumpling with emotion. He tried to cover it with his hand, and the show of emotion reached into her chest and squeezed her heart. "You saved me," he said, his voice cracking a little.

Haven smiled, completely overwhelmed by the perfection of the moment. "We saved each other."

Dare heaved a deep, shaky breath. "You're pretty fucking awesome. You know that?" he asked.

Her smile slipped into a grin. "I really am."

He gave a little coughing laugh and groaned at the same time. "Can't . . . laugh," he gasped.

"I'm sorry." She stroked his hair back off his face.

"Don't ever be sorry for making me happy, Haven. Because you do. Happier than I've ever been in my life. I didn't realize how little I'd been living all these years until you came along. So, yeah, we saved each other. And I just can't let you go. Not today. Not ever."

Which was exactly what Haven wanted to hear. "That's all I need, Dare. *You're* all I need. We'll figure the rest out."

His fingers toyed clumsily with a long strand of her hair. "Yeah, we fucking will," he said, strength filtering into his voice. "One day, one night, one ride at a time."

ACKNOWLEDGMENTS

The idea for the Raven Riders, a different kind of a motorcycle club with a protective mission at its heart, was inspired by a real-life organization—BACA, Bikers Against Child Abuse (www.bacaworld.org). BACA works with referring agencies to create a safer environment for abused children. Working with state and local officials, BACA members provide emotional support and a physical presence to help children feel safer and shield them and their families from retaliation or intimidation, often for the length of a police investigation and any court proceedings. I admire what they do so much I wanted to pay homage to the spirit of their mission in the Raven Riders.

A book is always the result of a collaboration, which was definitely the case with this one. Thank you to Amanda Bergeron for believing in the Ravens and for offering such thoughtful and insightful editorial guidance on the book. It's an amazing experience to have an editor really get your voice and vision and characters, all of which has made Amanda a great partner on all eight (!) of the books we've now done together. I appreciate that so much.

Thanks also to my agent, Kevan Lyon, who is always such an incredible source of support and encouragement. And thanks to KP Simmon for her positivity, generous spirit, and all the fantastic work she does on all of my books. It's an invaluable experience to work with such amazing women and have them on your side.

Next I have to thank fellow authors Christi Barth, who read the book right behind me and offered great comments, and Lea Nolan, who helped me out of more than one plotting problem. Their support, friendship, cheerleading, and help mean the world.

My next word of thanks goes to Liz Berry of the 1001 Dark Nights project for helping me kick off this series with my novella *Hard As Steel*. That opportunity gave me the chance to introduce readers to the Raven Riders world, and I appreciate her innovative, generous, and enthusiastic spirit so much. Thanks, Liz!

As always, I couldn't finish a single book without the amazing support and help from my family, so thank you to my husband and daughters! Much love to you! And thank you to the Heroes, my street team of awesome, who do so much for me—you guys rock!

Finally, thanks to the readers who allow my characters into their hearts so they can tell their stories again and again. Your support is everything. Ride on, my friends. Ride on.

~LK

Keep reading for an inside look
at the next heart-poundingly sexy novel
in Laura Kaye's new Raven Riders series,

RIDE ROUGH

Coming Fall 2016 from Avon Books

Maverick Rylan stared at the flower-draped casket and hoped this was the last funeral he and his brothers had to attend for a long damn time. This loss hit him and everyone in the Raven Riders Motorcycle Club particularly hard—because it had happened on their own turf. Inside their own clubhouse. And the victim—prospective member Jeb Fowler—had been too young and too good to get taken out in cold blood.

The proof of Jeb's goodness was sitting right beside Maverick. Bunny McKeon, Maverick's mother, whose face still bore the bruises and scratches from where she'd been struck and her mouth duct taped. But she was alive because Jeb had taken the bullet intended for her when a group of lowlife criminals had broken into the clubhouse looking for something—or *someone*—that wasn't theirs.

Mav's gaze slid over to his right, where the club's president, Dare Kenyon, sat with his girlfriend, Haven Randall. Three days out of the hospital, Dare's face was pale and dark circles ringed his eyes. He'd been shot twice in the same attack that had hurt Bunny and killed Jeb. An attack meant to force Haven back under her abusive father's control by whatever means necessary. An attack that had ultimately failed, despite the losses the Ravens had sustained.

It all could've been so much worse. Which was true even though Maverick felt like shit thinking that while sitting there in front of Jeb's coffin. Especially since Jeb had sacrificed himself for Bunny.

The service concluded and people around Maverick rose to their feet. The June air hung humid and gray. Almost oppressive. The weight of it was fitting. It was as if their collective grief had taken on a physical form.

Maverick held out his hand to Bunny. With her white-blond hair and dark blue eyes, she was still as pretty as she'd ever been. And every bit as feisty. Well, usually.

Accepting his help, she gave him a sad smile and rose. Her husband, Rodeo McKeon, steadied her from her other side.

"Thanks, Maverick," she said, stepping toward the casket. She pulled a long-stemmed red rose out of the arrangement and brought it to her nose. A moment later, she laid it on top of the lid by itself, her hand resting there for a moment.

When she turned away, her lips trembled, and when she made eye contact with Maverick, her whole expression crumpled.

Maverick pulled her into his arms, her tears like ice in his veins. "It's gonna be okay, Mom," he said, using a name for her he hadn't used regularly in years. *Everybody* called his mother Bunny, and somewhere along the way it had stuck for him, too.

From behind her, Rodeo rubbed her back. Mav met the older man's gaze and saw reflected at him the same pain and regret Maverick felt. Normally, Bunny was the youngest sixty-something you'd ever meet, but the attack and Jeb's death had left her fragile. And Maverick fucking hated it. Not because he thought her shakiness wasn't warranted, but because it reminded him of another time:

When Bunny's first husband—Maverick's father—had beaten her so badly she ended up in the hospital for days.

That had been seventeen years ago, but not a day had gone by when Maverick hadn't blamed himself for not realizing what was going on, not being there, not protecting her.

Maverick's gaze slid over Rodeo's shoulder to the casket. *I wish there was something I could do to repay you, Jeb. But you can believe I'll never forget.*

"I'm okay," Bunny said, wiping at her cheeks. She patted his chest. "Thanks, hon."

Rodeo gave Mav a nod that said he had her, and Maverick didn't doubt it. Not only was Rodeo one of his brothers in the Raven Riders, he was also the best thing to ever happen to Bunny.

"Are you coming to the clubhouse?" Maverick asked. Bunny hadn't been back since the attack five days ago, which was totally unlike her. Normally, she spent part of every day there, often cooking one or more meals for whichever Raven happened to be around or drop by.

"Yeah," she said. "We'll see you there."

"Okay," he said. With a last look at Jeb's casket, Maverick turned for the drive that wound through the rolling hills of the cemetery. Motorcycles formed an unbroken wall of steel and chrome almost forty deep. The whole club had turned out to pay their respects. As it should be when a brother took his last ride.

As vice president, Maverick's bike was at the front. Normally, he'd be riding second position behind Dare, but the gunshots to Dare's side and arm meant he'd be driving only four-wheel vehicles for the immediate future. So Maverick was riding point. Still standing, he brought the bike to life on a low rumble. And then he waited for Road Captain Phoenix Creed's command.

Like the black bands they wore on their arms—made of thin strips torn from a couple of Jeb's Harley T-shirts—they had traditions they honored when one of their own died.

A few years younger than Maverick's almost thirty-five, Phoenix normally wore a mischievous, good-humored expression. Not today. Not when they were burying one of Phoenix's closest friends not a month after Phoenix had buried his cousin. Their road captain had taken a beating the past few weeks, and it showed in Phoenix's unusual frown and his lack of joking around.

When everyone else started their engines, Phoenix finally started his own. Then he turned his throttle and revved his engine until it roared.

Every biker except one joined in.

Roar, roar, roar, roar, roar.

The five thunderous revs lodged a knot in Maverick's throat. Because the Last Rev was meant to alert heaven that a biker was on his way home.

And then all the bikes quieted to a low idle—except one. The one that had remained silent before now roared out. Ike Young, the Tail Gunner of the procession, revved his engine five times, as if Jeb was answering the club's call and saying his good-byes. One last time.

When the Last Rev ended, everyone mounted their bikes and the procession got underway.

Quietly and slowly, they made their way home—back to the Raven's compound on the outskirts of Frederick, Maryland. Maverick knew he had to at least make an appearance at the reception, though his gut had him wanting to go somewhere else—to the home of Alexa Harmon.

The first and only woman he'd ever loved. A woman who'd chosen another man over him five years before. A woman who'd shown up at the Ravens' clubhouse a week ago with a bruised and bloodied face, but ultimately wouldn't tell him what had happened.

Her brief reappearance into his life had triggered every one of his protective instincts.

And as if Maverick hadn't already been climbing out of his skin with worry over Alexa—whether she wanted him worrying about her or not—Bunny's attack whipped up all the old guilt inside him and made him *must* know that Alexa was okay.

Or, if need be, *ensure* that she would be okay. Whatever that took.

Because he'd failed a woman he could've helped once, and that failure ate at him a little bit every day, like a slow dripping leak of acid deep inside his veins. Even all these years later.

Then, Maverick had been young and naïve and weak. He hadn't realized all the kinds of evil that lurked in the world. But that wasn't him anymore. And he refused to ever make that same mistake again.

ALEXA HARMON TORE out of her car and ran into the house, her high heels clicking against the concrete of the three-car garage and then the travertine tiles of the hallway and kitchen. She was late getting home from work, and that meant she was going to be hard-pressed to get dinner on the table on time.

She bee-lined for the bedroom, already working at the buttons on her silk blouse. Despite being under the gun, she took the time to hang up her work clothes and put everything away in the walk-in closet that was nearly as big as her childhood bedroom had been.

Cole didn't like mess or clutter.

Slipping into a pretty blue blouse, jeans, and her ballet flats, Alexa's gaze cut to the alarm clock on her nightstand. She had twenty-five minutes. Twenty-five minutes to make sure her lateness didn't ruin their whole evening.

Damnit, Alexa. You should've kept your eyes on the time better.

It was true. She'd just been elbows deep in materials arriving for the model home in Cole's newest development. This was the first time he was letting her take the lead on the interior design of a model, rather than hiring their usual outside contractor, and she wanted it to be perfect.

She wanted to be perfect. For Cole.

Cole *really* liked perfection.

Alexa got it. Cole's perfectionist tendencies went a long way to explaining how he'd built Cole Slater Enterprises, the biggest real estate development and management company in western Maryland. Hell, Frederick was almost a company town, at least where real estate was concerned. There were more developments in the area with the words Cole or Slater in their names than she could count. Their own neighborhood was a prime example—Slater Estates.

Running back out to the kitchen, a low pleading *meow* caught Alexa's attention.

"Come on, Lucy. Come with Mama," Alexa called, heading straight for the cat's bowl. She poured dry food into the dish, spilling a little in her haste. The hairless sphynx brushed against her leg in a show of affection. Alexa gave Lucy's mostly blue-gray body a quick pet as she scooped up stray morsels of food with her other hand.

The clock on the microwave told her she now had twenty-two minutes.

She grabbed the package of two filet mignons from the fridge, along with a bag of fresh asparagus. Moving as fast as she could, she found the grill pan for the meat and the sauté pan for the asparagus, and got that much going. The baked potatoes she'd planned weren't going to be possible with this little time, and trying to boil water for corn on the cob would be pushing it. Her stomach knotted as her pulse raced. She buttered thick slices of Italian bread and seasoned them with garlic, then slid them into the warming oven to brown.

As soon as she turned the filets, she was back in the fridge. When her gaze settled on the container of chick-pea salad from the weekend, relief flooded through her. She'd forgotten they had that. Finally, she threw together a green salad with chunky fresh vegetables.

Keeping a close eye on the time, she set the dining room table—Cole always preferred to eat in the formal dining room. And then she was pouring the wine and plating the food with two minutes to spare.

Alexa might've fist-pumped if she wasn't so anxious about almost having been late. Her stomach was in so many knots she wasn't even sure she'd be able to eat, though it was her own damn fault.

Six-thirty came and went. Six thirty-five. Six-forty. Sitting alone at the dining room table, Alexa frowned. Finally, her phone buzzed an incoming text message from Cole.

I've got a dinner meeting tonight. Don't wait up.

Alexa stared at the screen for a long moment, then found herself blinking away threatening tears.

She let herself wallow for several minutes, then shook her head. "Stop it, Al," she said out loud. God, she really was over-emotional lately, just like Cole said she was.

Between her job, designing the model home, her classes, getting used to living with Cole, and their upcoming wedding, there was just so much going on. She felt like she should be juggling it all with more grace and enthusiasm. Instead, what she *really* felt scared her. Scared her bad.

Dread. Skin-crawling, stomach-dropping, run-while-you-can dread.

It was ridiculous.

Alexa was on the cusp of having everything she'd ever dreamed about. A beautiful home she could be proud of, a secure job that she loved, a man who worshipped her, and more money than she'd ever be able to spend. She wasn't greedy; that wasn't where her interest in money and a nice house came from. Instead, it grew out of the way she'd grown up. How *little* she'd had as a kid, how terrible the conditions she'd endured had been—against all of that, it was amazing to think about how much she had now.

She was grateful beyond imagination. Grateful to be safe and secure. Grateful to be able to help her mom, who needed all the help Alexa could give her. Grateful to Cole for making it all possible.

Which made the dread seriously ridiculous.

It was just wedding jitters. Totally normal.

Right.

Sighing, she dried her eyes and surveyed the beautiful dinner she'd managed to throw together. Given how scarce food had been when she was younger, Alexa absolutely hated to waste anything. Problem was, her appetite had been all over the place lately. Either she couldn't stomach the thought of eating or she was binge-eating a bag of potato chips while Cole was at work.

Knock, knock.

The quick raps on the front door pulled Alexa from her thoughts. She crossed the dining room to the wide oval foyer framed by a grand curving staircase. A glittering chandelier hung from the ceiling, casting colorful prisms here and there from where it caught the late-day sun through the large picture window above the door. Out on the front porch, Alexa found a stack of packages. She gave a wave to the UPS driver as he pulled out of the end of their driveway.

With only two weeks until the wedding, presents from the registry had been pouring in every day. Cole had so many friends and work colleagues that she'd never met, Alexa didn't know who most of the gifts were from.

She carried in two smaller ones, then two medium ones, and then found herself struggling to move the large square box on the bottom. It was too deep to get her arms around and not easily pushed. What the heck could it be? She crouched behind it to try to gain leverage to push, and was just about to give up when a strong breeze blew her hair across her face and she heard a soft click.

Her gaze cut to the front door.

"Oh, shit," she said. Knowing what she was going to find, she tried the knob anyway. Locked.

She was locked out and Cole was away until who knew what time. And she couldn't easily go anywhere because her purse, car keys, and phone were all inside.

"Shit, shit, *shit*."

She sat heavily on the stupid box and dropped her head into her hands. And burst into tears.

Not because of being locked out. But because of being . . . trapped with no easy way out of the situation? Suddenly, that felt like a crazy, accurate metaphor for her life.

If she was being honest with herself.

Which she really, really didn't want to be.

"Stop it, Al," she said in a rasping voice. "You're not trapped. Stop thinking that." Except, just then, she leaned her left cheek too heavily against her hand and sucked in a breath at the smarting of the healing bruise there.

The one from the fight she and Cole had last week. The fight that had started with Alexa leaving a big mess in the foyer from where she'd been unboxing another delivery of packages and escalated into Cole saying Alexa was just like her mother—something Cole knew cut her deep. The fight had ended when Alexa told him he was being mean and he'd kicked a box at her—when she'd tried to duck out of the way, she tripped over another box on the floor and fell, hitting her head against the leg of a console table in the foyer, giving her some nasty bruises.

Alexa had been totally and absolutely stunned, especially when Cole hadn't stayed to help her. Instead, he'd said her tripping had just proven his point and stormed out. She'd fled. To her past.

A past she'd left behind for a whole lot of very good, logical, and well-thought-out reasons.

When she'd finally returned home, Cole had apologized so profusely he'd gotten down on his knees and cried with his head in her lap. Never in the nearly five years they'd been together had he ever hurt her. At least, not physically. He could be short with her when he was stressed and occasionally his criticism bordered on the mean side. But the truth was Alexa *could* be messy and she could be disorganized and she could be forgetful, all things that drove him crazy. And Cole could also be generous and sweet and he'd done so much for her and her mother. Their lives were better because of Cole Slater.

"Alexa?" came a deep voice.

Prickles ran up her spine as she lifted her head—and found herself staring at her past, into the dark blue eyes of Maverick Rylan.

Alexa swiped at the wetness on her face and nearly jumped up off the box, her heart suddenly in her throat.

With his longish sandy blond hair, square jaw, ruthlessly masculine features, and Raven Riders cut-off jacket hanging on those broad shoulders, Maverick was the sexiest man she'd ever known. Had been when they were together, still was even now. No, he was hotter now. More muscular. More rugged somehow. More self-possessed. Utterly desirable.

Snap out of it, Al!

Releasing a shaky breath, Alexa met his gaze head-on. "Maverick, what are you doing here?"

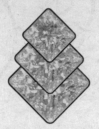